This is a work of fiction. Names, characters, places and incidents either are the product of the author's imagination or are used fictitiously. Any resemblance to actual persons, living or dead, events, or locales is entirely coincidental. Every effort has been made to trace or contact all copyright holders. The publishers will be pleased to make good any omissions or rectify any mistakes brought to their attention at the earliest opportunity.

First Edition June 13, 2021

Second Edition June 1, 2023

Third Edition November 22, 2023

Parly Press Publications,

an imprint of BarbLanell.com

ISBN ; 978-1-7356081-1-2 Paperback

ISBN ; 978-1-7356081-0-5 Ebook

PUBLISHED IN THE USA

THEY FLY SILENT

A Novel

BARB LANELL

For what we learn as children grows up with the soul and becomes united with it.
~Irenaeus Polycarp

Age considers; youth ventures.
~Rabindranath Tagore

THEY FLY SILENT

BY BARB LANELL

The beginnings and ends of shadow lie between the light and darkness and may be infinitely diminished and infinitely increased. Shadow is the means by which bodies display their form. The forms of bodies could not be understood in detail but for shadow.

~ Leonardo da Vinci

PRESENT DAY

MAY 3, 1988

NEWS YOU CAN USE

BY EDNA ROLLINS

TEXAS NEWS EDITION

The collard green fire is still a mystery to locals. A disturbed woman targeted an innocent woman's home by setting a large fire in her front yard with bizarre items such as men's attire, animal bones, deer horns, rugs, artwork, paintings and more. This and other aspects of the fire make this the strangest night on record that anyone in this town can remember. For the next few weeks I'm going to interview those who witnessed the atrocity. Today we begin with Mrs. Myrtle Holsomback who lives two houses down from where the fire started. "It was something terrible. Her face painted with red stripes and she was dressed dark like she didn't want anyone to see her but we saw her, plain as the devil himself. And I don't know what kind of enchantments she was saying but it was strange and outright devilish."

Myrtle said the strange event frightened her enough that she has taken it upon herself to call a town meeting in order to stop what she says is a cult forming at its roots. As a long-standing matriarch, she said she intends to cut it off before it grows into something evil. If you would like to attend the meeting, it will be at Shawnee Church, Wednesday, June 15th at 7pm. Until next time, tune into KTBR local radio news station 109.9. I'm Edna Rollins and that's news you can use.

THE DEVIL IN THE DETAILS

We derive our vitality
from our store of madness.
~Emil Cioran

I noticed the painting the first day. I saw myself in it—a strange embodiment of the person I was, or used to be, or am now, I wasn't sure. There I was in the blurry brushstrokes where the colors ran together, me out of proportion—in chaos—messy and mad. It stirred emotions in me, foreign, from another time and place, but so palpable I wanted to jump inside the frame. I continued to stare at what I perceived to be my life description, in swirls of reddish-orange sky towered above a long bridge and a blackened body of churning water. Watching from a distance, two shadowy figures conjoined at the edge of the bridge while the tortured soul at the forefront of the painting stood trembling in fright, terror in his face, his body melting, his skin slipping into the otherworldliness behind him, above him, beneath him, while an atmosphere of spine tingling texture, of unseen imps and demons, the tangled environment of touch, sound and sight, the elements of nature combined with the inner self, the spiral of all things seen and unseen dissolving around him. His hands were clasped around his alien-shaped head as if his mind had imploded but no one else could see it. His mouth was open in a circle while the hell of his internal existence excavated the invisible demons from inside him. I could see the demons because I had them too. Monsters always recognize other monsters. I stared into my own tragic soul while I read the inscription below the famous painting.

SUMMARY OF ART: Artist, Edvard Munch, painter of the famous and emotionally charged work, *The Scream*. He is said to have suffered from depression, agoraphobia, a nervous breakdown and hallucinations, one of which inspired *The Scream*. Mental illness also ran in his family, most notably with his sister. The Norwegian artist said of the relationship between his mental illness and his work, "My fear of life is necessary to me, as is my illness. Without anxiety and illness, I am a ship without a rudder … my sufferings are part of myself and my art. They are indistinguishable from me, and their destruction would destroy my art." In one of his journals he wrote, "Illness, insanity and death were the black angels that kept watch over my cradle and accompanied me all my life."

The words made me shudder tip to toe, the blackness inside me flittering around like wings of blackbirds. I wasn't sure how long I stared at the painting, felt its pain, and submerged myself within its energy. A door opened and closed. Noises filtered in and out of my ears. Yet, I could not turn, move or blink.

"Engaging, isn't it?" A female shadow appeared out of nowhere. "I'm inspired by the great work of broken, flawed people. Are you a fan of art?" I tore myself from the canvas to face the shadow beside me.

"I'm sorry, what?" It took me a second to gather my wits.

"I asked if you are a fan of art? These are reproductions of course, but aren't they just breathless?"

I nodded, "Yeah, kind of" I said unsure of myself. I remembered Maw Sue's love for great art and there was something else but I couldn't put my finger on it. The woman had interrupted my train of thought. And then it dawned on me, the woman is the doctor.

"Let me get your file and we'll step inside my office."

She motioned to the secretary who had been eyeing me suspiciously since I walked in the door.

"You've met Pearl already I assume?"

"Oh, sure, I met Pearl." I said lying and wasn't sure why. In truth, the secretary had avoided eye contact since I walked in. She knew who I was, like everyone else, probably from the newspaper. I had no doubt that me seeing a psychiatrist would also make the rounds in town, and probably straight to Edna's gossip column.

"By the way, I'm Doctor Telford." The woman turned and presented her highly manicured hand. "And you must be Cassidy."

"Yes, I am…or I was." I said shaking her hand. "Now they just call me the town arsonist. Or fire witch. Oh and divine cult leader." I laughed and glanced sideways at Pearl trying to get a reaction. With baited sarcasm I said, "You can read all about it in the local newspaper, right, Pearl?"

"In the *Gazette*?" Dr. Telford asked. "I thought people only read that to find out who got arrested or divorced?"

I raised my hand and smirked, "I fit both categories," I said, laughing.

"Well, Cassidy. Let's see if we can work on those categories. Follow me and we'll get started." She took a few steps towards her office and I slowly followed. For better or worse, I knew my life was about to change.

"Okay, Cassidy. This is my office. Make yourself at home."

"You can call me Cass for short, everybody does." I said trying to put on a masked exterior to protect myself. From what I didn't rightly know, but whatever it was, it made me tremble inside. I stopped short inside the doorway. Her office was like a cloud made into a room, or an entryway into heaven. The stark whiteness of everything made me adjust my vision. The ceiling went up, up and up. From the lobby, you wouldn't expect it to look this way. A miniature cathedral with white arches, large round columns and stained-glass windows. Sounds echoed and the walls swallowed them, as if they were holding thousands of secrets inside their bellies. I felt an eerie strangeness as if the room was as anxious as I was, anticipating my exposure, my secrets so it could eat for the day. I expected church bells to ring and saintly figures to come strolling out in robes and throw holy water on me. Everything was shades of white, except for a few flowers in vases, and some paintings on the wall, and scattered knickknacks. I felt like a huge sinful inkblot. I hesitated to touch the white couch with wooden arches and carvings adorned with white crème-striped pillows. I bent down and sat on the edge of the couch, uncomfortable and tense. My fingers tightened into clinched fists, an anxious behavior I'd had since I was a child. I rubbed my thighs until my skin was hot. *I pondered what happens next in places like this?*

My eyes scanned the perimeter of the room. Doc's petite frame sat in an oversized plush white chair. Behind her were bookshelves lined with medical and prescription books, and great thinker books by Maslow, Freud and Jung and others. I'd read some of them in my youth when I worked in the library during high school. To my right was a wall of windows and French doors leading outside to a pristine jungle of plants, waterfalls, birdbaths and feeders. A low blend of soft classical music played from a hidden speaker. Two Vincent van Gogh paintings were bookended on both sides of the wall. One I recognized to be *The Starry Night* but the other one I hadn't seen before. It depicted an old man sitting in a chair bent down with his hands on his face, hidden and appearing to be in anguish.

"Nice color scheme. You really hate white, huh?" I said laughing to break the tension in the air. And to cover up my anxiety.

"Can't stand it," she said smiling.

"I reckon you hear some pretty dark stuff in here, so you gotta offset the mood, huh? Just whitewash the whole place to get rid of the bad mojo, right?"

"It's part of the job, and the color white opens everything up."

"Ohh…is that what you're going to do with me? Open me up like a can opener…" My eyes glinted in anxiety and protest. It was a defense mechanism I never out grew.

"That's up to you Cass. Let's start shall we?"

My body flinched. "Sure thing, Doc" I sighed "Oh. I'm sorry, I mean Doctor Telford."

"It's fine. I'm not formal. You can call me Doc for short. It's all the same."

I nodded and glanced at the numerous degrees on the wall. I felt small. I had never let anyone inside my head before so this was a little off-putting and my mind unraveled in quiet desperation. I hoped she wouldn't notice.

"I see you got a divorce last year. You want to elaborate more?"

"Yeah, good riddance!" My sudden burst of emotion surprised me. I hadn't spoke about my ex-husband out loud in over six months in an attempt to erase him from my life.

"You sound angry, Cass. Can you tell me about it? A few days after your arrest, you told the police that your husband had been having an affair with Cynthia Stubblefield. The fire you *allegedly* set was in her front lawn with Sam's belongings, correct?"

"Hmpt! Allegedly" I said laughing under my breath. "Just like I told everyone else, I have no memory of that night, period. Believe me… if I DID remember, I'd take a lot of pleasure in it." I smiled one of those half-crazed hysteria filled grins that no doubt made me look guilty. The mere mention of Sam provoked chaos that led me to a dark place, lost in an effigy of shadows and slinks all the while trying to weave my way through to a light source that I felt was slowly slipping away, or worse, had never been there at all.

"Cass…what are you thinking?" Doc's voice was calm and predatory.

I felt trapped, an animal in a cage forced to confront what I don't want to see, hear, feel or touch and sure didn't want to talk about. I stared silently at Doc until the pressure burst forth.

"I hate talking about him, about her. It makes me angry. I feel as if I might self-destruct. I don't understand how talking about him helps me? Why can't I just let him go? I just avoid him, simple as that. Why can't everyone else? Why does everybody want to talk about him?" I bit my lip until it was numb.

"Cass. It's normal to have feelings of anger when someone betrays you. Anger is a healthy emotion when used in constructive ways. But just avoiding what happened is detrimental to your growth and healing. It's not easy confronting painful events, but avoidance and denial of our emotions is a sign of trouble. Emotional health involves being able to experience and exhibit all of our emotions in a way that doesn't cause harm to ourselves and others. I can feel the negative energy, so before we continue, I want to clarify something, okay? I'm not here to convict you. I'm not the judge or the jury. I'm here to help you. I am your advocate, not your enemy. I am not Sam, nor the police. I'm your therapist. I want you to feel free to voice anything you want. And we'll get there. It's not something that can be done in one day, or a week. Healing takes great courage. And patience and most of all, grace. You must give yourself a little grace each day and be kind to yourself while you heal. It's just day one and we're hitting the basics, feeling around but it will all come together eventually, with time. But remember, I'm for you—not against you. Now that you know where I stand, let's continue, okay?"

I let out a deep breath and nodded in agreement.

"The police and paramedics said you were knotted in a ball and speaking gibberish when they found you the morning after the fire. It's apparent you had some sort of breakdown triggered by something. It's important we find out what, so we can get to the why."

"Okay, Doc. You're the professional. Whatever you say." I shrugged knowing I really didn't have a choice. It's this or worse. I thought of Maw Sue and Castle Pines. My greatest fear was that I'd end up in that place, like she did. It was strange that I could only remember bits and pieces of my childhood, no details, just scraps, a few crumbs here and there. But I never, never forgot my fear of being locked up because of a broken mind. It was always there reminding me, that I was next.

"Let's start with the unusual. Let's talk about the bowl of collard greens. What do you think that was about? Does it have meaning? It's rather bizarre, don't you think?"

I laughed out loud. All I could think about was elementary school and my last name.

"Truthfully, I don't know, but if I was to make an educated guess, I left them for a statement. I mean, that's what I'd do today. You know, to make sure those lying cheaters knew exactly where it came from. And I say that because of my last name. The bowl of collard greens is basically my signature without signing my name. But the match, I'm not sure where that came from."

"You think so?" Doc looked baffled, "But why?"

"Hell if I know but I wish I did remember because it sounds pretty epic if you ask me. Now that I think about it, it's like a *Hallmark* card of the South. A big 'ole bowl of kiss my ass. *Burn, you bastard. Burn. Signed me, the collard green girl. Your soon to be ex-wife!"* Envisioning this made me start laughing. It was an off-the-chain hackle that made one of Doc's eyebrows rise as she studied me like a bug under a microscope.

"But then again, Doc…I don't remember. I'm just guessing."

"That's a pretty specific guess, Cass."

"Maybe, but with a name like Collard in the South you get bullied. *Here comes collard green girl. Gimme some collards and cornbread. I wish I had me some collard greens*, they'd say pinching my flat boobs or slapping my butt. Boys have their sexual innuendoes to really mess with a girls self-confidence, you know?"

Doc continued to scribble and I wondered what she was writing. Did she believe me? Or would she side with Edna's bullshit stories? My mind started to wheel into a dark place, a corner where I always think the worst.

"So…what's your assessment of me, I said with an air of smugness. Is the *Gazette* right? Is Edna Rollins a master of words and wisdom? Am I cultish and the devil incarnate? A witchy woman? Do we need to have an exorcism? Call a priest? Sprinkle some Holy water on me? Am I collard green crazy? Pun intended. Give it to me straight Doc. I can take it."

"Actually, I wasn't thinking any of those things." Doc smiled awkwardly as she jotted in my file and looked up. "You are actually unique."

"Unique?" I laughed under my breath. "That's what people say when they actually *think* you're certified crazy."

Doc put her pen down, leaned forward and gave me a serious eye-to-eye. "Cass, you were in a psychotic delusion when they found you, crouched in the corner of your house, wearing the same disheveled clothes witnesses said you wore the night before, and reeking of smoke. Plus, your face was painted with your own blood, not to mention your palm was sliced open and you were talking gibberish. The paramedics said you wouldn't let them touch you without screaming incoherently. You were saying, make me seven, make me seven over and over. Do you remember that? Even the smallest detail may help jog your memory and bring it back."

Hearing the word *seven* startled me and my hand flinched. I was fearful for the lost gaps of time and what remained hidden in my mind refusing to be seen. I glanced down at my palm. The wound was healing slowly now, scarring into a thick, perfect number seven and every time my heart beat, it pulsated and grew red like flames of fire. If I stared at it too long the voices would come. I felt branded and owned by a childhood I barely remember.

All I could think of was Castle Pines and the numerous times Maw Sue was locked up there when I was growing up. It was the spookiest place in Pine Log. All sorts of rumors spun around it dating back to the early 1800s. It sat like a huge dark beast at the edge of town, right off the main highway, three stories tall, made from stone and surrounded by a large piked iron fence. To my eyes it looked like a horrific open-mouthed gargoyle ready to swallow anyone that walked nearby. Even the older-than-time oak trees rising from the earth around the building seemed off, out of kilter, fractured, twisted and broken, as if the forest cast them out to shade the secrets looming in the walls of Castle Pines. Occasionally in passing, in the back seat of my parents car, I would try my hardest to see if I could find Maw Sue in the landscape dotted with zombie-like patients walking on the lawn, some in circles, some climbing trees, others chased by attendants, but mostly a landscape of lost souls isolated for merely being broken. I used to dream about Maw Sue inside the walls of that terrible place, hear her footsteps down a long hallway, rattling keys, locking doors, moans and cries for help. All of these things taught me that being different, outside the typical norm of society often leads to being cast out. And punished, and for Pine Log, that punishment was Castle Pines. Knowing this early in life, I began to clam up. Hide myself from others. Be someone I wasn't for fear of being found out and sent away, but now, here I am, one step closer to my worst nightmare. I came out of my mind meltdown to find Doc staring at me intently.

"What are you thinking about Cass? Anything? Can you tell me?"

"Oh, I'm sorry, Doc. I zoned out, not really thinking, just blah." But that was a lie. I was completely aware of everything, but numb, lost inside myself. If she'd been paying attention, if she'd looked a little deeper into my placid, red-rimmed eyes, she'd have seen the truth. She would have found a child crying and a woman dying.

But Doc was too busy studying the details of my dilemma. *And that was a mistake.* Maw Sue used to tell me that the devil *was* in the details: facts, items, objects, or features. And that's *exactly* where he is supposed to be. The obvious place. Trouble is, …*his* demons are not. The devil may be in the details but his sidekicks, his magistrates of misery, his demons of duty and determination lie scurrying outside the lines. They are obscure, they live in the abstract, they skid amongst the edges, they hang on to loose threads, they slip in unnoticed, unrecognized, and unknown. They are packaged, prized and ready to deceive all who befriend them. I would never reveal this tidbit of family history to Doc, *not now*. Besides, I'd been trained well in the art of denial from the queen herself, my mother.

"Okay, we'll continue pushing forward, no pressure, and then when I'm finished, I'm going to let you sit at that desk." She pointed to the small cubicle in the corner. "I'd like you to take a few tests for me. They will help me determine the best treatment for you. Lots of questions, don't overthink it, just go with your gut, okay?"

I nodded in agreement but my mind hesitated. It didn't know how to *not* overthink. It's automatic. It goes there. And once it does, I can't stop it. My eyes spanned the perimeter of the room without tipping off Doc to my paranoia. *They were here.* I could feel them as I always have. *Watching. Slinking. Lurking.* Maw Sue's words echo in my mind. *The devil is in the details; trouble is, his demons are not.*

For the remaining hour, she made use of her framed college degrees to pick apart my so-called destructive behaviors. In my mind, I bid her good luck. I knew those demons didn't answer to anyone but themselves.

"So, tell me about the cut on your palm. You told police you didn't remember cutting it, nor did you know how streaks of blood got painted on your face. Was this symbolic? Have you ever had feelings of wanting to hurt yourself?"

I blew out an exasperating gasp of air.

"I do now. You got a knife handy Doc?" The words flung out from a dark place, a tired of talking kind of place. "Who wouldn't? I feel interrogated and everyone in town is talking about me, as if they know me, which they don't. So yeah, suicidal thoughts invade me sometimes, but as far as that night? I don't remember."

"Why do you feel the need to hide your feelings with dark sarcasm?"

I squirmed in silence. A wrecked emotion, something dangerous and unnamed kept filling my lungs till I could barely draw air. I felt dizzy and disturbed but tried not to show it. I grabbed my right hand and rubbed the seven scar on my palm. It had been there since childhood, only sliced back open the night of the fire. It's weird that I have no memory of cutting it. *Why would I cut my own hand?* I was as puzzled as Doc on this one. *Did I try to kill myself? Did Sam drive me over the edge? But why my palm, why the scar? Why not just cut my wrist?* I pondered Doc's questions while I rubbed the wound until it burned hot and a vision erupted in my eyes with little fires. Each flame spoke a language I understood. A warning of what will come. Pain. Lots of pain.

A fear overtook me, followed by a faint partial memory. My mother told me and my sister that we got the scars from playing with old coke bottles. Meg ironically has the same seven cut on the same palm, same exact place. *How does that happen?* I don't remember playing with bottles, nor the cut, but I do vaguely remember another coincidence, a big one. Maw Sue had one too. Same scar, same seven, same hand. I never paid attention to it…*until now.*

"Cassidy…" Doc said patiently waiting and scribbling in her notebook. I came out of my mind doze to give her a satisfactory answer.

"Did I try to hurt or kill myself? Probably not, Doc." I fidgeted and sighed for the hundredth time. "Who knows at this point? Painting my face, cutting my hand, burning shit down. Crazy cult woman, so sayeth the gospel of Edna Rollins and the rest of this busybody shit show of a town. Everyone has answers but me. It looks like I'm no help at all."

The sound of Doc scribbling on paper with her fancy pen made me jittery. Suddenly all noises seemed filtered through my ears vibrant and louder, crisp and overwhelming. The classical hum from the speaker, the ink spilling on paper, the whir of air vents, a bird chirping outside the window, my mind racing. I shuffled from side to side. My squirming sounds echoed and bounced across the room. I was in my head, sorting, sifting and observing.

Doc sat in her queenly chair. Her hair fell in long silky strands of black fringe. Her face was pale and oval like an egg, with almond eyes and a tiny nose. She was petite, but her mannerisms and confidence give off a fierceness forged in hardship. Her blouse was red and flowed loosely over a short black pencil skirt.

Her legs were waxed and bare and had a fairy-dust sheen. Her feet were adorned with black and red peep-toe heels with fancy soles. She wore rings on every slender finger. She had a gold and black pen that was more like a magic wand. When she finished writing, without moving her head, her eyes would glance upwards at me and she'd twirl it between her fingers while it clicked against the rings like some hoodoo hypnotist, summoning a magic spell.

"I'm going to ask you a lot of questions and you can answer however you choose, yes or no, or elaborate more, it's up to you."

"Bring it on." I said since I didn't have a choice. A barrage of strange questions rolled off her tiny lips, each one a mini explosion rattling my core of being, forcing me to confront things I'd never thought about before.

"Tell me about yourself. When did you first know you were depressed? Are there any family problems? What about your intimate relationships? Have you ever felt unusually good or high? Any suicidal thoughts? Do you hear people talking when no one is around? What about hallucinations or delusions? Have you felt any of these things, Cass?"

I tried to answer the questions as honestly as I could. But mainly, I just wanted this session to end. I tensed up so much I was shaking and fully expected to see Doc push a red panic button sending in the men in white coats to cart me off to a modern-day Castle Pines. Just like Maw Sue. Letting a stranger in my head terrified me and sent me to a vulnerable place inside where I just shutdown.

"I don't know, Doc. I don't know, I don't know." I said grabbing my head to control the spinning.

"Take a deep breath Cass. I'm not trying to upset you. I'm simply introducing the possibility to your mind, so it can absorb the information, and ponder. The answers may come later. Right now, we're just getting to know each other. So, let's do this. You don't need to answer anything else unless you want to for the rest of the session. I'll do all the talking. All I ask is you give me a chance and listen."

I nodded in relief and leaned back on the couch. The thought of doing this weekly for twelve months seemed overwhelming. Doc began telling stories about other people with similar issues as mine, beginnings and endings, life stories with metaphors and lessons. I listened intently. Somehow the child in me took interest because it connected me to a time long ago. Storytelling was as familiar as my blood type. Knit in me, running through me, binding me to parts unknown.

As a child I told everyone if I was dying and needed blood, to make sure I got the blood type I needed. Type (S+) for storytelling. It was the bloodline of the timeless classics, Hemingway, Fitzgerald, and Twain. Or so I thought, and no-one could convince me otherwise. It started when Maw Sue told us we had the (S+) blood type. She was referring to our ancestors who were seekers, but I thought she meant storytelling. I didn't know it wasn't a real blood type. At doctor visits, the nurse would ask my mother medical questions, and when they got to my blood type, they'd say, Cass is (O-) but I'd scream out, no I'm not, I'm (S+). My mother would huff and say, stop that, there is no such thing. But I'd throw a wild-eyed fit. My mother would go into spasms of embarrassment and the nurse would get a good laugh.

Doc's way of storytelling was familiar and connected me to my childhood and my great-grandmother, Maw Sue. As kids, me and my sister would sit at her feet listening to outlandish tales of worlds, places and people long ago. We'd take long walks behind the pine curtain in the safety and terror of the woods behind our house. Listening to Doc tell stories gave rise to a yearning in me to remember, to pull up roots I'd buried or covered up. A gap of time was missing, gone from memory for reasons I can't recall, and not only the fire, but my entire childhood. Suddenly, I realized I *don't* know who I am. I am Cassidy Cleo Collard by name and birth, divorcee, town arsonist and witchy crazy cultist by social status, via Edna 'gossip queen' Rollins but otherwise, an empty shell of a person. Nonexistent, as if I have no core, no attachment, no bond to anything or anyone. Just bits and pieces of a childhood that eludes me.

Brrringgggggggg! A loud pulsated noise echoed in the room. I shot off the couch like a bottle rocket! Lately, I jumped at everything, even little noises. I glanced back at the door expecting the men in white coats to pounce on me. *Castle Pines, the ghosts say. Time to go, Cass.* Frazzled and filled with anxiety, I rerouted my ears to the noise clacking on Doc's side table. Her hand reached for the off switch on the loud bell timer bouncing across the surface until it was silenced.

"Geesh, a little warning would have sufficed." I said shaken and disturbed.

"Sorry, it is a bit loud isn't it? It signals the end of our session, so most of my patients look forward to hearing it."

"Good to know." I sighed in relief, mainly because there would be no Castle Pines for me. I made it through day one. Only three hundred and sixty-four days to go. I finished up my session by taking numerous psychological tests that managed to burn my brains till I couldn't wait to leave. On the way out, Pearl handed me my next appointment card and never met my gaze. I tried to get her attention with my whimsical sarcasm but she would have none of it.

I hurried back to work at the bank, but I didn't get much work done. Five o'clock came and I slipped out unnoticed. All the way home, my mind pondered the session with Doc, her questions, my questions, and all the unknowns. It was exhausting. I didn't know it yet, but this day would mark a crossroad in my life for irrevocable change for better; but everyone knows, before it gets better, it always gets worse. Doctor Trish Telford, MD, PHD, would become a big part of that journey too. She'd scribble in my file with her fancy hoodoo pen documenting the various details of the devil.

As for me...I was *still* dancing with his demons. Doc had stirred the cauldron of chaos inside me, to which they clung like flesh on a bone, so it wasn't long before they summoned me to return to my past, a childhood behind the pine curtain, deep in the forest where I left the disturbed little girl I hated. All it took was a prod, a poke at my mind, my restless spirit. And no one can provoke me better than my mother.

MOTHER MOONSHINE

Breathing dreams like air.
~F. Scott Fitzgerald

Talking to my mother is not easy. It has taken me ten minutes of pacing and two glasses of wine to calm down from a two minute one sided conversation.

"The store clerk asked me if I was the fire starters mom." She said furious. "What am I supposed to say to that? It's embarrassing Cassidy."

I laughed out loud, "Well you should have lit a match mother and cut loose…danced around the fire like that hag Edna said I did."

I felt a deep stab in my chest that left me winded. It was an instant gnawing once the words left my lips. The words summoned a ghost, something alive and festering inside me. It was unclear what, or why or how, but its presence is eerie and unsettling. I simply chalked it up to the strange side effects of talking to my mother. Our atypical bond always sets off bombs in me. And as usual, my cynical tone upended my mother, but it was my way of ending the conversation.

"Cassidy this is not funny. I can barely show my face in town. And your father just acts like you had a campfire and roasted marshmallows, I…I just can't deal with you two acting like nothing happened."

"Ohhh…I'm sorry mother…that I'm such a disappointment to you. I feel so bad that you are going through this because of me."

My sarcasm was sending her over the edge and I enjoyed it.

"Cassidy what is wrong with you?" She spat so forceful I could almost taste the sour spittle coming through the phone.

"Ask Edna. She seems to know everything about me." I said in finality. I had hit the bare minimum of time I could talk to my mother without a mental breakdown or a complete fury of anger by breaking a dish or destroying a chair. I needed to end it quickly so I just beat the end of the phone against the cabinet door a few times until I gained composure. It gave me a moment to make my escape.

"Gosh, did you hear that? What is that?" I said pretending. "Mother? Are you there? Hello? Mother?" I hit the cabinet five more times and slammed the phone down. I walk to the couch and bury my face inside the pillow and scream till the ghosts of my mothers womb are silenced. *Or so I thought.* For the rest of the night I lounged on the couch trying to mend the fracture that had opened the floodgates to my past, but it was too late. I stared at the cut scar on my hand in the shape of a seven. Under pressure my mind released quick flashes of time, disturbing and rapid bursts of yesteryear. I'm a child standing by a fire, hands dripping blood and I'm screaming. My vision tunnels and goes black. A memory is released, one I would never be ready for.

My parents both grew up in the small town of Pine Log. Dad had three brothers, Daryl, Sid and Mark. Their father, who we called Papa C spent weekends at the local race track. He was a top mechanic, could fix anything and loved the thrill of racing. As kids, my father and his brothers tagged along until they knew everything that he did and it was only natural for them to follow suit. By age ten my father could literally rebuild an engine better than any mechanic in town.

Papa C built a tinker shop behind their house out of tin siding and metal poles. It was a man's playhouse, a torture chamber for cars, machinery and boyish dillydallying. Tools, hoses and metal contraptions hung on prongs and strapped from ceiling to floor, or strewn on shelves, under cabinets or tucked under boards. Wooden carts on wheels were stacked three-deep with nuts, bolts, fragments, screws, plastic fittings, you name it. From what I hear, the Collard boys were drawn inside the tinker shop by a cosmic force only affecting the male population. Females have yet to comprehend this strange male bonding ritual. The tinker shop even had its own monster. A fire-breathing, spitting contraption that magically transformed metal into pieces of art. This metallic, fire-breathing power made men gather in groups and take stuff apart just for the fun of it. They hit iron, wood, and blunt objects, twisting, bending, molding, or burning them with monster's fire. Outside they pissed on tree stumps, and spit tobacco but inside the tinker shop they cursed like sailors, drank like fish and created magic like wizards. Those Collard boys could roll in a box of metal parts and three days later, roll out a shiny, souped up Chevy. My father didn't know it at the time, but this hobby would lead him to his future, not as a mechanic or a race car driver, but to the doorstep of a fortress of a woman so mysterious and unknown she would become his wife and bear his first born daughter. Then sacrifice her on a Southern altar to worship the Gods of silence and suffering.

My mother, Gabby Lancaster was barely eighteen and worked as a clerk at a shop furnishing custom fabric and leather upholstery. My father drove up in his Chevy to drop off two bucket seats to be recovered. She was sitting behind the desk and didn't give him a second glance. But when she did, one look at Mother's blue eyes and he was smitten. He showed up once a week to have work done and to get my mother's attention. She had no interest at first and it drove him crazy. He returned time and time again, determined to win her over. Neither of them knew what they were getting into. She finally let her guard down. Dad broke the ice by inviting her to one of his races. When Mama C would retell this story to me as a child, she said from the get-go mother was out of place, all prim, ladylike and proper sitting in the stands next to the wild brothers. She said it was like royalty and rebels. Side by side. Alcohol was as common as water amongst the patrons, so was loose lips and tempers.

My father won two consecutive stages in the pre-races, showing off for Gabby. This fired up his nemesis, Carl Ray Johnson, who had been riding his bumper all night. Carl Ray had bumped him illegally and sent him spinning into the pasture once already, and what should have been flagged, wasn't. This infuriated the crowd into an uproar and when rednecks go into uproars, nothing good comes from it. Daryl, Sid and Mark cursed, spit, yelled and threw beer cans. Dad was known as the Mad Hatter of the racetrack, so things were fixing to hit the proverbial shit fan and Gabby would be an eye witness to the carnage. Carl and my father exchanged hellfire looks between motor revs. The flag dropped and the race was on. Carl Ray was in the lead and my father on his ass. It was tight for the first few laps until my father gassed it on the straightway and rammed the hellfire out of Carl

Ray, which sent him spinning into oblivion. The crowd went crazy and cheered the Mad Hatter's retribution. Until the black flag came out. Apparently, my father was flagged for the same move Carl Ray pulled on him earlier, except Carl Ray didn't get flagged. He got away with it which was the reason for the initial uproar.

This was not going to fly for the racing fans. Tempers flared in the stands, but my father took it in stride. He'd seek revenge another race. His only plan in the moment was to impress Gabby. He made another lap and blew her a kiss as he revved the engine. She looked lost as ever, her head spinning from side to side as fans erupted into chaos, pure southern mayhem. Yelling and cheering, then booing and then the food fight started. Flying hot dogs, popcorn like confetti and fizzing beer cans exploded in the air. A punch was thrown, then another. Suddenly the whole stand was a free-for-all brawl. My soon-to-be mother ducked and dodged and watched with shock and horror. My father just laughed and did a burn out. He saw the commotion as just another day in the Mad Hatter world of racing.

The next month, my mother Gabby was not in the stands but behind the wheel of a race car and a newly initiated member of an all-girl racing team called the Powder Pistons. Most, if not all the entrants at the track were wives or long-time girlfriends of drivers; but there was one persistent tart who had been trying to convince someone's husband or boyfriend to provide her with a car. It was made clear through the racetrack grapevine: no man was to lend her a stock car. Well, poor 'ole Gavin, my father, "Mad Hatter" Collard didn't get the message. He sent the perky blonde tart out in his car. Laps later, after rolling his car in a heat, he moseyed across the track looking for Gabby. She met him with a palm smack across the face right in front of a packed and roaring bleachers. From that moment on, my father never lent his car to another woman. It was weeks before Gabby would talk to him again. I had a good hint this was when the *silent treatment* all started.

The G-Team, as they were called, Gavin and Gabby were unbeatable at the racetrack. Then came Myrtle "Messy" Waterford. She was a stout potty-mouthed female who didn't bother sissy racing with the Powder Pistons. She raced with the brute boys from the get-go, whether they liked it or not. Gabby, who had won every single heat and had the town talking up a dirt storm, double dared her to a race. Myrtle decided to cross over to the girls' side to prove a point. Myrtle "Messy" Waterford did indeed cause a mess, after she lost control and flew off the backstretch into a pile of hay, courtesy of Gabby "Lash" Lancaster, who dished out some serious lashes and had the bleachers roaring. Afterwards, a defeated and silent "Messy" Waterford stuck with the boys. Gabby became queen of the racetrack and crown of my dad's heart. Weeks later, Dad proposed from the window of his race car and the crowd went nuts.

Out of all the stories I heard about my parents, this one was hard to swallow. I tried to picture my mother behind the wheel of a car doing ninety to nothing and wearing a pink Powder Pistons jacket or sending Myrtle flying over the backstretch. It was inconceivable. This was the same woman who constantly nagged my father to slow down, don't turn the curve so fast, quit revving the engine, don't spin the tires, and whatever the hell else she could gripe about. If this was *indeed* my mother, then what the hell happened to her? If it wasn't for my grandparents telling me these stories, I'd never have known this side of Gabby "Lash" Lancaster Collard. She hid this part of her life just like everything else she hid—beneath the walled fortress of pale skin and blue eyes. *But why?*

It occurred to me that not only did I have a family tree on my father's side that was rooted in disturbing details, I uprooted another branch on my mother's side just as muddled. It made no sense for my mother to hide something like racing cars. She was well beyond the age of not caring. So why all the secrecy? And what else was she hiding?

As a kid, there were times I'd catch her watching me precariously. She was always there at the edge of the pine curtain, in the backdrop of my life with an ambiguous glare in her eyes, a struggle of sorts, one cold and distant, but the other yearning to be unshackled and join me in play. But I fear this is only something I dreamed up. Because in the same thought, my mother sees me for who I am, and it is equally terrifying as it is joyful.

I constantly observed my mother, curious as to her function and what made her, the way she walked, the way she dressed, the way she put on lipstick, twice around the lips, then pat once with paper. I learned to mimic this motion till it was perfected and I was a carbon copy, a shadow in the mirror reflection. I did not know that this would become a ritual to me, not for the sake of makeup but for survival. I'd find her lip prints around the house on notepads, receipts, scraps of paper and tissue—but never on me. I felt instantly cheated. So I'd find the lip prints and hide them in a wooden box called the mirror bin, a present from Maw Sue when I was born. Every day I'd go on a scavenger hunt to find them. Stacks of lip prints, colorful unearned kisses from my mother. One day I thought for sure I'd have enough kisses to fill the emptiness inside me. And every day I yearned for those kisses to come to life on my cheeks, on my lips, around my neck. I wanted the lips to grow a body capable of holding me and wanting me and telling me how much they loved me. But until then, at least I had the lipstick paper kisses.

In my eyes my mother was an exotic paper doll with beautiful coal-black hair, paper-white skin, and sky-blue eyes, fierce in intensity, but easily torn. As I grew older, I began to believe I was the cause for every rip and tear. It must have been my fault she couldn't hold me. Kiss me. For some reason, my mother grew as distant as the moon, unreachable, and I was only a shadow in her bright glow. I kept telling myself she couldn't help it. She was after all, just a paper doll, fragile and lame, who couldn't hold me or tell me I was valuable. Not because she didn't want to, but because she couldn't. *She was paper.* So, when I heard the stories of my mother's former life before I was born, I found it hard to envision this same broken doll used to race cars. Even now that I'm grown up, married and divorced, an arsonist on the verge of madness—*I don't believe it.*

But because my mind is broken, it has to punish me, apparently, because in that same thought, she appears like a ghost before me. She is dressed in a tight black jumpsuit, pink jacket and black helmet. She is sitting behind the wheel of a race car with a loud purring motor. She pops the clutch, presses the gas, squeals the tires and speeds off, leaving me stunned and choking on dust. The dust turns to sparks and the sparks bring another painful memory. The one I thought I erased forever.

It was New Year's Eve, a little before midnight. I was seven. Mother was lying on the couch drinking a glass of wine. Dad was six beers in and kicked back in his green wool recliner. Meg, my sister and I were laying on a pallet watching Dick Clark's New Year's Eve special. The countdown commenced, ten, nine, eight, seven, six, five, four, three, two, one—and then an explosion of fireworks. People yelled, kissed, hugged, threw confetti and toasted drinks. At the same time as the celebration on TV we could hear our neighbors up and down the street gathering, popping fireworks, shooting off guns and raising all kinds of Southern hell. We were nothing of the sort. Meg and I were dull as doornails and bored out of our wits. According to our parents, fireworks, sparklers, matches, anything flame related was too dangerous.

Mother disappeared into the kitchen. We thought nothing of it till she returned with an assortment of pots, pans, metal spoons and two wild slits in her eyes I'd never seen before. My father must have recognized this wildness, because he chugged his beer and said, "Mamma's cut loose."

Meg and I looked at each other. *What did that mean?* I didn't know it then, but it would be the first, and only time I'd see a side of my mother I never knew existed, except in the stories from my grandparents. The events of this night would linger in my heart for years, when the silence of the house ate me alive.

Meg and I sat up on the pallet, confused as she handed each of us a pot and a spoon. Meg and I gave each other sideways glances. We weren't sure if this was a hint to start cooking or what? Then the woman who resembled our mother skipped outside the front door like a phantom melting into the darkness of the night. Meg and I sat like bumps on a log as to what was happening. Seconds later, between popping fireworks and sizzling sky sirens, we heard clanging and banging, metal to metal, then strange howling and yipping and carrying on. We both looked at Dad for answers.

He just smiled and said, "Yeppp, cut loose all right" then winked at us nonchalantly and opened another beer. Meg and I didn't know what to do. It was uncharacteristic of our mother to act freely wild and crazy. We weren't too sure we wanted to participate. Her sudden feral nature gave us caution, but dad sat back as if this was something he'd seen before and took pleasure in seeing again. She banged and howled until we were compelled to witness this with our own eyes. We ran out the door and stood on the front porch like parade gawkers. Our mother looked like a ghost, an apparition, a barefoot night phantom in a thin white gown dancing across the lawn. She howled and sang and yipped and hollered while she banged on the aluminum pot like a rock goddess left over from Woodstock. She spun and clanged, thrust her hips out and in circles, she shimmied and shook, and tilted and vibrated like those go-go dancers I'd seen on TV. Our aloof mother was caught up in some strange energy, her head jutting upwards, sideways and back and forth. I caught the wild glint in her blue eyes reflecting off the light of the moon and forming prisms. They were like the white and blue flames that leapt from sparklers only twice, the second you light them and right before they go out in cinders of smoke. I was so mesmerized by this stranger, this ghost woman using my mother's body as a vessel, that I barely heard Meg ask, "How much wine has mom had?"

"It doesn't matter. I like it." I said running off the porch in a sprint. I joined my flamboyant, vibrant, wild slit-eyed, cut-loose mother. This event was as rare as a cosmic comet crossing the blackened sky. I didn't want to miss it for fear it wouldn't return for another eighty years. Meg followed. The three of us danced. Banged. Clanged. Hooted. Howled. Hollered. Yipped. Yelled. Laughed. Shimmied, wiggled and waggled. We were all caught up in a strange eccentric embodiment that had somehow embedded itself inside my mother. For the first time, *ever*, I felt inches from the moon. So close in proximity I could see the craters, the fissures and cracks, its fusions colliding with the galactic heat as it lit up and illuminated its great flaws and beautiful edges. I could see my mother, the one I always wanted. And there we were, three wild pot dancers cut loose under the shine of the big drop moon. I wanted the moment to go on forever.

Unhindered. Spellbound. Goddesses.

For ten heavenly minutes, I embraced a mother, a woman, a girl, a gypsy, a goddess and a vivid blinding moonshine I never knew existed. After the pot dance, we lit sparklers and went back to dancing in circles with our fire sticks under the light of the moon, behind the beloved pine curtain we called home.

I barely slept a wink that night. But when I did, I dreamed of fireworks, metal drums, moonshines, and mothers. Morning came and I leaped from my bed. My ears anticipated the sound of metal. My eyes grew wild while my heart waited to cut loose again at dusk when the moon rose up from the pine curtain. But just like the moon, parts of my mother were hidden away. Far on the other side where I could not see, reach, or touch. It was dark, shadowed and silent as if she never existed. I would never see this dancing, wild eyed, cut-loose mother moonshine side of her again.

She was gone. As if she had never been real.

Sometimes, I wonder if I dreamed it. I'd ask Meg if it really happened. I needed to know that I wasn't going crazy. Sadly, her answer was always "Yes Cass, it happened." Because of the sharp contrast of that night and our daily life, I put away the memory in my mind, pushing it deeper and deeper till I could no longer see it, or feel its power over me.

Only when I heard fireworks, or the sharp clings of metal did my mind wander back and grieve. Without answers, I pondered what happened to her. *Where did she go? Was she coming back, and when? Did I do something? Was it me?* When she didn't return, I'd get angry. I resented seeing the side of her touched by fire, shined by starlights, swept away by the moon and hidden by the shadows. I'd curse the darkness who I thought was hiding my carefree moonstruck mother who was held captive under people pleasing, coiffed hair, perfect makeup, colorful lipstick and brand-name pantsuits.

Anytime I saw fireworks, my blood would surge and my throat would lock. I'd stare into the star-studded night and be struck with incredible sadness. I'd see my mother moving and shaking in the sparks, tiny glimpses blowing up the sky and cutting loose. My arms reached upwards to touch her strange burst of colors. With each thunderous boom and crack, my heart broke. In vain I'd try to catch the disintegrated sparkles falling to earth, in hopes that I'd reignite what I believed to be my mother in the wild flames. I envisioned my mother moonshine rising from the ashes to embrace and love me.

But she never did.

And I could think of no-one to blame but myself.

PRESENT DAY

MAY 17, 1988
NEWS YOU CAN USE
BY EDNA ROLLINS

TEXAS NEWS EDITION

The collard green fire is still a mystery to locals. The following is my continued interviews with eye witnesses to the event. Today we are talking with Gladys Poland who lives next door to the victim of the fire. I asked her to give an account of that night. "Well, I had just arrived home from the women's quilting club and I parked my car and was almost on the front porch when I heard a whoosh and saw flames go up. The light lit up my lawn. The woman I saw was ranting and raving, singing and doing strange things with the fire as she danced around it. She was a terrible sight with red streaks on her face and just scary, as if she wasn't real. I went straight in and called the police. I am an upstanding member of the neighborhood watch and when I see something I call. But that night they told me it wasn't a crime to have a campfire in your yard. I kept telling them it was more than that, but they wouldn't listen. So I just went in and got my polaroid camera and took a picture. But when the police finally did arrive, long after she left, they said the picture only showed shadows and flames, not the actual person. But I told them I knew exactly who it was. It was an Ainsley girl. I'd know that family anywhere. I knew the grandmother too. I told them the story I knew and they won't soon forget it neither."

Well folks, you heard it here first. Until next time, tune into KTBR local radio news station 109.9. I'm Edna Rollins and that's news you can use.

SEEKERS AND SAGES

To live is the rarest thing in the world.
Most people just exist.
~ Oscar Wilde

It was three-thirty when I glanced at the bank clock in the lobby. I had just finished up with a customer when the flashes hit me. Bursts of fire, dripping blood, a child screaming, a never ending fall into a dark abyss.

"No, no, not here. Not here," I whispered out loud to no one and held my head somehow thinking I could detain them. I rushed to close my office door before anyone noticed my catatonic melt-down. I tried to stop it, will it away, but my dreadful past doesn't care. It stores up memories in the vault of my messed-up mind like a game of hide and seek, and hither they come. Tag! You're it, they say. It transfixes me to my desk and with a fervor the memory overpowers me.

I was six when I knew the fresh smell of pine needles was my scent of belonging. The plush haven of pines and thickets was my kingdom and I was the Queen of the pine curtain. The woods were my sacred place, my heritage, a story yet untold. Nature welcomed me as its own child and I took refuge in that. When life broke as it often did in the Collard household, I ran to the curtain of the pines to hide. The disturbed soil bore the imprint of my tiny feet, and somehow I feared, also held the horrors of my soul, the scattered seeds of sorrow, the ones I can't seem to recollect or dig deep enough to find and maybe for good reason.

This land had been in my family for generations. Big Pops (Jefferson James Collard) came in the nineteenth century and raised his family. His son, William Jefferson Collard (Papa C) married May Dell Adams (Mama C) and they raised four boys, the oldest being my father, Gavin Beck Collard. During Dad's childhood, May Dell's mother, Susannah Josephine Worrell, who we call Maw Sue, my eccentric great-grandmother, moved onto the property. Years later, my own father followed tradition by getting married and moving a few houses down.

Growing up with family on all sides gave me plenty of time to explore our barbaric ancestral tree. I had always been curious to know our lineage. I tried to acquire my younger sister Meg's help, but she scorned my request as if she originated from a line of nobility found in a jeweled oak tree, some scandalous fifteen-minute affair in the back room of the White House, JFK meets Maid Mary drama. Her efforts at obtaining royal status began at a young age when Maw Sue told her she was a seeker, a special kind with sparkle and shine. Meg learned to smell greenbacks like a bloodhound. She believed she was only temporarily punished to live in squalor. Her belief was a royal knight was going to drive up in a Mercedes while a squat chauffeur driver in a stuffy white suit jumped out holding a satin pillow with a sparkling rhinestone baby rattler with Meg's name inscribed. Documentation to further prove her theory of a royal bloodline. She'd hightail it out of this shit town and leave us redneck Southern saps to our pig-sticking.

But me, I bled the Southern way. I bled thick pine sap flowing from the bark of the wounded ancestral tree. From an early age, a sense of aloneness had found its place in me. I began to read books and absorb stories to fill the gaps of empty space. I became an eavesdropper of conversations, a watcher, an observer of my surroundings, people and mannerisms, and expressions. Once I started elementary school, teachers became annoyed with my chatty tales. No one needs to know about Mrs. Sparkman's gall-bladder surgery Cassidy, they'd say, and certainly not her husband's scandalous affair. And how do you know what that is anyway? Now get back to your desk and finish your drawing.

I knew a lot more than they thought I did. Kids are perceptive to their surroundings. I may not have fully understood what I heard but I listened. I grew up on the porches hearing stories. It was part of me. Words stuck to my skin like leeches sucking the blood from my Southern core. A yearning in me had to speak it, retell it, add my own elements as if it came natural, letters and words forming a shape to my reality and gave my altered vision a perception of place. My ears tingled as they absorbed an assortment of fishing stories, epics of war, dramatic narratives, biblical analogies, poems, fibs, death plots, love sagas, autobiographies, memoirs, cautionary tales, race car stories, outlaws, hogwash and a lot of cock and bull. Maw Sue said that the latter wasn't story at all, just the liquor talking. Tales flowed from porches to kitchen tables, to the liquor stores, beauty salons, tinker shops and house to house, neighbor to neighbor, church office to pulpit, and by the time it reached Edna Rollins' front porch, it was a legendary tale. She was the town blabbermouth and found a way to get paid for it by using her black tongue to become a journalist. No one was safe from Edna's typewriter, including Maw Sue. And now, me.

I loved Maw Sue's storytelling rituals. We'd sit on the front porch swing munching a carton of milk balls. Meg was usually there too, but I liked it the most when it was just me and Maw Sue. It was then, our gifts would engage. Sounds went crisp in our hearing ears. *Creak, creak* went the swing. *Crunch, crunch* went our teeth. *Swish, swish* went the wind blowing between the swing slats. *Eek, eek* went the rusty chain. And she told many a story on that old porch. Stories of side-spitting, gun-toting, bullet-brazen renegades always one step ahead of the law, finger on the trigger and sleeping with one eye open. Gunfights, bootleggers, murder, womanizing, cheating, knife-slicing, fist-fighting, poker-playing, dice-throwing hucksters hung off every branch of our family tree. My love for words was built on that porch. It was also the first time I sensed they could haunt me as well, though at the time, I didn't understand why. I wanted to ask Maw Sue about it, but I remembered her analogy. She said a porch is to be useful for two things, and two things only. *Storytelling or silence.* No arguing, no lies, no crying, no gossip. No tears, no fears. Just storytelling or silence.

Meg and I were typical southern kids roaming freely along the side streets kicking balls, digging up crawdads, catching tadpoles, swimming in the creeks, skipping rope and trailing through the big pine thicket making forts out of pine straw or picking blackberries. But in the heat of the summer everything slowed to a crawl. The humid Texas weather flogged us with three-digit temperatures and there wasn't a whole lot to do in Pine Log for entertainment. We had one Dairy Queen, a Tasty Freeze ice cream shop, a miniature Putt-Putt, a movie theater and a skating rink. But if you were my mother, you might venture to the Green Stamp store and gaze at the shelves. What Pine Log lacked in activities; the S&H Green Stamp store made up for in mass merchandise. Green stamps were distributed as a rewards program from grocery stores and other retailers. The appeal of collecting stamps for the latest gadget sent women into buying frenzies, including my green tongued mother, who had more kitchen utensils than sense.

When Meg and I ran out of things to do, boredom would set in and my mind hated idleness. It suffered the most in silence, so I sought out ways to stimulate it anyway I could. There were days I weaved between my mother and father as if I was trying to find my place, my core identity, a fingerprint, a roadmap to find my way. I could see parts of myself in my dad, the long-winded know-it-all part which was the vivacious, wordy, no-holds barred half of me, and yet the more mysterious half of me was my mother, aloof and distant, avoiding me at every turn, unknown, sometimes brooding and hidden, closed off, withdrawn, a blank disconnect. *This* was my dilemma.

My relationship with Maw Sue was different. She had her strange ways, but even so, her rituals and storytelling drew me in, and comforted me. We shared a strange mutual connection, a bond I loved and yet also feared for reasons unknown. Meg and I had heard all the old stories about our bloodlines being from a line of seekers with beautiful, wonderful gifts that we must use, less they become our curse. She'd bend down on our level and stare deep into our eyeballs and her voice would turn to a crippling whisper, while her crinkled lips cast the spell. "Girls, she'd say, you must always, always—make lovely your losses."

And there it was. The weight of four words on my shoulders like giants with smelly feet. Four words that broke my ever-loving Southern sap heart. Hearing it the first time, I grew heavy hearted with unknown burdens. Anytime I asked her what it meant, she'd tell me life would let me know, soon enough. Those four words were like sticky old wallpaper glued on my heart, and every time I heard them being spoken, an unknown force snatched a top corner of the paper and yanked it down, exposing my vulnerability. No matter how much got peeled off, it left a gruesome layer of pain behind. *Make lovely your losses. Make lovely your losses.* Days and nights I pondered what it meant. I feared a great weeping loss was always at my back. I spent a good majority of my childhood living on the verge of anxiousness, waiting to lose something. Even today, as I sit here with a porch full of losses, divorced, in therapy, in trouble, I'm still no closer to understanding what she meant.

Mama C didn't receive the storytelling gene, in fact she barely spoke but she could sew like a mad woman. She made a lot of our clothes, much to the dismay of our mother who preferred the bland modest JC Penney style. I wasn't that keen on the patchwork trend Mama C seemed to be stuck in, except for one outfit. Mainly because it irked the crap out of my mother who said I looked like a hippie reject, which I took as a compliment. I eventually had to hide the outfit to keep her from burning it.

It all started when the hippie gathering turned up in Pine Log at the campgrounds in 1971. They traveled through our small town in big painted-up buses, and vans, and barefoot women with flowing dresses, flowers in their hair, playing and singing music and carrying on about stopping the war. We happened to be downtown at the JC Penney store sidewalk sale when they paraded by. Meg and I ran beside them waving while our mother ran after us. We made it a half-block before she finally caught us but not before we saw everything we needed to see. Hanging out the windows of the cars were free-spirited girls with skimpy shirts and painted faces, holding signs saying, *Peace and Love, Stop the War*. Others danced in the back of pickup trucks, and some girls had no shirts on at all, which made the local men stop and gawk. The boys were loosely dressed with hip huggers, long hair and some had beards. That was the day the Moon Wanderers lit a fire in my belly and I began to mimic the hippie movement, what they wore, their hair style, and temperament, even their strange language which freaked my mother out, which only made me want to use it more.

The Moon Wanderers' wanton freedom of expression, despite the opinions of others, gave me great insight into a world I didn't know existed. Apparently, they stirred up controversy wherever they went, including Pine Log. This is when I discovered more about the blabbermouth journalist named Edna Rollins who had written about the moon wanderers in the daily newspaper.

After I read it, I didn't like Edna at all…and I normally like everybody. Sometime later, Maw Sue started acting different. She wouldn't sit or relax, or talk. Nor tell stories. Just pace, fret and mumble. It wasn't until a few days later I saw the newsprint of the *Gazette.* This time the blabbermouth was talking about Castle Pines Mental Hospital and there were references to members in the community, no names, but small details recognizable to people. Anyone could figure out who she was talking about. I grew to despise Edna Rollins. She gridlocked the town with her typewriter terror and used God as a weapon. It took a few weeks for Maw Sue to overcome the damage of those words, and she did so with grace. As for me, I held a grudge.

When Meg and I weren't listening to stories or modeling patchwork hippie clothing, or thinking of ways to hunt down Edna, we played games like any other southern kid bored out of their wits. Parcheesi, Monopoly, Checkers, Crazy Eights, and Go Fish. This is when I discovered my sister was a sore loser. Denial with a big D. It didn't matter if you won hands down, Meg refused to believe that she had lost. Once I remember triumphantly winning and enjoying the moment, so I ribbed her a little. Her eyes went slant. Her body tensed. Meg *couldn't* lose.

Not at cards, Hopscotch, Red Rover, Dodgeball, Chinese checkers, Old Maid—or *life.* Queen Meg did not get the game player gene; she did, however, get the over reactor gene and played it to the hilt. Since she couldn't lose, lest she die or something, she created a distraction, and not just once or twice, but every single solitary game. I mean, try playing hide and seek with someone who is clearly found but swears up and down she isn't.

I caught her in the act of cheating once, though she'd never admit it. We had just finished a game of checkers and against my better judgment, I let her win, but only because I despised hearing her whine and carry on. Plus, she pinched like a crab and I had the bruises to prove it. While she was basking in the winner's circle, we started playing a game of cards. I was ahead by three sets. Unfortunately, I had not considered the four glasses of water I drank earlier. My bladder screamed. I squirmed and called a time-out and warned Meg not to touch anything. When I returned—for the one hundred and fifty-seventh time—*disaster*.

"Act of God," she said all innocent and fragile. *Act of God, my foot.* Cards were strewn all over the porch, down the steps and across the yard. Checkers were littered on the grass and the board hung limp in the cleft of a sycamore tree. Another time she said a massive wind swept across the porch and disbanded from its swirling vortex a mob of ugly, hairy, big-nosed trolls who tied Meg to the porch post, and then proceeded to ransack the game like a bunch of Viking savages. Meg acted convincingly shocked. And more elaborate, to top it off, she said before they left, all thirty of them licked her cheek with their crusty inflamed troll tongues, then tickled her silly, untied her and ran off in the woods. I didn't know whether to be impressed with my sisters brilliant imagination or be fearful that she may actually believe her own storytelling to avoid loosing.

Collecting cicadas was another pass time in the South. When the hot brutal summers left us with not a damn thing to do, it was their buzzing, squawking, rhythmic high pitched whines of musical notes that drew us to them. We collected their dead carcasses and empty shells. These deafening critters fascinated me with their transparent skin which left my mind to wander to the empty holes inside me, the places where I'm fragile, void, hanging out, waiting, and always searching for meaning and purpose.

We learned rather quickly that if we mis-handled their shells, their thin barrel chests would cave in and their tiny feet would fall off, and they'd make the most awful bone-crushing sound since the dawn of mankind. For two southern girls with nothing better to do, it was a lesson which garnered a change of namesake. The encyclopedia bug name was *Auchenorrhyncha* which Meg and I agreed sounded like a hack of throat spit. Even their official name, cicadas sounded French and that was unacceptable to us. So, on a hot summer day in Pine Log, Texas, the cicadas died and the crackles were born. *And the South rose again.*

Over the years, we collected armies of crackles and stored them in shoe boxes. Last summer we counted sixty-seven gutless creatures staring back at us, along with their armored shells. We dressed them up into wild, crazy characters using leaves, moss, pinecones and grass. We had puppet shows, villages and towns of crackles. Two of them had patchwork hippie shorts like us. We even created a town similar to Pine Log. It had one Dairy Queen, one grocery store, one hundred and fifty Baptist churches, and one lucky beer joint on the other side of the Salt Flats River Bridge. If truth be told, Pine Log was the wettest dry county in Texas. When folks rattled off they were "going across the river," it had nothing to do with baiting a hook or fishing—they were talking about buying brew, hard liquor and rousing spirits.

Our favorite prank of all time involved two ninja crackles and occurred during the summer of flames, basically it was too hot for neither of us to have any sense and we were up to no good, and stayed in trouble. It was only a matter of time before we commissioned the crackles for help. They were experts at covert missions and willing to die for the cause. We had a pre-war ceremony, so their spirits could pass onto the otherworld after they died, although technically most of them were near dead anyway, but we felt it an appropriate gesture for their service to our troubled adventures. We painted their bubble eyes blood red with a yellow dot in the center and disguised their bodies with black coats of paint. We gave them honey locust thorns for swords and painted them silver and glued glitter to their wings until they glistened. We sat outside and waited till Maw Sue settled in for her evening nap, then tiptoed across the squeaky floor, snickering and giggling until Meg was a clumsy boob and hit the roll-away table. The wheels squealed like a pig, the porcelain statue of Jesus holding a baby lamb went down face-first and sent a jar of pencils towering like dominoes. We froze. The pencils rolled their last judgment, then fell silent. I gave Meg the OH-MY-GOD-THAT-TABLE-HAS-BEEN-THERE-FOREVER look of doom. Maw Sue snorted and rooted around while we held our breath.

"We're going to Hell." Meg lip-synched with a look of dire straits as she pointed to the overturned statue.

"We live in Pine Log." I whispered sarcastically. "I think we're already there."

Finally Maw Sue was in a deep sleep and we slithered in like serpents. Looking back on it now, I figure we should have turned coat and ran, heeded the baby Jesus moment as a sign. Instead, we turned heathen and mounted two ninja warrior crackles on the rim of her glasses. The hardest part was not laughing out loud. A few times, she'd jerk her arms or legs and we'd freeze up, nearly busting a gut giggling. Meg kept glancing over at Jesus and the squished lamb. On the way out, she picked up the pencils and uprighted the Messiah, as a way to get back in the Savior's good graces. It took a while to get out the door since we had to silence the loud clanging bell. We ran and hid behind the chicken coop for an hour, laughing and cutting up. We imagined her waking up from a dead sleep, staring into two bug faces. The enormous zoom on her bifocals would make them triple in size. The more I laughed, the more I saw the statue of Jesus giving me the stink-eye.

Just when I started to regret the whole thing, we heard a scream and a loud plunk. Loud plunks were never good signs. A few seconds later, she came barreling out on the porch. Her hair was wild looking and she acted madder than a boar hog with his nuts cut off. According to Dad, this is the maddest any Southerner can get. She paced back and forth a good five minutes, blowing and huffing and scanning the tree line. We didn't dare move but it was hard not to keep from laughing. Finally, she walked to the washing machine and slammed the lid down. The reverberating clang made our bones clatter. She reached on the wall to a rusty nail and pulled off the paint stick. Meg's knees started to knock and my heart hitched. Maw Sue lifted her flowery skirt and whopped her bare thighs a good one. Her skin sizzled and sent out shock waves of laughter. If there was one thing which hadn't lived up to its namesake, it was the paint stick. The stupid stick hadn't seen a speck of paint its whole life, but it could etch out the back side of our thighs in a heartbeat. We avoided Maw Sue for three days until neither of us could stand it. We loved her too much to go another day without seeing her.

The house announced our entry like an enemy approaching. The porch planks barked, the screen door let out an eerie squeal and the bell hanging from the latch clanged and gonged. Meg and I stood guilty at the executioners kitchen table. Maw Sue was sitting on the opposite side smoking a cigarette and drinking a cup of coffee. The air was thick and daunting as our bodies fidgeted. From across the room, the statue of Jesus melted us with his hot stare, and inside my mind I could hear the lamb bleeping with contempt. Maw Sue remained speechless. *She didn't have to say a word.* The message was clear. On the opposite end of the table, on top of the paint stick were the mangled remains of two ninja crackles. We learned later, that one of the cicadas was indeed, *not dead* and very much came alive buzzing on her face which resulted in an over-turned rocker and destruction of the living room. To pay for our misdeed, we had to wash both porches, all the windows, Maw Sue's car and the dishes. Afterwards, I concocted a memorial, an official badge of honor ceremony. We placed the remaining crackle remnants on the fencepost with a tiny flag we found in Mama's C's fabric scraps. On the fence in permanent marker is the words

Never forget!

The battle of crackles.

Meg and I still laugh about it today. We accepted the punishment, but the crackles…they died for the cause.

THE HOUSE INSIDE ME

The scariest monsters are the ones that lurk within our souls.
~ Edgar Allen Poe

I missed the next two therapy appointments. I avoided them as if they didn't exist, despite the fact that Doc's office called several times. I can't seem to make myself go. The barrage of memories that has already made their way into my mind has been overwhelming to say the least. A mixture of good and bad memories and I fear they are only the tipping point, a set up to lead me astray, to the edge of insanity, of no going back, no return. I'm terrified that Castle Pines is just waiting and watching to take me in, lock me up and I just can't make myself go back to therapy. But on the other hand, if I don't go, I'll go to jail and be locked up, so I'm not sure I have any other options. I am wrestling with my emotions. I feel like a child somehow, as if by magic all my problems will vanish. But despite my avoidance, inside me, a small voice whispers and tells me there is more at stake than I realize. I can't even work a full day without having a meltdown of sorts. It's affecting my job, my sleep, everything in my life. My troubles run deep and dark like the blackest ocean depths, the deep dark blue where creatures lurk unseen and untouched. In my mind, I am convinced no one can enter the deep, dark, blue black without turning dark themselves. It was natures way, the chameleon skin way, where light turns to light and dark turns darker. And I felt dark enough as it was. I wanted no part of the deep, dark, blue black.

I watched the clock on the wall slowly line up to five. I closed my desk drawer, grabbed my purse and noticed a pack of gum at the corner of my desk. One of my customers must have left it behind. I grabbed it to throw it in the trash. I wish that was the end of it. But the second it hit the metal trashcan it felt like a bomb went off in my memory. Whatever voodoo magic Doc did at our therapy session has unlocked and opened a doorway to my past that I cannot shut. It assures me, I'm going on this journey whether I want to or not. Before I left, I called Doc's office and left a message for Pearl to schedule me an appointment. By the time I pulled into my driveway I was barely able to contain all the memories that spewed from 1970's something.

Meg and I were pre-teens when we started collecting aluminum beer tabs and Wrigley's spearmint gum wrappers. It was a seventies vibe and everyone was doing it. We joined in the movement despite the disapproval of our Good Housekeeping mother who abhorred hippy trends. Spiraling through the ceiling of my room were train tracks of tabs, along with loops and weaves of folded wrappers made into a bridge. It tied all four corners together like a trapeze in a circus. We spent hours making them as pre-teens bored out of our wits. Mother thought it was the trashiest thing she ever saw, and tried to remove it. Dad would intervene and say it was self-expression and she better not touch it. Of course, it was his beer tabs since he drank like a fish, which mother also bitched about. How were we to know that gum wrappers and beer tabs would lead to friction between the two of them, which turned into heated fights, unresolved issues, which led to more arguments, which always led to silence, and if there was one thing our house didn't need, it was more silence.

I never understood the tenuous state of our household so I took the brunt of the weight upon my own heart. I took it upon myself to be the chaos controller, trying to meter out the moods of the family and fix them. Since I was invisible to Mother and her attention was diverted to Dad ninety-nine percent of the time, I turned to him for approval and love. I longed for him to see me, take interest in me. I wanted him to hold me, like he held that aluminum beer can. But I learned early on that alcohol is a taker, not a giver. It takes and takes and takes more. It never returns. It takes the bystanders, the onlookers, those close enough to fall into its clutches. Those who care way too much.

It was always something in the Collard household. The simmering silence permeated the walls, followed by slammed doors, popping beer tabs, scowling looks and skid marks in the driveway. Meg and I grew to fear the unknown. At any time, any second, life as we knew it would end. It's a terrible thing when the adults around you fall apart. There were shouts of blame. Dad seeing other women, mother threatening revenge. Dad worried, frantic and then more fighting. Mother would lick green stamps or go on a shopping spree for revenge. Dad would drink more. Mother would gripe about the drinking. Dad would gripe about the money spent. Then drink more. Mother would disintegrate him with her slanted blue eyes of steel. He'd scream, "This is horse shit Gabby!" and storm out carrying a six-pack. We'd hear the squealing of tires. This was followed by a solid ten minutes of breaking, slamming and crashing objects. During these moments of chaos, Meg and I would flee. Sometimes, we'd escape out my window and climb up the wondering tree beside my bedroom and try to drown it out with night sounds. Late at night, long after the house had turned into a frigid refrigerator, we'd hear his truck pull in the driveway and a sigh of relief would fall over us. The next morning my mother would go stealth mode. Without question this meant Dad was being punished. In reality, we were *all* being punished. Silence for days on end, the brutal, incapacitated, begging-to-talk kind of silence, as if an army of the dead rampaged our home refusing to leave. FOR THE LOVE OF GOD, SOMEONE TALK! It was followed by slamming cabinet doors, snubbed noses, burnt food and cold stares. I wanted to scream. Speak words to make everything right again. But I could say nothing. I had somehow lost my voice. And then, as if the tragic silence never happened, the polar ice cap would melt, and the days returned to normal that wasn't normal at all.

In my family forest, deep in the thicket behind the pine curtain of my life, two important giants were being struck down, and there was nothing I could do but watch the two pines timber and fall. The dismantled limbs and branches, the pine thistles and cones of debris scattered were just casualties of war, and I was the sap bleeding from their wounds.

To patch myself up, I learned to lie. I made stuff up. I wanted attention. I wanted approval. I wanted them to work it out and love me. Be my parents. Make this work. Hold this forest together. I knew if they fell apart, I'd fall apart. And the more they tipped, the more inventive stories poured out, eccentric, overboard, dramatic, and fabricated. I didn't know it at the time, but I was growing dependent on the feelings and lives of others to show me how I should feel, operate, think, act, perform, and speak for identity, and survival. It started early. I learned to people please. It gave me a false stability to function within the chaos.

Looking back at it now that I'm older, it's the common things in life, those daily mundane nuances most familiar to you, that never leave. Regardless of age, status, location or time—they are there, they return. The relics of childhood, the sounds, scents, smells, songs, objects, patterns, places and things—come back. I'm grown now but I figure no matter how old I am, the sounds that will haunt me the most is my mother in the kitchen.

Whisking, stirring, clanging spoons against bowls, the smell of bread, pies and cakes, cracked eggshells, scraped icing and the beaters' loud roar. I tried to help to be accepted, approved of; one whisk, one spoon, one taste, one crumb. I tried to gain my mother's love by using her most beloved affection—cooking. I would do what she did. I learned to cook from the early age of seven. Although it was a good incentive for my future life as a housewife, it was simply another mask I created out of necessity. It's something I did to receive. To garner love. Cooking is how I got close to my mother, her affection metered out in measuring cups. My heart told me, *I will cook. I will clean. I will bake. I will knead. I will whisk and whip. I will win her love and approval.*

Sometimes I actually saw the cold edge of her ice melting away, blending with the butter, flour and eggs. I licked the beater and tasted her love. I delighted in her expertise in the kitchen realm. I tried to do everything she did. I cracked the eggs like her. I beat the pudding like her. I mashed the dough like her. I iced the pies like her. I stirred the tea like her. *I will earn her love one bite at a time,* I vowed. As children looking for acceptance, we grab at whatever self-preservation methods we can find to get what we need, what we want. For me, *not* getting was sheer terror, measured one cup, one teaspoon at a time. Every day I sought with intensity to fill my cup: flour, sugar, butter, kisses, love, anything—*just not empty*. Yet everyday, I died a little more and more holding an empty cup.

When I wasn't trying to persuade my mother to love me, I was outside running the pine woods or at Maw Sue's house. From an early age, I recognized my sensitivity to noises. My hearing was so intense that even small noises irritated me. My eyeballs saw alternate visions, shadows and slinks, to the point I'd blink and refocus to make sure it was actually there. My dreams were vivid and filled with people from eras of time I didn't recognize and they would tell me stories I didn't understand. As a child I could tell no-one, except Maw Sue. She understood the anomaly of strange things plus she lived in a creepy house. I could be fifty feet away, and swear it noticed my presence. I heard it puffing and heaving as if the foundation wanted to crawl away. It came alive when you stepped on the porch planks. It knew it had visitors. It spoke its own language: squeals, creeps, moans, whistles, chirps, whispers, barks, bleeps or rattles. Inside every room, the corners slid off into a faded darkness, as if there was a slide to a hidden world, dark, damp and horrible. In those corners, I saw shadows in the shadows, figures absorbing light and others swallowing the dark. If I look too long, I felt myself being pulled and I had to flee and run outside. Her house was a labyrinth of holes and hidden things. For a long time, I thought it was me and my demented mind, my warped namesake, my gifts and curses, or the elaborate stories Maw Sue told us about our ancestors, the Seventh tribe. Day and night, candles and prayers, light or dark, moon or sun, still the inner workings of my mind haunted me, shackled me and tried to shut me up, push me down, or make me go insane. I could feel the entanglement of things hidden, their resistance against me. I couldn't see them, but their presence prickled my skin and hedged against my back.

Somewhere along the way in my fragile mind, I thought my mother would understand the stories Maw Sue told us, but in reality, it was just another way for me to hopelessly connect to her, gain her love and approval, some way, somehow. It turns out my mother didn't pay attention to me at all or care one red cent about stories. She glared at me fish-eyed, then cocked her head sideways like a confused dog. After a few fake eyelash twitches she'd mumbled and sigh and go right back to licking green stamp books and placing them in a cardboard box. On the side in big black marker was the word KITCHEN. It should have said DENIAL.

Maw Sue always said trusting our gift often means standing alone. But being by myself drove me crazy with overthinking, thoughts flitted in and out of my head like wild birds. Maw Sue was the only one who halfway understood me. I wandered for hours, dilly-dallying around the knick-knacks of her old bedrooms filled with stuff decades old. I liked to pick things up and think about their past life, their owners, and their journey. I figured everything had a story connection in some form or fashion. I got bored and ended up on the porch, dreading my future as a kid, but mostly as a grown up. That terrified me. I stared into the distance sky across the pasture and noticed it hanging on the post. One lone crackle. Meg and I had never found a group of cicada crackle shells, *always one, by itself, alone.* I considered this a sign, so I plucked it off the perch and commenced to create a world of magic. According to Maw Sue's philosophy, mayhem always follows magic. I sat the lone crackle on the railing and stared into the empty vessel. In the background, the sun set and dropped midway into the pine trees, and rays of light glistened into the distance. I must have drifted off to sleep for half an hour or more because when I woke up, I was flat on my back, staring at the square panels of the ceiling stained with abandoned wasp nests and a weave of spider webs. I sat up to find the crackle in the same position I left it. It suddenly dawned on me that I knew nothing about these cicada crackles. I pondered things for a second, then ran inside. I whizzed past Maw Sue, who was a haze of pastel flowers and smoke. I collapsed at the three-tiered bookcase in the dark corner of the living room. I could hear the slipping gurgles of things unseen. I grabbed the books I wanted and ran to the center of the room where the light was the brightest and the shadowy figures lurking in the dark corners couldn't bother me. It was then I thought of something Maw Sue said. Darkness wasn't to be feared in us—it's the brightest light in us that is more terrifying than any shadow, demon or dark pitch of night. She said the light in us, casts the shadows of our being—the one we know —and the one we don't. *And not knowing our self is something awful to fear.* Of course, I was scared of everything, so it didn't matter.

I spent hours pouring over encyclopedias and *National Geographic* magazines, page after page. I searched for explicit information about this cicada, aka crackle. I had to know its habitat, its purpose, its journey. But in hindsight, I think I was searching for my own. To my amazement and disappointment, I discovered crackles didn't have much of a life at all. I also discovered the reason Meg and I found gazillions of them. Their life span is like a strike of lightning, one day here, next day—*gone.* The only remnant of their existence is a tragic shell clinging to tree bark. For a second I imagined humans going out like that. One day you're talking to your neighbor George, and the next day his dead carcass is clinging to an old garden post. Talk about creepy death rituals. Something in my heart had to live for a purpose, a calling, a deep-seated human need, and I certainly didn't want to go out as a shell of nothing. I did discover one amazing fact which made me green with envy. A crackle spends the majority of its life as a kid. *A bug-child! They never have to grow up. What could be better?*

Crackles stay underground, digging out tunnels, playing in

dirt and sucking tree roots till they emerge, molt and mate, and then die. Needless to say, I had a meltdown in the living room. I figured I had a good ten years before I molted into a legal full-fledged, crazed adult like the rest of the population. I suspected life as I knew it was over so I threw the book back on the shelf, streaked past Maw Sue, hit the door wide open and plucked the lone crackle from the ledge. I hyperventilated a little, then had an epiphany, an effigy of fate. Maw Sue told us the heart was a source of great wealth and richness and the spirit of faith was a reckless and strange entity only known to the heart by surrender. I never understood those words exactly but I did feel a spirit blowing. It told me to make a vow. A solemn vow. So I followed the path of the universe. I vowed to never grow up. I would remain a child at heart. And that child played outside with the crackle long after the sun had dropped beneath the slender pines and the lanky shadows of the lesser light moved across the yard. I glanced up every few seconds while the hair on my neck stood up. I didn't like the dark regardless of what Maw Sue said. I played in every hill of dirt, sand and mud puddle I could find until I was a dirt ball with hair, teeth and eyes, a constellation of earth-infused madness. Regardless of my one-ness with nature, my mother opposed soil conservation. I came to this conclusion when I sat on the floor to take in some TV. Chunks of conservation fell on her precious rope rug she bought with green stamps. Her eyes expanded like two blue moons at harvest time. She went teetotal ballistic. She waylaid me with the damp dishrag, then dragged me outside and sprayed me with a water hose like a common house dog. If that wasn't bad enough, she dragged me into the bathroom, handed me a bar of soap and threatened to beat every speck of dirt off me and then some. My face twitched and my mouth drew up in snarls. My solemn vow gave me the wherewithal to stand firm and not back down to tyrants like Gabby Collard. *Moms who don't understand. Adults who don't get it.*

"Act like a lady, Cassidy!" she spat, her tone high and mighty. And her loudness was unnecessary because I was inches from her. This is when I knew I got a rise out of my mother and decided to milk it at all costs.

"You are eight years old young lady. Act like it." She said wiping bubbles from her brows. "Grow up, Cassidy," she snarled "Just grow up!"

My ears burned. In the South, when your ears catch fire, you are not responsible for your actions.

"Don't tell me to grow up." I fumed, spit and spat and sat on the floor like a protestor refusing to budge. I heard somewhere it was my constitutional right to do so, so I used it.

"I like dirt. I'm *not* growing up. And for yourrrrr information," I said fuming mad and with glaring glazed-over eyeballs. "I don't have to grow up!"

Apparently, my unconstitutional mother wasn't scared of protestors. "Who are you now, Peter Pan? Not going to grow up, huh?"

"If I want to be." I said with sass and sap. That's when my constitutional protest spun out of focus. A dull thud rang out when she swatted me with the Johnson and Johnson shampoo bottle.

"Is *that* all you got?" I laughed in rebellion. "A wimpy shampoo bottle! Hell, you might as well slap me with a feather!" That was the wrong thing to say to my mother. Sensing she was loosing ground, Gabby went code ten on me, which is repetitious Bible belt methodology—Jesus, Joseph and Mary shit. When it came to codes, this was the limit, the mother lode of mothers. I didn't know whether to be proud or scared shitless or both.

She jerked my arm, kicked off her black flats, and leapt over the tub like a graceful gazelle. All at the same time, which I kind of admired, but only slightly. She pulled me in and stripped me down like a banana and poured in a half bottle of bubble bath. I screamed and tried to escape, but she sprouted octopus arms and shifty tentacles while a militant brigade of soap plumes rose up like soldiers. I went into a Martin Luther King rally cry. *Defender of dirt, minister of mud, crackle crusader.*

"Suck root forever." I screamed and marched around the bathtub. "Dirt rules! Ban soap! Mud, mud, mud." I chanted and fist pumped my arms like the Moon Wanderers did in Washington protesting the war on the television. "Rule the kingdom. Take your life back. Moon Wanderers forever! Demand what's yours. Take your place, people. NEVER grow up! Never!"

"Be still," my mother screamed, fighting my emancipation. She wrestled me every which way but loose. "Stop it. What has gotten into you? Is Maw Sue filling your head again?" Her wet washcloth swished the air as she took swats at my legs. I felt no pain and no fear. I was in revolt.

"Never grow up. I am a seeker by God! Fulfill the namesake!"

"A what?" my mother said puzzled "Oh, my Lord." She leaned against the wall in exhaustion. Her wig was crooked and distorted, and she was soaked from head to toe with soap bubbles.

"What the hell is going on?" Dad said, poking his head in the door.

"Never grow up, Dad!" I shouted and raised my hands.

"It's your seeker daughter starting a revolution...or something."

I was counting on Dad for full support of my revolt, but the octopus intercepted with the bent eyebrow. The South refers to the bent eyebrow move as an act of aggression, and men steer clear when women use it. My father was no exception. Once the eyebrow arched, it was over. Dad skedaddled and left me with a crazed octopus hell-bent on pulling up my rebellious roots and squashing them. I declared she would have hell doing it. I was naked. I was fearless.

"No retreat! Rule the kingdom. Take your life back. Demand what's yours. Take your place, people. Be Ye seekers of the calling!" I yelled and yelled some more. My mother attempted one last scrub down. The room escalated into effervescent madness. Determined and relentless, she scrubbed me in a cat fight until I was raw and squeaky. I was so mad I threatened to go outside and roll in the dirt like a dog. She threatening to dust me in old lady powder and make me go to school in crusty patchwork shorts. Then I saw the bend of her eyebrow rise up. This was always a sign that if I dared cross the eyebrow, then I damn well better be capable of taking the punishment. I figured I had made my point so I backed down. I snorted in protest and marched to my room. I slammed the door. Opened it, and slammed it again. It was the best I could do to end it in my favor.

Later that night, I went to my dresser drawer and took out the fabric pouch that Maw Sue had given me. She showed me how to use medicinal herbs to be one *with* the earth when all hell broke loose *on* earth, which was pretty regular in this family. I crushed the rosemary leaves and lemongrass into my hands and rubbed myself down. The fragrance gave me a sense of aliveness, of calm, of one with the earth. Once I was in a better state of being, I pulled out the mirror bin, an heirloom, an amulet. The wooden box handmade by Simon Ainsley for his seventh-born daughter, my great-great-grandmother Joseymae, number seven. Maw Sue said the blood of every Ainsley sister was absorbed inside the wood and that is what binds their spirit to us, the life of each person to the next. As the bins are passed down in the family—so is the tradition. That night under glints of moonlight I wrote a vow to never grow up and placed it inside the mirror bin for safe keeping.

That little girl had no idea that years later she would break that vow, and grow up to be a broken adult, with a broken mind and a broken spirit.

ADAPT AND THRIVE

If you do not tell the truth about yourself, you cannot tell it about other people.
~Virginia Woolf

Mandatory therapy opened so many hidden doorways into my mind and past, I am having daily meltdowns. Fits of grief, strange and unusual grief without a source. I could barely keep it together through a day of work, my mind disoriented and dejected. By the time I got home, it was full on. These strange, violent images hit me like an electrical surge. A portal in my mind had been opened. A sudden flash of light, then quick bursts of images and sounds. *God, the sounds.* A mixture of laughing, crying, screaming, music, my voice, other voices, bangs, clangs, screeching, so many sounds. Then my mind tunnels in to view a slow movie, actions recorded from the past, memories fading in and out. I see a small fire. Inside the flames, a skull of hollow eyes. *Another flash.* Blood dripping into a wooden bowl like drumbeats. *Another flash.* A girl screaming, the emptiness of her mouth, a dark abyss drawing me closer and closer until it swallows me. Suddenly I snap back to myself visibly stunned and shaken. My head is bobbing and my heart is racing. But like a gentle wind after a raging storm, a memory enters in, not with force but like a warm, inviting hug. That ghost hug is Maw Sue. She wants me to remember. I take a deep breath and let myself go where the memories take me.

Her given name was Susannah Josephine Worrel. She stood four foot nine, a hundred pounds of piss and vinegar. Fire and ice. Wishy and washy. Rose petals and rusty nails. Mystical and mad. Her moods metered up and down like the red bubbles in a weather thermometer. We learned to tiptoe lightly around her till we established what frame of mind she was in. She was schooled in the ways of old, the ways of *seven.* This strange way of *seven* descended from a particular bloodline on her mother's side of the family tree, the Ainsley clan. Everyone has their spiritual beliefs, religious traditions, crosses, wailing walls and temples, and so did the Ainsley's. They believed in God, a majestic, all-powerful being. They believed in Jesus as the son of God. They also believed in divine messages and held a strange belief in numbers. The Ainsley's had their stories, traditions, their beliefs, just as others do. Like some say seeing a red bird is being visited by a recently deceased loved one, or how the Jews wrap up tiny pieces of paper filled with prayers and stick them into the crevasse of a rock wall, or how the Baptists dunk people in water, or the Catholics pray to the Mother Mary.

For the Ainsley family, if you were a believer, you were called a seeker, whose belief in numbers and earthly events coincide and lead to a particular pathway in life. These special meanings are to be sought after, interpreted and applied to life. My sister Meg and I learned all about the ways of seven in our youth, long before our belief system was tainted by the world's view of religion and its stifling methods of making converts and unbelievers. Long before we learned of hatred, division, judgment and shame.

Maw Sue was a direct descendant of this strange bloodline of mystical women. Not everyone in the family received the attachments of the gifted and cursed bloodline because it seemed to choose its subjects with care. No one knew how or why. Everyone had heard the old stories passed down, but not everyone believed them; therefore, some say, belief held the key and was the power to receive it. It was like a seed. The best seeds are pushed down into the soil of darkness and they must find their way out, straining upwards toward the light, reaching where their wholeness is found, sprouting, growing and maturing, and then the pain of pruning, snipping, cutting. Growth only comes from cutting away that which doesn't serve us. Maw Sue told us by this process, a seed grows in fullness. But if a seed is not pressed into darkness, it will be eaten by birds, or left to rot, never becoming what it should. Remembering this made my skin pimple and shudder.

Maw Sue's daughter who we call Mama C, did not receive the seeker bloodline, though she held some interest in the old stories. My father, Gavin, her firstborn son didn't receive it either, although he did receive a precious gift of being a water diviner. That man can find water with a forked stick in twelve counties and made numerous fat wads of cash doing so.

My story is different. The bloodline didn't skip me. It hit me full on. Cassidy Cleopatra Collard received the entire package. The whole kit and caboodle, the full shebang, me, the town arsonist in the making, the crazy collard girl took all the gifts and the curses, a complete seeker treasure trove. If truth be told, it's more than I ever wanted. As a child, knowing all these things was fun and belief was easy. Now that I'm an adult and my life is a crumbling wreck, nothing about it is fun, and my belief is tainted. *Is it possible? Is the bloodline real? And could this be why I'm losing my mind? As a child it was part of my natural nature to believe those around me, but what if Maw Sue was crazy like people said? And if so...what does that say about me?* Regardless of my thinking, belief or lack of, it didn't stop the memories from flooding in. Like seeds sprouting from the dark, they rose up from the soil of my soul seeking the light, and looking for purpose.

According to Maw Sue the gift came natural to me, because I shared similar traits to Joseymae, her mother and my great, great-grandmother. Maw Sue said that my birth was filled with mystical events, and because of this, she paid particular attention to me as a child. Sometimes I'd catch her staring at me as if some long-formidable ghost was haunting her.

My younger sister Meg received the genetic bloodline as well, which included attachments such as curses and eccentric gifts, but no-one could convince Meg of this. She was straight up a realist. From birth it was evident to Maw Sue she had considerable doubts as to the validity of the events described so often in our walks and story time sittings; therefore, her disbelief skewered and stifled the seed within her, causing it to be stunted and never produce the magic and mystery of the gift she talked so much about. She determined not to give up on Meg because she believed her natural sparkle and jackass stubbornness would allow her to accomplish the impossible.

Maw Sue did her best to teach us everything she knew about the Seventh Tribe, the bloodline and all the mysterious attachments, but Lord knows—it wasn't enough to stop the darkness from trying to destroy us.

. . .

As a child, I loved Maw Sue with an intensity so strong it felt like magic, something beyond anything I'd ever felt before, or since. We were connected by something neither of us could describe or discern. To this day, I remember every detail of her. Short and feisty. Square face, proud cheekbones, gray eyes like a storm cloud, a crooked smile, curly white hair swept behind her ears. She dressed in straight-line lounge dresses pelted with an assortment of flowers and snap buttons in front. She smoked, drank, dipped snuff and took pills like candy. Most importantly, she taught me to believe in the power of magic, of numbers and the old ways of seven. By her storytelling, she convinced me our lives individually point to something bigger, something way bigger than ourselves. Her favorite saying was only four words, but they were the most poignant words I'd ever heard. *Then…and now.*

"*Make lovely your losses,*" she'd say with conviction. For two sisters prone to believe their great-grandmother over everyone else, those words made us believe we had the power of magic. To make a bad day lovely. To right a wrong, to redeem a loss. We thought we held this tremendous gift inside us, so when troubles prevail or the bottom falls out of our lives, we can easily turn it around and make it lovely. It would be easy. Sour lemons into sweet lemonade. As a gullible, imaginative kid, I believed those four words had power. Now that I'm an adult my belief is tainted, my life is a mess and those four words make me sick to my stomach. It makes me angry she made us believe such nonsense. In my mind I argue with a dead woman, a ghost while I scream into the void where no one is listening. I can no more make lovely my losses than I can change the color of the moon. *I lost Sam. How do I make it lovely, Maw Sue? Tell me? I almost burnt down a house. Set a fire, supposedly. I'm the talk of the town. How do I make it lovely? And now I'm losing my mind, and seeing a shrink. Pray tell, Maw Sue, how do I make lovely all my losses?*

The memories shift something inside me. My nerves are on fire, my body tingles. It happens like before. A surge hit me. Again, the flashes, the images, the same as before, dismantling me to stillness, only to subside and return. I brace myself for the next onslaught. Quick bursts, images of fire, dripping blood, the horrible sounds and the child screaming, me falling, darkness, then gone. And just like before, the memory comes like a gentle rain.

Maw Sue had a coop with chickens roaming the yard, a wild vegetable garden, an herbal garden and a huge strawberry patch. Her property seemed straight out of a Grimm's' fairy tale. Adorning the tree limbs hung various objects of meaning, chimes, rags, beads, bells, jewels, bones, feathers and more. Her house was plain, a simple salt-box square, white with red shutters and black doors. A small step-down front porch, and a good-sized back porch for a washing machine, a freezer and two chairs. Walking inside was like stepping into a haunted box of crayons. Every room was a different color, unique in character, with its own language, smells, and embodiment. This house took on Maw Sue's personality and moods. It became one with its owner. The kitchen was bird's egg blue, the bathroom a Pepto pink, the living room a sunflower yellow, the spare bedroom was green like blades of grass, and Maw Sue's bedroom was the brightest lily white I'd ever seen. Her house was truly alive in many ways. Herbs and scents. Candles and crosses. Slinks and shutters. Clicks and clutters. Bells and beads hung on windows and doorknobs to fight bad spirits. Meg and I would run through the house smelling each bundle of plants and herbs hanging from the ceiling, sage, rosemary, lemon balm, spearmint and others.

We'd follow her as she would burn them in a bowl, walking through each room praying some ancient rites to rid away the bad.

Maw Sue was a spiritual soul, one with nature and the other-worldly unseen. She believed in shadows and visions, things others just shrugged away. Her belief was old belief, that of another time and place, taught by the ancestors, those called sages and seers. Those who left thick family chronicles with story after story, along with medicinal recipes, tonics and herbs, sketches and drawings, rituals and ceremonial events. I remember seeing those old dusty books, one of them particularly drew my eye because it had an eyeball on it with a huge number twenty-seven on it. It had something to do with vision, but I don't recall exactly. I did know that to the family, vision was a gift passed from family bloodlines, a gift allowing others to see things beyond the curtains of the pines, to a world only few have the heart and eyes to see. I never understood what she meant by that, until much later in life, but knowing this about her, made me love her more and drew me to her with its primal energy.

She kept Kool-Aid for us to drink, and gave us money to rake leaves, then treated us to soda pop and candy at the local store. I knew she loved us because even in her ever-changing moods, she was present, available, to talk, tell stories, take us for walks, help us draw, or read, or answer stupid questions kids have. She was always there. An eternal fixture two houses away, we only need step out our door and walk the dirt path to her porch. That is, until her mind wanderings. At times, she'd be troubled, agitated, pre-occupied, and even scarier, vacant. As if she was somewhere else. It reminded me, *of me.*

She first introduced us to the pine curtain by taking us on long walks through the forest of the big thicket. The dense canopy of Texas loblolly pines and sycamore trees muscled their way in like brute giants towering over us. Undercover were the yaupon, sweet gum, white oak and others. Maw Sue told stories of the boom days, before loggers trudged these woods to harvest the longleaf pines. She said it was a sight to see. Huge spectacular giants at least four feet in diameter dominated the forest. This was where my love for the woods began, with the beautiful trees, the strangeness of plants and flowers, their origins, their uses. It was in the thicket she introduced us to the baby Jesus. Meg and I were little, seven or eight years old, but this was a story we would never forget. We'd take it with us, as if the sap from the pine trees stuck to our skin, absorbing to our roots making us one with the forest, one with the unknown, those things we teared up and cried about without understanding. Things that would take a lifetime to work themselves out. I didn't know it then, but this would begin an immense internal struggle within me, a defining moment in my life of confusion, of spiritual awareness, of innocence and belief, and the sabotage of man-made religion on my mind, my identity and my journey of wholeness. It would take years to return to that place of innocence and discovery, of mystery and the majestic, and it would be upon the pine needle path, I'd come to know the truth. Until then, I would have to weed my way through the maze of memories coming back to spill their secrets.

Meg and I were anointed behind the pine curtain. It was a Southern sap of the sacred and holy sticking to our skin, a mark of something beyond us, bigger than either of us could imagine. We were queens of the pine curtain. We each had a crown made of locust thorns, green leaves, honeysuckle vines, brambles and Southern sap from a wounded pine tree. The hardest part was digging into the bark of the tree to release the thick sap. I felt as if I was gouging my own skin, but it was tradition dating back to our ancestors and a necessary part of the seeker ceremony. It signified we had powerful gifts and unimaginable purpose. Meg and I were proud seekers, the promised seed from the Seventh

Tribe, a great generation of yesteryears. To wear the ceremonial crown meant we accepted the gifts which created something magical, explicit and splendid, wrought by no other method on Heaven or earth. The crown was to ward off evil, and empower us with the visionary gifts of purpose, and the sticky pine sap bound us all together, crown, tribe and tree. Everything was to remind us of the suffering servant she called Jesus, his purpose and more so, ours. We had been chosen by the blood of our ancestors to bear the great, horrible, tragic, splendor of the precious gift.

Behind the forest of the pine curtain, we learned the art of medicinal herbs tucked away in plants, trees, shrubs and various seeds used by our ancestors for survival and well-being. Deep within the belly of the thicket was a place of wonder. Tall, drooping mulberry trees were the sweet gift of the gods. The burgundy berry was sugary on our tongues and what we didn't eat, we mashed and used for face paint and pretended we were tribal warriors fighting unseen battles and winning the hearts of all mankind like some female Robin Hood. The blackened dewberries were the edible jewels of a long-lost princess. If we found foam on the leaflets surrounded the vines, it was a warning a snake was nearby. Maw Sue long considered dewberries and blackberries a holy plant, as well as one of the earliest known foods for man. She often wore a wreath of brambles, woven with ivy and honeysuckle because it was known to ward away evil spirits. Brambles of blackberry were always planted around graves to prevent the dead from rising as ghosts. Legend has it, Christ himself used a whip of bramble to drive away the money changers in the temple. I used to cover myself in it but it never worked for me. The darkness came back. Shadows and voices rose up to haunt my mind, and I was continually running from them. Either I was doing something wrong, Maw Sue was flat-out Bessie bug crazy, or everything I've ever heard is a lie. My bets on all three.

Not only was Maw Sue a forest fanatic, she was a Southern-fried Farmer's Almanac full of whimsical, fascinating information. Chicken poop mixed with good soil was the magic ingredient to grow luscious strawberries as big as our palms and sweet as molasses. Honeysuckle was the sweet syrup enabling visionary empowerment, a gift from the vine gods and the forest fairies. Once again, it didn't work on me. I only saw darkness, shadows and strange slinky things. The nectar was indeed sweet—but the darkness bitter.

Maw Sue had a lot of tales but one struck me deeply. The story of the pine tree. I considered myself the barefoot queen of the pine curtain. I was one with the forest, one with the trees and one with my tribe. I was a seeker bleeding the Southern sap of my nature. Like the many acres of pines surrounding the land where I grew up, I would become like the pioneer species Maw Sue always talked about. Loblolly pines are the survivor trees tolerating low nutrients, shallow soils, fluctuating weather and drought. Where other trees fail and die off, a loblolly pine tree will regenerate naturally on disturbed sites where fires have occurred, or old croplands have been abandoned, or left vacant. Where everything else has died, these seed saplings learn to adapt and thrive. When Maw Sue told me about the tree's origins, something inside me broke and bled. It wasn't blood pouring out, but tree sap. Hearing the origins of the tree broke something inside me, and I felt a deep belonging. Maw Sue said a person can learn a lot from a tree's nature. When a pine tree is cut, or wounded, it oozes a thick, sticky sap from deep within the heart of the bark. Although the damage from the cut is permanent, something remarkable happens. The bark of the tree begins to grow over the scar, completely disguising it, yet beneath the tree's skin, the scar remains. The wound is ever present, but the tree still grows strong. It learns to adapt and survive. I didn't know it then, but one day I would need, *more than ever*, this resilient nature of a pioneer species in my own blood, my balm of Gilead, my own Southern sap.

As a child I believed without knowledge or understanding, just faith in something beyond but now as an adult with deep cuts, I am beginning to understand the meaning of it all. Back then, it was a warning. A prophecy of gifts and curses. Having life experiences in such matters, Maw Sue knew more than anyone that I would need this pioneer species, this core in my blood, this Southern sap nature.

To adapt. To thrive. To survive.

PRESENT DAY

JUNE 1, 1988
NEWS YOU CAN USE
BY EDNA ROLLINS

TEXAS NEWS EDITION

The collard green fire is still a mystery to locals. The following is my continued interviews with eye witness to the event. Today we are talking with Fred Ferguson who lives across the street from where the fire occurred. I asked Fred his take on the events of that night.

"It started earlier that evening while I was raking leaves. She drove by slow and suspicious. I didn't think nothing of it. It wasn't till after dark when the same truck stopped in the drive across the street that I knew she was up to no good. The bed of the truck was full of garbage bags and when she got out, she was dressed in black with long blonde hair, dark shades and red lipstick. The strange thing was she had painted her face with red streaks like a warrior going into battle and wore a necklace of bones and feathers. It startled me and left me a bit unsettled to say the least. But I watched her through my binoculars and the utility light at the corner gave me an unobstructed view. She jumped in the back of the pickup and started throwing garbage bags into the yard with a vengeance. The bags would bust and boots and clothing would spill out. She tossed lamps, couch cushions, pillows and paintings until she had a pile stacked up tall and wide. And then she picked up a huge whitetail deer mount and placed it in the middle of the pile. Some of the antlers had been covered in red and the deer face was painted up like hers. I felt like I was watching the beginnings of some weird sacrificial ceremony from medieval times. I had never seen such a thing, not even on television. I couldn't stop watching. It's like I was hexed. I watched her pour gas on it and then strike the match. The second it went up in flames, she seemed in a trance. But it wasn't long till she started chanting and singing all sorts of chatter. That's when I went out on the front porch so I could see and hear better. She never knew I was there. She danced, yipped and yelled, and held feathers in the air as if she was casting spells. She spun in circles around the flames, slinging her body in convulsions until she tossed her blonde wig right off her head. But that didn't stop her. She shook out her long brown hair and went back to fire worship. Then it got even stranger. She threw something into the fire that made it rise up in a shimmering cloud and it changed colors like one of them kaleidoscope prisms. I never seen nothing like it before. A time later, she got in the truck to leave, but stopped in front of the mailbox. I thought lord, what is she going to do now? Well, she got back out carrying a large silver bowl. Ohhh, and stranger yet, I swear on the Bible that I could see the reflection of the fire in the side of that bowl, but I'm telling you right now, there were people dancing around it. I kept looking back and forth at the fire a distance away, and the reflection in the bowl. She was holding the bowl, the fire was still burning, but on the bowl, I saw the fire and people dancing, shadows and stuff. It just messed up me. Then she walked to the end of the driveway and set that bowl down. She lit a match and dropped it in the bowl. And then she left. Just drove off. The fire was still roaring so I made sure she wasn't coming back and that's when I saw Gladys, and Myrtle and a few others by the road. I ran straight to that silver bowl. I looked all around it for those shadows but they were gone. They must have left when she left. All I found in the bowl was collard greens and a burnt match. It's the strangest night I've ever had in my seventy-six years of living in Pine Log. And I'm a war veteran so I've seen some stuff, but this trumps it all."

There you have it, folks. Three witnesses and detailed accounts to the event that has rocked this small community. We may never know what provoked this woman, witch or cultist to destroy a perfectly manicured lawn with such unprecedented behavior. Word is, she even had a blood sacrifice. We don't know the ends and outs of these things because we are God fearing but everyone agrees it points to the inevitable. Something is happening in this town. I say we join Gladys prayer chain and put an end to it. If we don't, just like the fire, it will spread. Just like it spread next door to Mr. Bailey's yard and ruined his prized Begonia flowerbed, destroying it to ashes. If you would like to donate to replace them, the quilting club has set up a collection so he will not miss out on next year's *Bloom Best* contest. You can talk to Sue Ann at the Holy Church of the Bride for information. Pine Log residents may never know what provoked this woman to insanity, but one thing is for sure. Folks around these parts will not be able to eat their freshly harvested collard greens without thinking of the terrible night Pine Log almost burned to the ground. Until next time, tune into KTBR local radio news station 109.9. I'm Edna Rollins and that's news you can use.

HOUSE OF SEVEN

When you look into an abyss,
the abyss also looks into you.
~Friedrich Nietzsche

After multiple therapy sessions my life isn't better, it's worse. I can't process my emotions and yet I can't run from them. I can no longer sweep them under the rug or pretend they don't exist. Therapy has opened a dozen doorways and behind every door is either Maw Sue, my mother or a child I hate or don't recognize. I embrace the memories of Maw Sue but it's a struggle with my mother. As much as I want to refuse the memories coming, along with the terrifying emotions they bring, a deeper part of me wants answers, from the child, from Maw Sue and most definitely from my mother. A part of me has to know her *now*, more than ever—some form of her, real and touchable. I need to know my mother exists. *Is Gabby Collard who she says she is? Or who I think she is? I feel she is hiding something*. I tried to know her as a child but she kept her distance, silent and brooding, a walled-off fortress. No one could get close to her. Just thinking about her causes wreckage inside me. And like all the times before, it dredges up a memory, right after the bursts, flashes, the images of fire and blood, snapshots of time, the terror of the sounds, the child's scream, me falling into darkness and then silence. Out of the silence a flashback to my past arrives, and with it, Gabby. The mother I loved and hated. The mother I tried so hard to figure out.

It's one of my earliest memories in the battle for my own mind. I couldn't have been more than six years old. Meg is tucked almost underneath her blanket asleep on the couch. The living room is dimly lit, the light of the television outlines my purple paisley flower nightgown. I'm sitting cross-legged on the rope rug in front of the television. My eyes glaze over staring into the cartoons. I drift inside the field of animated characters, inside the pasture where Elmer Fudd chases Bugs Bunny with his rifle. I can almost feel the green grass on my toes. A door slams in the hallway behind me. I am startled. My shoulders stiffen and lurch upwards. The air is charged like electricity. The soft fray of hair on my arms lifts up. An army of fingers marches up my spine till I shiver. My skin begins to buzz to the point I can almost hear its hum. My breath suspends itself. My back locks up. My hands draw up into fists. My boney knuckles grind into my thighs, making red slashes on my pale skin. My body is on high alert. My spirit is alive, restless inside. It needs to escape, run away. When it cannot, I am forced into a ritual I can neither avoid nor stop. My body starts to rock forward then back, swaying as if someone nudged me on the back, my torso with invisible springs attached, bobbing back and forth, my eyes glazing over, my mind freezing up and then melting. I will myself into the animated forest of the television, my only escape for what I know is coming. Behind me in the dining room, my father sits unaware. He drinks his coffee and reads his newspaper in front of a half-eaten breakfast plate. I manage to turn my head just in time for the stalky shadow to appear on the wall, growing larger until I hear its voice. It's shouting, but I will my ears to only absorb a whisper.

"Where were you last night? With her? With the boys? LOOK AT ME! Why won't you look at me? Aren't I enough? Talk to me, damnit!"

My eyes expand. I see the shadow clearly now. It's in full form standing inches from my father, naked and plump with rolls of tender fat. His eyes never leave the newspaper. He is avoiding the shadow, like I will myself to do, but cannot. The smell of stale beer, burnt toast and overly fried bacon permeates the room.

"Goddamn you! Just damn you!" The shadow screams and slams her fist on the table. The walls shake and dismantle. My mind wants to escape, it melts and merges into the cartoon. Reality meets an altered dimension. *A sign hangs on a tree. It says RABBIT SEASON OPEN. Boom! Elmer Fudd shoots his rifle.* I jump. I can't breathe. I realize I've been holding my breath. An animated cartoon symphony of music plays. In reality, a few feet away, my mother stands disrobed, naked and angry with intense eyes. She starts pacing the dining room like a panting horse after a race. Huffs, snorts, fumes. To see her in the flesh disturbs me, as if I shouldn't be here. *Don't they see me?* I want to run far away to the thicket, but I am heavy and weighted to the floor. There is a trickle of wet spit on my mouth. It dribbles down my chin. My teeth hurt and my saliva tastes like copper pennies. I untangle my knotted fingers to wipe it away, now realizing I'd bit my tongue. The blood pools in my mouth and I can't seem to release my teeth from the grip.

Yelling. Arguing. Cartoon symphonies. Elmer Fudd. Bugs Bunny. Daffy Duck. RABBIT SEASON OPEN. Boom!

Two worlds collide in my mind, a cartoon and real life. I feel myself falling…without falling, a slow descent into the worst of the worst, the place of nothingness, the gut-wrenching absence of everything. *Silence.* A silence that takes prisoners. Unspoken words, deep stares, eye cuts, slashing sighs, stomps, slamming, crashing and banging—but seldom words. My parents' squabbles always ended with a stewing silence, battle lines drawn, a war with one potent deadly weapon. Outbursts, arguing, yelling, objects thrown but always, always followed by an intense, unresolved silence. The sword that slices and rips away your flesh before you even know you've been cut. Subtle movements, slight actions of the hand, desperate eyes, blank facial expressions, ignoring, avoidance, jerking away…*but not words.* Rabbit season was open in the Collard household. But it didn't have anything to do with rabbits, only the killing of souls.

Watching these battles between my parents quickened something within me. A need to fix and fill in the silence with words that I imagined should have been said, to make things right, to heal, to end the war, to sign the peace treaty, to take down the open season sign. It was an honest gesture, one made out of love, but what I didn't know was how it would turn against me. As an innocent child with a vivid imagination, I had no idea that I could not control the outcome. In reality, I had *no* control. In my imaginary mind, I did. I became a caretaker of the unspoken words, the words to fill in the silence of the house. Words to diminish the chaos. Words to mend the mess. I didn't know what I created out of love to fix my family would only lead to madness and my demise.

Maw Sue taught us that words have power and so does silence. In addition, we all have a foundation inside us, a House of Seven, a place of wholeness with rooms of our own making. No matter how lost or far we go in life, the House of

Seven is our haven of wholeness, our refuge in times of peril and deep spiritual questioning. It's ours to build and to tear down. We create the landscape and the surroundings to suit our fancy. It's who we are, what made us, who built us, it's all the good and the bad woven together. Inside my fragile mind, construction began. My house was built on a foundation of fixing, mending, repairing. I began to collect language, and letters, and epistles of unspoken words. I watched and observed the function of my family, its ups and downs absorbing everything and anything that could help. I imagined what should be said to mend the argument, being my mother or my father, and by this I could see a final end, a favorable one. But I didn't realize it was only my imagination. My hopes. My desires. My prayers. The dim reality was that my parents fought and there was nothing I could do about it.

Nonetheless, hope endured. I turned to the stories of my ancestors. For the seventh tribe being seven meant wholeness. It was the core and the reason for the House of Seven. *The fullness of self. The absolute. Oneness. Totality. Complete.* As a child with faith and belief beyond, I needed to be seven, to be whole, more than anything. Because if I was whole, then my family would be whole. The House of Seven was my escape from the upheaval of our home and I set claim to it. I built it to fit my needs. I sketched it out on manilla paper visually capturing its mystery just as I had seen in other drawings in the old chronicles. It had a dilapidated front door and the sizzling number seven carved into the pine. The seven glowed with an amber hue against the edges of the wood like many moons set on fire.

Maw Sue said our houses inside ourselves take on our own nature, our embodiment of self over time. It was just natural for my home to be behind the curtain of pines, under the cover of giant Loblollies and a lush landscape of oaks dripping with moss. Once I began drawing, it seemed to take on a life of its own. The moss spilling from the branches became hair and that hair was attached to moss girl creatures with spirited eyes that glowed from otherworldly places. They were half-tree and half-human little girl creatures inspired from playtime. Meg and I used to hang upside down on tree branches and our long hair draped towards the ground in flowing strands matching the moss on the branch beside us. Hanging like bats, we'd take strands of moss and tangle it up in our hair till it reached the ground and we'd pretend we were whimsical creatures made from the earth, the trees, the roots, the leaves. Birds perched on our knotty bark legs and sang while woodpeckers pecked at our sinewy limbs.

My imagination had found a place for all the chaos. When my little mind and body could no longer contain all the words that should have been said, could have been said in the family battles but weren't—the words would rain down on me like a broken alphabet. They would pile up in a silent whisper, dead and void and useless. I would frantically capture the words on paper by drawing a skeleton and on the bones I would write the words that should have mended my family. I would pray the scriptures to God, the one that I had heard Maw Sue talk about where a prophet had prophesied to the bones and said, dry bones, hear the word of the Lord and I will make breath enter you and you will come to life! If there was ever a more magical use of words, I hadn't heard them. This was it. I prayed to God that he would bring them life and in my vision, he answered. The imprinted dry bones rose up with all the words I had written on them like chapters in books.

I adapted, thrived, survived, the only way I knew how. Every day, every argument, every battle I willed the dry bones to life. My little hands carved the words, etched, painted, scribbled on the skeletons. The unspoken, the broken syllables, the simmering confessionals unuttered, the resolved, the forgiving, the redemptive word bones. But the chaos continued in the Collard house. I must fight harder, be stronger, resilient and brave. I must be more,

I told myself. I am the seed growing in disturbed, uprooted soil. I must adapt. I must survive. I must thrive. But my mind began to fill up too fast. It splintered with all the verbiage I had hoarded up and began to falter. *I resisted. I cannot let the family fall apart.* I did not know the dry bones would turn against me and take on a life of their own. It began slowly as mumbles, but increasing more and more, until night and day, every minute my mind heard the voices, the words coming to life, skeletons speaking what was written by my small hands, and prophesied by my lips. My mind could not contain the chattering, the speaking, the unresolved drama of what was. Fix this, mend that, do more. I could not live with the hundreds of screaming word skeletons at my front, my side, and my back. They slept with me. Walked beside me, sat with me while I ate, cackling, clanging and banging on my walls when I tried to close my eyes. The words glowed with amber letters on their chalk bones like embers of fire, and their whispers demanded what I could not give. *Resolution, forgiveness, and redemption.*

I had to silence them, before they drove me mad but I remembered that Maw Sue said whatever is prophesied cannot be undone. So, I would bury them instead. Shut them up. It was my only solution. I picked up my pencil and drew the Hush Cemetery on the landscape beside the House of Seven. I put my forefinger to my lips and whispered a long drawn out shush. The spirit eyes of the moss girls seemed to fade dark, and then back to a spooky glow. In my vision, only the Hush Cemetery could hold such a relic of creation as the dry bones and cradle them beneath the soil and silence the rumblings. To keep them mute, I placed brambles around their graves like Maw Sue taught us to keep the ghosts from returning. I didn't know it yet, but the grave could not silence the groans and whispers of the dry bones. They would come back to haunt me. Because in the Collard household, nothing *ever* got resolved.

Despite my efforts, every year it grew worse. It was bound to happen. One morning my little mind fractured. I woke up to a brutal, disturbing silence. The chattering had stopped. It was eerie and yet strange. I wasn't sure which was worse, the sounds, or the silence. But it was too late to debate, or go back. I had split. And because my heart was as big as the shine of a full moon and my mind was a fragile cicada shell–a little girl identical to me appeared as if I magically drew her on paper to exist outside myself. She was there to do what I could not. She stood up when I crumbled. She took air when I lost my breath. She rose up when I could not lift a finger. I watched her walk my footprints through the dirt path under the pine curtain, straight to the glowing front door. This was the first occupant of the House of Seven but not the last.

BACK TO THE PAST

I love those who can smile in trouble, who can gather strength from distress, and grow brave by reflection. 'Tis the business of little minds to shrink, but they whose heart is firm, and whose conscience approves their conduct, will pursue their principles unto death.
~Leonardo da Vinci

For the next few weeks my mind dove face first into the past and would not let me go. I was overpowered, out of body and watching it all play out before me, a spectator to my own wrecked life. The quicksand of memory had me sinking deeper and deeper into the mysteries of my mind and the perils of denial. It would take me under and I would not be released from the walk down memory lane until it had forced me to see what I had purged and put behind me.

It was 1970 something. Meg and I heard Maw Sue's story so many times, it felt like it was a part of us, tangled up in our thoughts, in our heads while we slept, whispering to us, leading us along until it became one with us. We'd sit at her feet and listen to the story told time and time again, and we never grew tired of hearing it.

Maw Sue was a fragile child born at 3:13 on March 3, 1903 and named Susannah Josephine Worrell. Her mother, Joseymae, a seeker by old tradition, knew all too well of the meaning of numbers, how they played a part in our gifts, our curses and the journey we take. She knew preparation was necessary, as her mother Brue had done for her and her older siblings. She performed the birth ceremony, and the baby's entrance into the spiritual void, the gap, the passing over, and back to the earthly realm, where she would continue to teach her the old ways. The ancient stories of the Seventh Tribe, the bloodline, the traditions, rituals, ceremonial fires, the gathering of the brambles, the animals of sacrifice, the rite of passage, the prayer in smoke, the chants of ancient ones long before them. She needed her to recognize the gifts, the curses and the interceptors who come to steal, kill and destroy.

Sweet Susannah was only twelve years old when her mother died. For a time, having troubles and mourning her loss, Susannah obsessed over the mirror bin because it reminded her of her mother. She felt connected in ways she couldn't explain. Her father, a traveling book salesman named Carvin Worrell, became worried about his daughter because she was way too obsessed with the rituals to a point of self-harm. She'd stare into the mirror as if some ghost would return unbound, bringing with it her mother whom she missed with her whole being.

It had been one year and seven months since Susannah had lost her mother. The loss was still as brutal as the first day and sent her to a place of violent suppressed weeping. Bouncing from one emotion to another, she clung to the ceremonial journals and the mirror bin her mother had given her. This, along with the stories of the Seventh Tribe, was all she had left. For a time, her father calmed her but after a while, no one could. Susannah would stare at the mirror reflection on the outer lid of the wood mirror bin and see her mother's face melt into the pewter and then her voice would echo in her ears. She'd spend hours reading the old ceremony books to try and decipher their meaning. Her fascination with the mirror bin and the epic tales grew more intense each day.

They moved town to town, making their way across many states until they made it to a bank of river called the Trinity, in Eastern Texas. One day she noticed the face of her mother growing dim and faint. An army of unrecognizable voices replaced the soft maternal tones and drove her mad, unstable and displaced. She came undone. The horrible interceptors of which she had heard so much had now claimed her mind, her body and soul. Her eyes appeared wet all the time, her teeth set on edge, and excessive manic energy poured outward. Highs and lows tormented her soul, so much she was unable to sleep, the voices loud and terrible as she grew more distressed by the shadow interceptors.

She was alone and distant from the outside world and her father grew weary of her condition. Most times she was simply a corpse with breath. During her episodes of darkness, Susannah did not know that her father had been courting a woman named Earlene Codsworth. Soon after she came out of her state of neurosis, she was shocked to find Earlene and her father had married. She eyed the woman with a keen clarity, suspicious of her intent to replace her mother. After much observation, Susannah saw a different woman than her father did. When he would leave for work, Earlene became controlling, mean and held contempt for her. Earlene had her mind set on having her father all to herself. The next thing she knew, her father made plans for her to go live with her mother's sister. Susannah was blindsided with grief and outrage her own father would abandon her. In her next breath, she was standing in Aunt Raven's yard.

Susannah was frightened and had only heard about the woman through stories from her mother. Aunt Raven was sister number one, out of the seven she was oldest and the most eccentric. Suzannah remembered her mother vaguely saying whatever fractured the great Seventh Tribe started with Aunt Raven, something terrible and mysterious, yet her mother would never go into detail. This fact made Susannah cautious. *What if it didn't work out? Why did the family split? Is she dangerous*? Susannah's mind worked overtime imagining all the ways it could go wrong.

Aunt Raven was peculiar in her ways. She was a tall, lanky woman with bulbous ears and black silky hair she wore in a bun. Her face seemed unable to show emotion, without a wrinkle, as if she'd never smiled nor frowned, her expression always stoic and glazed. Susannah never forgot her first impression of Raven standing in the yard, as if she had just got off a bohemian bandwagon to live in the forest amongst the animals and herbs. She seemed to blend into the very nature of the forest itself, as if she could disappear at any second. Her wardrobe was as limited as her lifestyle. She had three black skirts with clattering beads off the hemline signaling her whereabouts like cat bells. She rotated shirts as if they were symbolic of days and seasons. In winter, she wore dirt-colored ponchos and knee-length boots. For the summers, skirts of assorted colors, and either sandals or barefoot. She wore a strange green scarf she never took off. It was either tied at her waist, around her neck, wrapped on her arm, or in her hair. This green scarf would later be passed down to my sister, Meg, along with her mirror bin.

Aunt Raven was as distant as the clouds. Untouchable,

moving in and out as she pleased without so much as a glance. Susannah observed her curiously as she was left to herself, most of the time. Her aunt seemed to enjoy the solitude and didn't know what to do with a young girl at her side. She was well in her fifties but looked years younger. The story is, she had never married and was content with a solitary lifestyle. If Susannah had not been there, she might have simply talked to birds, wild animals or herself. She rarely left the boundaries of her house, taking refuge in her wild herb garden, which consisted of five acres of torrential vines, massive cascading trees and an abundance of wild perennials, evergreens and herbs. The iron bell at the door never rang. No one visited. The only door knocks came from a delivery boy every two weeks with grocery and household items.

Over time, in her own weird way, but not all at once, Aunt Raven doled out increments of warmth here and there. She learned that sister number one was highly gifted and had a teachable spirit. Life skills were of importance to her. So was arts and literature. Because of this, Susannah learned to sew and fell in love with books, and her favorite place in the huge house was the giant library with floor-to-ceiling books in the upstairs loft. It was in the library she discovered a tribe of people with similar life issues as herself. She became keenly aware of mind suffering and those who wrote stories about madness, a fragment of a broken mind, people stigmatized by society as crazy, unstable, maddened. Yet with all their faults, their mind troubles, they created genius. Their books, writings and short stories garnered an enormous impact on society and inspired their creative genius. Without the mutated gene, without sufferings, without the curse, none of the masters would have created anything worthwhile. Aunt Raven acquired this conclusion through much study and observation. Susannah and Aunt Raven along with others before her, knew there would be no masterpieces of art so popular in novels, in plays, in paintings, in sculptures, without the affliction. Their *differences* made them stand out from the crowd. Sufferings paved the way for purpose. It set them apart. It inspired their gifts. Susannah marveled at her findings because it gave her hope for her own broken mind.

This inspired her to read more and document her findings. Charles Dickens was known to have depression, but look at his writing. Vincent Van Gogh had bipolar disorder, a mind-altering Dr. Jekyll and Mr. Hyde complex, but look at his accomplishments. His art was brilliant and moving. Depression followed Tolstoy, Nash, and Donizetti, and even our president Abraham Lincoln had his moments of clinical depression and thoughts of ending it all. Despite it all, each one honed and chiseled a curse and made their suffering into their best work. They channeled the pain into art and were willing to touch it without falling into its clutches, and by touching the pain, they created masterpieces.

Susannah wondered how she could convert her mind wanderings to good works. It was unthinkable at times, considering the vast canyon of her pain, her losses. Then one day, Aunt Raven was sitting in the parlor with a box in her lap. Susannah recognized it immediately. It was almost identical to the mirror bin. Susannah ran in a sprint and sat at her feet to touch it.

"It's just like mine." She burst with emotion.

"Yes," Aunt Raven said with a hint of contempt in her tone. "I reckon it is, but mine was first." Her chin lifted upwards. "My father crafted it for me, inspired by my birth, my raven hair and the white streak down the side, see? It is the same." She pointed to the dark black walnut coloring on the bin with a white streak in the wood identical to the streak of white in her hair.

"I was the beginning of it all, it was for me, all me. My father said a rare white raven flew into the window before I was born, a sign of my coming arrival, and the white streak in my hair proved it to be true. When the bird flew away, it dropped a feather, this one here." She pulled out a beautiful pure white feather.

"That is stunning!" Suzannah said with excitement. "So, you were the beginning, being number one, and my mother was the ending, being number seven." She watched Aunt Raven's eyes change to a dim glow of garish gray but her face remained emotionless.

"Do you want to see my mirror bin?"

"No, I do not." Aunt Raven said quickly and uninterested. "I've seen it before, remember?" Suzannah frowned sadly and pondered what could have happened between her mother and Aunt Raven to cause such a rift. She was about to ask when there was a knock at the door. A delivery boy dropped off a letter.

"What is it, Aunt Raven? Who is it from? Is it father? What does he say? Oh, I can't wait to hear it, tell me…"

"Child," Aunt Raven said in slow motion pulling off her tiny round glasses. "Earlene has written. Your father has passed. He fell ill with a chest cough and never recovered. He was buried last week at Tremolt Cemetery in Garrison Falls. It's a town about four hours from here."

Aunt Raven handed her the letter with a picture. Her father's brown eyes stared up from the curled edges of the image. Standing beside him was Earlene. The air felt sucked up into another vortex of place and she couldn't catch her breath. The feelings of being abandoned by her father surged and her hatred for the woman who took him away inflamed her. Her face turned hot. She grabbed the picture and ripped it in half and threw it across the room.

"I hate him. I hate her. I wish she was dead too." Susannah stormed out of the house and into the garden and dropped down at the edge of the large rosemary bush near the fence line. The death of her father brought to memory her mother and the times they had together as a family, before Earlene, before her mother died.

How she wished she could return. It was hours before Aunt Raven found her. "Come, child. It's time for a ceremony. Pluck some rosemary and lemongrass before you come." Susannah looked at her, confused and tearful.

"No questions now, just do it."

Susannah obeyed and followed behind her, head slumped and grieving. Along the garden path, Aunt Raven stopped at the section of lush roses and wildflowers.

"Now…did your mother tell you about the petal people?"

Susannah sniffled. "No…what people?"

"So, you mean to tell me you don't have a rose for your mother, for when she died?"

"No," Susannah answered, a little more confused. She tried to remember the stories her mother spoke of, but it was hard to remember a time and place of sorrow after she left. It was blocked from memory.

"Well, let's get to it, shall we…"

"Get to what?" Susannah questioned.

"Oh, for Pete's sake. Your mother was always a tenderfoot and could never buck up when it came to doing the hard stuff, always had to have others do it for her. She had more of Simon in her than she did Brue, but no, neither one of them understood. They had it all backwards and I'm the only one who saw it." Aunt Raven spun around and picked up her gardening shears. "Here… cut a flower that reminds you of your mother. Think hard. Don't just willy-nilly it. It's important. This flower shall represent your mother to you in memory for the rest of your life. Do you understand?"

Susannah tried but her memory of those times with her mother was lost somewhere in her broken mind, only coming in bits and pieces. She lifted the shears to one flower and then hesitated and looked to another one, and then another, and finally stopped and looked up at Aunt Raven in tears.

"Mama used to have some rosewater that made me lovesick when I held her. I can almost smell it now. It's like some witchery of a plant has besieged me terribly. I cannot remember the name."

"Hmmm…" Aunt Raven looked at her with a peculiar expression. "And what color was this rosewater, was it tinted?"

"Yes, it was. It was a tea rose, from what I can remember, velvet."

"Awww, yes, velvet. Perhaps your memory is better than you think." She spun Susannah around to face the most beautiful rosebush she had ever seen. It was the hybrid violet tea rose, her mother's favorite. Susannah buried her nose in the thick velvety petals and for a moment it felt as if she was in her mother's arms again.

"Child, are you going to cut a stem before it gets dark, or do I need to start a fire?" Susannah smiled at her and cut the rose. "Now, you'll need to find one for your father as well."

"But he left me…for Earlene." Susannah said bitter.

"Boo-hoo. It doesn't matter none, Susannah, he is still your father. We all do stupid, terrible things, especially to the ones we love the most." Her eyes drifted away lost and sorrowful. "You did have some memorable times together with your parents and you need to honor this."

Susannah was angry and grieving for her losses. Every inch of her was crippled, her mind, her mother's illness, her death, left behind by her father, now his death.

"Fine." She stomped toward a wild rosebush with pale yellow roses and clipped it off. "Will this do?"

"Suit yourself, now follow me." Susannah trailed behind Aunt Raven's long flurried skirt with the bells dangling and clanging, while she held flowers of her mother and her father. Memories came in scents like how he smelled like paper, old books and worn leather, and she often thought of him while reading. The last time she could remember seeing him, he smelled of strong ale and there was no rose for that.

At dusk, Aunt Raven had a strong fire built at the other end of the property where the moss dangled from low hanging limbs and the winds howled a peculiar strange sound and made the fire crackle and pop. This was where Susannah learned of the ceremonies held for the dead, the long-held tradition of the flowers, the petal people. The Everlastings Immortelles Poem was read that was written by Sessa, the second-born sister. It was then she began to remember some of the stories her mother shared when she was young, and they began to make sense. Aunt Raven handed Susannah the torn picture of her father and the other half was Earlene. She motioned with her head toward the fire.

"Do what you will." She said without emotion.

Susannah held her father's image close and threw Earlene's in the fire and watched her burn. Her mind was ravaged with horrible thoughts she couldn't control. The anger was still there and she didn't know what to do with it. She tried to look at her father's picture and grieve, but she was too mad at him. But Aunt Raven told her the story of looking into the gaze of God and forgiving him, accepting only the good she remembered. Susannah learned that love looks. Even if you're mad. Even if they hurt you terribly, if you've ever loved them—you must look. *Love always looks.*

After the rose petal fire ceremony of burying the dead, Aunt Raven showed her how to place the flowers in a mason jar to keep forever. She explained how the rose petals transform over time to the faces of the loved ones, and how the Immortelles Everlastings take our grief, so we don't have to bear it.

Susannah tried to pull herself together in the coming months, but dealing with the death of her father, the anger and her mother's death all over again did her in. It took her to a dark, dark place. It was a trying time in Susannah's life, but every day she managed to get out of bed and attempt to make a life for herself despite her great loss. Aunt Raven gave her tasks each day, something new to learn and acquire skills. She would learn a new herbal tincture, or a pain salve and her favorite was making perfumed soap from the ashes of a fire. She would make Susannah write down her feelings of loss and what she wanted to release into the world, letting it go so she could move forward. Then she'd have her build a fire and say a prayer of release as she burned each piece of paper. Then once the ashes had cooled, she scoop them up and make lye which would be used to make perfumed soap.

"See…" Aunt Raven would say, "Something good can come from bad, with a little skill and some good smelling herbs."

And though Aunt Raven rarely showed emotion, Susannah felt a kindred spirit with her. Days, months, and years passed until Susannah grew accustomed to life with her eccentric Aunt. There was a warmth in her heart she hadn't felt in a long time.

One morning after reading she skipped inside the oversized den with a book in hand and mind full of questions. She found Aunt Raven asleep in her chair. It was normal for her to take small catnaps during the day, but she'd always wake up intermittently. Susannah tiptoed closer, but with each step her vision changed. A dark, ominous cloud hovered like gnats stirring and grew in size above Aunt Raven's tight black bun. Before it could confirm itself, sink from her mind to her heart, she knew the horrible, the terrible had happened. Fear consumed her in seconds, and within the gnat cloud a face formed itself. It was her mother reminding her of loss. Susannah's thick thumbs gripped the pages of the book and her mind went to the place of the dead. She moved closer, hoping against hope what she saw was only a bad dream, and Aunt Raven was still alive. Surely, any second she'd raise her hand, or rock her chair or blink her eyes. But in the dead spaces, no one moves, no one blinks or breathes and no one stirs but the shadows.

Aunt Raven sat stiff and lifeless in the same position she had been in the night before, when Susannah told her goodnight. Aunt Raven had replied with a half-smile, as usual, and then Susannah would do what she always did: grab the ends of the green silk scarf and rub it between her fingers. Aunt Raven had never been the touchy-feely type to begin with, but when Susannah first came to live with her, her clingy nature was a bit overbearing to Aunt Raven. She could not lend herself to affection of this kind, so instead she offered up her silky scarf, which was the next best thing.

Realizing her aunt was dead, Susannah collapsed. Her fingers kneaded the scarf while she wept. She rubbed till it felt like sandpaper and rats clawing and scratching at her brain. It was hours, or days later, she did not know. Time was simply lost—fading in and out into the dark of the house, into the dark of her mind. The abyss of thoughts put her in a catatonic state of being, without feeling, numb to all. Her fingers were raw and left holes in the scarf, but she could not let go, so she unwrapped the scarf from Aunt Raven's hair to keep it for herself. She swiveled it around her neck and for a moment felt it tighten like a noose and then loosen.

"I will take my hug with me, Aunt Raven." Her voice cracked. "Goodbye, Auntie. You've been good to me. I will miss you."

She rode into town to find the delivery boy she had come to know when he made his monthly deliveries. She paid him well and asked he find a few men to give a proper burial.

Susannah watched four men put her aunt in the ground and something inside her broke. After the men left, she gave Aunt Raven her ceremonial dues. She built a fire, and sheared a rose from one of her aunt's favored rose bushes. She wanted her aunt to be proud of what she had taught her to do. She gazed upwards as the flames rose to the sky and knew Aunt Raven was close, because soaring overhead was a white raven.

Weeks later, Susannah realized the desperation of her circumstance. She was a few months over eighteen years of age and alone. *Her greatest fear.* The house and property were passed to her and she stayed on and tried to live as Aunt Raven did, but she was not the solitary type. She read to pass time, or tended to the garden but days and weeks and months dragged by like a slow death. The desolation of aloneness drove her mad. The silence drove her insane.

When she could no longer take the solitude, she made a plan. Susannah retrieved her favorite books from the library and packed what little belongings she had in a large trunk. She collected Aunt Raven's mirror bin and her own. Along with her treasured mason jar of petal people. She passed through the kitchen and collected the stash of money Aunt Raven kept for emergencies inside a tin container. She walked out the door and into the garden to bid her home farewell. She passed by all the rosebushes grown by Aunt Raven, the lush landscaped garden of bliss she had occupied for the last few years, and she gave a long, mournful cry. She lifted her hands into the air toward the heavens as Aunt Raven taught her. She prayed a silent prayer of gratitude. Weeks ago she had managed to sell the property to a new family in town, with the help of the delivery boy she had come to know. She was starting a new journey, but she would not break tradition. She would pass all the life and family skills onward. To whom, she didn't know yet. As painful as it was to go forward into the unknown, it was better than being alone, so she took one step and then another until she reached the end of the driveway. Susannah slung the green scarf around her neck, turned and looked with love one last time and then, she was gone.

She rented a small bedroom above a storefront a few towns away, close to people and places, noises and activities. For a time, it was just what Susannah needed. A change, noise, and people. Months later, fate intervened with its curses and gifts. Days came and went without recognition, simply vanishing into thin air. The rose which sat stoic inside the mason jar became some sort of ghostly figurine, taking a rather ghastly appearance of Aunt Raven in its petals, and shortly afterwards, the rose of her mother, and her father did the same. *This* was a different madness. What used to bring her comfort, now brought her suffering. Petal people talked to her in her dreams. Time warped and swirled.

And then, weeks later she woke up inside a hospital ward with no recollection of how she got there. Doctors at the clinic told her she checked herself in, with the help of some of the women she had met at the corner cafe where she ate most evenings while looking for work. Doctors told her during her stay that she had undergone shock treatment, along with other mind methods and had improved incredible, since day one.

Suzannah had no memory of such things and it scared her but she was ready to leave the grounds of the asylum and get back to life so she tucked it all in the back of her mind and moved forward. The doctors put her on medications to help her mind wanderings, but they also silenced the visions and the voices. Her newfound cafe friends helped her find a job at a sewing factory, so she could keep herself busy and her mind occupied. She enjoyed routine, like walking to work every day since it was only a few blocks away from the cafe and the room she rented.

One evening after work, on her usual route, she crashed into a star. It was a heavenly meeting of two bodies on the corner of Third and Bryant Street. Jefferson Starbuck Adams was love-struck with Susannah and had every intention of marrying her. Though she played hard to get, he came stubbornly to the same corner every day to crash into her again, and again, until she said yes.

Susannah was happier than she ever knew she could be, but

most importantly, she wasn't alone. She had found the love of her life. He brought out the best of who she was and she loved him dearly. While he was around, her mind was stable and at peace. The first year was more than she dreamed a marriage could be. Next came a house full of children and seven years of blissful love and family, but in the latter months of the seventh year, a terrible fate would render its curse upon the family, and Susannah's mind. Jefferson Starbuck Adams quickly fell ill and died of pneumonia. Susannah's heart froze as hard as the ice forming on the gutters. At first, she was in denial, then depression, then anger. Somehow, what used to represent wholeness and spirituality in the number of seven, her past, her present, her future was now ripped away in the seventh year. Seven should have been fruitful, purposeful, whole as she had been taught, but it was the opposite and doubts plagued her. What used to represent wholeness was now nothing but heartache and grief and a great loss of the only man she had ever truly loved with her whole heart. Having Starbuck in her life gave her stability, purpose and discipline, but most of all, peace. After Starbucks death, Suzannah was never the same again. Her whole world became dark and gloomy. The madness returned. Being a mother began to wear her down and her mind tormented her with grief. Everything, including the children and the mirror bin heirloom was a reminder of what had been taken from her. The amulet would not let up on its requirement of Suzannah, even with her losses. It continued to demand of her, things she could not give. Would not give. Refused to give. And so…the voices, the visions, the mind wanderings returned full force and Susannah went into a dark, wounded core of herself. Consuming air but not breathing, living in body but absent of spirit, broken by life, mourning of love lost while her soul wandered for connection. When Maw Sue told me this part of her story—I broke too. It was then I understood her more than ever. And most fearfully what it meant for me.

17 YEARS EARLIER

JUNE 11, 1971

NEWS YOU CAN USE

BY EDNA ROLLINS

TEXAS NEWS EDITION

The Moon Wanderers are traveling through town in the coming weeks and we need to be prepared. If you don't know who they are, well, have a listen and I'll tell you. The Moon Wanderers are a loose affiliation of individuals from all walks of life, some nomadic, homeless and the like, from all parts of the country who have joined up with a group, forming a larger group until it's a massive cult with no leader, just a bunch of wandering souls gathering and camping from place to place, state to state. They call it Moon Gatherings which to me signifies hippies so I'd be cautious and lock up your belongings. They tend to barter mostly, none having real jobs. I'm told they walk around half-naked; they are prone to smoke strange substances and even have large tents set up for ceremonies with tonics that cause hallucinogenic visions. Sue Ellen Bonner says her cousin over in Whissett County spent some time with them, being a fugitive of the law and he said they were free-spirited, open-minded free thinkers, with no rules, no laws, and you can basically do anything you want as long as it is in harmony with nature. If that isn't just a bunch of malarkey if I ever did hear such a thing. If anything, it should be a threat to our organized society. We need rules. We need laws. We need boundaries. We can't have that free-thinking spirited hippy-go-lucky happy camper movement come in here like Woodstock and change our community and stir the pot. NO. What in the Lord's tarnation would become of our fine town? Until next time, tune into KTBR local radio news station 109.9. I'm Edna Rollins and that's news you can use.

CASSIDY'S BIRTH STORY

Numbers are the highest degree of knowledge. It is knowledge itself.
~Plato

In addition to Maw Sue's birth story, I also heard about my own birth story, so much that both tellings intertwine, connect and converge.

It was 1963. John F. Kennedy was president, Beatle-mania had hit America like a storm and the first episode of *Bonanza* hit the television airwaves. And I was about to make my appearance known in a rather unusual way.

Click. Click. Click. Maw Sue's tiny heels announced her entrance to the third floor, across the shiny buffed hallway of the hospital. Her nose twitched. Her heart beat in raps, filling in the space between the clicking of her shoes. She didn't like coming here because the smells, the sounds and the closed doors reminded her of places she'd rather not return to. Castle Pines was much worse than the hospital, but the familiarity was too close. It was her duty as a Seventh Tribe member and a great-grandmother to fulfill the tradition for the newborn despite her fears.

She knew even though the bloodline had skipped a few generations, the child born this day, October 31, 1963 at 3:33 AM would be gifted. It was in all the signs. When she turned to face the door, she noticed something she hadn't before. Her eyes blinked in disbelief. *How—could—she—have—missed—it?* In bold black numbers it read, #333, and underneath it on a piece of paper slipped inside a gold bracket was the name, Collard.

Her mind shuffled through the memories of the past few months. A foretelling of what was to come. Like the day she went to the chicken coop to gather eggs. She put one egg aside for her breakfast with some bacon and biscuits. But when she cracked the egg against the pan, it spilt out a triple yolk, something she had never seen. At first, it sent a racking spell of shivers down her spine and she almost threw it out, but she didn't want to waste an egg so she looked past her silly notions. After all, she had put away the serious, superstitious side of herself long ago. Days later, she went to pick up a tablecloth at the catalog counter of Sears and Roebuck. The clerk handed her a ticket while he went to the back to find her package. Her heart literally jumped into her throat when she saw the ticket number, #333. The clerk came back and handed her the package and she just stood there besieged by an unknown. A week later, things got even stranger. Her alarm, although she sat it for six AM every morning, instead went off radically at three o'clock, scaring the bejesus out of her. Then just as she got settled in again, it went off at 3:13, and then again at 3:33. She did not sleep after the third ringing. She made some coffee and pondered what strange things were happening. But as Maw Sue did, she put those things away, tucked them back into the folds of her broken mind where they would not do their damage, as they had done in the earlier years. But later in the week, the Brickery Grocery receipt was exactly thirty-three dollars and thirty-three cents. She was breathless but at this point her mind was overloaded with worry and stirrings of the past, and she did not want to return to Castle Pines because of something as silly as multiple threes. So, she put it away. But regardless, it returned, over and over again, until now. Now she understood. It was the birth of the child. The longer Maw Sue stood at the door, the more she realized it did not happen by chance: she was given advanced notice in preparation of the child's birth. Her mother had taught her everything, especially that numbers pointed to something—a message was there if you looked hard enough.

Susannah had always feared the unknown. Plus, her mind madness often went into a siege if she put too much thought into things. But as it were, the messages always found her. She was disappointed she didn't figure it out sooner. A phone rang loudly from the nurses' station only a few feet away, startling her out of her dark thoughts and back to reality. She couldn't stand outside the doorway all day.

In her hand the mirror bin seemed to hum, almost vibrate in her hands, awaiting its mission. It was old and ancient as if salvaged from the *Titanic*. It was beautiful, intricately carved with swirls, mysterious symbols, and ancient etchings. It was strange and mysterious, hand-wrought and instilled with vision, foresight, and preparation. Simon Ainsley was a meticulous carpenter and everything he built showed it with craftsmanship to last a lifetime. Every mirror bin for his seven children were as different as each girl. This one belonged to Maw Sue's mother, Joseymae, and inside it was the carved number seven. Today, there was an urgency about it. It seemed to nudge at the souls of anyone who glimpsed it. On top of the wooden bin was a square mirror, ancient and older than the wood it sat on. The mirror was filled with insidious black bubbles and beady threads forming squiggly lines. They lay underneath as if the mirror trapped them there, holding accumulations of time and layers thick with secrets as old as the people who'd stared into its reflective depths, seeing themselves for who they were, and who they were not, while their spirits dissolved and melted into the cloudiness of the silver, trapping their stories inside its slick and mysterious realm. The mirror held many descendants, great and lowly lineages of families long gone, voices and screams muted by time and silenced by oppressors.

"How is the little one this morning?" Maw Sue said entering the room. She held the mirror bin like a tray of food. Gabby, my newly appointed mother looked up at her in distress. Her eyes were droopy and worn. Her legs were sprawled halfway inside the cover and halfway out and I was laying on a blanket between them and kicking like white fire. Maw Sue said I was fighting the forces around me even from birth.

"Are they always this restless?" Gabby said with dark moons under her eyes.

"Ohhh yes, sometimes." Maw Sue said as a quiver rolled up her spine. *Knowing. Remembering.* She nudged the door closed with her elbow and walked toward me holding my destiny in her wrinkled hands. *It had begun. There was no turning back. Nowhere to run. Only forward.* She laid the wooden bin on the nightstand alerting Gabby's attention.

"What's that?"

"Oh, it's a gift. It's for the baby." Maw Sue said cautiously not wanting to give out too much information.

"Ehhh…well know this, I am *not* burning sage in my house for some cleansing ritual, and it better not be a bell or some ridiculous tree chime because I'm not doing that either. No offense, Susannah but that isn't me. Keep your ancestral traditions in your own home. Not mine."

"Calm down, honey. I left my voodoo dolls at home." Suzannah laughed. "It's a precious box my great-great-grandfather made by his own hands. Articulate craftsmanship, wouldn't you say? Isn't it gorgeous?" Susannah lifted the lid for Gabby to see, trying to convince her it was just a box even though she knew it was much more.

"Yeah, it's pretty. Your grandfather, huh?"

"Yes, his name was Simon Ainsley. I think your daughter would love it Gabby, and as she gets older, she can keep trinkets in it and you know, teenager stuff."

"Well, I guess it will be fine since it's an heirloom."

"Oh, I appreciate it so much, Gabby. It's been in the family a long time. It's called the mirror bin."

"Sure, sure…whatever Suzannah. Can you take her? I have to pee like Niagara Falls."

"Go ahead, Gabby. She'll be fine. I got her."

Maw Sue swooped me up in her arms. While my mother was away, a number of magisterial events took place. The mirror bin hummed a low noise and vibrated across the nightstand, establishing a connection to me. It was time to bestow its gifts and idiosyncrasies. It threw off light beams from the mirror reflections and the room filled with a thousand faces, generations of family members, all dead and gone, screaming out their stories to me. A barred owl flew to the ledge of the windowsill. Maw Sue's face was filled with wonder and curiosity. She knew the old stories. She knew what was happening. The light transfixed us both, as the mirror bin hummed, beamed, and bounced, transferring the gift from Maw Sue, its former owner, to me, its new vessel. She held me tenderly with care until the mission was complete, until the room returned to normal, which wasn't normal at all.

"Little one," she said. "I'm your Maw Sue. You are going to fulfill your namesake, honey bunch. You will do what I could not. You are a seeker. I can see it in your eyes, sweetheart. They are the color of water, the deep blue sea, way below in the unknown depths of hidden things. That is where your destiny swirls. It was meant to be. The numbers never lie." Her heart swelled inside her till she thought she might burst. "This time—I will do right by you. I will. I promise you, I will."

Susannah Josephine Worrell held redemptive flesh. Seven pounds of second chances, a way to right her wrongs and Lord knows, there were many of those. Through the firstborn, Cassidy Cleo Collard, the great-great-great-grandchild of the Seventh Tribe—she would be made seven. By this, my great-grandmother, Maw Sue, would finally make lovely her losses.

ROOM TO BREATHE

In nature we never see anything isolated, but everything in connection with something else which is before it, beside it, under it and over it.
~Johann Wolfgang von Goethe

This generational mess I'm in started long before I was even a thought. It started with the seven sisters. Sister number one was Raven. Number two was Sessa. Padillia was three, Minneola was four, Bagette was five and Cymbal was six. Wrapping it up as seven was Joseymae who was Maw Sue's mother. And this is how the bloodline trails to me. As a kid I heard the strange, unbelievable, mysterious story a million times over. You see, Joseymae almost wasn't. She actually died at birth, having lost her breath for seven minutes. Mourning with their tearful mother, the six sisters started praying over number seven as their mother did. Sessa, number two, grabbed a freshly cut rose stem out of the vase in the window and began reciting a poem out of her head as if the words just came to her. She held out the rose, now wilted and dried as if the eyes of God had scorched it in the otherworldliness of prayers and the unseen. She crumpled the death rose in her hand and let it fall upon the child like white ashes. Time passed as slow as a broken clock but in the seventh minute of time, as if by a miracle of sorts, number seven, Joseymae, returned to life and took breath. The sisters rejoiced that their baby sister had been spared. It was a divine sign and afterwards, the Ainsley's celebrated life and death through ceremonial traditions each of them created, inspired by numbers. Because of Joseymae's miraculous birth, death, and rebirth, seven became the number that represented life. The lifeblood of the family, of wholeness, heavenly blessings, both supernatural and mystical .

They say Joseymae entered the void, the place where the lines between this world and the world beyond are thinly separated. Brue, the mother, began to call them the Seventh Tribe of Seven Sisters. Their father, Simon Ainsley, a carpenter by trade, built each daughter a box as a keepsake with the number of their birth carved into the wood on the inside. Attached on the outside was a beautiful mirror so they could each see the beauty of themselves, as he did for each of his daughters, equally. He called it their mirror bin.

Brue continued to teach the girls that numbers were mystical. Each held messages, with meaning and purpose, and signified the spiritual perfection of each person. She taught the sisters to seek with all their hearts the mystical meanings of their lives, and their purpose by using the ways of old, which was part Celtic, her heritage, and others of her own making, which she believed was divinely inspired. She kept journals and wrote down anything useful for her children to find their way in life. She believed seekers were those who live in the middle, not completely of this world, and yet not of the otherworld. Always tangled up, broken by the topsy-turvy elements of life where they don't feel they fit, yet all the while holding the realm of the untouchable unknown, a faith of the divine otherworld.

They had gifts and talents passed on by blood but there were curses too. Brue warned each child they would face difficulty throughout their lives, because suffering always follows passion. What she did not know, was a bitter root sprung up among the seven sisters, one of jealousy and spite because Joseymae received excessive care, attention and doting from her mother, more than any of the others. This bitter root would breed discontentment, tearing the family apart years later. Though they scattered, each sister going their own ways, they took their teachings with them and passed them down, each adding their own belief, ceremonies and traditions.

Maw Sue continued the strange, eccentric tradition of stories, numbers and messages. As a child she warned me of powerful agents working against me, seeking my demise, a shadowy figure of my soul, a mind menace with an army of strange imps bent on oppressing me. I'm beginning to believe what she said is true. They are everything I've ever feared thrown together, both carnal and supernatural growing up with me, attached to me, a second skin I can't shed. I understand why she called them interceptors. They *intercept* evil thoughts into my mind, which sends me fleeing to the house inside me. A house built by childlike hands filled with haunts and horrors, leading to harbingers of doors marked with nameplates that lead to rooms that contain compartments of my past. This and other unmentionables, I've never been able to explain to anyone, except Maw Sue.

As a child I shared my fears about my mind, how the shadow voices hover beside the light and feed off my fear, my insecurities and my want of answers I never get. They study and observe me, my desires or lack of. My features, my tears, my brokenness, my weary cries of yearning and loss for something I can't find nor describe. They hunger and pinch my loathing and gain strength from my weakness. Where darkness is—*they are there.* Where light is—*they are there.* They are hedged in the lesser light, right on the edge of it, the place where daylight meets dusk, dawn meets the day, and the thin line separates the light from the lesser light. *They are there.* They sit on the brim and wait. It's the moments of in-between I fear the most. The long, drawn-out lapses of silence, void of space, time and presence where nothing exists, nothing cares, and nothing matters. This is when my mind is afflicted in the worst way. It cannot still itself for fear of destruction. I fear silence. In the small gaps, something ethereal from a nether world slips in. I can't see it, but I can feel it. It lies in wait, tangled in the seconds of time after I scream, after the eerie calm, after my voice grows mute, when the aftermath of silence is left to crawl on my skin. I've endured an apocalypse without memory, only the trauma. I am a survivor of sorts, a conqueror of something dark and eerie, saved from the horrible, the terrible, yet I can't tell you what it is.

Maw Sue used to tell me everything has a thread that leads to salvation. And salvation, as we know it, actually means much more. More than any of us realized. For those dwelling deep in the midst of the mystical God, always learning, always changing and growing, it held a power unlike anything of this world, an unyielding enchantment. In the ancient language of seekers, prophets and kings, sages and seers, *salvation* meant *room to breathe*, a belief in something bigger than ourselves. We relinquish control because we realize we don't have any. A higher power holds all control, all deity supreme. When we let go, we have room to breathe. I held a lot of darkness inside me as a kid, so those three words struck me as mystical, life-changing. *Room to breathe.*

The air was sucked from my drab bones and cast into the atmosphere of Heaven's portal, and before I could faint, it was pushed into me, different, not of this earth, abundant, effervescent, fresh and redeeming, a gasp of new wind for my soul. I pause in awe and wonder as if I'm standing at the precipice of eternity. And then, the pine curtain is pulled back. For a few glorious moments I'm allowed to peek inside my past and my present. The light mixes with the shadows of darkness and merges in oneness. A connection where I comprehend my pain in the otherworldly realm where all things collide and give understanding. For a mere moment, I felt seven. I felt whole, and I never wanted to return, but I always did. Right back to the dark, the pain, the suffering.

Maw Sue loved paintings, sculptures and strange artistic things. Though she could never afford the real thing, she did acquire a book of all the great artists of the world and their masterpieces. I was eight when Maw Sue showed me the book and her favorite picture of Michelangelo's famous painting, *The Creation of Adam* in the Sistine Chapel. My eyes darted straight to the hands and fingers of God and Adam and the infinite void of time between their fingers. This divine touch was what brought life to Adam. Made from the dust and stirred to life with one touch. The small distance between the fingers of Adam and God is what Maw Sue's ancestors found to be the mystical void, the space of time invisible, the gap between this world and the next, the place where all things connect and find substance and wholeness. Maw Sue's mother and her sisters were taught God was wholeness, and wholeness was the infinite meaning of the number seven, which intimately connected to her mother, since she was born the seventh child. Her mother doted over her amongst all the rest of the siblings. Thus, seven became a goal to master, the innermost part of one's soul, to find a purpose and a place, only by converging in spiritual places between the fingers of Adam and God.

As soon as I saw the painting, the space between the fingers, I felt it also. I believed I belonged in that tiny gap, waiting to be connected to the Almighty, waiting to feel whole. To be seven. As a small child with big hopes and dreams, I thought when I got older, I'd travel to Rome and see the painting in person. I thought if I could only see it, just once, by then, surely to God, *by then*, the fingers of Adam and God would be touching. If so, then so would mine. *And all would be right in the world.* I would be whole. The world would be whole. Even Maw Sue's mind would be whole. Even now, remembering it makes me weep. Pieces of me shift, dislodge and reconnect. When I can no longer take the pain, the little girl inside the House of Seven, inside me, closes my eyes and whispers my salvation. A whirlwind of colorful leaves spin in my warped vision. The little girl makes lovely my losses. She gives me the salvation of my childhood where I have room to breathe.

In therapy, Doc says I will not begin to heal until I forgive the silence. The skeletons of unspoken words have snacked on my soul since I was a little girl, nibbling on the word bones till it was only bits and pieces of fragments. I don't know how to begin. *Where to start? What to do? Regardless, I must try.* Doc says it begins with words because they had power over me as a child and this is the key to my release, my healing. Each day, even if I don't feel like it or actually believe the words I'm speaking, I forgive the silence. I make peace with the skeletons even when they resist and rattle and clatter. I say the words. I pray the prayers. I journal the words as if writing them on bones. I do it even if I feel nothing. Days, weeks and month's pass. *No change. No forgiveness. No healing.* Just the silence of haunts. And the haunting of words. And then…one day, miraculously, everything was different. It was like the masterpiece painting had moved. God's and Adam's fingers touched merely for a split second, then parted but the gift was left simmering in my soul. It rose to the surface where I could see it for what it was. The suffering did not present the wound until I was able to acknowledge there was one…in the girl with no voice, living inside the House of Seven, inside me. I denied her for so long she was woven into the core of my inner being, the internal makeup of my madness.

According to Maw Sue I was born with it. An innocence untouched by the raw brutality of the world, the spirit of childlike faith unaffected by the world's enmity, a serenity she had long ago forgotten. When she held me in her arms as a newborn her heart stirred. For a moment she felt whole, forgiven, unified for a common cause and loved purely from the heavens. A warmth of transcendence shined from the sacred places where a proud Seventh Tribe, a majestic generation smiled upon her. Her parents faces appeared, glimpses of childhood, rare moments of contentment when the past and the present merged and formed crossroads of future journeys, where aged hands possessed new flesh and crumbs of life were sought by seekers true to their calling. But then, as quickly as the symphony of love and light enveloped her with its enigma, she heard the black laughter. It crept in to spoil the new fruit and taint the seed of a new generation. Maw Sue tensed but refused to retreat. In the past she'd fled turmoil, a life broken and ruined, but my birth changed everything. I gave her hope despite the familiar knife that hedged her back and the oppressive spirits that hovered around her inside the hospital room that night and the days, weeks and months following.

Later in years, when I was able to understand the story more clearly, I grew as tense as she did. Her rocking chair screamed out eerie squeals and the old house came alive with creeps and jitters.

I lived with the seeker gift, so I knew the darkness long before it knew me. *I wore it. Drank it.* It was bile, putrid and dank, rising in my throat and fermenting in my stomach. I shared a cell of familiarity with Maw Sue without definition or meaning, just a knowing. Sometimes, she'd stop dead silent and get lost in the walls of the room, falling without falling, remembering some dark, dreadful unspeakable she couldn't bear. There were times she was so frenetic her sudden movements would scare the crap out of me. She'd bolt to the medicine cabinet and take an assortment of blue, green and white pills. She'd return calm and distracted, as if a curtain had been pulled over her eyes.

Despite her issues, because of her, and other storytellers, I see the world in which I was born through vivid eyes of imagination and magical interpretations. It was so real to me, I used to think I wasn't born at all. I simply fell out of the back cover of a whimsical, weird fairy tale. Delivered to my mother in the hospital by an owl on a stormy night. Maw Sue made me feel as if I had to fulfill some prophecy, some grandiose event foretold ages ago. According to the old ways, the seven sisters, the Seventh Tribe, a mystical power guided all things, all tribes and nations, and I was part of it. *She believed in me.* Even though I was little, and didn't understand the complexities of life and adulthood, her belief in the magic of a heart, and soul, her belief in me, so powerful, it bestowed a kernel of faith in me. A belief that despite it all, the seeker part of me, combined with the blood of my ancestors, the mystical, the mad and the unity of the journey, above all, being seven meant wholeness, a connection to the divine. And I could think of nothing I wanted more.

MAKING BEDS, LIVING LIES

A dreamer is one who can only find his way by moonlight, and his punishment is that he sees the dawn before the rest of the world.
~Oscar Wilde

My past was not finished with me. It not only spilled out secrets of my ancestors and my childhood, it was now going to take me further inside my deep insecurities and longing for love. A place so out of touch with my heart and so empty, that to fill the void within me, I'd marry just about anyone who threw me a crumb.

It was six months into our marriage and I wanted out. It was bad from the beginning so I wasn't surprised. The fixer in me, the chaos controller told my empty cup, otherwise known as my heart, that if I just loved him more, did more, gave more, that it would make a difference. Of course, that never worked, not with my parents and not with my husband. I continued to pour from an empty cup and loose a piece of myself with each desperate attempt at reconciliation. His cheating, lying, and manipulative bullshit sunk me deeper and deeper into mental struggles. But daddy didn't raise no quitter. I fought harder. I held on tighter. I clutched and clung and gripped. My feet were cemented in disturbed soil and I had no plans of letting go. *Adapt, survive, thrive.*

Everything was in shambles but it was all I had left. I barely had a life of my own. I pushed away all my friends trying to control and maintain what was left of the pitiful marriage bed, so I had no one to talk to. I felt alienated, desperate and needy. In some weird way—I was merely a child in an adult body crying out for answers, for help. I do not know why my mind routed to my mother, but it did nonetheless. I dialed the number in a dispirited, dismantling, coming-apart-at-the-soul sort of crumbling. In fear and panic of what she may say, after the second ring, I almost hung up until I heard her cautious voice.

"Hello," My mother answered in her usual fists-up tone. It's as if she expected an overly zealous salesman to be on the other end trying to sell her a carton of Ajax. I put the phone back to my ear as my mind scrambled with thoughts. I longed to hear my mother moonshine, but that was only in my dreams and distant memories. My mind started in on my mistake. *Cass, now look at what you have done. No salt of the earth to be found here. The whole goddamned world must be coming to an end for you to call your mother, of all people. You have done it now. Go ahead and accept the punishment, young lady, because you know it's coming.*

My desperation made me vulnerable and the cork exploded off my never-talk-to-my-mother bottle.

"Mother," I whimpered, "I don't think I can do this. I don't think I can be married. Something's missing—I think *I'm* missing…yeah, me. I'm not here or something. I don't feel like myself. I'm not sure I ever have…" My voice was fast and frantic. My body shook in spastic ticks while I sat on the edge of the waterbed. The inside of my knees held my body steady against the sideboards while the rest of my upper body bobbled like I was in the ocean. I hated this bed like I hated this marriage. Both left me exhausted.

In truth I hated every piece of furniture in this house. It was all Sam's. I might as well be the maid. Nothing in this house said that I lived here. Besides, modern contemporary is so stuck-up. I'm early American, bare-foot-on-the-lawn kind of style and for god's sake, give me real wood, not this laminated bullshit. And the worst, half of the house was a trophy room for dead animals, wall-to-wall, eyes peering, skulls, horns, deer skins, tusks, snakeskins, pelts and more dreadful atrocities I hated. Returning from one of his exotic hunting trips, he'd drag another trophy in and say, look what I killed Cassie. All I wanted to do was scream out, "You know what else your killing? *My heart*, you're killing my heart."

Of course, that never happened and even so, it wouldn't have mattered none. The kitchen was the only area Sam let me choose whatever I wanted, in a barefoot and pregnant kind of way. The rest of the house was modern masculine, the brown and beige rugs, the icky yellow stripes and the horrible paintings on the wall, weird splotches and designs as if someone dropped a canvas on the sidewalk and let birds shit on it. I held the banana-yellow phone receiver to my ear and wrapped the coiled cord between my fingers while my disjointed mind came undone. My anger for the man I married had reached a boiling point.

"Now don't make something out of nothing, Cass, you…"

"I'm not YOU!" I snapped, cutting my mother off. Something angry and hissing came out of me. "And it's not nothing. It's everything! Don't make this about you, Mother. I'm not like you at all. I—can't—just—sit—back—and—take—it!" My voice went up an octave with each word until I was shouting.

"I can't. And I won't." I wasn't sure who I was trying to convince at this point, her or myself. My voice felt fractured, tempered with a spark of madness which scared me, as if I temporarily left my body, a mandatory evacuation of sorts, and I had no control. On the other end of the phone, my mother remained silent. Battle lines were being drawn. As a child, I watched my mother use silence as a weapon of war, strategically and without mercy. Questions soared in my head. *Could six months of marriage make someone feel completely helpless? Had I reached a point of no return? Why else would I have called my mother?* Not my younger sister, Meg, who might have had words of wisdom, but my condescending mother. I weaved and bobbed on the waterbed till I got motion sickness. I was exhausted emotionally and physically. I got up and paced the floor, coiling the yellow phone cord around my hand till it was as tangled up as my life. My mother and I have never, ever been able to talk. Yet, here it is, the one-sided conversation about relationships, God forbid! *What the hell is wrong with me? Am I a glutton for punishment?* Deep inside I believed in a forever marriage, the *death till we part* kind, the *happily ever after* kind and *for better or worse* kind. I was a fool.

"Mother, I should have left the first day. Six months ago, I should have left. I should have left the first time I caught him in a lie. Or the first time he cheated or when I found a stack of porn and videos. I SHOULD HAVE LEFT. I mean, why am I still here? Honest to God, what in the hell is keeping me here? I want to leave, I do. But either way feels like death to me. Is that weird or what? Why would I feel like that? That's not normal, it can't be…can it?"I paused a long time, waiting for words, but hearing only the silence as if I wasn't talking to anyone, then I started to ramble again.

"It's like there is this control, this force, this unknown power over me and I can't even explain it. Hell, I can't describe it to know what it is. It's just there. I feel it…it's pressing me."

I froze momentarily stunned at the buried memory resurfacing like a dead corpse in my watery lungs. I gurgled and laughed a crazy, deep, disturbed mental laugh, the kind that comes only when something inside you has cracked, and broke, and disengaged from its central core allowing you to see the hidden. It was bigger than I could work out in my head or make sense of. And then it hit me.

"It's you." I spat in revelation and remembering. "Oh my god. I would have *never* married him…if it wasn't for you."

"Meeee?" My mother replied in ice cubes. I could almost see her coral lipstick coat with a chilled frost.

I laughed at my naive servitude. "Yes, you mother? We were living together. We didn't even know each other. You reminded me over and over we were living in sin and needed to make it right, make it legal, quick-like, you know, bound and under God. I had no idea what I was doing anyway. Truth be told, I left home and moved in with him to get out from under you. But day and night, you were in my head. Babbling and chatter. I had to do something. You were never going to let up, so I gave in. I persuaded Sam to marry me. Hell, I barely liked him and that's what so messed up about it. We fought all the time plus he drank all the time and I mean, drunk kind of drinking, not casual. It's like I picked the worst fucking guy I could find with every deep, dark issue. Hell, I knew he was cheating too, *even then.* I mean, I know all that now, but what shocks me the most is why did I listen to you? Huh? Why? It's puzzling to me. I don't get it. Whyyyyy does *your* opinion matter to me so much? No really… tell me. I mean…why is it all I could hear was your voice in my ears? *Your voice* drowning out my own."

I could feel the water well up in my eyes and my chest began to ache. "Why? Why is it, mother? Please tell me why?" I sat dizzy and disturbed. Anger rose up in me burning hot while my skin flushed.

Silence.

I waited in the familiar I knew so well.

"Of course. I know this game. You're not going to answer. Just obey. Follow the rules. Live like Gabby Collard, right mother? Sweep shit under the rug. Shush. Don't say anything. Deny, deny. Live like nothing happened."

"You listen here, young lady." Mother said snapping back in a low monotone. I could tell from the background noise she was in the kitchen. With each word she spoke I could hear the knife slice as it hit the cutting board.

"I don't know why you're telling me this Cassidy. I. Have. Nothing. To. Do. With. This."

"You have EVERYTHING to do with this!" I said enraged. But as usual, classic Gabby is speechless. Just knife cuts, slicing and dicing between the edges of the weapon she used best. Silence. A disturbing, brutal, condemning silence. A war without words. This was the figurehead I knew. This was the mother I grew up with. This was the war of familiarity. A war I couldn't win. My broken spirit began to sob uncontrollably as if I was a child, though I fought it venomously. Crying around my mother showed weakness and weakness could be used against me.

"Mother?" I sobbed. "Motherrr?" I waited in vain. In the seconds following, a sequence of events took place. A door opened and closed within me. The room spun slightly out of kilter. My tears dried up. I felt numb, disengaged and lost in myself. My voice went mute. Then, as if summoned one after another, trotting into the bedroom, appearing in front of me like a play, a cast of characters, little girls of all ages, different time eras, each with their own pain and struggles burdened on their backs. Talking to my mother had resurrected the bedfellows of my childhood. The House of Seven inside me rumbled on its unsteady and crumbling foundation, the disturbed soil underneath it cracked and the ground split. The Hush cemetery surrounding it was no longer a hush. The dry dead bones, the unforgiven, the unredeemed, the unresolved had risen and every little girl that had entered the house had vacated and hoisted a skeleton upon their backs. The letters on the word bones glowed eerily, from skull to thigh, to the tip of the toe. Words, promises, hopes all etched, scribbled, carved, branded and painted by childlike hands.

What is happening? I blinked to wash the vision away, daydreaming perhaps, the stress of talking to my mother, but each time I opened my eyes, another girl appeared, a different age, a different era of time. Assorted outfits and hairstyles and time periods, but I was certain every single one of them was me.

This startling revelation rattled me. One minute I'm talking to my mother. The next minute I'm losing my mind seeing ghosts, childhood versions of myself shackling with tattooed skeletons on their backs. The literary bones were mere whispers all run amuck, colliding with the chatter of teeth till they sounded like the wind howling in a soft mourn. Combined with voices of the little girls it was almost too much to bear.

"Shall we bury them?" the little girl speaks sorrowful and expectant. Another follows, same words, and this repeated itself over and over again till the whole room was swallowed up by little girls' voices.

"Shall we bury them?" A six year old pleaded.

"Shall we bury them?" An eight year old sternly asked. Every age and era followed suit. Their voices caused the skeletons to clatter and whisper as if speaking the words written on their bones kept them alive. With every whisper, the carved, etched, painted and tattooed words on the chalk bones gave off a burnt amber glow of being awakened, and the energy they emitted surged foreign molecules inside me to ping and pong until I felt like I might explode.

"Shall we bury them?" A ten year old girl asked eagerly, further on edge and uneasy. Frenzied, I had no idea if this was real or a delusional hallucination from breaking tradition and phoning my mother, whom I NEVER call. The onslaught of words filled the room until my mind spun out of balance. I couldn't talk back to my mother. I couldn't hang up and I couldn't answer the little girls' pleas. I gripped the phone, my throat swelled with knots and my ears gave off a strange humming.

"YES! For the love of God. Bury them!" I shouted. My eyes zipped from girl to girl. My mother spoke but I heard garble. I was too preoccupied with being absolutely fucking crazy. As if commanded by my voice, one by one, the little girl ghosts with the skeletons on their backs walked away, disappearing into the walls like a dense fog. It was the disturbing aftermath of sounds that haunted me the most, the skeletons clacking and rattling, the etched words were whispers rising and haunting my ears with hidden meanings, sinking deeply into me, shrouded like a mystery, each word on their bones a clue to seek and find answers.

My mind's eye followed the girls in a dream state, their feet swiftly trampling through the pine straw of the forest behind my parents' house, down the pig trails until they arrived at the place of my terror and my safety, the Hush cemetery and the House of Seven. I watched as the girls dug holes and buried the word bones, covering them in perpetual darkness of the disturbed soil while the moss tree girls swayed like demented bats with their spirit eyes the color of gold dust. When the last speck of dirt covered the bones, they walked in formation towards the House of Seven. I stared at the large seven carving in the door that glowed like a thousand roaring fires. I grabbed my hand and rubbed the scar on my palm, the one in the shape of a seven exactly like the door. I felt it pulsate and my blood ran hot and a voice called me, a whisper, a distant flicker, faint and garbled words rose up from the smoke of a long smoldering fire. The vision faded as fast as it came. I found myself in the bedroom where I started, still holding the phone, and a mountain of air churning from the other end. I had no idea how much time has passed.

"Cass…" the graveled voice said. "CASS! Can you hear me? Bury who? What are you talking about? Who died? Are you there?"

"No one died Mother, no one. I'm sorry I called," I said in a serene hypnotic voice. At this point, I was done talking, done for the day, the week, year, just done. I was just about to hang up when she finished me off.

"Cassidy Cleopatra Collard. You are about to do me in. This is nonsense."

"Likewise" I said nonchalant.

"You made your bed—now you lie in it," she said with a fury and spite that was classic Gabby. Old school Gabby, the one I remember all too well. And then she hung up. Her words were like raw spittle and fluid damnation. I gulped what felt like a large, jagged and menacing stone down my throat. Her voice held not one hint of affirmation. No sympathy, no advice of motherly wisdom, no hopeful consolation, no pulling me back from the cliff I was hanging on by a thread, just absolutely nothing but make your bed, Cassidy Cleo Collard. Lie in the mess you made. Beds and lies. Just beds and lies."

What the hell was I thinking calling her in the first place? What did I expect to get? What is this controlling power she has over me? Why do I want something she will never give? Shit! You just set yourself up, Cassidy. It's always been this way. Why did you think you'd get anything different?

Disturbed. Pissed. Undone. Rattled by visions and hallucinations, I felt broken without anyone to understand. I sat on the bed I made, unable to move, listening to the many accusations in my head going off like tiny bombs. I was vulnerable exposing myself to my mother in the first place. I should have known better.

There is no hope. No hope for you, Cass.

Now go make your bed. Lie in the mess you made.

My distracted mind drifted. As a child, I was keenly aware I was a bit more vocal and chatty, a little overwhelming for others. I was the X in extra, a force of magic and childhood imagination. A voice to be heard, acknowledged, validated and accepted. I was fire and energy. Flames, atoms and protons. *I was more. I was much. I was a mountain.* But I had a weakness. The tender seed of neediness and approval would be my downfall. Before I ever got a chance to bloom, sink into the soil, root outwards, the seed was squashed, abandoned, trampled upon, isolated and left to adapt and thrive on my own. Thank God for Maw Sue's stories, especially that of the Loblolly pine and how it grows in disturbed soil in which nothing else survives. THAT little girl, the 'too much, over-the-top child is still there—somewhere. I hear her and I feel her.

But...

Something happened to her.

Happened to me. Happened to us.

Sometimes I feel as if she might unzip my flesh and step out, take charge, leave my unknown skin lying in the dirt, and disappear to live her own life, leaving me behind. I'm not sure what changed us, but I *do* know I should have never looked to my mother for my identity. *Then...and now.* I feel like two personas. Two pieces of a whole and each of us were trying to find the pieces of ourselves and come together. Twins of myself, one wild, extra, rebellious, free-spirited and ready to conquer the world, and the other yearning, timid, anxious, overwhelmed and filled with such fear she felt completely alone. The extra little girl, split from herself and everyone around her.

For reasons unknown to me, my mother feared a three-foot frame of pale needy skin, blonde hair, desirable blue eyes and a chatty mouth. *Extra. Too much.* The world was far too dangerous to host a tempest storm like me. My mother set out to stop it before it ruined me, ruined her, ruined others. I'd see those twins of myself occasionally when I would look into my mother's blue eyes, a reflection of the duplicity setting fear in her bones and poisoning my will to hope, to dream, and to love myself. Whatever damage my mother carried under her skin had long ago seeped beneath mine.

By this time the waterbed had me dizzy and swirling, almost sick, combined with other events of the day, my mother, the ghost girls and every other severe crack in my brain that had me under siege. A few tears puddled from my eyes.

"Don't do it. Do not cry. Do not let her break you. You know how your mother is. It's your own fault. You shouldn't have called Cass! Get some grits about you. You are strong seed," I say to myself, for myself, of myself, in myself. "You are sap by God! You learn, you adapt. You survive. You thrive!"

With everything the broken child, the broken adult, the broken woman in me could muster, I composed myself. I put on my mask. I took a deep breath. In a trance of Southern etiquette and grown-up protocol, I got up from the bed I made and began to live the lie. I walked to the kitchen of my identity and opened the cabinet beneath the spice rack and took out the brand-new aluminum pan my mother gave me and Sam as a wedding gift. I held it in front of my face and saw my mother's stone reflection in the pewter and heard her demanding voice. "That's it, Cass. A good Southern girl. It's our duty to make them happy. Women can't be alone. We need our men too much. It's not about love, honey. It's just the way it is. Now get along with your business. Make them happy. Do what you've got to do, dear."

My eyes were catatonic, unblinking and hot. I slammed the pan on the burner, turned the dial and watched the blue flicker of flames leap and dance and burn my life away. I cooked. I cleaned. I gave my body. I gave my sex and my soul. I performed my duty.

I made the bed. I lived the lie. Until it damn near killed me.

17 YEARS EARLIER

JUNE 21, 1971
NEWS YOU CAN USE
BY EDNA ROLLINS

TEXAS NEWS EDITION

Frank Bullard of the Forest Service says there isn't a thing he can do about Moon Wanderers coming into our campgrounds. It's public domain and if people want to camp then it's their right to do so. I disagree. And for that reason, we at the Eternal Order of the Sisters of Salvation feel it is our duty to stand up to this atrocity and demand action. We voted. We came to a decision. I will go and witness to these lost and damaged souls because it is the Christian thing to do. Understandably, if my late husband, Jimmy Don was here, he'd have a cat fit, me going off in the wild to witness God knows what, but I feel it is what needs to be done. The Lord commands us to go…and I will. Don't worry, I shall be safe when facing the heathens because I will have Mr. Billy Ray Thomas as an escort and we all know he visits Get Fit Gym on a regular basis, so I will be in good hands. I would advise that you do not camp the weekend of the gathering unless you plan to end up smack-dab in the middle of all the shenanigans. I ask for your prayers and guidance. Until next time, tune into KTBR local radio news station 109.9. I'm Edna Rollins and that's news you can use.

ROSE PETALS AND RUSTY NAILS

Optimism is the madness of insisting that all is well when we are miserable.
~Voltaire

Since my psychotic break down, I think of my great-grandmother Maw Sue a lot. How much I wish she was here to tell me how to handle this unsorted mess I've gotten myself into. Memories of her are like time traveling to my childhood. I see her just as she was, gray hair, false teeth, her wrinkled face, her raspy voice, her flower dresses and vintage aprons. I can smell the scent of her skin doused with rose powder, the waft of herbs hanging in the kitchen and the pungent ammonia of moth balls discreetly tossed in closets, and the overpowering scent of transformation stacked in square blocks in the bathroom cabinet. That's what I called her homemade soaps. It came from the story she told when she taught me and my sister how to make lye soap from fire ashes. This is when I thought her hands were magical to be able to make something that smelled so good out of dust and debris. The story was used to illustrate how God can transform a life, because fire signifies both a consuming, and an anointing to be used and set apart by God for a special task, a transformation by the Holy Ghost indwelling within a person. Remembering this now, after everything evokes fear and a fondness in me. I'm understanding a little bit more of the all-consuming fire part of God especially how it can undo a person's life but not yet the transformational part of God, not yet anyway. I'm not sure what he's doing in my life and I'm pretty sure I failed any task he might have put before me. A tug-of-war ensues inside my soul, tangled with love and indifference. But I try.

I was always mesmerized by Maw Sue's small but effectual presence, an unseen force of magic I couldn't see, describe with words or touch, only a feeling. I'd catch myself studying her from across the room. Her pale gray eyes staring into the distance void, a place of unknowns, intently driven by some never-ending storm hidden behind a pair of white, horn-rimmed glasses with three tiny diamonds at each point. I used to wonder if those diamonds had grown sharp points while she dozed off in her rocking chair, piercing her skull and clawing at her mind and causing her to lose her grip on reality. I wonder if the same thing is happening to me. But mostly, I fear I will end up where she did. Castle Pines State Hospital on the Southeast edge of town.

The mere thought gives me caution. I'm careful with my words and my behavior, as much as I'm able, especially with my psychiatrist, Dr. Telford. Even though she says she is helping me, she still has the power to lock me up. I share what is necessary, but I keep a good portion to myself. According to Doc, I have dissociative amnesia caused by a stressful or traumatic event which triggers a loss of memory. So far they have pieced it together like this; the night in question, I had a psychotic break from my recent divorce, re-cut the scar on my hand, and torched my lying, cheating ex's belongings on the lawn of his mistress.

After Edna Rollins got hold of the story for her gossip column, the whole town is convinced I'm guilty and part of a fire burning cult movement. I can't go anywhere in town without stares or whispers. I read the articles out of curiosity and it's complete hogwash but folks around these parts are bored for entertainment and they'll believe just about anything. When I was a kid, Edna did the same thing to Maw Sue after she caught sight of her leaving Castle Pines after an extended stay. Townsfolk ate it up and that's when the name calling began; crazy old bat, nutcase, mad Sue, basketcase, lunatic, coo-coo and a host of others. I fear I'm next in line. They'll call me mad Cass, crazy collard girl, coo-coo Cassidy. Everyone knows my family tree, from Maw Sue to the Seventh Tribe, and because we think differently than others, we are always a target, especially for Edna Rollins.

Doc is doing everything in her college educated mind to pull the memories of that erased night out of me, but so far, it's only bringing out childhood snippets here and there, which for me, is far more terrifying. I'd prefer they stay where they are. In the past, *thank you very much.* But the more I try to elude them, the more they persist. The memories like dark shadows claw at my feet. I can see their outline, dark edges and cloudy figures fading in and out, smudges, ghostly elements seeking my demise. Intense emotions overtake me when the dark dimensions call out to me with voices I've long ago silenced and put away behind the pine curtain of my youth.

Maw Sue always said, we didn't get to choose our gifts or our curses. We only get to decide *how* we'll live with them. I'd curl up my nose and snarl in defiance. She's been dead for years now, and I still feel the same. I couldn't live with it then—and I don't know how to live with it now.

I came to dread my therapy visits. I walked into the lobby and plopped down on the couch.

"Hello, Pearl." I had a lighter in my hand and playfully

flicked the flames a few times as to get a reaction of her. "I'm here for torture."

"Doctor Telford will see you now," Pearl said never looking up and her voice as rigid as a claw hammer.

"Great talk, Pearl." I flicked the lighter endlessly while scooting down the hallway. Still no response, not even a blink. Pearl's coffee table personality about did me in and I was determined to get a reaction out of her.

"Hi Cass. How are you today?" Doc said, setting the timer on her side table.

I closed the door behind me, "Fine, Doc, just chatting with Pearl."

"Really? That's odd, Pearl rarely talks to anyone…even me."

"What can I say, people are drawn to my natural charm."

She smiled. "Well, we have a lot to cover today. Let's see…I spoke to you on the phone last week because you no-showed, so let's talk about that. What happened?"

"I know, Doc. I know. I'm sorry. The memories made me a little on edge. I lost it a few times, I missed work too. I don't know what's happening to me on a daily basis. It's like I don't know who I'm going to be when I wake up. It's weird. The memories are random, sporadic, out of nowhere. I feel like a ticking time bomb of emotions, a ball of energy and I don't know what is going to come out. I'm losing it. I'm sorry for calling you…a thousand times. You're the only one I can talk to about this stuff."

I felt helpless as if I was in quicksand trying to explain this to Doc. "It's like I'm lost, literally lost and all I do is overthink. And feel. Oh my God! I FEEL so much that it makes every bone inside me hurt. My head, my heart…I just want it to stop. I panic, then end up calling you. I'm sorry."

"Feeling emotional pain does cause physical pain, Cass. But *not* feeling is even more dangerous. Think about it. People who are alive, feel. They feel pain and joy, laughter and crying. It's a pendulum. You have to learn to keep the balance in the middle. But in your case, you're panicking because you don't know how to process the pain."

"I'd rather be dangerous and feel no pain."

"No. You wouldn't." Doc said nodding sternly. "You're feeling repressed pain. It's uncomfortable. Your wall is being broke down. That's why it feels like you're being violated. Invaded by emotional ghosts of your past. The pain you are feeling now—is pain from your past that wasn't dealt with. It wasn't felt back then. It wasn't allowed a release, to grieve and flow, cry or mourn, get angry or sad. People who do not feel their emotions, clam them up. Put them away. Deny them. This can cause you to repress your memories, *and* the feelings that come with the memory. But your mind and your body know it's still there, it's basically unfinished business. It doesn't matter if it was twenty years ago. Unfinished business always returns. Usually in dangerous and destructive ways, alcohol, drugs, substance abuse...pick your poison."

"Fires," I said with a shrug.

"Yes, possibly fires. I know you're being sarcastic but that is a form of acting out, a destructive way and since you brought it up, it is possible there are some repressed memories, and past feelings emerging possibly triggered by your ex-husband betraying you. I'm simply putting feelers out since we don't know yet but the point is, whatever feelings you are dealing with now have to be examined, talked about, and dealt with allowing you to move on.

"For instance, last week, the two times I did talk to you on the phone you were out of control. You wouldn't tell me why and I can't help you if I don't know what makes you react, or what makes you have the feelings you are having. So, do you want to talk about what happened last week?"

I sat on the couch and stewed inside myself. Doc was right. I was out of control. Memories came and the feelings attached to the memories always provoked a destructive reaction in me. I called in sick at work, and then called Doc's office over and over again. I drove Pearl crazy, it's no wonder she hates me. So much information and so much intensity left me reckless without knowing how to control it. It was so painful I thought I'd literally loose myself, my mind, everything. In hindsight, I ended up testing the limits of Doc's profession. Instead of working it out, myself, I came to co-depend on her. I pushed her buttons to the extreme. In reality, I drove my therapist crazy with *my* crazy. My broke set its sights on breaking her. After all, it was in my nature to break things. *Make beds. Live lies.*

When the childhood memories came, from Maw Sue to my mother, I acted psychotic, ups and downs, from depression to manic behavior and isolation. It was a new undoing and it was all about Sam, what he did to me, and why. How he couldn't love me but could love others and on and on. The two times I called Doc and left long winded messages, it was all in reference to him. The rest of the week just spiraled from there. I wanted today to be different so I did what Doc told me. I trusted her and let go. I loosened my grip on reality and my past and I allowed myself to break in safety. As the tears poured, I felt a tremor inside the House of Seven and the many cries of wounded little girls.

"Cass. This is good. Feel the pain. Let it flow. It's okay to get it out. Let it come, but don't let it take you under. You are safe here. No-one can hurt you." Doc could tell I was fighting for control and spiraling into a downward siege of panic.

"You have the power, you are in control of your mind, no suppression, just feel it and let it go. You are in charge. It's okay. Your feelings are a part of you, but they don't own you. You are in control. You control the flow. Turn it on, let it out. Pull back… breathe….then let go again."

Doc talked and consoled me but I was in my own bubble of

pent-up pain. This menacing, demonic, subliminal, unjointed burst of emotional refuse sprung from the deepest of the deepest places inside me. Pain of being alone. Pain of coming to know myself, all of me, good, bad and ugly. The divorce, the rejection, the unmet desires, the anger, all of it exploded into the cathedral of Doc's office. The whiteness of the walls and the blurriness of my vision through a flood of tears transformed each word, branding it to the office walls, much like I did when I was little with the dry dead word bones, until it looked as if I was sitting inside a book, a book of my life. I was careful only to tell Doc what I wanted her to know. I held back the knowledge of the little girls, and anything regarding my mother. That was too fresh and fragile to touch, or comprehend.

In the days following my session, I freaked out again. Turns out I'm a hard learner. Without Doc physically there to tell me—remind me—coach me—teach me—I drifted in a galaxy of melt-downs. I'd find myself calling her office. If she didn't answer or I got her recorder, I would leave a gazillion messages.

"Doc. I'm crashing and burning. Please call me back," or "I can't sleep. I'm losing it again. I don't know what to do. These goddamned feelings are tormenting me. I can't do this. I'm not coming back. I'll gladly go to jail, to hell with therapy." I'd slam the receiver down and then five minutes later, call back apologizing and pleading for help. My next appointment I learned why. I was co-dependent. Somewhere starting in childhood, I latched on to people as if I needed their oxygen to breathe. As an adult, Doc was one more hose to drain. My need to control people and things was necessary for my survival. I was also a reactor. My life had been so chaotic for so long—control was my only vice to maintain some semblance of peace. *I didn't know I had no control over my circumstances. I didn't know there was a solution.* I needed to control my own doctor as if *she* revolved in *my* world. I needed *her* planet in line, so I could function, turn, face the moon, rotate, align the stars, feel the sunshine, coat the darkness. Doc believed it may stem from the emptiness the divorce created but it started long before Sam.

Looking at it now, days later, it was a bit overreactive but in the moment, it was all I knew. Inside me was a world of its own making. Some dark apprentice lived inside the House of Seven within me, pushing buttons, turning knobs, whispering, talking, telling, and demanding. Doc began to teach me why. It has to do with *family origins, roots and the root extensions.* I learned about myself in the process, information I didn't like. Turns out I was controlling, manipulative and angry. I was bored, empty and undefined. I yearned desperately for love, yet I pushed people away. I sabotaged good. I gave and gave and gave until I was depleted but could not receive from others. I accepted bad treatment as if I deserved it. I provoked. I blamed. I felt shame and guilt. I felt condemned. Learning all this put me into a state of denial. One to be expected.

Examining myself made me reactive in a negative way because it was too painful, so instead of focusing on my internal self, I projected everything outward and it landed on my ex. All I could think of was Sam. *I blamed him.* He was the reason for all my pain. *Him,* I screamed, *him.* Then I'd reverse and blame myself. I must have done something wrong. I was the reason he cheated, lied, rejected me. Then came the loathing, self-doubt, criticism, guilt. Then it would flip-flop. Eyes off me and back on Sam. I'd hate and blame him again, then myself, then my family, then Sam, then everyone was a target. I was a dysfunctional mess.

In the days and weeks following the next two appointments, my life unraveled. The pendulum swung side to side. I couldn't get things done. I had no energy or too much energy. I couldn't get out of bed and other times I paced like a trapped wild animal. I had fits of rage and hostile tantrums. I denied the feelings bubbling out of me. I pretended it wasn't real. *It didn't happen. Not to me, I said. It's not true. Not Cassidy Cleo Collard. Nope. Not me.*

But deep inside me, inside the House of Seven a little girl wept with muted lips, trapped and held captive beneath my skin, a shield for *her* protection, *our protection.* I knew she was there, *I've always known.* She wants to talk things out, but her words are painful and too horrible to mention, so I keep her silenced in a solitary room inside the house, far away from the other girls as to not influence them to rebel like her.

Doc said everyone has an inner child inside them they either accept or deny. I kept silent as to not mention my inner child for reasons unknown. But I felt her sadness every second I breathed. The air leaving her lips and sweeping through my inner ribcage like sorrow and regret. Her fingertips were pokes and prods, her movements undoing me, the twists and turns, and her voice like a thousand crickets chirping rendering my eardrums numb. Her cries endless, her desperate pleas a nightmare. Her balled-up fists beat against the wall of my heart causing me to clutch my chest in pain but I could not answer her, let her out or give her a voice. To accept her meant I would have to accept what happened to her. And I cannot do that. *Not now. Not ever.*

During sessions I could see her intermingle like a ghost spirit, in and out of the walls and around the room, staring at me with those eyes of truth and danger. Sometimes, she sat beside me like a warrior in full armor ready to fight battles and other times, she floated above me, a weeping angel, tarred and black from the life I put her through. Her hot tears would drip and land on my skin, disbursing into tiny smoke angels dismissed to Heaven.

There were times I left therapy reassured and ready to face the world, and a day, a week, a month later—I'd crack under pressure. The world turned, the world broke and I broke with it. A stress factor, a work drama, seeing couples in love, a trauma trigger, a word, a memory, a flashback. Minor things set me in motion. Anything that reminded me of my marriage would send me into orbit. I'd find myself calling Doc's office and talking to a machine. "Tell me what to do. I don't know what to do?" On rare occasions she'd return my call. Her calming voice was like a tranquilizer gun on a wild elephant.

"You have the skills, Cass. I taught you what to do. I gave you the tools necessary to work the problem out. Stop being irrational in your thinking. Stop reacting to each situation. Take a step back. Renew your mind. Detach."

"But…but that bastard…," I'd stutter.

"No buts or bastards Cass. This is about *you.* Not Sam. Do the work. You cannot depend on me, Cass. I am not your savior. This is part of the cycle of co-dependency. You are the one to break it. You can't move on until then. Do the work. Yes, it is painful. It's brutal and hard. But your alternative is staying sick and in the same place. And aren't you sick and tired of being in *that* place, Cass?"

"Yes…," I'd blubber like a child.

"We've talked about the two pains. The pain of staying sick and in a destructive cycle repeating the same pattern over and over staying stuck. AND the pain of breaking that cycle and doing the therapy and the hard work to overcome it. One pain lasts horribly forever in a stuck cycle and the other pain is recovery and healing, but it only lasts as long as you are willing to keep it. There is incredible healing and LIFE in the second pain and it is worth it. Now which pain would you prefer? You don't seem to be doing too well in the sick stuck phase…so let's try the latter, shall we? Yes, it hurts, it's supposed to hurt but it won't last because healing follows. So practice the twelve steps. Stop reacting. Believe in yourself. You can do this. You are stronger than you realize Cass."

Her manner of calmness irritated me to no end. Her poker face could stare down Charles Manson without a twitch and offer him tea without so much as a blink. These twelve steps that Doc referred to had changed me, made me accept and try a new way of life. But they didn't work unless I practiced them, and applied them to my life, every single day, hour, minute. God! It was work. Excruciating mind and heart work. Hence, steps. Baby steps, all twelve of them. Repeat, backtrack, mess-up, steps, move forward, back-up, step, repeat. It was like learning to walk and talk again. *Re-live. Re-learn. Re-love. Re-form. Re-do.* Basically, learn how to do life differently than before. The steps helped me to balance, focus, and reclaim my life when it tipped over too far to the left or right but it was a second-by-second attempt that took all of me.

And when I was done wrestling with myself and the uncontrollable world around me, I finally surrendered my messed-up, chaotic, reactionary life to a higher power. I even named my madness. *The broken knob.* My mind. My messed up, irrational brain is my broken knob. It's the only term I could come up with to explain what happens when I lose control. A knob inside my mind randomly turns on and off at will, and I can no more control it than I can control the earth spinning. This is where cognitive behavioral training came in. Another hard work step-by-step therapy based teaching Doc was putting on me. But the broken knob kept doing its damage.

Appointments came and went but one day out of nowhere, a shift. I felt the knob turn. Click. Rattle. That had never happened before. It occurred when the loud, clanging bell timer went off signaling the end of my session.

"So, Cass, next time we'll dive deeper into family, maybe talk about your relationship with your parents, and we'll start with your mother."

I gave Doc a deer-in-the-headlights, horns-in-the-windshield, blood-and-guts face. I let out a long, exhausting, terrible gust of wind and dust particles left over from 1970-something. Perhaps, a breath I'd been holding since childhood. No memories came, but the weight of their presence was heavy and pending. My mind flashed only mere snapshots, the parents, threats of divorce, drinking and fighting, barefoot feet in pine straw, tree limbs swaying, flames, screams. It was enough to make me withdraw.

As a child, Maw Sue said I was a seeker, but I was beginning to think I was a keeper instead. I internalize stuff, other people's stuff. I take it in and touch it, feel it, wear it, keep it and make it my own. I keep stuff I should have let go of a long, long time ago. I hold it to my chest. I swaddle it and give it comfort and try to understand it until it soaks inside me. Layer after layer, it becomes a part of me. And now I don't know how to discard it without feeling naked and vulnerable.

Therapy sessions came and went. Doc never forced the "mother" from me. Forcing her from my lips was a call to arms, as we both discovered. Someone else would rise up in me, an angry shadow, a scared little girl, a fearful woman. Doc made the mistake of pushing too far once and I cracked. The next thing we knew I was crouched in the corner by the window, my arms locked around my knees and my face wild and in fury, repeating the same words over and over again.

"Don't burn it. No Mother, noooo."

Why my past seems to invade me with fire and smoke references, I couldn't tell you. It's eerie and fills me with dread. All I can think of is the all consuming fire of God and me in ashes. After coming out of that terrifying incident with no reasoning of why, Doc used caution when discussing *the mother*. For me, it was a trigger pull, which provoked a memory emerging over which I had no control. But before the memory could waylay and dislodge me with terror and fear, I would shut down. It was then I realized I had more than myself for company. It was the inner child that Doc spoke of and she was in charge, not me.

Long ago, when war was declared amongst the Collard family, my heart summoned a protector, inside the house within me. A shadow warrior to protect the little girl who resided there. The knighted warrior swore my allegiance to silence in her name. I only spoke of the things she told me. Sometimes, she surprised me with her words, her stories, the things she remembers. Other times, I turned away. But since the fire, slowly, as I began to listen and trust her more, I raised the pine curtain to peak deeper into the blackest part of my childhood. Shockingly, I would soon discover even though my mother and I were separate, cut at the umbilical cord, and different in every way imaginable, we were inexplicably bound to a darkness neither of us would identify until it was too late.

BEHIND THE PINE CURTAIN

My crown is called content,
a crown that seldom kings enjoy.
~ William Shakespeare

I got up earlier than I normally do. There was a nip in the air and the dew was still glazed over the plants and blades of grass on the lawn. The sun with all its magnificent colors was peeking over the pines, rising up like a yellow god. I sat on the porch swing. The creaking eek-eek noise of the old chain made my heart yearn for simpler times. I glanced toward the pasture. The forest beyond the fence line called to me with a voice only a child would recognize. My house was surrounded by national forest land, which was the reason I was attracted to this rental house to begin with. The next thing I know, I'm manipulating the barbwire and crawling through the fence. I could almost see Meg and I as kids behind our house, heading to the woods, her holding the wire up while I crawled under and Meg saying, *hurry up fool, we ain't got all day for you to roll around in the grass.* I found myself walking a trail barefoot and still in my white cotton nightgown. The pine needles on my toes and the red dirt beneath my feet made me whimsical as if I'd been touched with magic. My arms reached side to side, touching various trees, shrubs and greenery. I had forgotten how quiet it was in the deep woods. Only small rustling sounds of nature nestling in uncertainty.

I had momentarily closed my eyes to take in the sacred moments, my arms outstretched with invitation. I exhaled and opened my eyes, only to freeze up. I blinked to make sure I wasn't dreaming. But it was still there. An owl, a real live owl only a few feet away near a puddle of creek water. I held my breath and my movements to stare at the amazing creature. The owl rotated its head from side to side and watched me mysteriously and as curiously as I was to it. Maw Sue used to tell me owls were messengers of spirited things. There had been an owl outside my hospital window when I was born but she never understood the message it brought. As a kid it made me feel special, connected to nature, but as I grew older, I never thought much about it, *until now*. I stepped forward slowly to get closer. The owl lurched upwards and straight at me. All I could see was those long talons growing larger as I fell backwards flat on my back. There was a sharp pain in my arm, but I hardly noticed because time seemed to slow down in my mind to see everything in slow motion. The widespread wings and flapping feathers were spiritual fans. My vision sharpened with every detail and pattern. It had sharp, massive talons partially encrusted with thick clay from feeding in the creek beds. And then it was gone, returning to the sky it mastered. The sacred moment was over but I had been stirred to stillness. When I finally moved to sit up, I felt a sharp pain in my arm. A long gash with blood trickled down my arm where I had fallen and scraped it against the sharp thorns of the locust tree. It occurred to me that I hadn't seen a Locust tree of swords since childhood.

And then without warning—or maybe the thorn scrape *was* a warning, who knows, but regardless, a childhood memory emerged.

A leaf drops from a tree branch, my little bare feet scruff against pine straw and my toes sink deeply into the hot, crunchy red soil. Birds chirp from treetops, water trickles over sand and sifts through the creek bed while the hot Texas wind licks my skin like a damp dishrag. Sweat beads across my neck and soaks my hair making it sticky and matted. Meg and I were gallivanting down a pig trail following Maw Sue's footsteps. The tops of the pine trees bowed over us like guardians. They shut out the sun with their massive upper bodies and formed a tunnel of dusky shadows weaving in and out of the underbrush and played tricks on our eyes. A tangled mass of weeds, grasses and a variety of small hardwoods—oaks, elm, hickory, and sweet gum—had strangled the narrow path, making it hard to walk. I was hedged close to the tail end of Maw Sue's skirt. Meg was behind me, her fingers locked into the belt loops of my shorts.

Maw Sue was our forerunner through the dense woods, slashing, chopping and breaking a pathway. Small prickly bushes grabbed us with long boney fingers and scraggly nails. They pinched our thighs and left bleeding scratches. The forest could be a beautiful but dangerous place. Deeper and deeper it swallowed us until we reached a clearing. Acres of twisted vines snaked around numerous trunks, a highway of limbs spiraled above us, loops and drops, twists and turns connecting each tree. The mouth of the forest opened wide and we walked freely on its pebbled teeth and soft palette of mossy growth and a carpet of reddish-brown pine straw. Meg and I found plants, herbs and various other flora and asked Maw Sue a gazillion questions. She knew a lot about herbs, nature and medicinal recipes passed down from the Seventh tribe. It was important for her to pass tradition down to us. On this particular walk, she told us to gather up honeysuckle vines, dewberry brambles and scrapings of sticky pine sap and we were happy to do so.

We were wading in the creek bed when Maw Sue approached a tree we had never seen. It was a Locust tree. A sword tree, a warrior tree. Tiny swordlike points sharp as needles stuck out all over the place. In my mind, tiny creatures of the forest would break off the swords and commence to do battle. Maw Sue snapped off a handful of swords and stuffed them inside her apron pocket along with a handful of green leaves she plucked off another tree. I assumed it was for herbal potions since she swore, she was a door knock away from death. She had more aches and pains than anyone I knew but she could whip up an herbal remedy in no time flat.

She sat on a tree stump and told us to take a break. We knew what was coming. This was storytelling mode. My ears perked up and waited anxiously for a new story or some other grand tale about the newly found locust tree. She emptied her pockets and began sorting. She sifted through the wild arrangement of leaves, brambles, and honeysuckle vines on her lap. Then finally, when I couldn't stand it anymore, she began her story. As she spoke, she sewed, twisted and wrapped. I listened and watched her seamstress fingers meticulously weave a strange and wonderful creation. Her fingers sewed a gift—while her lips sowed a seed.

We were transported to a whimsical place of childlike wonder. The story was about a baby named Jesus and his miraculous beginnings. The words impregnated the forest with life as if Bethlehem were tucked under the haven of pine trees a few feet away. The power of it made my heart hurt. So much I clutched at my chest and pondered its profound ability to make me tear up. No other story had done this to me before. I was prone to being overly dramatic sometimes, but this was ridiculous. *I was a mess.*

She spoke of his mother too. Her name was Mary, a simple woman whom God favored for no other reason than he knew she would say yes to anything he asked of her. God was right. *Mary said yes.* She did so without questions, without answers, without any knowledge of what the future held. *Mary said yes.* This thought kept running through my head over and over. I could never call her Mary. It didn't seem fitting. I had to call her by her identity and her identity was in her faithfulness, and her faith was in her answer. *Mary said yes.* Her impulsiveness astonished me; her reckless abandonment gave me pause. Heck, I could barely go five minutes without asking twenty questions. I pondered this *Mary said yes* woman till my ears burned. Then the story got even more radical. The baby was God's son. The son came from the womb of *Mary said yes* and all because *Mary said yes.* I mean…*hello?* It sounded so simple yet unbelievable. Plus, he was born poorer than white trash and under less than desirable conditions. More like scandalous! *Mary said yes* was an unwed mother.

"Like Emma Parkinson?" I bleeped.

"What?" Maw Sue stopped sewing and looked at me strange.

"Emma Parkinson." Everyone in this town knew everything about everybody. "You know…Maw Sue." I stuck my hands out over my stomach and blew it out huge like a baby was inside. "That blonde woman with the big belly, the cashier at Pick-N-Pack. People say she's having a bastard. Did Mary have a bastard? What is a bastard anyway?"

Maw Sue got choked. Her face turned pink and she spit a big wad of brown snuff on the ground. My nose curled in protest.

"That snuff will kill you Maw Sue."

"Mmmhuh…" she mumbled and spit again.

"Well, did Ms. Parkinson say yes to God too?"

Maw Sue hem hawed, rolled her eyes and fidgeted. "Child, she said yes to somebody, okay. Now are you going to listen to the story, or ask questions?"

"Well…I guess listen to the story," I said sulking and drawing in the dirt with my fingers. Supposedly, the story goes that *Mary said yes* was taken in by a man named Joseph who cared for her and asked her to be his wife so he could protect her and the baby. It's a good thing, cause shortly afterwards they would flee Egypt to avoid some madman who hated male babies and wanted to kill them. *Mary said yes* ended up in a barn and gave birth to her son surrounded by animals. Somehow, magically, a bright star announced his birth. He was visited by great kings and wise men who rode on camels. They brought him presents too. Special gifts, magical treasures that told him who he was, who he was to become, his identity and his purpose. Studying the heavens was the kings' job, so they knew the star fulfilled an ancient prophecy that signified a birth of a messiah who would lead his lost people home.One king gave him gold. It meant kingship because only wealthy kings could possess precious metals. The second king gave frankincense, a fragrant oil to symbolize he was a priest, a man commissioned to represent God on earth for the people. For some reason, my mind reverted into deep thinking. *Why can't I have hints? Where is my star? Where are my gifts to tell me my identity? Where is my Mary Said Yes plan? Have I missed my important moment? Who am I and how shall I know?*

I was young and yet tormented by a quest for meaning. *Why am I here? Why was I born? What does all this mean? What am I supposed to do?* I was relentlessly questioning my mind, my body and its desires, its ups and downs, or my heart's ability to cope, to fall apart, to love and hate, to sin and worship, to break and recover, its resistance, its barriers, its resilience, its strengths and its weaknesses. I was tangled up in a collision course of my own making. I feared on a deeper level I had no identity. My three wise kings were tragically lost, and my shining star plummeted from the sky void of light and direction. *And I missed it. I missed it all.*

My body was at war with my mind. My mind was at war with my spirit. My spirit was at war with my heart and my heart was tied to the chaos of a crazy world. Folks around these parts yack and yack about a place called Hell. If there is such a place, I lived it in my mind long before I knew I could be saved from it. I came out of my mind-wandering identity crisis only to discover the third king was a freak. He gave the gift of myrrh, which was a scented oil used to anoint a dead body. *What kind of a stupid gift is that?* Meg and I looked at each other awkwardly. This was the worst story Maw Sue ever told. It was heading in a direction neither of us cared for. This dude named Jesus was born with a purpose. His purpose was to die. And we didn't like that one bit.

"Well, that's just stupid," I yelled out. My heart sank. "I hate this story." At the same time, I felt the earth split while I waited to be swallowed while Maw Sue finished the story. The pain in my heart overwhelmed me with grief and guilt and odd feelings I had never had before. Maw Sue said the gift of myrrh foretold of his sacrificial death on the cross for our sins.

"What's a sin?" I interrupted for the umpteenth time. Maw Sue looked at me confused.

"Didn't they teach you this in church, Cass? A sin is a sin. It just is."

All they told us in vacation Bible school is a bunch of sentences we had to memorize and if we could recite them, we got a dumb certificate, a soda pop, a chocolate bar and recess on the playground. If I'd known that, I'd never have done all that work to memorize. I don't get it. They said Jesus would take them, take the sins, so I figured okay, sure, take mine, but how am I supposed to know what he's taking if I don't know what a sin is to begin with? It's just bullshit, Maw Sue. Don't make no sense."

"Well, I don't know how to explain it no other way….the Lord said he came to save us from ourselves by the cross." Maw Sue said deeply in thought. Then she hem-hawed and crawfished and spoke long words till I felt my head hurt.

"Girls, I reckon if you feel bad about doing something then

that's a sin you need to rid yourself of or it could destroy you, simply as that. And yes, man made religion, the rules of men and all that nonsense in the church, and *this* town, well, you're right, straight-up bullshit."

Finally something I understood. I *did* know the reference for bullshit and heard it quite frequently from Dad, my uncles, and Papa C, with a conversation that would go something like, Gavin you see that car over there? It goes a hundred miles per hour in six seconds flat on a straight run by god" and they'd answer back with, that's a crock of bullshit. Ain't no Ford can do that."

I'd heard several scenarios where the word was used. I was just shocked the church was using it too. For a mere second, I imagined the Pastor at the pulpit saying, Jesus sat with the little children and told them stories and all kinds of bullshit. I giggled but I wasn't sure it fit him just right, but who was I to question the called. And then I heard the snap of fingers. It was Maw Sue pulling me out of my daydreaming.

"Can we get on with the story now?"

"Yeah, Maw Sue. I'm good." I smiled and lifted my hand in agreement because the next time I saw the church reverend I planned on calling him out on his bullshit.

Maw Sue continued her story of the man named Jesus who was born to die. I listened but suddenly things got strange. Feelings inside me burbled up like a deep hole in a stream. The saliva pooled in my mouth. A frog crawled up my throat and clogged the pipe. If I didn't know any better, I'd say I felt responsible for the dude named Jesus's death for some reason, and I'm guessing sin was the cause of it. Maw Sue tried to reassure us it was his life mission. I finally swallowed the frog down my throat after almost choking but at least I could get words out.

"Naahhhh," I said in disbelief. I held my hand up to push the words away but some deeper part of me uprooted. Dislodged inside my chest cavity. I had no idea what came over me. I felt my bones detach and I struggled to catch air until my heart started flip-flopping in my chest. My eyes leaked and leaked until I couldn't blink them back. My body rocked forward in little ticks. I was restless. I wanted to run. Run away from my feelings, run away from the story, run away from what it meant, the deep inner message that stirred me, undid me. I felt a shift inside my heart, my soul. I was plucked to an otherworldly place. My eyes took on an altered sense of reality. My vision crisp and my hearing keen. It was like God came down to meet me. He pulled the pine curtain back and walked on in. He sat down beside me like common folk. If I had sin, he sure wasn't concerned with it. I looked up at Maw Sue to see if she noticed, but obviously it was just me hallucinating, or maybe it was really happening. He could tell Maw Sue was talking about him and he seemed to enjoy it, which was weird because when someone's talking about your death, it seems odd to smile about it. Of course, my opinion didn't matter none. Maw Sue was finishing up her story and personally, I didn't give two shits because in the end he died. *Some story.* But then the tables turned on me. I was wrong. Well, half-wrong.

He did die, but then he rose up. It was like magic. Then he told everyone to follow him and they would rise from the dead too. My jaw dropped. I didn't like the idea of a lot of dead people rising up and walking around. It sounded too Edgar Allen Poe-ish. Turns out, before Jesus left, he passed out ghosts named Holy as a free gift to everyone and then he up and skedaddled. By this time, my jaw was jacked open so wide a mockingbird could nest in it. I was plain irked with the whole concept of this unbelievable story. I looked at Maw Sue and then at this spirited Jesus man sitting beside me. I wanted to roll out the questions on him and get some serious no-bullshit answers, but that would alert Maw Sue and I didn't need no more trouble, so I kept it to myself, but I sure did give him the stink eye. *I mean, who gives ghosts for presents?* While the mystical presence made my insides roll around like magic marbles, Maw Sue had finished sewing. In her lap were two beautiful locust leaf crowns intertwined with honeysuckle vines, brambles, pine sap and the flowers Meg and I collected. She slipped them over her wrist and stood up. They dangled in the air like magical hula hoops.

"Okay, girls. We are going to have a Seventh Tribe ceremony."

Meg and I looked at each other. We had no idea what a Seventh Tribe ceremony was—but if Maw Sue was involved, it was going to be a doozy. I mean, we had heard all sorts of stories about the seven sisters, and the tribe, but not a ceremony. I turned to look at Jesus and he was gone. I was almost offended that he didn't say goodbye, but then I remembered the ghost and obviously I had one somewhere and I was just about to start looking when Maw Sue snapped my attention back to her.

"Are you ready, girls?" Maw Sue stood up and held one of the locust crowns in her hand and walked in front of Meg. She held the crown high over Meg's head. Meg was wide-eyed and bushy tailed and bowed her head like a true princess.

"Meg Collard. You are a child of God gifted with a precious and beautiful gift. Anointed from a great line of seekers. You are empowered with the blessing of the Seventh Tribe." She placed the crown on Meg's head and reached her hands to the heavens, closing her eyes.

"Birds of the air, oh the lilies of the field. Great stars of Heaven. Meg wants to be whole and complete. Make her seven. Send her crumbs so she may consume and make her life a beautiful bloom. In honor of the seven. Amen."

My heart pounded like distant drums. Maw Sue walked in front of me. I bowed my head. *This was it.* It was my *Mary said yes* moment. Inside my mind I screamed, yes, yes, yes! I was being anointed. In my heart I knew who I was. My personal identity was tied to this man king, this Jesus. I was Southern sap. Queen of the pine curtain.

"You, Cass Collard, are first born. You are a child of God gifted with a precious and beautiful gift. Anointed from a great line of seekers. You are empowered with the blessing of the Seventh Tribe." She placed the crown on my head. I felt my gut heat up on the inside, my skin hot and clammy. I felt dizzy. She reached her hands to the heavens and closed her eyes. I wanted to do what ceremonial people do—but I didn't want to miss anything either. Instead of closing my eyes, I saw everything magically manifest. I had to see the words come out of her lips, see the heavens accept them, pick out a star for my identity and take in the whole moment of my rebirth.

"Birds of the air, oh the lilies of the field. Great stars of Heaven. Cass wants to be whole and complete. Make her seven. Send her crumbs so she may consume and make her life a beautiful bloom. In honor of the seven. Amen."

I felt a whoosh in the air. I lost track of words, time and thoughts. The heavens spun with clouds, angels and prisms of blue, yellow and white.

After it was over, Meg and I floated down the dirt trail like newly anointed queens of the pine woods. A gentle breeze licked my skin and goose bumps broke out on my arms and tingled up my spine. I glanced back and the common man's savior was still there, as if he'd never left. I waved and skipped ahead to catch up with Meg.

Together the magical and mysterious burned me slowly from the inside out. The pine curtain was ablaze. A veil had been lifted in heaven and on earth and the Collard girls were never the same.

The childhood memory had overpowered me so much I forgot where I was. For a second I thought I was still in the past, in that moment of the sacred, but then I noticed the blood streaming down my arm and onto my nightgown. And then I remembered falling back against the Locust tree when the owl flew up. I glanced over at the Locust tree and plucked a few swords from it's limbs. Holding them made tears pour from my eyes and my heart was heavily burdened. I sat in grief beneath the warrior tree of my childhood. The pine guardians of the forest stood watch around me while I cried. *Where is this little girl now? Where did she go and why?* I had no answers but for the first time in a long time, probably since childhood, I felt the touch of a mystical God emerge and make me tremble in his realness. After all, he is the common man's savior.

When I was able to stop crying and gather my wits about me, I walked back to my house. I cleaned and bandaged my cut and then made me some coffee. Still rattled from today's events, I felt the blue lines of my journal calling me. I jotted down my Locust tree adventure, the owl, the memories, the little girl. I wrote of the beginnings, the madness, sleeping long hours, rarely going outside, numb to myself, to my mind, my emotions, the pain. The times I cared not for living—but could not will myself to die. I wrote of death and being alone. I wrote of darkness pulling me under. I dreamed of death, saw visions of my death, and heard whispers of dying from those voices I constantly had to shut out. Those were the deep soil days of darkness where I wandered inside the House of Seven, inside my own body, building each room from whatever mindset I was in at the time. I constructed this whimsical and weird haunted house inside me, board by board, misery by misery, fear by fear, nail after nail. The shadow guard, a truth teller, a soldier, a strong female presence stands outside the house holding a sword at her side. She's always been there, but only now, after the locust tree cut me, do I realize who this shadow is. The shadow is only an altered version of me, the protective one I created at one time or another, and she holds a locust sword, sharp and ready to slice, safeguarding me at all cost. She is the shield and the sword who protects the little girl inside the house, the girl who couldn't protect herself. There are times in my dreams I visit the little girl inside the House of Seven without fear, but when I wake up, I will not let her come out. The broken knob clicks and madness prevails. Pain is unbearable. There are nights I cling to the shadow soldier and beg her to stab me with the locust sword and be done with it. She refuses. Instead, she whispers words riveting my backbone with steel girders. "You are grit and courage. Blood and tears. Stars and moon dust. You are faith and hope. You are beautiful clusters and constellations of promise."

I want to believe her words but can't. On rare occasions in my daydreams, when I am under the control of the knob in my head and my soul is restless, the little girl will throw out her magic and put me under a spell. I believe the little girl inside the house with the magical words, and the spirit of belief and wonder. Once she persuaded me to let her out of her room to roam freely with me. I agreed, with the understanding she had to go back in. I wanted her to realize how cruel it was outside. I wanted her to see she was safer inside the House of Seven. Safe in the darkness, alone without anyone to hurt her. She was not convinced. She'd try to sway me with stories of great and marvelous things, of people and places, of families and of love. *Great love.* An unfailing love. One I hadn't seen or felt until today behind the thick curtain of the pines on the forest trail when the locust tree pricked my skin and opened me up to bleed emotions and remind me of the suffering servant. *The greatest love of them all.* She made me feel hope. Maybe for the first time. Hope I could eat like crumbs off a beggar's table. Hope like the brisk fingers of the wind on my cheeks. Hope like the common mans saviors kind of hope. I should have known it wouldn't last long. Soon after, a hideous fear rose up and snatched hope away. My eyes grew dim. The light was too bright. *What was I thinking?* I could never be *her* again. Not after all the bad things I've done. So I doubled down. I said no. I can't. The little girl was screaming the whole time, "But you said yes, just like Mary, you said yes."

I clamped down on my lips and in a low voice said, "I said no. Now leave me be." I shoved the little girl back inside the House of Seven. I locked the door and shut out her screams. Maw Sue was right. Words have power. And so does silence.

PRESENT DAY

June 18, 1988
NEWS YOU CAN USE
BY EDNA ROLLINS

TEXAS NEWS EDITION

The annual Pine Log Summer fest will be held at the Taylor Martin Zoo as it is every year since the wall went up in 1952 when the first animal was donated.

Sloan, the infamous hippopotamus, has entertained the masses of children and adults for years. Sloan quickly became the locals' favorite zoo animal, but many do not know the details behind the thick-skinned, toothy animal and the stories that ran rampant around town before the zoo was ever constructed. After all, when you receive a gift like a hippopotamus, rumors are bound to float. Today, some thirty years later, questions remain. Legend has it that Mr. Martin received the hippo as a gift for his birthday in 1951 after a hunting trip to Africa, yet no one can say who gave it or where it came from. Speculation abounds and of course, a lot of questions were raised, such as, who gives wild animals for gifts, a hippo at that, which weighs over 4000 pounds and is nearly impossible to hide, not to mention the transportation to get here from overseas.

Which brings us to our next question: does the hippo have a deeper meaning, possibly with family ties? Local residents have asked these questions and more for ages. In a small town of twenty-thousand, it's hard to hide an animal as big as a hippo. People caught glimpses of a large truck with a huge crate making stops in town, where strange sounds were heard coming from it. Then country folks started saying they had spotted an unusual beast outside a farm on the outskirts of town, but it wasn't till hunters started tracing the pine woods to scout this creature that they found him floating in the Southerbees' old fishpond. It was private property so they couldn't get close, but they did snap pictures of it, and a few folks saw it, until "highfalutin" gatekeepers and a wad of cash mysteriously made the picture vanish. But by this time, the rumors around town of a hippo in hiding became commonplace. It wasn't till the official ribbon-cutting ceremony of the zoo's opening that the hippo was presented to the community zoo. The town went crazy with delight and children wanted to visit the zoo almost every weekend to see this huge creature. Of course, accusations, table talk, laundry line chat and a whole slew of questions still reverberate through Pine Log, even today.

You see, before the zoo opened, committee members were sworn to secrecy, but why? Is there something more going on behind the scenes? What is more astonishing about this legend is the other aspects of the story. At the time, Mr. Martin was a widower, having lost his wife to illness three years prior. The housekeeper Eloise, an unmarried black woman from Mississippi, had worked for the family for fifteen years, but disappeared a year after the wife died, and then reappeared with a child. A child named Sloan. *Coincidence? Happenstance?* Whatever it was between the hippo, the zoo and the wild accusations around town, it was too much for Mr. Martin's housekeeper. Within a few months, they were gone and never heard from again. Mr. Martin lived till 1978 and saw his dream fulfilled of his beloved zoo become a place of wonder and amusement for children and adults alike. It housed over 800 animals from all over the globe, but Sloan remained the most popular of them all. Sloan lived to an old age and probably would have outlived us all, had it not been for some brat throwing a ball into the pool. Sloan swallowed it unaware, which caused intestinal blockage upon which they were unable to save her. As you can see, this town has unanswered questions to fill in and that's why I come to you, residents of Pine Log. Can you fill in the blanks? What other legends of Pine Log do you have to share that may help? Give Edna a holler and we'll get to the bottom of it.

Until next time, I'll see you at the festival. In addition, it has recently been suggested that the city move or discontinue the annual fireworks exhibit at the zoo, due to the undue stress it causes the animals. Unlike humans, animal ears are more sensitive. Just imagine if your hearing was intensified 300 percent and fireworks were exploding all around you? That's how the animals feel. According to sources, protesters will be out and about with petitions to sign, as well as suggestions for a new location. Have a safe summer. Until next time, tune into KTBR local Radio news station 109.9. I'm Edna Rollins and that's news you can use.

BLACK ANGELS

Light does not come from light
but from darkness.
~Mircea Eliade

My days are filled with thoughts of my mother. My past, *our past.* Our connection, or lack of. Our relationship was as ambiguous as my emotions. Or my whole childhood for that matter. I was selfish. Back then, I wanted all of her. I wanted the parts of her I couldn't find, couldn't see or comprehend. I was desperate for her love, acknowledgment, and validation that she even existed, and if so, then I existed. We existed together. But that was not reality. And because of that, I'd often daydream or worse, my mind went savage, my vision taking eerily roads of its own. I saw myself plunging my hand into her beating heart and pulling it out. My teeth sinking into her heart flesh while the blood pumped and spilled down my arms, as my body surged with her taste, a final all-knowing, a yearning fulfilled. It was those visions that scared me. My unmet needs and desires made my mind shift and crack. Other times, it would surrender to the crumbs. The only sustaining substance that kept me surviving.

Hope. A desire that one day I'd finally get what I wanted so badly. Growing up, I would catch glances of it on my birthdays. Each year I received a cake and a party. Mother planned and prepped everything. It was a big deal to me. I felt special. Celebrated. Loved. But when the day passed, the candles were blown out and all the gifts were opened and played with, my mother disappeared into her shell. The wall reconstructed. The fortress secured. Her obscurity returned. Her silence resumed. I may have been a year older, but things were the same.

No matter our distance apart, she was beautiful in my eyes. So beautiful I wanted to show her off. I told my elementary school friends she took two showers a day and wore red lipstick. Why I felt the need to tell them, I don't know. I mimicked her motions with the lipstick and how she patted her lips on paper and I collected them as paper kisses. When I got home, Mother was coming out of the living room and I told her how popular she was with all my friends. Her face turned bleak. Her Ivory skin crinkled like crushed paper. Her perfect arched eyebrows raised their black flags and her red lipstick turned to a murky scowl. She scolded me with her long-painted fingernail.

"Young lady, don't you ever do that again. Don't go around telling anyone about me—do you hear me?"

"I…I…didn't…mean…," I stuttered, not knowing what to say. I walked away with a horrible fear I'd done something wrong, yet for the life of me didn't know what.

A few weeks later, I found a picture of her dressed as Dorothy in *The Wizard of Oz* for Halloween. I took it to school to show my friends. I forgot it was in my pocket and it fell out in front of her. She went ballistic. "How many times do I have to tell you to quit talking about me to your friends? Did you take this to school?"

I cowered in fear. My face revealed what my mouth couldn't utter.

"Don't ever, ever take a picture of me out of this house. Do you hear me?" She stormed off to the cabinet holding the photo albums and ripped through it like some mad scientist. She took out every picture of herself and put them in a shoebox. Whenever I look at the photo album and see the blank blocks between the other photos, I am reminded of a mother who didn't want to exist. There were other incidents afterwards, but I soon learned not to speak of my mother, in words, in beauty, in thoughts, in deeds or in kindness. She didn't want to exist in my world, and there was nothing I could do about it. Months later, something in my family broke. My parents' relationship began to unravel, and since my strings of existence were held together only by their cleaving, even as dysfunctional as it was, I lived on the constant verge of snapping—cut loose in the most horrible way—forever lost without an attachment. In my forest, two tall trees were cut down, leaving mere stumps, and I was a tender, fragile sapling at ground level with no shade and no roots, only the intense heat of the sun and all the dangers and exposure to elements. Their distance and unavailability were a knife to my heart. Maybe I was too needy of a child, I'm not sure, but what I wanted the most, I didn't get.

Despite everything, I wanted to be every bit the woman my mother was. Or maybe who I imagined her to be. I acquired a vintage shawl from somewhere, I'm not even sure where, I just remember having it. It reminded me of her, and I loved its feminine appeal, the way it draped over my delicate shoulders and showed my bare skin, how the flirty beads clattered along the fringed edges while I spun in circles and danced like those Egyptian girls in the movie *The Ten Commandments*. My mother saw me swirling across the room one day and jerked it off me so swift I thought I'd been hit by a cyclone. She didn't say a word, but her eyes told me everything I needed to know. *Do not be a woman. You are awful. You are bad. This is inappropriate. Do not act. Do not feel. Shame on you.*

It was like the picture I took to school. I didn't know what I did wrong, but whatever it was, it offended my mother to a degree she turned on me. It was also evident the summer I wore a bikini. It was a two-piece floral with ruffles on the edges. Meg and I had been playing in the sprinkler and Mother came out with a camera. She was all smiles at first. We posed on our matching beach towels. I laid on my stomach and hiked my knees up, arching my hips, and smiled just like I saw models do in magazines. I heard the click and she lowered the camera and I could see it in her eyes, the disgust on her face for me. Her lips curled like the edges of burnt paper.

"You think you're sexy, don't you?" Her eyes burned my skin like a scorching sunburn. I was confused. My smile turned to shame. A negative image of myself clicked an imprint in my mind. I didn't actually understand what the word *sexy* meant. But I could tell enough by my mother's words to know it was bad. And it was in me. *Skin deep. Cass deep. Cluster deep.* I wanted to wrap myself in the towel, run, hide, and disappear. This moment and others began to define my core being. The all-encompassing grip would give shape to a lifetime of shame, confusion and a warped sexual identity. I didn't know it yet, but the worst was yet to come.

I couldn't shake my mother's words. All I could think of was Maw Sue's story of Jesus dying because of our sins. I still wasn't clear as to what sins were but I knew it had to be bad. Therefore, I must be sin. Something in me was bad and my mothers actions towards me confirmed it. Because of this terrible thing in me, I had summoned without knowledge a darkness, and bewitched a monster from the deepest thickets of the pine's underbelly, and it was going to show me how awful I really was.

The weight of my pen is heavy. This powerful memory of my past disturbs me. I stop writing on the blue line. I get up and pace the room. I feel an overwhelming presence with me, a slow exhale of stale breath marking me, oppressing me. My heart races while the memory pushes back in refusing to let me loose.

Confront it, feel the pain but don't let it take you, Cass. Doc's words drift in. So I surrender. I go where I don't want to go. I pick up my writing pen and face the blue line. I hold on tight. The memory comes forceful and violently and unlike the other memories, this one comes directly from the sword and shield girl. The girl that was done hiding and keeping secrets.

In my vision, I am standing on the front porch of the House of Seven inside me. The wood planks are as uneven as my life, squeaky with the pressure of my feet and their squeals are things of my nightmares. I stand still as to not hear them and stare into the dull black-and-white vision I've always had when I visit this dark hole in me. Behind me the creepy house, large door with the carved sizzling number seven and the broken doorknob. Across the landscape I created was a vision of thick pine trees, a curtain of comfort, along with the hushed cemetery with all my skeletons buried. I can hear them now—louder than ever before. Something is off, different. The tree moss girls with glowing eyes are whispering and grow louder until all the sounds seize me with terror, like a chorus of locusts invading my mind. They start moving with their tree limbs legs and arms, knots and moss, yellow eyes. They tangle and intertwine with each other. They mesh in a labyrinth of provocative positions, seductive like growing vines snaking up a tree. Their moss hair slithers and slinks, curls and bounces and their whispers drive me mad.

The next thing I remember is screaming and running inside the House of Seven. I am not alone. I stop to gain my footing, my bearings, my sanity. Something about the house is different. Suddenly, like a ghost, the little girl appears in the foyer where it is dark and shadowy. I am frightened for what is to come. She is the little girl I was, *used to be.* She raises her hand and curls her forefinger, and without saying a word, she calls me forward. I am fearful, so terrified I can barely shuffle my feet on the creaky floor. Screams claw my throat, unescapable. Commanded by her spirit, together we walk the long dreadful hallway of shadows leaping and hands reaching. The noises drive me deeper inside myself. Doorknobs turning, letters shifting and scrambling, and scrapes, doors opening and closing, strange sounds. My hands shake. Sweat beads across my lips. The girl stops in front of a door I don't recognize. The nameplate is missing. Fear rises in me for reasons I can't explain. A deep terror sickles through my veins so much I feel as if my heart might stop. For whatever reason…*I don't want to go inside.* But it's too late. She pushes me in with only a glance. In a half second, I am forced to watch, see and feel. My mind conjures the memories I have buried. In the Hush cemetery the skeletons claw their way out from the graves and walk the forest of the pines, their clattering bones with engraved words blazing like flickers of fire, lighting up the blackness of the night and whispering things I don't want to hear. A memory disengages from the depths of the house inside me. I am subdued. The terror of what I have feared all my life is now before me playing out as if I'm reliving it. It convinces me of what I have always feared. It is me. I am the sin. I am the demon coloring outside the lines, I am the monster.

I was seven or eight, I don't remember which, but too damn young for what was about to happen, that's for sure. I was eating a praline. I had climbed up on the toilet to get to the upper cabinet in the bathroom. I was looking for lipstick to match the paper kisses I collected from my mother's lip prints. *Kisses for Cass.* In my mind, I had convinced myself instead of loving me as my mother should, she had left me paper kisses instead. Even when she threw them in the trash, I told myself it was a game and she knew I'd find them, like a treasure hunt. I loved putting on her makeup and face cream and using her cosmetics when she wasn't looking. I tried to be all grown up in the mirror and mimic her motions. I'd put the lipstick on my mouth and pucker up and make my own paper kisses for my mother. I'd save them because one day, she'd want them, I was sure of it. I had just found Candy Crush Pink, my favorite color, which was also my mother's favorite. Instead of climbing down, I jumped but didn't make the landing and hit the bottom flooring of the cabinet. A wooden plank popped up. The sound made me flinch. I was just a kid, an innocent, curious little girl. I didn't know a demon could leave its mark.

A sound like a hiss drew my eye underneath the plank. It was a page from magazines or scrap paper. When I got closer, my whole body revolted in tingles and shocks. The pictures pulled me in with their obscene mannerisms, while a bent light drew me inward. I moved the board to see what it was. Immediately my vision took it in. I could see every detail: the sweat from their pores, the naked bodies twisted and contorted, faces in agony and pleasure. The monster swallowed me whole, clawed his mark upon me and took my innocence. The snap inside me broke, the forbidden door swung open, never to be shut. Inside the house, inside me, a room formed. A room I didn't know was there, hidden in the shadows of the grunts, moans and horrible noises. My ears felt punctured, wounded, bleeding. I tried to close the door—make it close, make it lock, erase it, retreat, go backwards, pretend it didn't happen—but no matter what I did, it wouldn't budge. The door hung in its place by a metal hinge, swinging back and forth with a squeal. This squeal would forever become a demon's whisper in my ears. He manifested himself from the darkest dark and attached himself to me like a second skin. I could not rid myself of him if I tried.

My eyes burned. Piles and piles of naked bodies, page after page with black bar lines attached over their eyes like square masks to hide their shame. As much as I wanted to run, I could not put the magazine down. It aroused a need in me, a yearning I didn't know I had. Secret flowers bloomed in me. I became ripe with hunger, and not for food, but for something I couldn't even describe. Just a physical ache from deep within me. My mind retained the images, almost photographic, even the most disturbing pages. They held a magnetic dark power over me. From the first glance, I knew a monster had me and was never going to let go, and to be honest, I didn't know if I wanted him to. Everything I could have been was gone the second I saw the mangled bodies, the twisted arches of backs and muscles flexed, toned and V-split legs, writhing arms, private parts of men and large-breasted women exposing all of themselves.The world I used to know was no more. It was now a dark place and I feared what I did not understand.

I finished eating the praline and turned the pages, over and over until my fingers stuck and wouldn't let go. I ripped pages trying to free myself from the grip of the monster, the sounds wretched and horrible. At the same time, the black bars latched to my face and grew their dark mask on me. The monster had me and it was not letting go. It was visceral, my physical yearnings turned uncontrollable and yet I had no one to tell, no one to ask, no one to share this terrible awful splendid thing with. How can something so bad, feel so good? It was the most confusing moment of my childhood. I did not speak of it. I was sure if anyone knew, I'd be punished. Even God would never look at me the same. *This was the monster I feared all my life.* I treated the monster as one would treat a feral cat or dog, feeding it, yet maintaining a safe distance. Wild things can turn on you at any second. Underneath all the fur and fluff, a savage, vicious animal is waiting to rip your heart out and eat you alive.

Weeks later, I watched the movie *Old Yeller*. I cried when Travis had to shoot his dog to save it from suffering. In my heart of hearts, I knew one day in my future, I'd have to kill something I loved in order to save it from suffering. My fears mounted while the monster had its way with me, black bars tacked on my eyes, masking the pain and hiding its control over me. Worst of all, it confirmed the badness in me—the horrible awfulness my mother had recognized and found unlovable. *How could I blame her? How could anyone love a monster?*

I kept waiting for someone to pull out a gun and shoot me like Old Yeller. Put me out of my misery. *Please.* It was awful and wonderful at the same time. My tongue held a taste for the forbidden. The monster taught me a woman's need to be dominated, controlled and ruled over as a sexual object. It taught me the unrealistic and distorted view of sex in our culture and most often it did so through demeaning and violent imagery of women. It taught me to be subservient to men as a slave, an object to be played with. I could never tell anyone, or confess my secret and in my heart, I knew the God I loved had abandoned me because of my terrible sins. The monster whispered and called me back again and again.

Fear and torment. A desire. A need. A sin. A shame. Marked by the monster. Surrounded by demons. It was a menacing, cavernous depth of willful transgression I could not stop. By the time I was eleven, I possessed a wealth of deviant knowledge no kid should ever know at any age. I observed the gestures, the movements and mannerisms on the pages, while the black-lined bars on the men's faces told me who I was. My body betrayed me and constantly confused me. I felt out of control and yet controlled. I no longer saw the world with childlike eyes. A film of gray had clouded my vision. I was disconnected from the world, void of feelings and place, and basically numb. I kept everything hidden inside the house of my demented dark mind. I created a room for the bad girl with no place and no voice. From thereon, I grew up understanding men wanted what women had—

the awful, terrible, splendid playthings on the pages of the magazine. In my young impressionable mind, if women gave men what they wanted, then women would get what they wanted, which for me, was a great everlasting love.

I was deceived.

A DOOR CALLED DEATH

"Me too. That moment when you find out that your struggle is also someone else's struggle, that you're not alone, and that others have been down the same road." ~Unknown

Memories rush in. Flashes, surges, image bursts, and sounds. At this point my only outlet is the blue line. It was a good thing I took Doc's advice and started journaling my thoughts, my memories, the black gunk that terrifies me. Getting it out of me helps but it's a painful process.

"Black angels to blue line. Get it out. Bleed. Pour. Get it on paper and out of my head." I say over and over again, as my ink pen scribbles on the blue line.

For as long as I can remember, there has been a great pain held up inside me, an embodiment captive inside the House of Seven. Yet I can't see it or tell you what it is or how it got there or why. It sits inside the house under heavily guarded walls. I know the answer is there. I can see the doorframe, the archway, the molding. I rattle the doorknob, trying to gain entry, but my mind refuses to allow it. So I continue writing. Once I've gotten a good portion of memories down, I spot it in the corner of my bedroom like an idol of worship. It triggers a mood and a memory. I view the object with fondness and resentment. The maple wood hope chest is three feet long, eighteen inches wide and carved with intricate details, metal clasps and doodads. It was a sweet sixteen present from my parents, which was shocking and to say the least, odd, and extremely awkward for a teen. I'm not entirely sure what transpired between my fifteenth birthday and my sixteenth birthday for my mother to do a complete one-eighty. Birthdays used to be simple, cake, ice cream, presents, a few friends and maybe a party at the skating rink if I was lucky, but when sixteen hit, it was the goddamned apocalypse. My mother, aka housewife extraordinaire, went on and on about how I could fill it with household items for when I got married. Jesus ever-loving kitchen Christ! I was sixteen years old when she presented it to me like the Royal Crown. I thought I was in *Betty Crocker* hell. Plus she had filled it with grown-up stuff. She yakked about the blender with its state-of-the-art turbo blades for chopping, mixing, and blending. Who the hell gets their child a blender for their birthday? *Gabby Collard, that's who.*

I remember standing there frozen, my friends looking on, trying to pretend to be interested. All I could think of was moving to Alaska, checking out of school, running away. My ears burned with her continuous housewife chat mode, weddings anniversaries, cook-outs, recipes and holiday brunches. I felt like I was in a Hitchcock horror movie. I prayed the eight-inch state-of-the-art jagged cook's knife would rise up and stab me. Put me out of my misery. I summoned the 180-thread-count pearl white bed sheets to unfold like a flying carpet and whisk me away to *never-a-housewife* land. Surely it existed somewhere.

"...and this is why they call it a hope chest," my mother said grinning like a Cheshire cat. I cringed. *Dear God, is she ever going to shut up?* I was embarrassed to death. For Gabby Collard everything that existed for a woman could only be found inside marriage, inside household goods—inside a freaking hope chest. My mind swirled with thoughts. *Where is Mother Moonshine? Where are the wild-eyed slits? What happened to the motor-revving, howling, no-holds-barred Gabby "Lash" Lancaster?*

My heart raced and I snapped like a green pea in my mother's pea-shelling hands. My arms went stiff. The blood in my face ran hot and turned my skin red.

"Can we just get on with the party now?" I closed the lid of the freaking hope chest and stomped outside. My friends followed. "I'm sorry about…whatever that was," I said leaning against the porch rail hoping I'd just disappear. My friends looked on while I went off the rails. "I'm not even out of school and she's trying to marry me off. What if I don't want to get married? What if I want to tour the world? How do I lug a monstrous wood box up a mountain in Scotland, huh? What good is a kitchen blender on an iceberg in Alaska? Pfffftttt! That's *her* life. It's not mine." My friends rallied around me and tried to cheer me up, but it was useless. My mother had embarrassed the crap out of me. I'd never live this down at school.

Even now that I'm grown, the wooden hope chest is a kitchen curse I can't outrun. It sits against the wall like an unfulfilled prophecy, a cross to bear. I drag it wherever I go. *Make it work, Cass. Use the kitchen gift. Be the housewife. Do what you should do! Who gives a shit about your plans, they don't count. Be the good Southern girl.*

Sometimes I open the lid and scream, "HOPE! What hope? Where the hell is hope? Huh? Who gave you your namesake anyway? Stupid, stupid, stupid hope chest." I'd slam the lid down and swear and be damned if I ever heard the word 'hope' again, I'd burn the sucker to the ground. But I never did. The hope chest and I endured. We've been back and forth more times than I could count. Do-overs and repeats, try and try again. Hoping Sam would love me. Hoping he'd stop cheating. Hoping my mother would understand me. Hoping I'd understand her. Hope and more hope. Me looking for hope—desperate for hope. I'd sit on the floor and lean against the chest, wounded and broken. Searching, wanting, and needing, but hope was deferred.

In therapy, I have learned that journaling on the blue line brings other memories to the surface, all threaded together waiting for their moment of truth. One prodding another, giving its approval to emerge. Today is no different. Another disheartening memory arrives like a wave that takes me under.

I was twelve. Big Pops was Papa C's father who lived next door. He was old and brittle and useless with words but he was the only one I could sit with and remain comfortable with silence. We'd porch sit or piddle in the gardens for hours on end. We had this connection without words like I've never had with anyone. I never expected him to die. No one had ever died in my family before. I was unprepared for the pain and sorrow. I felt my heart being ripped out. A fear rose up in me I'd never had before, a fear of death, and the unknown. My only coping mechanism was to climb the wondering tree outside my bedroom window to the highest limb. I slipped into a place inside me, the inner realm of mystery, the old ways of seven, the one I was born tangled up in, the gap between this world and the next, where I lay within the secrets, lies and madness, between the living and the dead, between the seven sisters and Maw Sue, between the blood and the roots, between the common man's savior and the cross.

In the space of the unknowns, I whispered a prayer, a long benediction of words pleading the blood of Jesus. I envisioned a long list of prophets and sages speaking the exact prayer in perilous times, two thousand years ago when lions stared them down and stones were cast, bodies burned and hung on crosses, all pleading the blood, petitioning the heavens to come down. But the blood didn't save them. *They died.* When I questioned Maw Sue about this dire situation of compelling evidence, she of course, had an answer, as she always did.

"Some things weren't meant for our knowing, Cassidy" Maw Sue said, "Having faith doesn't mean we'll always get what we want or keep those we love in this life. Death comes to all. The petal people will always come. We know not the time or place. But our loved ones are always near us."

It was the strangest saying. *Petal people?* It gave me chills just thinking about it but as much as I wanted to find out more, I didn't get to ask, plus my mind was full of haunts already and I wasn't going to add to it. But life interjected and did it for me. And then, I wish I'd never known how the rest of the story played out.

Maw Sue had just gotten out of the asylum after having one of her spells, as they called it. When I heard she was home, I ran to see her. The atmosphere of her house had changed. It was a warning to me. I wanted to ask her what happened in that place. Maw Sue was stoic. Pale and sad. In her rocking chair she swayed, darkly disturbed, back and forth with placid eyes staring into the nothing of the room. In her cryptic wrinkled hands, a horror story and a saving grace—*I just didn't know it yet.* They clung tightly to a pint-sized mason jar full of dried roses she called the petal people. This is where my belief in what I could see and what I could not see had to suspend itself into another realm of being—where the natural and the supernatural collide. I had to go where the seven sisters went, to the gap, the void, the space of time where this life meets the otherworldly. I was scared. The roses were dark and brooding, almost lifelike, their petals took on faces and their stems and leaves seemed to want to sprout legs and arms and leap out of the jar and start walking. The energy inside the house was insufferable. My knees were weak and ready to collapse on me. I felt consumed with the unknown. For Maw Sue, each rosebud in the jar was a representation of a loved one passed into the eternal light. A single rose plucked from a funeral wreath, casket arrangement or flower bed. At first, it gave me the heebie-jeebies. She talked of the petal people as if they *were* alive. The more I looked, the more they seemed alive, which freaked me out more.

I was young and didn't understand death when I heard the story of the mason jar and the petal people. I was terrified, fascinated and petrified. I had hope and yet felt fear. My nightmares became my own versions of petal people. Sights, sounds, shadows, whispers, stories, and voices. She told me they are my loved ones speaking from beyond the grave. It didn't make sense to me at first, but Maw Sue said it would as I got older and grew into my gift and the old ways. The petal people could talk to me and tell me their stories through my dreams. Unfortunately, even though I was a seeker, I didn't know what to do with all the words, stories and influx of information. I had too much in my own mind; I didn't need anymore voices eating my soul. I wanted the gift—but I was also haunted by it.

The petal people inside Maw Sue's mason jar were special to her. A single red rose symbolized her first husband, Jefferson Starbuck Adams, the love of her life and no other, she'd say with a smile as big as Texas. He died of pneumonia seven years after they married and left her with five children. She went plum mad afterwards and never fully recovered. Her oldest daughter, May Dell, who we call Mama C, found a diary of her father's stuffed away for years and years, one she never knew existed. The journal was a tanned leather binder with *Starbuck* in the center with a picture of a moon and one bright star in the top corner. She loved reading about the father she barely got to know. Sometimes in my dreams, he told me stories too. I wanted to tell Mama C about them, to comfort her, but Maw Sue cautioned me against it. It was between me, Meg and Maw Sue, our secret. Besides, no one else understood the gift like we did.

Standing next to the red rose was an orange rose for her second husband, Sully who had died from plain meanness. She was so desperate for companionship after Starbuck died, she just grabbed the first blockhead who came her way. Sully was controlling and manipulative. Plus, he drank like a fish. Turns out, whiskey killed him. His liver just quit or Maw Sue killed him with some herbal potion. That was the gossip in the town back in the day, once again thanks to Edna. It's still a family story of mystery and people have their suspicions. The white rose was her last husband, Morton, a gentle, quiet soul who kept to himself. He stayed with her the longest and died of a heart attack. The other roses in the mason jar were hard for Maw Sue to talk about but she managed to get through it. Once I heard, I understood. I never looked at those dried-up flowers the same again. With each sight it was as if they were waiting on eternity to bloom for the first time, because they never got the chance to bloom on earth.

One tall violet tea rose towered above them all. It was her mother, Joseymae. No one talked about what happened to her. It affected Maw Sue in the worst way, enough to never want to talk about it. Not even to me and she told me mostly everything. The other two peach roses, identical, were Lorinda Lane and Lizzy Lynn, twin girls. Each rose cradled together, clutching one another with wilted arms intertwined with locks of curly blond hair and pink ribbons. Two other roses, burgundy in color were for her sons, Luke and Larkin. The twins died of a sickness, a few months apart, and the boys died in the care of neighbors a few years apart.

After Starbuck died, leaving Suzannah with five children, she went into a slow decline of madness. This is when the petal people ritual became an obsession. The tradition, however strange it may have been to some was comforting to Maw Sue. It was the only way to keep loved ones alive in her memory.

When the passing of Big Pops occurred, Maw Sue took this as opportunity to pass on the flower petal ritual to me and Meg. We'd heard stories of them before in passing but she never fully shared the ritual with us, until now. I was extremely attentive to the realities of the otherworld. I didn't understand it, but I felt it often enough to know it was there. I was sensitive to life and death matters, those of the spiritual nature, those gaps of time and place, between this world and the next. Places where I seemed to be stuck, all tangled up, where I took other people's grief and sorrows to myself and clutched them to my chest like a plunging sharp knife, unable to stop, even though it pained me terribly. It was a seeker gift and a seeker curse. Maw Sue seemed to understand both of us, even Meg's distance with the subject. She took us aside at the cemetery. My mother looked on curiously from a distance, almost suspicious, as if she wondered what kind of baloney we were being dished.

"Girls, now listen to me. Life doesn't end in the grave, you hear?" Maw Sue said holding our hands and squeezing. "It just turns to a spiritual plane, a new level of being, another realm of life. So go on now, and pick a flower that reminds you of Big Pops."

My eyes glazed over the wide assortment of flowers surrounding Big Pops' casket. Meg ran straight to the basket of marigolds and returned with not one, but two. I wasn't even sure she understood the concept of Maw Sue's words, but it didn't matter. Maw Sue smiled. Later in the evening we trotted over to her house, me carrying my peach rose and Meg with her marigold. She took us straight to the back room and inside the cedar closet, the creepy hideaway Meg and I swore was haunted with voices, knocks, and frightening sounds. We looked at each other as if we weren't too sure what was fixing to go down. A light bulb with a pull string hung from the ceiling with a spool of crippling wires. Maw Sue pulled it and shadows seemed to run, dispersing themselves into the thick row of wool coats and clothing on wire hangers. My mind jerked. Trembled like a motor trying to start up. My skin pimpled and the house inside me stirred with spirits and whispers from the mouths of people I didn't know. A thin white string ran from one side of the closet to the other. Clothespins hung limp from the old string like meat hooks in a butcher shop. Maw Sue took our flowers and placed them upside down, clipping them to the string with the clothespin. At this point in the private ceremony, it was story time. Maw Sue was always dramatic, detailed and mystic, as if she was caught up somewhere else altogether. In most cases, I loved Maw Sue's tales, but this one about did me in. It was personal.

She told us the French used dried flowers to immortalize their dead and called it *Immortelle*, a symbol for longevity, resurrection, and immortality, which meant everlasting.

They used chrysanthemums, Amaranthus, strawflowers, and asters, or just about any flower, but Maw Sue preferred roses.

"Do you believe in magic, girls? The mystery of the unknown, the unseen?"

"Yes. Of course, I do," I blurted out. In my vision, the room was engulfed with spirits of the dead. I could feel them around me though I didn't know if I could say it out loud. Meg shrugged her shoulders and looked at me as if she was completely distracted. Bored, even.

"Well, it's okay to believe and it's okay to have doubts. Life will let you know eventually what it's trying to tell you, whether you want it or not." She looked more so at Meg than she did me. Meg wasn't the least bit concerned. "Just believe even when you don't want to. Life can be utterly cruel, but use the gifts, keep the magic going even when it gets the darkest. I see the gift in both of you. Of hope and everlastings. And never forget that the real magic is in you, right here." As she pointed to our hearts.

Hope and everlastings. I simmered inside myself. Meg had already plucked a coat off its hanger and was deep diving into the pockets to find treasures like we usually did when we played dress-up.

"But why are we putting it in the dark closet?" I said curious. The string looked awkward and creepy as all get-out with the upside-down flowers hanging oddly out of sync. My mind envisioned dead-of-the-night fairies casting spells using flower petals to summon a thousand monsters from the black earth. Maw Sue bent down, rustled around against the back wall and came up with a dusty thick book as big as an encyclopedia. The outside was bound with leather and I thought I saw the name *Sessa* carved in it with an abundance of flowers and swirls below it, but I couldn't be sure. Maw Sue opened the ancient-looking book. The dust appeared to make me dizzy. She flipped the pages open to a flattened rose, burgundy red like wine, wilted with time, crinkled and dried between the pages. She picked up the rose delicately and held it with tenderness. A loud sigh left her lips.

"The darkness allows the petals to grow into their spiritual fullness, just like people, Cass. People grow and learn the most in darkness. Now, this is a poem written by my Aunt Sessa, a Seventh Tribe member, one of the seven sisters, and her gift was words, poems and great wisdom." Maw Sue held the book like a prophet on a mountain gleaming with light. "Sessa wrote this poem when my mother Joseymae, sister number seven lost her breath and died at birth. Of course, we all know she was reborn in the seventh minute, but the words had already formed themselves as fate. The poem became part of the ceremonial tradition." Her words were mysterious and magical as if she were some fairy godmother about to grant me a wish. Maw Sue began reading and my bones trembled. My eyes leaked. My heart fluttered. Something happened I couldn't explain.

Everlastings By Sessa Ainsley #2

Time goes quickly day to day
Petal after petal we pluck away.
Life is here—it comes and goes
As quickly as the flowers grow.
One day here—then gone the next,
Blooming and wilting—life perplex
We live life but death we fear,
It takes our loved ones, those so dear.
Pick a flower from the casket,
A wildflower for your basket.
Take the flower—dry it well.
Petals, petals, cast a spell.
Take our grief, our tears.
Absorb our unspoken fears.
From the grave, our loved ones speak,
Alive, alive voices we seek,
Shouts and whispers and shrieks.
The door of life, the door of death.
Petals, petals do tell;
Petals, petals cast a spell.
Take my grief forevermore;
Until I meet my loved
ones at the door.

The sounds of time broke like aged glass. My soul seemed to crack with it. I watched Maw Sue break as well. Old grief leaked from her eyes and formed streams flowing into the dry riverbeds of her wrinkled face. I was spellbound. The words, the meaning, the mystery all held up in the everlastings. *In her, in me, in the mason jar, in the petal people, in the Seventh Tribe.*

Right then and there, a room built itself inside the House of Seven, inside me. The walls were made from the tall pine trees. The windows were the blue skies and the petal people lived there, rose faces, stalk stem limbs, leafy arms and slim necks. They chatted as if they were still alive, having never left this earthly realm. They were immortal inside me, in the House of Seven, they were the Everlastings. The *Immortelles*, the petal people carried the grief in their petals so we didn't have to. The rose from Big Pops absorbed my wicked suffering and my burdened cries. It took to its stemmed chest the moisture of our tears.

Meg was unimpressed. Distant, distracted and still rummaging through the closet like some junk-seeking junkie. But I was thoroughly enchanted with the entire process. For the first time, I understood Maw Sue's weird obsession with the mason jar and the petal people. The curse of death took her loved ones over and over, without understanding, without explanation, without answers. She was so overwrought with grief, all she could do was cling to the petal people in the jar, the everlastings, the immortal symbols carrying our grief because they remind us that life doesn't end in the grave.

A few weeks later, Maw Sue presented us with our first everlastings, along with a copy of the poem by Sessa. Sitting inside a simple mason jar was my first Petal Person rose of immortality, Big Pops. Inside the plush soft rose petal, I could see his face, his form take shape. The stem formed his body, the leaflets his arms, his legs. He was my first protector of the petal people realm. I felt an odd sense of relief, as if I didn't have to endure life alone. The *Everlastings Immortelles* was as beautiful as the day I plucked it from his casket. And Maw Sue was right. It did exactly what it was supposed to do. The dried, fragile rose took my grief.

Meg looked at hers a long time as if she was trying to figure out what to do with it. I think she expected it to change, or transform. She seemed disappointed and left as quickly as she had entered. But for me—it was life-changing. It wasn't long after that the petal-faced flower people from Maw Sue's jar crept inside my visions, day and night walking the rooms and the hallways of the house, and each held a mason jar of their own, with flowers, everlastings of their own. I did not know my own private losses, combined with my broken knob of madness would tangle up and escalate into something I feared, something terrible and terrifying. I lost control. I could no longer push it away. My tears and madness would sweep me to this room, without consent, without control. Over time, all was meshed together, the dreams of strangers, the whispers they spoke and the petal people in the room, inside the House of Seven, inside me. I could not bear it any longer. Instead of allies in this world, they became monsters, the frightening, awful things that helped to haunt me. It drove me mad to be inside the room, see them, hear and feel them. Their traumas and tragedies were drawn to my own. Their morbid expressions and afflictions drawn in their petal-dried faces were the things of my nightmares. And no matter what I did, they'd gravitate to me like moths to a light bulb.

The tragedy of my childhood manifested itself inside the House of Seven, a compound of rooms, a shelter for the little girl I used to be. I gave my gifts and curses a haven, a house of refuge. It was in this House of Seven, behind the pine curtain of my heart, where petal people wandered the hallways with mason jars and one little lost girl cried out in my dreams, "Make me seven. Make me seven." She waited to fill the void. She needed to be whole, the all-encompassing oneness of spiritual connection with the almighty God. But I could never tell her the truth, that she would never be seven, never be whole, never be good. I had ruined that for her. And I hated myself for it.

LOVE LOOKS

Love looks not with the eyes,
but with the mind; and therefore,
is winged Cupid painted blind.
~William Shakespeare

If my memory serves me correctly, it's going to serve me to the front door of Castle Pines if I don't gain some sanity and quickly. As powerful as the memories are, they have a grip on my soul but I have no choice but to examine and pick them apart even if its painful. Doc says the more painful it is—the more I need to confront it—and the more growth and healing I'll gain.

The timeline of events in my journal is as fractured as my mind. I am putting dates and ages with them as they come, as to really get an accurate look at my past. Journaling has proven to be helpful. It's strange when I go back and read what has transpired over time as a child, a teen, and a woman. I'm amazed at how powerful the mind is, how it operates, putting away, denying and overcoming.

My next memory is when I was nine. Mama C was recovering after surgery in the ICU behind a little blue curtain. Only two people were allowed at a time. Meg and I went in to visit. She was lying on a bed of ice to cool her high fever. She had a tube in her mouth attached to a machine. It pumped air every few seconds and made a god-awful racket. There were wires running all over her body. Her feet were exposed. Since we were both seekers, we decided to do our gifted part in hopes it would send healing vibes to Mama C and speed her recovery. I spied some lotion on the table beside the bed and told Meg I would massage her feet and seek her healing. We chanted prayers like Maw Sue taught us. It was going great until bells and whistles went off. Mama C's eyes popped open so wide in terror it made me flinch backward. It was as if she saw a monster. Meg flung herself against the wall. Before I could turn around, a slew of nurses zipped past the curtain and pushed us out of the room. Mother took us to the waiting room. All I could see in my head was her marbled eyes.

Twenty minutes later, the room was a wailing mass of broken people. Mama C's lungs had exploded. Meg leaned against me and cried. Her tears burned through my shirt. I couldn't move. All I could do was stare at my hands. *My cursed hands*. My terrible, awful gift wasn't a gift at all. At the time of Mama C's death, Maw Sue had been in Castle Pines on lockdown. The family, for whatever reason decided not to tell her for fear of making her condition worse.

My father was a total wreck. Losing his mother turned him into a leaking faucet. He cried almost every day. I was with him when he had to tell Maw Sue the truth of what had happened while she was in the asylum. She cursed him in disbelief. After that, I didn't have the heart to tell her I killed her daughter. My cursed hands took her because I didn't have any magic in me. I was flawed. I was a failure.

To try and convince her of the truth, my father took Maw Sue to the cemetery and showed her the grave. She went into some blind stare, stoic and distant without words. Denial is a horrible master. She simply walked away from the tombstone with a stone glaze in her eyes.

One thing I hadn't told Maw Sue, is that while I was at the funeral, I felt it my obligation to pick the flower for her to represent Mama C in the mason jar of petal people, since she wasn't there. I dried it the ceremonial way and placed it inside her jar sitting on the nightstand, next to all the other petal people dried flowers. For weeks, Maw Sue remained in psychotic denial. Each day she'd ask Papa C where May Dell was.

"She's dead, Susannah, I already told you. She's gone." He'd say heartbroken. Maw Sue scowled, spit and cursed him. Normally, he took no shit from her, and they would banter and bicker back and forth for days on end, something that brought them both pleasure; but in this case, he simply waited until she had no words and he walked away. I had watched this horrible scene play out from the side of Papa C's shed, where I heard the shouting. It sent me to a deep place of pain inside myself. I had avoided going to see Maw Sue for this very reason. But it was time. I had to go no matter the consequences.

The next day, I walked inside to find her standing in the living room, frozen in place, staring at nothingness. In her hand she clutched the peach rose, the one I plucked from Mama C's casket to represent her among the dead, among the petal people. She didn't see me standing in the doorway. I was silent as I watched her collapse and crush the rose in her hand, the brittle petals falling to the floor like snapped bones. Denial had been broken. Her daughter was gone and she had missed the burial. She cried like a pack of wounded animals. To see her like this broke my heart. I had always believed in the stories she told, but watching her break down gave me doubts about these so-called petal people. I didn't know it then, but in the upcoming teen years, I would be just as crushed, just as broken, just as damaged. Like her, I would need a slew of grief takers, petal people and mason jars.

A year later, I reached the pinnacle milestone of ten years old. My body turned on me like some evil twin hell-bent on destruction. I didn't know who I was. Empty, mindless and scattered like the windswept leaves in fall. What happened next was punishment. To make matters worse, I believed I deserved it.

I was in the bathroom looking intently at one of those girlie magazines I had found on accident ages ago. I remembered the exact day I found them. It would become a dark harbinger imprinting its mark on me, never to leave. I figured out through process of elimination they were Dad's magazines. And yet, even though something deep inside me told me it was wrong, vile, awful…I could not turn my eyes away, as if possessed by a darkness I could not control. My father's vices had become mine. The black bars tacked a shameful mask across my face when the door flew open. My mother stood there shocked as if she had to look at me twice. Her pale skin turned beet red.

"Where did you get this filth?" she said, snatching it from me.

"I-I-don't know. They…they…" I stuttered, afraid to say too much, to get myself in trouble along with my dad. From the girl talk at school, every red-blooded Southern male had dirty books stuffed somewhere whether or not his wife knew about it. Apparently, my mother did not know, until now. The house of silence flipped upside down. Gabby became the mother I feared. The one I saw glimpses of from time to time when she and Dad fought. She rolled up the magazine and slapped my thighs, my arms, my back, and wherever she could reach.

She bent down and squeezed my jaws, "Bad. Dirty. Nasty

girl," she said with a disgusted tone. "Shameful…do you hear me?"

I heard her all right. I trembled and stared into her eyes seeing my own terrible reflection. Whatever horrible thing happened afterwards; I don't recall. Dad came in, more screaming, chaos, throwing dishes and slamming doors. The rest is blocked from my mind. *Gone. Removed.* Maybe to protect me. Help me survive. Whatever lies in the pitch black of my memory is hidden for a reason. But bad attracts bad. Unaware, I had opened a doorway. I had summoned every dark hidden creature inside the pine forest straight to me, straight to my mind. Squeals, howls, screeches, teeth snapping, snarling, growls and scratches. They were hungry. *I was the dark thing they craved.* I deserved punishment. Unable to bear some of the aftermath, *I split in half.* I could literally feel myself drifting away. Mind madness, unlovable, monsters and shadows. Later in the evening I skipped supper and stayed inside my room. I cried long and hard, and violently. A fake Cass rose up from deep inside the House of Seven. *The girl who would survive for me…control my life outwardly, do what I could not do.* The unloveable Cass went away for good. I tucked her deep inside. *Buried. Beneath. Below. Behind the pine curtain.* That night the House of Seven received another occupant.

It took my mother a long time to look at me. She walked around me as if I wasn't there. She didn't want to see me. In truth, she had never seen me at all. I didn't blame her. I didn't want to see me either, and as days passed, pieces of me disappeared. I began to wonder if my mother had been the same way as a child, where parts of her just vanished, never to return, and then I wondered why? Was this the reason she was so distant? Regardless of her avoidance, the left-over pieces of me still tried.

"Hey, Mom, look at this doodle bug," I'd say. Or "Look at this cool cicada shell," trying to get her attention, but she'd look at me listless and blank. In her eyes I saw my reflection glaring back at me, the unlovable monster. Every night I'd stare at the moon and confess my troubles, and wait for the petal people in the mason jar to take my grief. When dawn came, I'd try once again to win my mother's approval.

She was sweeping the living room and deep in thought. I asked her a question, trying not to get in her way. I don't even remember what I asked. Probably something stupid, but I just wanted her to speak to me, say something, respond, reply, nod, blink, anything. She responded all right. I became the trash she swept out. With the broom she brushed the straw bristles against my bare legs as if I wasn't there at all. When I didn't move, she did it again, and again until I was out the front door and on the porch. The awful pricking sensation of the straw on my skin and the *tsk, tsk, tsk* sound it made condemned me to a thousand hells. *Tsk…tsk…tsk. Shame. Shame. Shame.*

She stopped sweeping and leaned against the broom, while her back held the door open. Her eyes slanted and her mouth wrinkled. "Sexpot," she said in a disgusted tone. I swayed on heavy feet while pieces of me detached and drifted away like puzzle parts lost in a windstorm. I stared at my mother's candy-colored lips unable to free myself from their torment and lack of affection. Cass wanting something she would never have. Candy crush colored kisses from her mother's lips.

My mother swished the broom a few times and slammed the door. I felt destroyed. I didn't know what the word sexpot meant, but I knew it was bad, dirty as the dust settling on my skin. I quickly ran away and climbed the wondering tree to hide in its chandelier of leaves. Inside the House of Seven deep within me, I bawled. I squeezed my eyes tightly through tears and envisioned myself pacing the landscape with moss tree girls who had now taking on my mother's disapproving spirit eyes as they watched me with disgust. Voices, words and letters swarmed my head. It was such torment, I dropped to the ground and began to dig. I dug up the skeletons, grabbed a rock and began to carve the horrible words that had intercepted my mind; shame, dirty, bad, disgusting, sexpot, all of these and more, until I had filled up the dry bones instead of my mind, which was already deeply exhausted. Then I buried them in the Hush cemetery.

When I came to myself, I climbed down from the tree and found my mother's cutting shears. Remembering Maw Sue's stories, I cut a rose stem from a nearby bush. I plucked a rose for Gabby Collard, an *Immortelles, Everlastings.* I placed it inside a mason jar. *It was done.* She was dead to me. I was invisible to her —so I made her invisible to me. Performing the ritual was the most painful moment I can remember. But finally, the petal people did what they were meant to do. The petals took my grief. Bore my burdens.

In the coming weeks, I fell in and out of delusional states, overwhelming fits of rage, and then sadness. My body became a haven of aches and pains with no cause. I slept a lot and then none at all. My interests in life waned and I'd wander alone a lot. I didn't want to listen to stories or play with Meg anymore. Since she couldn't reach me, Meg hung out with her friends more and more. Dad would occasionally call me over from under the hood of a car inside the tinker shop and ask me if I was okay.

"Sure," I'd say without emotion. I could never look at my dad without seeing those magazines. It was strange and unnerving to me.

"Well, your mother thinks you're going through girl changes, teenage stuff…are you sure you're okay, Cass? Is it something else you'd like to talk about?"

"No, Dad. I'm fine," I said, turning away. I was unavailable to everyone, including myself. The shadow interceptors took me. The dark ones Maw Sue often spoke of. They were the rot of my brain. There were times I enjoyed a sacred refuge, only occasionally during periods of time when my mind seemed stuck, neither off nor on. A sense of balance stabilized me, a time to gather my thoughts, and perspective. I longed for this stillness to remain but those moments were short-lived. The House of Seven within me continued to fill up with rooms and occupants, a variety of ages and versions of Cass I no longer liked, or could not endure.

It was the summer after I turned fourteen my life changed. I spent most of my time reading books. Meg had grown accustomed to her rich flamboyant friends, so I barely saw her except in passing. Books became my sole companions. *Huckleberry Finn* and Henry David Thoreau, my personal favorite, along with other classics.

One evening, I was fumbling through an old box of books in Maw Sue's bedroom. Two books caught my attention. One was a leather book filled with handwritten prayers. The pages were soiled and stained. The writing was cursive and a torment to read. The loops and curves broke my heart. The impact a thousand pains. I absorbed the first few pages like crumbs. The words, the aspirations of its message, the internal conflicts, the afflicted writer, long groping and grasping, riddling with struggles and long on hope. A tear rolled down my cheek. I felt as if I had written it.

But since I was short on hope and prayers went unanswered, I sat the book aside and picked up the other book. I wiped the dust off its hardback cover to read *Lady Ledbetter in Love*. It looked interesting enough, plus darn near every girl at school had a boyfriend except me. I thought Lady Ledbetter might teach me a thing or two. *Oh—she taught me things, all right...*

I couldn't stop reading. I devoured the words. I was in the room with lady and her lover so much I felt I might go up in flames. In my mind, sex got love and love got sex. Between the pornographic images burnt in my mind from the early exposure to monsters and the explicit sexual stories of lady and her lover, I came to my own conclusion of love. I began to watch others. I observed my surroundings, couples, adults, their relationships, my parents, teens at school, in movies and on the streets in passing. I mastered seduction at an early age. I was molded and made to attract and seduce a male with cobra eyes and poison in my red Southern blood. *The message?* If I gave, I would get. I knew no different. There were no sexual discussions in our house, no preparation for the adult perversions of the world, no teaching of man and woman, no sexual definitions. I didn't learn the art of modesty or feminine rituals. *Just punishment, black bars, monsters of shame and sexpot.*

My body held strange aches, yearnings and desires, a wanting of something yet not knowing what it was, just an ache, raw and desired underneath the pulsating throb of my heart. It surged hot through my veins to other parts of my body. Shame told me it was wrong to think like this—but no matter how much I tried, the thoughts remained.

Silence. Shame. You are unlovable. You are an offering for a man, a slave to his desires, you do not exist. You have no voice. Black bars, black bars, black bars. They were always there to remind me of who I was. When the thoughts wouldn't go away, the black line mask would rivet itself across my eyes and bind me to the darkness inside myself, while the men in the magazines had their way with me. I'd ask God to forgive me, and every night when I lay in bed underneath my white blanket with pink roses, I'd feel the thorns ripping away at my skin, clawing at a film of shame covering me, controlling me. In the heavens, between the void, the place between God's and Adam's fingertips, I saw myself slipping away. The glare of God's gaze gave me nightmares. *Undeserving—unworthy—shameful girl.*

Something had changed inside me. A dark birth. It was alive and wanted to be fed. A hungry mad dog. Hidden underneath my bed were the light and the dark. Two books I read, alternating one and then the other. Both held my affections, my curiosities. I had so many questions. No answers. *Just trapped. Marked. Bound.* The images of naked bodies burned inside my camera mind and conjured up haunts and monsters I couldn't kill. Tiny vibrations exploded underneath my skin and little hot eruptions would flame up and down my frame, ripening my loins from within. The explosions set off mass quantities of electrons and protons bouncing around, crackling against my bones, rattling and shaking every hormone I didn't know existed. It felt good—but shame told me it was bad. *Disgusting, shameful. Tsk…tsk…tsk. Sexpot!*

The lady and her lover assured me it was okay but the book of prayers told me I had committed the unpardonable sin. Whatever that was. I was a prisoner under both spells. A battle waged within me, pulling me in every direction, and away from the little girl who danced behind the pine curtain. Feelings of right, of wrong, and the forbidden plagued me. The locust crown Maw Sue had given me as a young child, the thorny and flowery anointing of mercy and unfettered grace had been exchanged with black bars. The childlike heart had been isolated, pushed down, denied, stolen, taken advantage of and betrayed by her own cursed hands. I lingered in a misunderstood world. I was lonely. I grew depressed. Disengaged. The more I tried to fit in with everyone else, the more I felt left out. Different. Alone.

In my dreams, Maw Sue was locked up in a clinic again being poked and jabbed and shocked with therapy. Machines and doctors, nurses and carts, pills and liquids. Inside the house within me, inside the everlasting room the petal people marched and chanted and held mason jars. The room was lit with a solitary candle while slithering shadows slipped between their stemmed bodies, to and fro. When I finally managed to wake up, I was in a drenched sweat. A violence filled my head. It spilled into my mind as if Michelangelo were painting the Sistine Chapel but not with paint, with blood, and not the Sistine Chapel, but my own inner house of horror, and not Michelangelo. It was Maw Sue. *She was gone.* I knew it before I knew it. The House of Seven inside me gave me warning. It rumbled on its crippled foundation and accepted her inside.

"No…No…. No!" I screamed. But it was too late. She had finally joined her Seventh Tribe. Brue and Simon, and the seven sisters, joined May Dell and Big Pops, joined all her little children who died long before they ever lived. She was part of the petal people now. *The Immortelles. The Everlastings.*

In a daze, I sat on the corner of my bed in shock. In a burst of anger, I reached across my nightstand and raked whatever my arm hit. Everything fell in slow motion, my makeup mirror, my watermelon lip gloss, a few pens, a tiny flip calendar, a book and my mason jar full of pennies tipped over and spilled out seven pennies on top of the calendar. The House of Seven shook on its foundation. I fell back on the bed in a trance of nothingness. The doom of what I knew overtook me. I'm not sure how long it was between the nothingness and when Dad opened my door to sit beside me.

"Cass, you need to get up. I have to tell you…" Before he could finish, I cut him off.

"I know, I know, Dad." I said rising up from the bed. I stared at him with an awful, terrible sadness and a touch of anger I feared in myself. "I know she's dead! Maw Sue's dead."

"What? No, no she's not. Cass, what on earth…she's not dead. She's in the care clinic. It's bad this time—they don't know…"

"No. No. No. She's dead," I screamed jumping up and storming across the room, tears invading my eyes. Dad tried to console me, but I was ravaged by intangible ghosts. I was tormented by the grim shadows he could not see. I was lost in angel tears and bright stars, dark of the moon, shine of the sun. A spinning sensation erupted inside me, inside the House of Seven. It was one I'd experienced countless times. A terrible moment when I was gripping the edge of the world and my fingers were slipping and I couldn't hang on any longer, so the world fell off its axis and took me with it. The last image I saw in my vision was the scattered remains of my stability.

In one quick, desecrating moment I slipped away. I became disoriented, displaced and disengaged from the world. I dethroned myself and smashed anything I could grab, my lamp, my glass unicorn figurine, the angel statue in the corner. Then I collapsed into darkness.

17 YEARS EARLIER

JULY 27, 1971
NEWS YOU CAN USE
BY EDNA ROLLINS

TEXAS NEWS EDITION

It is with great pleasure I give you my update on my recent missionary work while engaging the tribal people known as Moon Wanderers who passed through our community last month. I am late on my normal publication, and I apologize, but it was rather exhausting to minister to lost heathens who engage in all sorts of shenanigans right in front of my face. I endured naked bodies, loud, obnoxious singing and dancing all hours of the night, moonshine, spirits and more spirits, campfire games, mud Olympics (who knew?) and so much more I can't list them all. I am happy to say the Wanderers accepted me in and even invited me to all the activities without question. It was hard to talk to them about Jesus with all the goings on, but I persevered and several lost souls came to Jesus, or at least I think they did. It was hard to decipher the language sometimes. I got a lot of yeah man, and peace-out, or that's cool words sister, we hear you, but not much else.

Billy Ray was an exceptional bodyguard and kept me safe even though we got separated a time or two, me pulled one way and him pulled another. All in all, it worked out fine. With exception of one thing which has still got my feathers in a tussle. The rowdy crowd picked me up and tossed me around like a tomato in a salad. I kid you not. It was a ritual of some sorts, an acceptance into their tribe, although I strictly prohibited it, I could not keep them from trying. We had only planned on staying the day but Billy Ray convinced me that people are more receptive to Jesus at night, which I thought was absurd, but turns out there is some truth to it. For some reason, be it the alcohol consumption or the plants they were smoking, there was an interest in my storytelling, of which I shared my testimony and the love of Jesus to all of them, regardless of their substance abuse. I even saw a few tears run down their dirty cheeks. I'm glad I made the trip and it was a gospel success. Until next time, tune into KTBR local radio news station 109.9. I'm Edna Rollins and that's news you can use.

THE FUNERAL

One does not become enlightened
by imagining figures of light,
but by making the darkness conscious.
~ C. G. Jung

The memories of the funeral came next. Along with me in a deep black hole. In and out. Darkness. Voices. Chants. My vision blurred. A high-pitched sound pierced my ears until they bled. A damaging squeal of a pig, an owl or both together, a terrible death squall like winds ripping into insanity. I saw angels, a choir of them, tarnished and fallen, despaired of voice, trying to sing but only screaming. Bodies jerking and squealing a rhapsody of vile contaminations as if possessed by dark shadows. Thrashing bodies, twisted and contorted like snakes expelling moans not of this world. Hearing the dead—I felt it uncurl in my chest, something horrid, dank and unnerving. It waited for me inside the house, inside the deep crawl space, beneath and below. It had knowledge of all I'd done. It knew my secrets.

The next morning when I came out of my blackened pit, my father confirmed what I knew to be true.

"I told you," I said. My mind blank, head empty, emotionless. No tears, no nothing. "I want to be alone, if you don't mind."

"Okay, Cass. But…but how did you know?"

I stared at him. He was visibly shaken. I could see the worry in his eyes.

"We were connected. I just knew." I said glancing away.

"We all loved her. I'll miss that kooky woman."

"Umm-hmm." I turned over as he closed the door. The wondering tree outside my window seemed droopy and sullen. My mind slipped into the darkness of what it knew best.

Brother Lester talks and talks. Last words, eulogies, prayers. I fidget on the pew and want to run. Music starts to play. I can't move. Everyone crawls around me. My mind spins. *Get to the porch, Cass. Storytelling or silence. Look for crumbs. Make lovely your losses. Use your gifts.* My body moves back and forth in small ticks. It's here. The time of last looks, final viewing, end snapshot, the last kiss, and the last bitter cold touch. Everything in me refuses to cooperate. I'm hyperventilating. My eyes blink rapidly through the tears. I'm here, but not here. I'm in a place of in-betweens, a realm between this world and the next, the one place I can never explain or understand. Suddenly, without knowing how I got here, I'm standing in front of the casket. It's like a dream, a nightmare. It doesn't seem real. Maw Sue's body lies stiff and lifeless like some wrinkled old porcelain doll. Instead of her normal face, I see her petal people face, a perfect flower dried and preserved, forever to bear the grief and live inside the petal room, the *Immortelles*, the Everlastings. I see myself there too, as a black rose squished beside her, our wilted leafy arms curled around each other, taken by the shadows, the afflictions, the curse neither of us were able to defend ourselves against. The next thing I know, I'm trying to crawl inside the casket and Dad is pulling me away and I'm screaming.

At the cemetery I stare at the casket morbidly and daydream. I wonder what a tree feels like when it knows it's been picked to snuggle a human's dead body under the dirt, in the darkness of the underworld for the rest of its life. Does the tree sap pour out underneath the dirt and surround the human body, covering the wounds of the person it wraps in its bark, like it does when the tree is cut? *Does it resist? Can it refuse?* Does it say, "No God, please not me, choose another tree, but not me, I simply cannot do what you ask. Let termites eat me instead. Let me rot and decay to dust, but not the casket. Please not the casket."

Amazing Grace plays from the speakers. The musical notes grow muscled fingers and clutch my throat until I break and choke. The last note holds on and on, and on until I am sure every tombstone shall shatter with grief. The sounds bounce off headstones, pewter vases and angelic statues with chubby faces. They split rocks, crack the earth and shake the heavens. I stare into the vast portal of scattered souls laid to rest in different times, decades apart. My vision blurs and goes foggy. I feel removed from everyone around me. I'm held inside a thin strip of space where two worlds intersect, each yearning for the other. *The in-betweens. The realm of gaps, of voids, of waiting for wholeness.* It's hard to remember what happened afterwards. The hours and weeping ran together. I did not die. But I did not live either.

Weeks came and went. I gave off a faint odor of decay, the scent of the insane, those doomed to mind afflictions and broken knobs, little girls lost and haunted. I couldn't get out of bed, wash my face, brush my teeth or go outside. My bedroom changed like the seasons of time, except it would mimic the landscape and the rooms inside the house within me. Darkness and light. Depression and joy. All rotating each room, each mood. Creepy moss tree damsels hung from my ceiling, eyeing me with their spirit eyes, and petal people strolled in circles with mason jars while crumbs fell from the wondering tree. Crushed crackle bugs clung to the walls while the door of seven blazed a hot sizzle and shadows slipped in and out of the cracks. The new mason jar, which my father had replaced after I broke the other one in a fit of rage, began to spin like a carnival ride as it sat on my nightstand. I had crazy delusions Maw Sue would come back to life. I'd sit at her feet and Meg and I would listen to stories again. It was weeks before I remembered what actually happened at the cemetery.

The ceremony was over. Dad's lighter flicked and clicked from the front seat. I smelled tobacco mixed with Mother's strong perfume and hairspray. Meg was sitting beside me, fiddling with clanging bracelets. Dad cranked the engine and the car started to pull away. My tearful red eyes drifted to the casket underneath the awning in the distance. My hands reached up to touch the window. And then I freaked out. I had forgotten to say goodbye. Not the regular-everyone-else's goodbye, but the ceremonial goodbye. I banged on the glass and started screaming and scrambled to open the door. Dad barely got the car screeched to a halt before I barreled out and dashed for the casket. *How could I?* I had completely forgot to pluck a rose for Maw Sue, the Everlasting *Immortelles* to represent her in the mason jar. For the petal people, for the Seventh Tribe. For my House of Seven. To carry my grief. And I had plenty to carry.

Then I saw the perfect one. Not from the gifted flowers or the casket, but the wildflowers of nature. It was on the other side of the fence bordering the cemetery. I ran over and reached under the fence and plucked the most beautiful wild white rose I had ever seen. A lush, pure flower which doesn't worry with the cares of the world, for its creator takes care of it, come what may. Maw Sue always spoke of this. Her desire was to be like the lilies of the field, the wildflowers tended by God, nurtured by the rain, the warmth of the sun and the glow of the moon. Now…*she was.* She was free and wild like she was born to be, as nature intended, free from the confines of this crazy brutal life. Free of mind madness and interceptors, free of cares and worries, free of the curse. She was *whole.* Her fingers were now touching God. The connection was finished. The gap was closed and she was seven. Forever whole.

I dropped to my knees and wept like I had never wept before. The little girl inside the house cried and cried, our tears matching with each droplet. I felt a hand reach for mine and squeeze it. It was Meg. I looked up at her and she was holding a blood red rose.

"I had too," she said, crying. "It was part of her and in some small way, I did believe, Cass. I did." Her voice was soft and broken in bits, as if this was something she couldn't admit all the way. It was good to see the old Meg—the one who used to believe —even though she rarely showed it now she was a teen. Together we got up and walked back to the car hand-to-hand. Dad was leaning against the car lighting another cigarette and inserting the pack under his rolled-up shirt sleeve.

"For the mason jar?" he said with a half-smile.

"Yep," I said with a sniffle.

"For the petal people," Meg said.

"For the Seventh Tribe," I said in agreement. We looked at each other and smiled. When we arrived home, I hung the rose with one of Maw Sue's clothespins and clipped it to a rope inside the darkness of my bedroom closet. Every day afterwards, I would go in and check it. And every day it would gradually form her face in the petals, her body in the stems, arms in the leaves, everything about Maw Sue and who she was. Weeks later when it was dry, I placed it inside my mason jar next to Big Pop's flower and May Dell's, along with my mother who didn't know I existed. Each night in the darkness of my bedroom, I lit a candle and faced the darkness. It was the deepest darkness I'd ever known. I tried to remember what Maw Sue taught me. I sat in it and let it overcome me, rule me. There were times I was sure it would swallow me and I'd never come back. Without Maw Sue to ground me, confide in and tell me stories, I felt lost. *No storytelling or silence. No porch. No forest walks, no ceremonies, no rituals. No hope.* Just mind chaos, and shadows. I had no idea it was the beginning of my descent into a deeper, darker pit than I ever imagined.

MAD DOG

In diving to the bottom of pleasure
we bring up more gravel than pearls.
~Honore de Balzac

Age fourteen was my kryptonite. It was a year of many firsts. First drink of alcohol. First cigarette. First kiss. I had crossed over into an exhilarating, exciting and scary world. My mind rebelled against me, worse than it had ever done before. Numbing it became essential to calming the storms wrecking me, and alcohol became my go-to. I should have seen it coming. I was forewarned. My family line was littered with substance abuse. Our trees were nurtured with alcohol, not water. It infiltrated the sap and cut off the roots. My father struggled with it, his father, his mother, and so on and so forth. The fermented apple fell straight to me. The seed embedded itself as a taste bud on my tongue. I wanted what I wanted. I learned to sneak it from the refrigerator. It was tiny sips of wine at first, then swallows, then gulps. Its maddening effects grew on me. I grew braver and careless. I'd sneak out with wild boys who had their driver's license and could buy alcohol, and we'd hit the back roads of life drinking and smoking and talking about adults who didn't understand us. Over time, I just didn't care.

It was 1977. I was wild as a March wind, wilder than my daddy predicted at my birth. The same kind of wild which would later put me in a psychiatric office at twenty-five.

Junior High was a year of tragic perceptions for a young girl already fueled by anxiety and moodiness. It wasn't long till I lost my moorings. Scrambled classes, an unfamiliar environment and crowds of people. It became overwhelming and my mind fragmented, misfiring and short-circuiting. Simple tasks became unmanageable. I'd panic, fall apart, my concentration futile. Words spun in my head in a vortex of confusion. I lost my way to class, over and over again. My mind could not and would not maintain the information. I'd catch myself standing in the hallway looking around, fearful, surrounded by a sea of student bodies moving around me in slow motion. Where was my next class? Was it here or there—this building or the other? Why couldn't I remember? English or math? This hallway or was it the other? I'd try to establish period one, then two, then three, or was it reversed? My life had been instilled with numbers and meanings, yet I couldn't remember one of them. Not then, not now. I'd walk inside a classroom and it'd be the wrong one. The teacher and the students would all look up at me. Wrong class—wrong period—wrong time. I would run out embarrassed, more anxiety, and mind madness. It seemed the harder I tried to double down and focus, the more I lost control. I'd end up in the office requesting a copy of my schedule, multiple times, and then re-tracing my steps, mapping my way through hallways trying to reset my brain and my memory from erasing itself randomly.

Keeping the schedule helped for a while, until the siege on my mind began. I lost it rather rapidly. The schedule and my mind. I deteriorated in torturous ways. In literature or math, I'd read the same passage over and over again. Line after line, nothing stuck. I had no memory of what I'd just read. My mind lapsed into another time zone with racing thoughts. It was a constant struggle to find my locker. I felt like a rat in a maze trying to find the cheese. The lockers and books and classrooms were playing hide and seek in my mind. *Was it in this hallway? Or this one? Was my locker in this building or the other?* My decline continued. I misplaced schoolbooks, notebooks, paper, pens, and homework assignments. My mind went on lockdown. This intensified the panic under my skin because I held no control over it. It held me captive like a slave. I felt embarrassment because I couldn't get it together. I felt shame for being different from others. I was out of control. This began my phase of keeping to myself. The less contact I had, the less chance anyone would notice my struggles.

Episodes were sporadic in nature, lasting days or weeks, sometimes months, shape-shifting from cluster to cluster. I cycled from one to another. The depressive can't-find-my-classroom Cass would go inside her cave and out came the extreme buzzed-out Cass, rising up cathartic with ideas, jet-fueled energy and creative enthusiasm. I'd whiz through homework as if it was nothing. But at night when I tried to sleep, making my mind rest was akin to those Viking battle scenes. My thoughts raced from subject to subject. My eyes stayed open simply because the Vikings wanted to fight a war inside my mind. The ceiling would spin, my mind pinging like a strange machine unable to shut off. After a few weeks in the mission mode phase, my manic clusters would grind to an exhaustive halt. The dark shadows would return to take me captive, pulling me to the depths of blackness. I'd lose my will to do anything. I lost interest in school, people, and places. I grew tired, depressed and my weary mind wished for death, decay and danger. I'd sleep and sleep and not get enough sleep, dull and drained and dying. I had no preconceived concept of what was happening. My mind wouldn't let me think about the troubled seriousness of it. It was just the way it was. It knew feast or famine, all or nothing, do or die. The knob inside my broken mind did as it pleased, clicking on and off at will and I followed the mechanism of the machine.

THE SKY IS FALLING

What makes the desert beautiful
is that somewhere it hides a well.
~Antoine de Saint-Exupery

In high school, as a sophomore, I learned to mask my broken knob inside my mind and masqueraded as a highly functioning basket case. It was exhausting hiding a state of neurosis I didn't understand or control. In the darkness of my room at night, cloaked figures appeared as shadows whispering while my head spun with strange thoughts of death and decay. My moods cycled. I was tethered to madness. A mind bewitched. I felt different, awkward, and out of place. It was hard to navigate my way, isolated and alone. At school, a maze of chatty students filled the hallways and I floated by in slow motion, invisible. Sometimes, I wandered outside until the bell rang trying not to get caught by a teacher. I was an island of loneliness surrounded by great bodies of water. No one was able to cross over or reach me from the island of self and the House of Seven inside me. Occasionally my mind would drift to the thicket behind the pine curtain where I heard the story of the son of God, the common mans savior who would rescue me from myself. I'd picture the little girl with faith and the locust crown of thorns. The hope lingering in the mist of those morning walks with Maw Sue. *Where was this girl? What happened to her, and why did she leave? Why did I rid myself of her?*

One major victory for me in school was a job working in the library. It was the only stability I could cling to when the broken knob would allow it. Reading stories gave me a temporary place to fit in an otherwise lonely world of existence. One day out of the blue, the librarian asked me if I would fill in as the lead character in a play for elementary students, and I said yes. In hindsight, I should have asked who my character was first. I was Chicken Little in the play *The Sky Is Falling*. Indeed.

Falling. Crashing. Burning.

I reported to the library for makeup and a costume fitting. We were leaving between fifth and sixth period, so I had to put the bright yellow makeup paste on my face beforehand. My only consolation was I didn't have to wear the whole chicken suit around school, only the face makeup. The bell rang. I grabbed my books and headed off to second period. I immediately felt the stares. It wasn't the normal, *I'm not here,* invisible glances as usual. This was different. I was dressed in bell bottoms and a blue T-shirt with white Keds, and my mousy brown hair was pulled back in a ponytail so it wouldn't mix in with the yellow makeup. Odd looks, second glances, awkward gawks. Classmates, strangers, groves of students gave me the eye. Giggles, sneers and gasps. I realized something marvelous. No one had any idea who I was behind the makeup. I had everyone's attention and it was riveting. The yellow mask made me incognito, unrecognizable, disguised from the girl I was, the one I hated, the one with the broken knob, broken mind, broken spirit, broken life. It was strange and invigorating. People who never looked my way suddenly spoke to me, stopped me in the hallway and asked me questions. Curious spectators, drawn to me by a mask. Being Chicken Little transformed me into someone else, a youth bold in speech and words, confident and less shy, emblazoned and free, less modest, empowered.

At night while I lay in bed, I plucked the shy wallflower petals off my skin and told myself I could be anyone I wanted to be. Throw away the Chicken Little mask and make your own. *Masks give power. Masks get attention. Masks are magic.* Attention was what I had always wanted, craved, and needed desperately. Now I knew how to get it. I found people I liked, admired, sought to be. I eye-plucked pieces from them like skin scabs and attached them to myself. When one person's characteristics or mannerisms didn't fit, I'd pluck another. By the end of the ninth grade, I was a collage of people pieces. My skin wasn't me anymore. I was a little of Susan, a lot of Carol, a smidgen of Marie, buckets of Kathleen. More of her, and her, and her. A little of him, them and they. Somewhere along the way I convinced myself I never existed at all—Cass had disappeared long ago. There were times I heard the screams deep in the dark night to remind me. The little girl inside me, deeply hidden away, who knew the truth screamed and threw fits and told me NO. She was the real me and I was a fake. *Stop it!* I could not accept her words. I pushed her down. Deeper and deeper until her voice was muffled.

The mask of people pieces became me. I attached each characteristic, each pattern, or unique persona of others to suit myself like some mad teenage Frankenstein. I became all sorts of characters; geek, nerd, cowgirl, introvert, extrovert, metal head, rock-chic, punk, preppy, princess, slacker, and others. I remade myself, built a new identity out of people pieces. I lived a life that wasn't mine to live. *I. Lived. A. Lie.* The sky had indeed fallen, and Chicken Little had morphed into this people-pleasing, approval-seeking shell of someone she wasn't. Cass became semi-popular, outspoken, a party girl. I ran with the wild crowd, boys who smoked weed, drank whiskey and did whatever the hell they wanted.

Half a year went by in a blur. People pieces aside, I had no idea who I was. *Still.* Half the time I didn't care. I was just trying to hold the world up while it spun in my hands. My broken knob accelerated to maximum speed. Mask after mask didn't fit. I teetered between highs and lows in virtually no direction, just following whoever happened to be in front of me at the time. Party at your house—I'm there. Bonfire in the woods—I'll be there. I was aimless, drifting, and my chameleon nature of changing suits to fit others' expectations and gain their approval had taken its toll. I had no real friends. I fell into a state of catatonic drag. There were days I couldn't get out of bed. Days I couldn't do homework or find my classes. Days I just stared into the blankness of my own existence and cried. I hated looking in the mirror. I hated who I was. I hated my face, my body, my skin and my clothes. I hated my family, my life. Meg drove me crazy wanting to tag along with me when I left the house with friends. I didn't have time to deal with her problems, I had my own. Our parents looked on as if we were strangers, moody teens invading their houses with pimpled faces and loud music, slamming doors, hormones and hades. We stayed out of their way as much as possible. Basically, life in the late seventies for teens was raising yourselves. As long as you didn't alarm the parents' antenna of trouble—you could get away with just about anything. Seventies parents were occupied robots. And we were the kids left to their own ways.

There were times I just wanted to hoard up in my room, avoid places, people and things. Just thinking about any effort on my part exhausted me. Making decisions was torment. Yes. No. Maybe. Yes. No wait, okay, yes…no, no, never mind. If I *did* make a decision, which was a miracle, I'd later change it. Regret it. Or not make a decision at all. I simply could not get it together. I formally, officially, unequivocally hated myself, inside and out.

It changed in December at the skating rink. Jeff was tall and limber but muscled like a runner and caught my eye immediately. He had a splatter of freckles across the bridge of his nose and deep auburn hair like an overripe peach. His eyes were as green as a fresh blade of grass in spring. He noticed me when no one else did. He gave me one of those long lizard stares. It made me flinch. He was from Prairie Grove, a town twenty miles from Pine Log. I crushed on him hard. He was the first guy who paid me any mind at all, but since we were from different schools, we only saw each other at the skating rinks on weekends. We were talking on the phone when I eyed my mother's car keys lying on the stereo like a shiny symbol—a northern star. My parents were gone for the day. Meg was with her high society friends and I was all alone. I hung up the phone, grabbed the keys, hopped in the car and drove to Jeff's. I had no license but here I was breaking the law in my parents' brand-new Lincoln Continental four door we'd named Alligator Ava. I was speeding down the highway like I knew what the hell I was doing. To make myself appear older I put on Mom's bug-eyed sunglasses.

I picked up Jeff and we drove to a nearby park and sat under a maple tree tucked away at the edge of the woods. After small talk he bent down and kissed me. My skin tingled and I laughed. Then he pressed me to the ground and kissed me some more. I melted into his lips and he made his way down to my neck, sucking and licking. He smelled like hot Dr. Pepper. I broke into goose pimples. His hips gyrated over mine and his hands roved between my legs, almost too quick, so I locked up. He felt my constriction and leaned up. "You are beautiful—those eyes," he said, leaning down to kiss each eyelid. I loosened like a budding flower. My heart pounded. My body ached for something it had no words for —only an assortment of images and dark spaces, black bars. I wanted him to like me, love me. His tongue explored my mouth. It was an explosion of heat and fire. The house inside me burned. In my ears another flame erupted—my mother's voice. Shame fell over me in a film. The spittle of her lips hit my skin, sizzled and branded the *Scarlet Letter* on my chest.

S for sexpot. I could feel the prickle of the broom on my legs, *tsk,tsk,tsk! Shame!* I saw her steely blue eyes condemn my female prowess to the deepest darkest hell. Not able to handle the pressure of Mother's shaming stare and her condemning voice, I pushed Jeff away. I took him home. He called and called but I would not speak to him. I stopped going to the skating rink. We never saw each other again.

Not long after, I found my group, my people. A place of belonging. A place of acceptance for the first time. I was one of *those* girls. The ones who don't quite fit with the girl groups, not with the cheerleaders, or the dance teams, not with the geek band types, nor those cheery gossip girls and cliquish fashion chicks. I seemed to fit right in with the boys. Rebel types, the smokers, tokers, drinkers. The hell-raisers, the ones most likely to be suspended with the exception of one, the peacemaker, Terry Bradbury. Terry and I became best friends. He was ruddy with freckles and had the lean body of a baseball pitcher, a sport he loved more than food. His hair was sandy and wired like the bristles of an SOS pad. He wore an Atlanta Braves cap and dipped snuff. I'd poke the knot in his cheek and kid him about it. He said he'd give up snuff if I gave up cigarettes. It was a bet neither of us cared to entertain. We had nicknames for each other: I called him Snuff and he called me Smokes. It was the purest friendship I've ever known, genuine and authentic. We talked on the phone almost every night for hours, about everything and nothing. Terry was a knight to every girl, very protective, a lover not a fighter and a brother through and through. I didn't remember feeling this safe with anyone, since Maw Sue passed. Looking back now, he was a Southern gentleman, a good guy I should have been attracted to—a guy every girl should marry. *Every girl but me.* I didn't deserve a guy like him. He was *too* good. Cluster Cass had to pick the most damaged of all men, someone as damaged as herself, someone with black bars and snarling teeth. Someone who would prove she was of no value.

Mark Addington was the dark horse. He was a stallion breed of man, oozing charisma and charm. Girls drooled and went google-eyed around him. He had long legs towering him above the crowd, well seen and he liked it. His dark mane of hair was like a finely groomed horse, slick and straight. Square face, perfect nose, ink eyes, the kind that spill out and stain you, mark you as his, just like his name. I felt it like an arrow filled with poison. Every time I looked at him, I would fall off a cliff, falling—falling—falling as if I didn't care if I hit the ground in a million splats and splintered bones. He was the only one in the group I kept my distance from. He had shark eyes, dark and mysterious. He was a fish exploring the deeper places in me with his eyes and it made me a nervous wreck. I had heard through the school grapevine of gossip, Mark Addington always got what he wanted. Knowing this scared me and thrilled me at the same time.

The other guys in the group were Todd Swain, a short blond with chubby cheeks and a permanent smile, and then there was Pepper, who smoked more weed than all of the 1960s hippies combined. His nickname came from being the only pepper in a sea of salt. He had a towering afro and he talked real, real slow, and dramatic. We were always like, "C'mon Pepper, for God's sake, spit it out already!" He was older than all of us and the only one with a driver's license and a 1969 four-door Cadillac Deville.

Caddy was our ticket to trouble. The other was Robert Tipton, aka Tip. They say he came out of his mother's womb drinking a beer. He was loud and rambunctious, risky as hell and always doing dares. We were quite a bunch of rowdy rule breakers. We got together on the weekends as far away from the population as we could get. While everyone else was at football games and preppy parties, we were in the woods around a campfire.

I had managed to keep a safe distance from Mark for a long time, but one night I glanced up and he was next to me. I guzzled a beer and lit a cigarette. My heart was pounding. We were at the river a half mile from behind my house, a shortcut through the woods from my backyard. Meg and I found the jewel of a swimming hole when we were little. A pooled-up cavern of water from a river run-off and natural spring. It was our secret place, until we were older and I took the guys there. It soon became our weekly gathering place. I could sneak out anytime and stay past curfew and my parents hadn't a clue. I never told Meg I shared the location, until she caught me crawling out the window. She blackmailed me to let her go or she was going to sing like a canary to the parents. I let her go, but I was not happy about it. Before I headed to the cooler to get a beer, I introduced her to everyone.

"I got this, Cass. You just have fun. Do what you normally do," Meg said walking to the fire. I rolled my eyes. She started talking to Snuff who gave me a side-eyed glance as if he didn't know what to say. I shrugged my shoulders and smirked. I mimicked smoking a joint, and then I found one. Where there's smoke there's weed. Where there's weed, there's Pepper.

"What's up, guys?" I said chugging my beer.

"Got a tagalong…" Mark said.

"Yeah. Harmless." I laughed, coughed and blew out puffs of smoke. The rest of the night went like normal. Terry stayed at the fire entertaining Meg, but he watched me with a keen eye as he usually did. I lay back on the hood of Caddy in a stoner daze and watched the night stars twinkle and blink and tell me things. The band Journey played a ballad of loving, touching, squeezing. Words I sang in a whisper as I lost myself in an anthem of teenage lust and a dreamboat who had joined me. I swore I saw two stars align as if it was a sign. This time, for whatever reason, I did not turn away. I accepted his advances. I acknowledged his presence. When the evening drew to a close, Snuff had grown irritated and took me to the side.

"Smokes, you know he can only be trouble for you. Be a friend but don't fall for him, I know, Smokes—I've seen him work girls before, and it's exactly what he did with you tonight. If he touches you, Cass, I will beat the shine off his teeth. I will."

"Dang, Snuff…the wedding isn't till next month." I pressed his chest with my fingers and laughed. "Calm down. It isn't what you think. Geesh…quit being militant."

"Cass, I'm telling you…"

I cut him off annoyed. "Okay, Daddy Snuff." I rolled my eyes.

It was late, clouds were rolling in, thunder could be heard in the distance, so everyone packed up. Todd left on his motorcycle while the rest of us loaded up in Caddy. Pepper was going to drop me and Meg off so we didn't get caught in the rain. Mark slipped in beside me and then Snuff on the other side. Meg sat in front between Pepper and Tip. In the darkness of the backseat a hand grazed the top of my thigh. Mark's touch sent electricity up my spine. I gulped so hard I thought I might choke. Pepper cranked up the stereo. *Cheap Trick* sang out from the speakers, a song of wanting and desperation that I could feel deep in my gut. The whole ride I felt conflicted. A little voice whispered I could have him. I could have Mark to myself. While another voice whispered it would be at a high cost.

17 YEARS EARLIER

AUGUST 15, 1971
NEWS YOU CAN USE
BY EDNA ROLLINS

TEXAS NEWS EDITION

We have a community alert folks! Keep your eyes out and your ears open. As you know Billy Ray helped me on my mission trip to minister to the Moon Wanderers a few weeks back and now he's missing. It was only a few days afterwards, that his mother realized he hadn't returned home. She is worried sick, bless her heart. If anyone knows his whereabouts, please contact the Pine Log Police Department. Everybody stay cool, drink sweet tea and go to church. Until next time, tune into KTBR local radio news station 109.9. I'm Edna Rollins and that's news you can use.

BLACK ANGELS & BLUE LINES

KNOW THYSELF
~ Inscription in the forecourt of the Temple of Apollo at Delphi

When I started journaling, I wrote down the beginnings, my first appointment, meeting Doc, even Pearl, the bland coffee-table receptionist, to Edna the old gossiping goat from the *Gazette*, to all my newfound memories of Maw Sue and the beloved forest we called the pine curtain. Time passed quickly and before I realized, I had finished an entire notebook. I had fallen into a trance unlike anything I had known before. Words poured out of me onto paper. It was strange, beyond me, as if the broken knob in my mind clicked and the pen obeyed, writing the words on the blue lines. They found their place. A peaceful rest on paper and no longer controlling my mind. I was amazed. It was just beginning. I learned that whenever I wrote, I would get lost in the story, as if some mystical convergence occurred and I was a tool. I thought of Maw Sue and her teachings. There were no coincidences in life, only crumbs. Fate, messages, intervention, circumstance, part of the journey to wholeness and being seven. On the blue line I poured out my crumbs of life to decipher, internally consume and work out. I ended each writing session with Maw Sue's words.

A plea. A hope. A divine prayer.

I wanted it more than anything.

"Make lovely your losses" she said softly like the wind.

I wish, Maw Sue, I wish.

Once the broken knob in me found the blue line, nothing was off limits. I wrote about my initial diagnosis; major depressive disorder, anxiety disorder, and level one bipolar disorder. A few attachments, partners in crime, and mild tendencies like self-defeating behaviors. I have family of origin issues, along with major co-dependency which is a need for dysfunctional relationships and reliance on others for approval and identity. Doc spoke of clusters too. People have one or more personality clusters. Turns out I have some borderline personality traits, plus I'm a highly functioning bipolar with highs and lows. I'm a skilled overachiever, over-doer, overkill tee-totaller until I crash and burn. Which is exactly what happened. I crashed and the town burned. Well, almost…according to Edna, that is. Knowing all this an emergence ever so slightly comes to the surface. Somewhere in the recesses of my mind a fire is burning and I can smell the smoke. It's coming for me and when it does, I pray to God, it doesn't consume me.

At my next appointment, I had planned to share some things with Doc. But before I tell her all the memories I've written down, the ones I'm scared to talk about, of Maw Sue, the family gifts and curses, the Seventh Tribe, the ceremonies and rituals, the times she disappeared to Castle Pines, all of it, I have to ask her a question. Then and only then, I'll decide what secrets to reveal and what to keep hidden.

"Doc, before we begin, can…" I stopped mid-sentence and sighed. "Can I ask you something?"

"Anything. What's on your mind, Cass?"

"So, I don't know how to say this, other than just say it. But I also don't want you to think I'm totally crazy when I tell you. Like lock-me-up crazy. You know?"

"Let me stop you right there, Cass. Let me clarify my methodology of healing. The word *crazy* is a label I rarely use. Others do, but I do not because of the stigma related to it. Mental illness in whatever form it may arise is a manageable disease, with medication, and self-help and doing the work it requires to understand the inner child, the family trees, and much more. I believe crazy is a superpower if one uses it to bring good." She smiled and I saw a twinkle in her eyes. "If you are going to use it, use it for a superpower, real power, the power of the mind. So, with that being said, if there is anything you are hesitant to tell me, I promise we will work it out."

"Okay, Doc." I sighed and prepared myself fidgeting as normal. "Do you believe in magic, not the witchy movie stuff, but the unexplainable, the otherworldly, the supernatural, the mystical connection between this world and the next?"

"I do," Doc said without blinking an eye. "Is there something specific you're referring to?"

"Uhmm, yes and no. Honestly, Doc, I'm scared to death to tell you. I'm scared you'll lock me in a psych ward and I'll be labeled mentally insane."

"Cass, hold on," Doc said setting my thick file on her desk. "I have seen plenty of mental illness cases. Extremely sick, sick people. But you are far from that. Yes, you have mental illness in several forms, but they are manageable if you stay on your medication, and do the work. From what I've observed from all our sessions, you have the potential to rise above all of this. Now, let me dive a little deeper into your question so we're on the same page and you feel comfortable telling me whatever you are hesitant to share."

I nodded. Doc seemed sincere but it could be a trick. Spill my secrets, then boom, lock me away. I wasn't sure.

"I am not a religious person. I was raised Catholic but I don't attend services. Growing up I had my own spiritual experiences which led to my belief in a higher power. I believe there is a world beyond us, seen and unseen, and unexplained. I believe in good and in evil, in gifts and curses, I've seen both, but I also believe in the mind. The power of thoughts, and how those thoughts shape our reality, and we are the master of them. Say, for instance, I give you a present. It's a blue basket. Inside is an ancient hand-carved stick and the tales of it speak of anyone who touches it has the power to make the wooden stick do magic. You try. You attempt many times to make the stick create something but it fails. You begin to believe you have no power and no magic. But it's not true. You have power. You have magic. The power is not in the wooden stick, the ancient tales of the stick or the blue basket it came in. The power and the magic are in the holder. It's in you. We are the little blue basket and we hold the power of our gifts, our thoughts and our future within us. This, to me, is the magic. We fail when we believe other people who point us to the wrong magic, the wrong basket. But when we believe in the power inside us—it opens up the whole universe and its magic pours into us, because our thought process has changed. We can still use the basket and the wooden stick, because we know the magic is in us. It's like the blending of all things connecting, us to animals, and the earth, water, sky, wind, fire… all the elements swirling and coming together to make up life as we know it.

"Do we get sidetracked, lose our way, experience trials and pain and loss? Yes. It's the journey. We apply the magic of healing and move forward. I'm not sure this helps you, Cass, because I have no idea what you are struggling to tell me, but I assure you I will examine it with an open mind. Will I have you locked up in Castle Pines? Highly unlikely, unless your destructive behavior takes a turn, or if you are a danger to yourself or others. The fire? It was destructive behavior which we'll discuss and get to as we go along, but I have to put all cards on the table, Cass. It's my job. It's my work. My passion is to help others get better. Now, what I have to do, to make it happen, is up to you."

I sat tangled in her words wondering if I should tell her everything, or nothing. Her last sentence set me on edge. I didn't trust myself, my mind, my behavior, my dreams or my thoughts. It seemed the only option was to trust Doc.

"You okay, Cass? Any questions, anything you want to tell me? I see you brought a notebook."

I squirmed while my journal sat in my lap like an elephant. An animal weighted with my memories, my secrets, the gifts, the curses and the magic. If there *was* magic in me, and I had the power to use it by compiling my thoughts with pen and ink, then this notebook was full of *my life*, my so-called troubled, distorted and mysterious past. I took a deep sigh, and opened the journal. I poured out all the memories I had filled my journal with. The wild, and eccentric memories of Maw Sue, what she taught me and my sister, the family stories, what I could remember of them, along with the rituals, the manic phone call with my mother, my meltdown in her disapproval, followed by the disturbing appearance of the little girls, the word bones, and what they might mean, the bloodline, the House of Seven, all the stories I heard growing up, my parents, my distant relationship with my mother, how it pained me, how I coped, how I lost myself, created another version of me, my imagination, my inner house, my disturbed mental status, the pine forest and the magical, mystical elements of those things I felt, but could not see, the otherworldly, the stories told to me as a child, along with the delicate, fragile things from birth because of the mirror bin, the Ainsley clan, their beliefs, and how all these things shaped and impacted my life.

Doc picked apart my regurgitated monologues with meticulous candor and sorted the clusters into a category. Layers of Cass, the inner child, the broken woman. I let a stranger inside my head. I showed her my dark inner house. The one I'm so afraid of. Doc's wholehearted belief in her craft made me want to believe it too. She believed she could help me to help myself. Her insight into the crazy me, the sane me, the broken me, the seek-to-be whole me, the little girl me, the adult woman me—*all of me*—gave me hope. My listening ears. My keeper of secrets. Doc accepted me as I was, all of me without judgment. Cassidy Cleo Collard may be a hot mess but in Doc's eyes she was a constellation with promise. After I was emptied of all thoughts, I felt exhausted. The bell timer went off as usual and I bid my goodbyes and scheduled another appointment. As I was leaving the lobby, the artwork that had drawn me to it from day one, was now calling me again. I studied it from afar then slowly walked closer and stopped. It was oddly different, as if the brushstrokes had changed from the first day. I smiled and closed my eyes and thought about the journey. I knew it wasn't the painting at all, but me. I had changed, and therefore my perception of the world around me had changed. I opened my eyes and read the inscription of *Edvard Munch* again.

> **"My fear of life is necessary to me, as is my illness. Without anxiety and illness, I am a ship without a rudder … my sufferings are part of myself and my art. They are indistinguishable from me, and their destruction would destroy my art." In one of his journals, he wrote, "Illness, insanity and death were the black angels that kept watch over my cradle and accompanied me all my life."**

I read it twice, letting the words sink deeply inside me, finding their place inside the House of Seven. The broken knob in my head clicked and turned and burned hot. *Black angels,* I thought to myself. *The broken knob is my broken mind, but it is also my black angel and the blue line of my journal is the art it creates.* "Oh My God!" I blurted out loud. "It's mine. It's all mine."

Pearl looked up from the desk with an odd expression as if she wasn't sure what to say or do. I couldn't believe she even made eye contact with me. That was a first.

"It's okay, Pearl. I'm good. You're good," I said with tears streaming down my face. It stunned me to realize that something so simple and overlooked could be my gift, my art, my purpose. Even in pain, or destruction, sanity or insanity, no matter what, it was all mine. All me. Inside and out. Gifted and cursed to do with as I chose. I owned it. **It. Is. Mine.** For the first time in my life I knew without a doubt, even in all the pain and suffering—*I was created for more.* A simple, profound more.

MAKE LOVELY YOUR LOSSES

Man is least himself when he talks
in his own person. Give him a mask
and he will tell you the truth.
~Oscar Wilde

Looking back at it now, with clear and focused, and partially healed eyes, after the divorce, my life virtually stopped. Because the only substance I knew existed in a vow, in the matrimonial ceremony and without it, I was a zombie picking scabs off of others just to feel alive. Pain and suffering were my companions, my only point of reference. The depression didn't help matters. I had lost weight, my skin was pale and my head always hurt with a heaviness I couldn't explain, like too much information was held there, with no way out. I remember constantly grabbing a pillow because I had to have something to hold—in order to hold myself together.

Long before therapy I desired nothing more than to rid myself of this monster, this gnawing malaise, a damaged organ inside my wrecked body. The broken knob, my curse. If I'd known what it was, I would have yanked it out with my bare hands. My existence was on two planks, all or nothing and pain or numbness. There was no in-between, no gray area, no middle ground. When you're crazy, days mix with the nights, the sun collides with the moon and everything is blackened. Being alone after the divorce had left me literally lost and empty and so maddened in my mind, it's a wonder I got through each day without being locked up. But Cass Cleo Collard wears her masks well.

I am leaning against the window, daydreaming drifting in and out of memory, listening to the wind blow the leaves across the lawn as if they are running, tumbling gymnasts. The tree limbs bounce up and down in slow motion as if they are waving and trying to get my attention. *Wake up, Cass,* they say. I sigh loudly and hold my pillow tightly to keep from dying and slipping into no-man's land. A place where I'm alone. A place of spinsters and cat ladies, beggars and bag ladies. I lean into the windowsill, lost in what is and what isn't. Sorrow and sadness. How my whole life has changed in just a few months, how I'm changing, learning so much about a past I left behind, but I know there is more to come. It's getting harder and harder to deal. I'm beginning to crack and lose my stability. I'm trying. But it's hard when the broken knob clicks and I have no control.

I lean my cheek against the warm glass and watch the ferocious wind whip the Chinese tallow tree as if it's a spoiled child in need of punishment. They grow wild around these parts, sprouting up everywhere. The one outside is almost identical to the one near my bedroom window as a child. Meg and I called it our wondering tree. We'd sit on its branches and wonder about life. In the springtime I'd leave my window open. The smell was my version of heaven, slightly sweet, not overwhelming. The tree bloomed with yellow-green clusters of spiked flowers, and attracted thousands of bees. The buzzing was so loud my room vibrated. I felt transported to a peaceful state of mind and solitude. It was like riding the back of a bumblebee with no cares, no silence, no crazy, no feeling different, no maddening houses, just floating inside a long chant of the universe. When autumn came, the leaves dropped and the bees disappeared. The silence of my bedroom returned and drove me insane. It summoned me back to the house inside me. As a child unable to cope, I returned to it, the House of Seven, again and again.

Looking at any tree reminds me of this. But I am no longer a little girl with whims and wanderings. I don't have time to sit in treetops. *Or do I?* Suddenly, I catch a glimpse of something I'm not sure is real or imagined. I unhinge from my pillow and open the window. The air rushes in and a slight dislodging occurs in my chest. The Texas humidity slaps me like a damp dishrag. Orange, red and brown leaves flutter from the spindly limbs like chandeliers. I come undone. High in the treetop it hangs, waiting for me to acknowledge its presence, bow to its kingship and grovel in its majesty. It's lush and dripping with morning dew. The drops glisten and bounce across the fabric of its sticky weave. Its craftsmanship astounds me and leaves me in awe. Something so small can create such beauty time and time again, over and over. The spider web is three feet across, stretching from one limb to another and draped with a gallery of crisp, colorful leaf curtains. The small brown spider bounces like it's on a trampoline. What holds my gaze and makes my heart drop is a tiny cicada shell clinging to a brown leaf. It hangs loosely from a single thread frayed at the bottom of the web. Seeing it brings a rush of childhood memories and a teardrop from another time pools in my eyes. The leaf spins in the air and my vision goes blurry. My mind connects, drifting from past to present, yearning for something unknown, unseen. Something hidden in the wind, the leaves, the web, the cicada shell. On impact, I emerge into another realm, a world of forgotten magic, held up in a lost, forgotten childhood seeking to reclaim me and take me back. I hear Maw Sue's voice again.

Make lovely your losses, Cass.

My heart shatters. I want to scream at her spirit words. A deep quiver rumbles from a dark place, a hidden room inside the house. Underneath. Below. My vision goes dark. Pure black. Fear trickles up my spine. I feel someone grab my hand and pull me into another realm. My vision opens up to a colorless view, a landscape of black and white. Moss trees girls hang from every branch, different than before, now they are demented versions, the bad and awful parts of myself that I hate and they swing and drape and watch me with haunted spirited dark eyes telling me things I don't want to hear.

The House of Seven is different too. It's creepier than ever before. It sits rough, abandoned and disjointed. Beside it a large locust tree with dull swords clinging to every limb and standing in front is the shadow soldier I see in my dreams. A girl, the persona of who I was, at one point or another. Suddenly I find myself inside, walking the hallways in a haze, passing room after room. There is a familiar blue blackness, as if I've been here a thousand times before in the belly of the house. The foundation that rules and controls me. Suddenly, I stop in front of a doorway. I can't read the nameplate. LERACKC. As soon as it enters my mind, the letters move and scramble to spell out a word.

"Crackle." When I say it, the doorknob rattles and the heavy door swings open. A phantom force pushes me inside. The door slams loudly behind me. My heart bolts. My flesh gooses out in a cold sweat. I feel clammy and filled with fear. Everything is different. Everything is the same. Something is, and something isn't. I am me. But I am her. I am Cass the child...and Cass the adult. It is odd, ethereal, a drifting in of two worlds.

In the earthly realm, I am an adult clutching my pillow. In the otherworld, inside the house, I am simply a child staring at the room I built. It's like being inside my own memory skeleton, bones, muscles, blood; a persona of my life manifested in stone and wood, a house of Cass, a House of Seven. Without warning she rips through the walls like a torrential ghost. We are inches apart. She is the same as I remember. Everything I used to be. Everything I wish I was now. Our eyes blend together, blue to blue, transferring our energy, one to another. *She* is a deeper part of me, unknown and complex. A conflicting twin who knows things—disturbing, awful things. Pine curtain secrets.

"Accept me. Let me go! Let me out!" she says with piercing intention.

"No. No. No." I shake my head in protest. "You know I can't do that." In a rage, she disappears. Behind me a door opens. I am yanked up like a rag doll and dragged down the hallway by an invisible force. I am dropped in front of a door. The door is black. The nameplate reads letters EMMROY ZLINGZUM. I feel a hot stench against my neck.

"Stay here in your favorite room, Cass," the voice hisses. "The coping room. The leave-it-be room. It-never-happened room. Don't-go-back-there room. Denial room. Silent room. *Go ahead.* It shall be your suffering room." The letters on the nameplate scramble, but never make words, they just shift and sort. The doorknob transforms into a slinky ghostly hand of smoke and shadows. A chill runs the length of my spine. My mouth feels muted, captive, silenced. The door opens and I am swept inside. An escalation of terror enters me. A fear so intense I find myself screaming, but no words escape my mouth, just polarized air. Out of nowhere, I am suddenly back in my own house, still in my bedroom, clutching my pillow in intensity. I feel this sadness enter me, a menacing depression, an enemy with cupped fingers reaching to suck me down to a cavernous depth of black hell. I see him for the beast he is, his figure transforming before my eyes, his oppressive beast-like body on top of me bearing down, a savage pressing my pores, riding me, bedding me as his bride while he fondles my breasts and licks his forked tongue across my cheek, his hot breath igniting the hairs on my flesh as he slides his sword into my privates, twisting and slicing away my innocence. I feel his darkness flowing through me as he ejaculates a thousand demon babies inside me, scattered and roaming to do their harm. He is a master of me, robbing me of myself, physically, mentally and spiritually, and when he takes me, he takes me down for weeks at a time. I have no desire to do anything, to talk, to get dressed, to bathe, or brush my teeth or comb my hair. My lungs exhale and smell as stale as a dog. I have no strength. To lift my arm is more effort than I can bear. My mind is a road map, red lines sprouting in every direction, and yet I go nowhere. In rare times, I rise up with a sudden gust of energy, supernatural in nature, I cannot explain it otherwise, and it reckons me with aimless pleasure to pick and pilferage for landmarks, a road, a doorway, a map or a memory, a hidden enclosure, but all I get are the adamant cries from a voice I barely recognize screaming inside me. I retreat internally to cope. I struggle to hold her inside me, keep her where she belongs. I fear the walls are not strong enough. She is growing violent and adamant and determined to find a way out. I feel tiny ruptures as if the foundation of the house splinters and shifts under her stomping protest. Voices slip through the cracks of the house, of my soul. I rise up from my death bed, eyes wild and alert. What happens next, I cannot explain. My room becomes a bridge, a connection to things buried, stored away, hidden, forgotten, abandoned, denied, an entryway into my past—a voice silenced long ago. It isn't a cosmic boom or a thundering awakening. It isn't phenomenal in the grand sense of things—quite the opposite. It is simple and transcending. My heart beats rapidly, my senses alive, acute and responsive, vision crisp, scent anew, tongue tasting and skin feeling. It is strange. I find myself saying a prayer, a way forward, to repair the damage of my past. I must deal with all the clusters of my life, no matter the cost, no matter the darkness.

PRESENT DAY

August 12, 1988
NEWS YOU CAN USE
BY EDNA ROLLINS

TEXAS NEWS EDITION

When Texas heat rolls around, folks get a taste of what hell will be like. It is also when souls get restless and wander away from God's law. As ladies of the church, we have our eyes and ears out into the community as to be overseers of his children, so we can guide those back to the place of the sacred. Lately, we have upsetting reports about a considerable amount of drinking at the Pulp Mill after shift changes. Husbands were not home after their evening shifts as they should be. Folks say they gathered on tailgates and drank till the wee hours of the morning, talking about the fish they caught, or the motor they overhauled or the upcoming hunting season. Second report is even more disturbing. Our teen populace has some wild habits they will need to overcome if they are ever to become graceful adults. On an average Friday night, teens can be found tracing all over theater row, and while some are inside the theater, they are not watching the movie. Kissing and other scandalous behaviors have been noted. The ones that don't make it inside, are seen leaving with older groups in cars or the backs of pick-up trucks and are usually found at Buttermilk Road in the pasture gathered round a bonfire, drinking and Lord knows what else. The most troubling behavior is teens discovered slipping off behind the theater where there are pockets in doorways and obscure hiding places. Let's just say that if you have a redheaded daughter or your son drives a beat-up green Ford, you might want to talk to them about abstinence and the Lord's view on sexual purity, and how babies are born, before you end up with an unwed mother and a wayward son. Until next time, tune into KTBR local radio news station

109.9. I'm Edna Rollins and that's news you can use.

THE GREAT SADNESS

Repetition compulsion; we unconsciously seek out people, events, situations that duplicate our core trauma, in the hope of eventually triumphing over the situation that wounded us.
~ Freud

I walk inside Doc's office. She greets me with a smile from her high throne chair. I usually look forward to visits but something is off today and I can't pinpoint it. I turn to sit on the couch and feel the instant attack. The vision splits my soul wide open and leaks a torment of voices, whispering, screaming and crying. Sitting inside the bay window is a mason jar of wild white roses. Doc always has flowers in the window, but this is different. This feels like a part of me, as if my heart sits soaking in water. A vile taste rises in my throat while a palpable resistance enters the air around me. My vision is altered, skewed. Sweat excretes from my pores. *Is this some kind of reverse psychotherapy Doc is using on me?* She knows about the petal people. My fears, the old stories, and Maw Sue. She knows about the Seventh Tribe, the long-held beliefs my grandmother had, the truth behind the words. Doc knows all my secrets. Why would she do this, knowing how it would affect me?

I sit quietly on the couch, unable to speak, just staring into the folds of the petal people standing in the jar as if they want to speak and tell me their stories. Outside the windows are overcast clouds, mist and fog. The jar draws me to it like a snake charmer. I hear a rumble inside me. The house awakens with fears. The petal people rise up and whisper. "Cass," they say. "Come to us. *Immortelles.* Everlasting. Death is the only way out."

"Cass, are you okay?" they say one after another.

"No…no, I'm not okay," I reply. "I'm not okay. I'm not okay." And then I realize it's not the petal people talking. It's Doc.

"Cass," she says concerned. "What is it? Do you need some water?"

"No. No—thank you." I wipe the sweat from my forehead and gather my wits about me.

"Just try and relax. Why don't you lie back on the couch and close your eyes for a minute?"

"Okay," I say as the cushion pulls me in. I inhale deeply. I close my eyes. Instantly a fragrance captures me and I am helpless to fight against it. It permeates my nose and fills me like the waves of many oceans. In my vision is the House of Seven, the house that built me, drives me, sustains me, and makes me crazy simultaneously. Around it I see the large cascading trees with the drooping moss tree creatures and their spirit eyes, hanging upside down and eerily staring through me, knowing me, wanting something from me. And then I hear the familiar clatter of bones. A rumble unsettles the ground beneath my feet, the earth splitting, crumbling. Beneath the soil I hear them, coming out from the graves in the Hush cemetery where the little girls buried them. Laid to rest, yet never asleep. Forever tossing and turning in the grave and in my mind. Each headstone has a mason jar with its own petal people at the base and a small lit candle burning with a creepy glow while the wax drips with a black sludge.

I feel a change in the air. The mossy-haired spirit damsels start dripping what looks to be tree sap, raw and oozing, sticky and thick. It runs down their tree people faces and trickles through their thick moss hair and drips slow and morbidly to the ground, and creates a river flowing toward me. A thick fog moves in and the whole landscape begins to change, growing creepy and eerily spooky, but then a voice perks my ears. It comes from inside the House of Seven a few steps away. I quickly walk up the cobblestone path and face the door with the carved seven. The broken doorknob rattles and turns. A thousand fears rack my bones. I am hesitant to go inside; I may never come out. Trapped. *Forever.* I can turn around and run. Right now. *Go back. Live the lie.* Never see the truth. *Or….*

I tremble. My lips twitch. My shaky hand reaches for the knob and before I can touch it, the door opens. I enter and come face-to-face with *her.* I am frozen in my tracks. Finally, after all this time, *she* shows herself and I know exactly who she is. Or maybe I just allow my eyes to see her for the first time, really *see her.* She seems so incredibly lifelike standing in front of me. I reach out to touch her, feel her, and make sure she is actually flesh and blood. One touch leaves me winded and taken aback.

It is me. The child me. The truest form of myself. An authentic embodiment of sacred rituals, trust, story and words, crowns and crackles, love and mystery, innocence and spirit. Of want and wonder, of passion and fury. She is the little girl I was but always thought I didn't deserve to be.

"Cass. Take my hand," she says. "You are grit and courage. Blood and tears. Stars and moon dust. Faith and hope. You are a beautiful cluster. A constellation of hope."

"Go on," she says as I move forward under her trance. My legs are wobbly. I take her hand and we conjoin. Our mannerisms combine. Everything about us is in sync, eye blinks, smiles, nods, shrugs, turns, everything—all is one. Twins of self. Together we walk the hallway of the house, bare feet, pure Southern sap, queens of the pine curtain.

"I have to show you something, Cass," she says mysteriously. "It will not be easy to see, but you must confront it to move forward." I hesitate. She seems to read my thoughts.

"Look. You trusted Maw Sue, right?"

"Yes, of course," I say pinching my lips together, remembering. "That was a long time ago."

"No…seriously, it's all or nothing. Do you trust me?"

I look at her for what seems like hours, but only a few seconds pass. "Yes. Yes, I do." Suddenly with our thoughts converging on dark things, the shadows slip out. They seep out under the doors and out of the cracks in the wall. Inside the house I see them differently, as they truly are. In the outside world they are just a thick oppressive spirit, but here they are in bodily form, like fallen angels, burnt black with large feathers materializing and then vanishing, coming to life then disappearing in black smudges. We stop in front of a door. The letters on the nameplate read, NATDODING.

Instantly, they scramble. GAINTODND. I glance at her, puzzled.

"Touch the doorknob, Cass." Her eyes are weepy and cause a knot to swell in my throat. "I can't do this for you. You must do this all alone."

"Do what?"

"See the truth." She sniffles. I turn away to face the door. I touch the knob and feel a pulse of dark energy. I flinch. The nameplate scrambles the letters. My teeth chatter. I watch the letters form a word. Terror sinks inside my skin and my whole-body trembles as I remember.

It reads ADDINGTON.

The door opens violently and I am thrust inside. I haven't thought about Mark Addington in years. *Why now? Why him?* He's just a guy I had a crush on. What's the big deal? I glance at the little girl for answers.

"You'll see soon enough, Cass," she says. Suddenly the room transforms like a picture screen, as if I'm out of my body, and seeing it in real time. My past unfolds before my eyes. I am in the woods. It's nightfall. The stars are bright in the sky, the moon blinks halfway between the pines. Creature's chirp, buzz and croak. Water laps against a creek bed at the river of our old hide-out, our gathering place. I see a light coming from the trail at the woods edge. Holding the flashlight is a sixteen-year-old Cass. It's strange watching myself in the past at this age. Standing face-to-face with a teenage me is kin to staring in the mirror and not knowing who you are, not trusting what you see is real. Was I *this* girl, really? Not knowing who you are separates yourself from your own identity, as if everything you should know, is tied up in someone who looks like you, yet, is foreign to you. I feel tormented to look at her, or rather, look at me. Hormones and icky feelings gurgle up and make me uncomfortable. She senses my anxiety. The little girl stands beside me and assures me with a glance that this is what I need to see, so I continue to watch in wonder as events unfold around me. In my mind, I'm figuring the guys or Meg will show up any minute. I wait. I watch. I wonder. I feel a familiar terror in the woods at being alone. *Then, and now.*

I watch the teenage Cass make a fire while I hear the sounds crisp and crackling. Suddenly, a red Plymouth veers around the corner in a dust storm with bright headlights and loudspeakers blaring. The car engine kills. I hear laughter and a deep rumbling voice but its not coming from the car, it's in the wind, through the tree branches and rising up from the earth. Watching this scene play out makes my breathing intensify till I'm almost hyperventi-lating and I don't know why. The little girl grabs my hand and I subside to calm, yet my mind is raging. My body feels an epic variety of feelings of another time and place. Teenage hormones, the love sick giddiness of hope, wants, fears and expectation. Everything the teenage Cass felt back then—I feel it now.

I am boy crazy about Mark Addington. Despite all the warnings Terry gave me to stay away—I didn't listen. Despite all the rumors at school, I was stubborn. If truth be told, I was desperate for someone to love me. Pay attention to me. Talk to me. Resolve my life. Forgive my trespasses. Save me from my own internal damnation.

We planned it earlier without anyone knowing. He asked me to meet him there long after everyone else had left. I grabbed my handy flashlight, rolled some watermelon gloss on my lips and climbed out my window. Walking the dark trail of the pine woods, I imagined this would be the night my life would change, for the better. He'd give me his bracelet, the leather one with his name carved in it. The girls at school would be so jealous. He would be mine. He would kiss me by the firelight, tell me he liked me from the beginning. Little Cass would fall in love.

Right off the bat he is demanding, almost pushy, unlike his demeanor around the guys.

"What's going on Cass?" He says putting the cooler by the fire. "Let's get this party started." He sets his open beer down and removes his shirt. "What are we waiting for? It's time to go skinny-dipping?" He winks. "I've had a six-pack already. Grab a beer, young lady. You need to catch up."

"Dang, Mark. Slow down. You just got here. I don't want to go swimming." I laugh as if he's kidding. *Is he kidding?*

"I didn't say swimming." He winks again and it unnerves me. I was hoping he was joking.

"You chicken?" He starts squawking and flapping his arms. Then he starts taking off his shoes, his pants, then his underwear. My eyes widen with disbelief.

"What are you doing?" I say loudly and cover my eyes. Underneath my eyelids I see the black bars and hear my mother scream, "Sexpot!"

"Whooohoooo!" Mark screams. I turn to see him running butt naked, hooting and hollering and leaping into the swimming hole.

"Oh my God, Mark, you are crazy." His head pops up from the water as a darkened silhouette. I laugh but on the inside I'm fearful and weirdly can't shake an impending doom. *Stop it Cass!* I think to myself. Just have fun, let loose, enjoy the moment.

"Well, you coming or not?" He dives underwater, shoots up like a porpoise and then under again. I am shy about the no clothes part, but I like him so much that a part of me doesn't care. A part of me tells me it's innocent enough, no harm done, just a little skinny dipping.

I stand up and lift my shirt over my head. Mark whistles. "Stop it," I say, feeling my face flush. I quickly strip to my bra and panties. That's as far as I will take it. I walk shyly over to the edge of the water. Mark playfully grabs my leg and swiftly pulls me in. I go under the water but come up laughing in his arms. I can hear my own heart beating relentlessly out of control. He is only a shadow against the firelight glow, and I melt into the darkness of his ink eyes, under his spell and drowning in a deep well of danger. His embrace is passionate but changes almost instantly, growing intense, almost smothering.

"Owww…Mark. That hurts," I say trying to make him stop. I don't like the way his eyes glaze over as if he doesn't hear me. His lips lock forcefully around mine until I feel swallowed. I have no air. His hips grind into mine. The playfulness turns to heavy hands, pressing, groping and grabbing. My mind spins with thoughts. *He doesn't want me. Not Cass Collard. Not the girl. He wants the object. He wants what the men in the magazines wanted. He saw the bad girl. It's who I am—always have been—always will be.* Momentarily, his eyes lock onto mine. In the reflection, I see what he sees. Tacked around my eyes are the black bars, the dark mask of who I am. The real me. The monster. The sin.

I try to get away, to settle things down a bit.

"No," I say, pushing his hands.

"Aww, come on, baby. You know you like it." His tone is playful, slightly different. "You've been wanting me since you met me, admit it. I see how you look at me."

I start to second guess myself, my actions, his intentions. Maybe I was wrong. Maybe it's just me. I'm overthinking things. *Lighten up, Cass.*

Mark lets go of me and falls back into the water, submerging under the surface. I watch the bubbles pop up one after another and then my feet go out from under me and I'm pulled under water. I slip into the dark of the underworld where I feel his arms wrap around me and rush me up out of the water into a breath of air. My back plunges against the embankment of clay. He presses his body into me, his face dripping water drops one after another. I see the dark of his eyes. The way he looks at me, like I'm not a person.

"No, Mark. You've got the wrong idea. I'm not doing this, I'm not. I can't." His eyes spill over into nothingness. They are the dark waters, the depths of the murky, deep, blue black where monsters lurk and feed. He doesn't hear me. He blocks my words with soft kisses as to tempt me, deceive me and it works for a second, but then it changes to a hard bite of my lips. The metallic taste of blood pools in my mouth.

"What the hell Mark….no, stop it." I yell and fight him harder now. But his actions intensify, heavy-handed, pushing, groping and grabbing. I'm confused, scared and in a state of panic.

"No, Mark. I mean it," I say firmly. I push against his shoulders and beat on his chest but he is an iron crush of weight that I cannot budge. I squirm but he pins me to the clay dirt. I feel his manhood against my hips and tears flood my eyes because I know what is fixing to happen and I cannot bear it.

My mind is screaming with words I can't speak. They are stranded in my throat. Not like this. This is not what I wanted. This isn't the way it works. Not like this. No. Stop. No. I am not the monster! I am not the sexpot! I am not black bars! I am southern sap, a queen of the pine curtain, I am anointed!

I exhale and gather enough strength to scream as loud as I could. "NO," I say with force. "NO!" I say it over and over but it lands on deaf ears. "Let me goooo…I mean it, Mark. Just let me go." The echoes of my voice in the wild are like demons taunting me and turning into laughs. He doesn't hear me. *No one hears me.* My voice is a night scream of an animal being wounded, killed, unable to escape, until the screams turn to whimpers, wet tears and torn flesh. Exhausted from fighting, I can only cry in silence at the brutality that invades me. In that moment, a kingdom desecrated, a queen dethroned, a crown destroyed.

An hour or so passes, and I gain some form of clarity, some realization that Mark is gone. What he left behind is ruin. It is then that I, the grown-up Cass watching this play out, beside the little girl, hand-in-hand, can no longer stand. Crushed by emotion and repressed memories of this moment coming back in real time, makes me collapse to the ground. In duplicity with my younger version of self, I sob with her. I scream with her. I beat the hard ground with her. Together, adult, teen and child weep so hard the loblolly pines start to leak thick sap, their limbs scratching and swaying, crackling and crumbling, breaking, breaking, breaking for their weeping queen.

My mind, my body, my spirit crack into a million broken pieces, clusters, fragments, particles of light and dark. Somehow, I leave my body and spill into the twilight of stars and glow of the moon until I am one with the universe, drifting and floating till I reach the dark, tangled place of the void. The gap, the place of wholeness Maw Sue loved so much, but could never touch, not until she passed over. I stay in the void trying to find a place of sanity until the river laps at my neck and the clay dirt is caking my face. The water pulls me out of my trance. I am leaning against the clay river banks, my body imprinting the tragedy, indentions in the soil. It is marked with him, as I am marked with him. I stare into the darkness of night lost in myself, unable to comprehend the magnitude of what has happened. My tears are blurry and scattered in my eyes and I notice the stars seem to fall one by one, burning long threads of smoke tendrils across the sky till there is nothing. For some reason, my mind drifts to me at school in the Chicken Little play. I hear my words. *The sky is falling! The sky is falling!* Indeed. The sky has fallen.

I slide down into the water slowly. It would be easy to drown myself and rid my body and soul of its aches and pains. Take my life like Maw Sue tried to take hers even though she denied it. I understand her desperation now, her pain. The feeling that you can never go back. I feel sick to my stomach because I realize I can still feel him. I turn and vomit on the river bank edge. And then the tears begin again. Frantically, I try to wash his handprints off my skin, my face, my body, his taste, his smell, his imprint, his mark, but deep inside I know the truth. His seed is inside me. Forever marked from the inside, out. I throw up again. There is no removing what he done.

I dive under the water and want to drown but instead float to the surface on my back. I imagine myself to look like a dropped flower with some of its petals ripped away, torn and damaged. The river water laps at my ears and my skin like soft pats of comfort as my eyes take in the blackened sky. Underneath the moonbeams and the blinking stars I feel my lifeblood slipping away, draining me of everything. In the waist-deep soggy river bottom I cry and pray, and beg to be washed of the blood, a saintly baptismal with river angels where the terrible awful will vanish and the great sadness will wash downstream, my sins eaten like fish pellets. I sink underneath the water in hopes of a Godly cleanse, to be untouched, untainted, and washed. *But that doesn't happen. I feel a rot from the inside, out.*

In a slow, begotten hypnotic trance, I walk out of the river. I get dressed and sit by the fire. I am transfixed on the flames and try to think of rituals, stories, or what Maw Sue might do. But it is useless. I'm trying to erase it all—make my mind forget, but denial removes its mask. I get up and walk around only to collapse near a brush of trees and roll onto my back and scream into the sky, hoping it will swallow me. Exhausted, I roll into a fetal position holding myself together momentarily. I catch it out of the corner of my vision. The shimmering doesn't look real and I wonder if I'm hallucinating. It's a large wild bush of white roses. I take in its beauty and at the same time, a face emerges within each bloom. A wild bush of petal people comes to life with energy and illuminating light. Faces I recognize, along with faces I've seen only in pictures. It is magnificent and frightening, splendid and sorrowful.

"Take my grief" I whisper softly over and over. "I cannot bear it, take it, please take it." The *Immortelles*, the *Everlasting*s, the petal people do what Maw Sue said they would. They absorb my pain. They take my grief and whisk me away to the otherworld.

Time passes, the fire is flickering and the woods are growing darker and more wicked by the minute. I hear coyotes howling and a nearby owl. I know I need to get home. Before I leave, I break a wild rose off and press it against my nose but all I smell is the nectar of shame, my scent of suffering. My vision goes black. I spin off into the depths of the deep, dark sky and feel as if I will never come back.

But that was then, and this is now. I do come back, but it's years later sitting in Doc's office. I jerk upright, breathless and terrified. Doc is sitting across from me writing in her notebook and studying me closely. I can barely talk but I manage to get a few words out in stutters.

"Did, did, I just…tell you what happened? Did, did …oh my god! Did you see what I saw, what happened? Did I say it out loud?" I say in a panic.

"Yes, Cass, you spoke it out loud. It's okay." Doc says trying to calm me. I notice someone beside me that wasn't there before. I turn my head slightly and she takes my hand. Warmth surges within me. The inner child Doc is always referring to is there beside me, just like she was moments ago, in memory, remembering the terrible awful sadness with me.

"Cass, take a minute, take as long as you need. This is a traumatic memory and it will take time to process." Doc says. "This repressed event is horrible, despicable but it is necessary for you to confront it in order to move forward and understand where you are now. You've done all this work so far—to get you here. Most of all, you need to know it wasn't your fault. You did nothing wrong. What he did was awful, and he is a terrible, evil person. He is the badness, not you. He took advantage of you. Now that I know this story, I truly believe that this is when the shift occurred and the great sadness as you refer to it, took you away—*for good.* You never told anyone, so no one knew. Because it was so traumatic, you tried to will it away—even the rosebush was part of it, wanting the flowers to bear your grief when you could not. Pretend it didn't happen—ignore and deny it but it *did* happen, Cass. *It did.* But it doesn't define you."

"He took my innocence. It wasn't supposed to be this way." The magnitude of my words was heavy on my heart.

"I know, Cass. He did. You should be angry. Feel it. Whatever you need to do to deal with this constructively is good, but I need you to know you can move on from this. Until then, let it process…Right now, this is a lot to take in, so give yourself grace."

Doc's words rumble through me, sifting and sorting. I hear another voice and my hand is squeezed.

"Cass…" the little girl says, "She's right. I've held this secret inside the House of Seven for years because you couldn't handle it. I endured it for you. But I've been here the whole time watching you grow, seeing how you handle things differently now, and I know that it is time for you to move on. Besides, I would really like to come out. I would like to live. I'm supposed to be freely living within you, sharing your life as it should be. Please don't shut me out. Do what you have to do to heal, but let go. Set yourself free. Set me free. It's the only way."

Let go. Let go. Let go.

I hear the voices of petal people all around me. I stare with blurry tear filled eyes into the face of the little girl as she speaks words from my past into my present, into my future.

"Remember, Cass. You are…wait, I meant, WE are grit and courage. Blood and tears. Stars and moon dust. Faith and hope. Together we are a beautiful cluster and a constellation of hope. And remember what Maw Sue always said, make lovely your losses. This is a great, great loss, no doubt, but together we can heal and conquer life. Together, hand in hand. I love you. I have always loved you."

THE TERRIBLE AWFUL

Hell is empty and all the devils are here.
~William Shakespeare

Remembering the terrible night at the river unleashed a plethora of skeletons rattling in my soul. More repressed memories came with the same dreadful entrance as always. Flashes, images, sounds.

This particular one was the morning *after* the great sadness. My head was dead weight on the pillow as my eyes opened. My mind spun with thoughts of what I hoped was just a nightmare. But once my eyes adjusted to the light, I saw it hanging in my closet.

The dead one. The wild white rose might as well have been me, strung up lifeless, limp, frail, violated, void of life and purpose. After a minute staring and remembering what I did not want to think about, I moved slightly under the covers and immediately felt my body revolt, sore, damaged, broken. I tried to turn over and get up but felt restricted. My legs felt bound. I panicked, adrenaline surged and I jerked upwards, in a fight or flight mode throwing the covers off me. Once I untangled myself from what held me down, I saw my sister Meg moaning and rolling over.

"Shit!" I said breathless trying to stop hyperventilating. My whole body was shaking in fear. *What is she doing in my bed? When did she come in?* I had to calm myself, so I sat on the side of the bed and took deep breaths. My level of anxiety was off the chain. I focused visually on the wild white rose with silent prayers until I could feel it taking my grief from me. Taking from me what I could not bear. The next thing I remember was taking a bath but the sounds of the water sent me right back to the river and the terrible awful, with raging flashbacks. I quickly washed, got out and wrapped myself in a towel. I turned from the mirror avoiding my own reflection. My eyes knew the truth and I could not look into them. Facing myself would mean accepting what happened. And I couldn't do that. It would kill me dead. I would never recover. So I doubled down. *It didn't happen, I told myself. Not to me. Not Cass. It didn't happen. Just move on. Close the door. Shut it out. It. Never. Happened.*

I opened the door to my room to find Meg sitting upright gripping her pillow. She had a long scratch across her face. I stared for a second pondering if it was there before but then turned to get dressed. I didn't speak. Didn't nod. Didn't care. I was numb.

"Hey, I wanted…"

"I don't want to talk this morning Meg." I said cutting her off. My tone was stoic and flat. "So, whatever you have to say—just don't. I'm in no mood for it."

"But Cass, I need…"

"But nothing, MEG!" I spat violently, my body tensed, stiff and angry. "Just go away! Why are you in my bed anyway? Aren't you too old to be sleeping with your sister? Go to your own room. Leave me alone." She clutched her pillow, sullen and defeated. I turned to get dressed and heard the door shut behind me. For the next week or so, I fell into this dark abyss. I barely spoke. My parents were clueless. I heard them mumble something to each other about teen moods, hormones and typical growing pains. Everyone just went their own way. Snuff called four times the next day and every day after. I avoided talking but I heard Meg speaking to him like they were worried I might cliff jump. I skipped school a few days to avoid the chance of running into Mark. The day I returned, Snuff tracked me down and cornered me.

"Cass, are you okay? Why won't you talk to me?"

"I don't know," I'd say. "Just don't feel like it."

"We need to talk, Cass. We're buds. Come on, Smokes. Let me help you. We're best friends."

"Help me?" I paused and stared at him hard. "Why do you think I need help?"

"Just a feeling."

"Well, you're wrong." I snapped. Being the nice guy he was, he just lifted his hands and walked away defeated. As for me, I was paranoid at every corner, afraid of running into Mark. Afraid he had told the whole school I was a slut. Lied and made stuff up. *Was this why Snuff wanted to help me? What if everyone knew a version from Mark?* Besides, no one would believe me. I'd be the talk of the school, the infamous rumor mill of gossip and grins and slut shaming. No one would know the truth. Just thinking about it almost gave me a panic attack in the hallway. No one ever believed the girls story anyway. It was always because we asked for it. We flirted or led him on. We wanted it. We dressed provocatively. We consented. We drank too much. And the list goes on and on. The overwhelming dark whispers inside my mind told me I deserved what I got. I was bad and bad attracts the deep dark blue black murky depths of hell. You can't live there without turning black yourself.

The day drudged on, me still not fully aware of my surroundings, lost in my mind, in the nothingness of everything. I left fifth period to go to the bathroom. A classroom door opened ahead of me. A tall, dark shadow walked out. I froze. Breath left me. My head swayed on my neck. My feet sunk into the tile floor. Mark Addington walked a few steps to his locker and opened it. His eyes lock on mine. His right eye was blackened with green edges and his nose was shades of purple and black. He looked like he'd been hit with a baseball bat. My skin crawled and my body shook. I forced myself to turn and walk away. I heard his locker slam and a door close. When he was out of sight, I ran to the toilet and hurled. Just the sight of him made my stomach turn and flashbacks of the river filled my head to the point I thought I might pass out. I had no idea what happened to his face and I didn't care.

For the remainder of the school year, I planned my route to avoid him. Our group never gathered again even though they tried. Snuff and I drifted apart. The world was broken as I was broken. Nothing was the same. Everyone went their separate ways. One night altered our entire universe, rerouted our fate. The night the terrible, awful sadness took me away.

Eventually, I repressed this memory, and all the others to survive. What I didn't know is that turning it inward, also caused all the energy of the traumatic event to turn inward as well. The emotions, anger, sadness, guilt, shame and more were tucked away, silenced. Never to feel, confront or acknowledge again. *Until now.*

Doc says traumatic energy cannot be contained. It will come out in one form or another, reacting it's way into our lives often in destructive ways. According to my body, my mind, my spirit, my energy, my cells—they all think this event just happened. They hold no concept of time or space. They only hold energy of the moment and *that* horrible, terrible moment is ripe and raw inside me with every single emotion waiting to be released. Vented. Cast out. Confronted. Condemned. Inside me, the House of Seven is ready to implode. The Hush cemetery will not be silent any longer, it is rumbling and splitting the earth. I can hear the boney fingers scraping and digging at the dirt making their way to the surface. It's like claw marks on my brain. The resurrection has begun. The bones will speak. They will live. And they will do it with or without my consent, freely, unchained, unbound and I must deal or die.

PRESENT DAY

AUGUST 25, 1988
NEWS YOU CAN USE
BY EDNA ROLLINS

TEXAS NEWS EDITION

If the heat doesn't kill us in Pine Log, alcohol will have a chance to take up the slack according to Lola Bess, owner of the Cut & Curl on Fourth Street downtown. If you mention this ad, you'll get $5 off a haircut. According to Lola's numerous clients, word is there is a petition floating around town and come to find out, Cletus Herrington started it. Cletus owns the River Shack Bar and Club across the Moss Belt river line, into Maple County which is just a crow's fly from Pine Log community. Cletus wants to make Pine Log wet like Maple County and if he gets enough names, he'll be able to put it on the ballot for folks to vote on come election time. And by wet, we're not talking water, folks, we're talking the devil's juice. If this passes it would mean that every corner store and grocery would sell alcohol. We'd soon have beer joints and liquor stores on every side street. This is how the devil gets in, folks. There is no two ways around it. He starts with one finger and inches his way in, until he is there and then it's too late. Everybody knows what goes on down at the River Shack Bar & Club at night, so let's not pretend we don't. This cannot happen to our fine town. We have started a petition of our own against this hedonistic idea and you can sign it at the Streams of Life Baptist Church, or just ask any member of the Eternal Order of Sisters in Salvation of which I am a proud, and long-standing member. We can stop this and we, in Jesus's name, plan to.

Until next time, stay cool, drink sweet tea and when the powerful rays of the sun shine down on you and you feel the heat, just be reminded that it's only a taste of what Hades is like and this town is heading on a fast track there, unless we turn it around. Until next time, tune into KTBR local radio news station 109.9. I'm Edna Rollins and that's news you can use.

SISTER CODES

Nirvana is not the blowing
out of the candle. It is the extinguishing
of the flame because day is come.
~Rabindranath Tagore

I called Doc to cancel my appointment and reschedule. It was after-hours, so I left a message. All I told her was that I just added another flower, another petal people to the mason jar. She'd know exactly what that meant.

It meant Papa C took his last breath—*and I lost mine.* I came undone again. He was eighty-nine, the last of the greatest generation, the last of my childhood. He was now a part of *the Immortelles. The Everlastings.* Another petal for the mason jar, another flower to take my grief. After news of his death, I unraveled like an old sweater. Meg and I sat in the living room of our parents' house with its haunted walls of silence to contemplate our loss. Disbelief ravaged me. *He'll walk through the door any minute now I thought and plop down in Dad's ugly green recliner and say, "Girls, did I tell you the story about..." and then the world will return to normal, Meg's normal. My normal. Pine curtain normal. But deep down I knew it wouldn't happen.*

Death does strange things to people. Meg and I were sitting at the kitchen table trying to get through a conversation without breaking down. Papa C's spirit hovered over us with unbearable emptiness. Dad had his moments too. But he didn't stick around for us to see it. He'd mow the yard, or tinker in the shop or pop the hood of his truck, cut firewood or trim the hedges. His denial was to avoid feeling by keeping busy. My mother was a whole 'nother story. She did what she always does, *cook*. The pear cobbler was cooling on the counter. The room simmered scents of cinnamon and sugar. Dad came barreling in the kitchen with a familiar *I—need—a—beer*—expression. He eyed the cobbler, plucked a corner piece of crust and was just about to eat it when Gabby, having eyes in places no one else does, caught him.

"Gavin Beck. That's your daddy's cobbler." She says popping him with the spatula. The room went deadly quiet. Dad froze inside the refrigerator door. I couldn't breathe. Meg gasped. No one knew what to do. We were Southern fragments submerged inside a dome of wrecked humanity. The refrigerator made a weird noise. Mother fell apart and Dad rushed to comfort her.

"I—I've baked him one every week, Gavin, every week for years. Ever since May Dell died. I don't know how NOT to. I just…I just…" Her voice was disjointed and out of sorts. Meg vanished in sobs. I sat, unable to move and weighted by some force. The dead don't eat cobbler. My mother was doing what Gabby does; avoiding the inevitable by cooking, caretaking, cleaning, feeding. The cobbler cooked with love would remain untouched sitting on the counter, a stone marker, sacred and holy.

I lost count of how many breakdowns occurred afterwards. One minute we'd be talking about Papa C and then the next minute, one by one, we'd disappear to grieve, to remember, to cry. We worked out our grief in different ways. Dad tinkered. Mother cooked. Meg disappeared to who knows where and I went to my internal House of Seven to process and ponder a profound revelation.

It took a damn peach cobbler for me to see my mother, maybe a mere glimpse of her for the first time. I had always thought she was withholding of love and affection, but now I think she gives love the only way she knows how. There were no fireworks, no Mother Moonshine or pot dancers in the dead of night. Instead, there were pots, pans, silver spoons and lots of food. As a child I missed this. How did I not see this? It's so clear now.

The kitchen is where I remember her the most, collaborating, concocting, cooking, canning and cleaning. All in the name of love. It's strange how death can make you see a person in a completely different light. As a child I longed to know her, and I still don't in many ways, but *this* I know for sure. If you received food in any form, at any time—you can bet a cast-iron skillet, it was pure love from the heart of Gabby's kitchen. She insisted Meg and I inherit the kitchen gene too. By six, I could cook hot dogs and had my first cookbook thanks to Imperial Sugar. Ironically, it was titled, *My First Cookbook.* At age nine, I mastered French toast and by ten, the highly prestigious Southern dessert of all time, pecan pralines, or more properly pronounced, pee-can pralines. By the way Gabby went on and on about the recipe, I thought it was a prerequisite for marriage.

This knowledge of my mother sent me to a vulnerable place, a place that I could not deal with right now, so I made my way of escape. I ran outside to find Meg. I looked everywhere except for the one place I did not expect her to be. I looked up and there she was in the branches of the wondering tree.

"Aren't you a little too old to climb trees, Meg?"

"Aren't you a little too old to start fires?" she said sarcastically.

"Owww…that one hurt, sister." I laughed and climbed up the opposite limb beside her.

We sat in the silence of the damp Texas wind with the rustling of the leaves to soothe us. It was peaceful and we were used to it, the absence of words, of resolution, of answers. As much as I struggled with the house inside me, the horrors of my own mind, my sister Meg had her own. I couldn't tell you what they were, she never spoke of them. Ever since we were young, there was always an anomaly of silence between us, mute mouths unable to communicate the horrors beneath, an abattoir of family and personal secrets.

Meg was the pebble you carry in your pocket. It's there, it exists, you can feel it and rub on it, but it doesn't speak. It carries secrets in the hard stone, heavy burdens, polished and shiny but ever silent. She'd creep into my room at night, half-asleep, cradling her pillow and blanket and nuzzle up to me. In order to fall asleep, she'd have to touch me somewhere, a foot, toe wiggle, a leg wrap, or a hand on my back. Something to tether her to earth in case the world spun out of control as it often did in our house. Meg finally broke the silence.

"Hey, Bill is out of town. You want to stay with me tonight? You can sleep with me like old times" she winked. "You know you want to."

"Sure, why not. I love being tangled up in Meg vines."

Deep inside all I could think of was the morning after the great sadness when she was in my bed. She had tried to talk to me. After all these years, I wonder what it was and if she even remembers it. I started to ask but it didn't seem like the right timing. For the moment, we were grieving our loss in our childhood wondering tree, a place we'd been a hundred times before. Two sisters staring from the treetops into the pine curtain of their magical, brutal kingdom.

Meg grabbed my hand like she did when we were kids. I

noticed she had fat squalls sliding down her cheeks. It was rare for her to let me see her in pain, so I said nothing. I just squeezed her hand. We sat in the wounded bitter silence, surrounded by the comfort of the wondering tree, our childhood hide-away, each of us cradled by slender bark and bountiful leaves and the hush of the winds. It was magical and comforting. The tree held us together, sister to sister, child to adult, adult to child, wounds to bark, past to present, behind the pine curtain of secrets, shadows and sevens.

Later that day, I grabbed a few clothes and something to wear to the funeral and headed over to Meg's for the night. This was as rare as a comet. I hadn't slept near Meg since we were kids. I had no idea a sleepover would set me back thirteen years. I lost count of how many tequila shots we had. Papa C's death took us back to our childhood.

"You know Mother is going to be pissed if we show up hung over to Papa C's funeral, don't you?" I said taking a shot. "Can you believe the last storyteller in the family is gone?"

"Not true." Meg says. "You are a great storyteller."

"I'm not the one who said a band of trolls licked your face, and oh…oh, what was the other thing….oh yeah, flying frogs." I busted out laughing.

"Yeah, well, I had to get you back for cheating in cards."

"I never cheated." I said in my best Southern drawl. "You were a handful for the parents, you know?"

"What do you mean?" Meg looked confused.

"You don't remember all the parent-teacher meetings at school? The time you hit a boy over the head with a yard stick, and kicked another boy in the groin. Or let's see, when you drew stick figures on the neck of that kid named Roger while he was asleep during reading or when you cut a girl's hair for calling you Meg the Smeg."

"Oh my god, I barely remember." she said giggling.

"You were mean as hell. I think I still have teeth marks on my arm where you bit me. I think a few classmates do as well."

"I wasn't that mean? Was I, Cass?"

"Uhm…yeah. You were pretty mean when you wanted to be. You couldn't help it though. Dad raised you like a little boy, hunting, fishing, horses. It's a wonder you weren't in bar fights." We both started laughing.

"Remember the crackles?"

Meg fell back on the edge of the couch. "Lord, do I. Best prank on Maw Sue ever. I can still see her face waking up to find those damn things on her glasses. Oh my God she was so mad."

We belly laughed until we were both laugh-crying and our stomachs hurt. It felt good to laugh. To actually share stories and talk, to be together. I sat for a second in wonder.

Here we were. A sparkly diamond and Southern sap. Suddenly the atmosphere turned serious. It's inevitable when the seeds grow from disturbed soil. When the word bones are buried alive. I should have seen it coming. I was unprepared. I was about to learn a side of my sister I never knew existed.

"See this?" Meg said, pulling up her shorts. I was stunned for a second, trying to figure out exactly what I was looking at on my sister's thighs. Red, rough lines, up and down her thighs, some raised, some more subtle, but all of them apparently cuts. I was speechless, trying to comprehend what I saw and fit it with the sister that I thought I knew.

"What…I…" I said gasping for air and loosing my words.

"And this too," she said holding out her arms in front of me, palms up and her fingers tracing the lines on her wrist. Instead of the lines, my eyes went to the eerie scar in the shape of a seven on her palm identical to mine. Identical to Maw Sue's. In my warped vision it glowed a strange amber sizzle from beneath her skin, and my scar answered back with the same glow.

"Yeah, it happened." Meg nodded pulling me out of my seven trance.

"No, that can't be" I said confused, baffled. My mind spun. "How could I not know about this? And why? Why did you do this?" Tears welled in my eyes.

"It's not dinner table talk, Cass. Mom and Dad couldn't face it themselves. They got it taken care of and never spoke about it again. It's like it never happened. Even if I could talk about it—I couldn't explain it. Not then and barely now. I didn't know what it was. I couldn't get it out. I was a mess. It was this strange inner chaos of power that took over me and I was defenseless to stop it. I just remember not knowing who I was. I felt sad all the time. I wandered around. I felt disconnected from myself, from you, from Mom and Dad, from everyone. I was aimless, bored and useless."

I was shook by my sister's words. I thought I was the only one messed up in my family. But not my sister, the diamond. Not Meg.

"Where was I when this happened?" I said pouring another shot while words spun in my head. *My own sister…the curse… spirits…. secrets.*

"I was seventeen, almost eighteen, I'm not sure, Cass, I don't remember things like you do." Meg poured a shot, licked her wrist, and sprinkled salt on it. In my vision, the white crystals lay like tiny gems, sparkly diamonds littered against her skin, her scars, ready and able to cut, to slice, to open up and pour out the madness. I had to blink several times to get the image out of my head. Meg licked her wrist, downed the tequila and bit into a lime wedge. I felt a siege within myself, inside the House of Seven with all this newfound knowledge of my sister. Meg could sense my anxiety.

"I'm married to Bill now, Cass, so it all worked out. He's good to me. Even with my faults. I have a lot of those. He does too. Actually, he's a little controlling at times, and we butt heads. You know I don't take shit from no one, but at the end of the day, we're on the same side. Occasionally though, long ago, there were times I really didn't want to live. Something's not right about that, huh?"

I closed my eyes. I shuddered, knowing what I know. It went deeper than Meg wanted to admit, seeker deep, Seventh Tribe deep, secrets and sevens deep. The darkness tried to take her too. As it did with me, and Maw Sue, and others before us.

Meg was a seeker in her own right, a shiny diamond. But those diamonds can do damage, cut to bleed and wound. Even herself. But Meg wasn't finished yet. She began to spill out secrets and hidden things that would alter my life forever as I knew it.

Meg's curse, the one she didn't believe in as a child would manifest itself in adulthood years after the slit wrist and cut thighs incident. It would emerge darker inside her marriage and she would keep it hidden from everyone, including herself. My little sister Meg had her own slew of masks and inner houses. I wasn't the only one with people pieces.

Her marriage was not all bliss. When it was good, it was great, but when it was bad, it was hell. Both strong-headed individuals and neither one would back down during a fight or argument. It grew into endless battles. When neither could surrender, they turned to alcohol and pills. This evolved into explosive tempers from both. This was a side of Bill I never knew existed. Meg said no one did. As for Meg's temperament, she was always a powder keg, even as a child, and she never backed down, which made her even more dangerous.

"Cass, it's strange. We were out on the lake, just Bill and me. We had been there all day and he was ready to leave. I wasn't. I wanted to see the sunset but he was adamant that we go. It started a stupid argument. He was pissed, I was pissed and there we are in the middle of the lake screaming like a bunch of crazy loons. Then he just snapped, threw his shit down and cranked the motor and took off. I fell backwards against the boat and hit my head, enough to bleed a good bit. I screamed but he kept on going. I started throwing his fishing poles out, one by one and then I reached in the cooler, grabbed beer cans and started chunking at him. One hit him in the head and knocked his hat off. The boat swerved and he stopped suddenly which made the waves swamp the boat and rock it so hard, when I stood up, I fell out. When I tried to get back in, Bill noticed all his fishing tackles and rods were gone. I started laughing in a vengeful tone and he turned beet red. He was madder than mad. He gave me a go-to-hell glance, sat down, cranked the boat and drove off. I thought for sure he was just bullshitting me, trying to pay me back for tossing his fishing gear, but I was wrong. The seconds ticked away and he grew tiny in the distance. My head was still bleeding and I had to swim to a nearby tree to hang on until an hour or so later, a boater came by and rescued me. You should have seen his face."

"HE LEFT YOU THERE?" I yelled, "In the middle of the lake…that bastard."

"Yeah. I know. I couldn't believe it either but hey, I did get to watch the sunset." Meg laughed but it was a cynical laugh born from pain. I recognized it too well. I had it myself.

"But Cass, I've done some crazy stuff too. Once, I can't remember what we were arguing about, but whatever it was, we were both too drunk to be driving, that's for sure. You know Bill and how fast he drives, well, I kept poking the bear and wouldn't let it go, and he just kept pressing the gas getting madder and madder. I had been drinking all afternoon. But that's not the worst part. It's like my mind just imploded. I had nowhere to run from it. I couldn't escape it. Bill's screaming, the radios blaring, the trucks flying down the highway and this horrible thing is inside my head just eating away at me and telling me to end it now. *Just do it. Stop it now. Let it all go. DO IT!* It was awful. Of course, I'm sure the alcohol intensified it. But it drove me. Pressed me. This dark harboring voice would not stop. Louder and louder until I just reacted. The next thing I know, I'm reaching for the door handle, the door is open and I jump. I feel the gulf of freedom for just seconds before the impact of the ditch sent me into a painful rolling howl."

"You did what?" I punched her in the arm. "Jesus Christ, Meg!" I could barely listen to her because I knew the voices that drove her. Those horrible, terrible interceptors—the shadows, the black angels Maw Sue warned us about as kids. Meg wore her mask well. All these years I thought she had her life together and I was the damaged one. What a fool I'd been, what a fool we'd both been.

I poured Meg a shot and poured myself a double. I let Meg's words settle into my spirit, while my own restless life felt the need of confession. If I didn't know her as well as I thought, then there was a probability she didn't know about me either. I downed one more shot of tequila and let her rip.

I started at the beginning, my earliest memories of what I had recently remembered of my childhood. I told Meg everything—start to finish, all the memories emerging of us as kids, teenage years, of seeing myself as a monster, to the magazines I found, to my non-relationship with mother, to the madness of my mind, the intermingling of Maw Sue's madness, my fears of Castle Pines, to the old stories of the Seventh Tribe. I told her of my unflinching belief in everything Maw Sue told me, and how I was convinced it was real and there was more to it than we ever imagined. I told her about the night at the river, the terrible awful sadness, the white rose and sacred ritual of petal people and bearing my grief. When I was finished the room seemed a tad out of the ordinary, as if the combination of secrets spilled out made it momentarily a mixture of magic, mayhem and madness. Or it could have been the alcohol. I wasn't sure anymore.

"Cass, I think..." Meg said before I cut her off. A plunder of tears ran down her face.

"Meg, I'm not finished. That was just a portion. I think my mind had to take a break or I would lose it. So please...let me finish. I may never be able to talk about it again. Okay?"

She nodded and leaned against the couch cushion while I sat in the pain of the memories that poured out. I told her about Sam, our marriage problems, his cheating, me losing my mind, the phone call to mother, seeing the little girls, ghosts with word skeletons, me making the bed and living the lie. I told her how I lost myself long ago, lost my voice, and the little girl I used to be. I told her I believed in the House of Seven. But I didn't know if I'd ever find myself again, not fully. Not like the number seven Maw Sue said we should live up to. I feared I'd be broken forever. I'd never make lovely my losses. When I finished talking, I glanced up at Meg. Her face was red and her neck was dripping wet with tears and her lips trembled. Right then, our bedfellow returned to pay us a visit, as it did many times when we were children.

The power of words. The silence of secrets. The gap of time, void and lengthy where nothing fits. The collective knowing of dark things that bound us as one. The strange hole of surreal emptiness.

I leaned over and grabbed Meg's hands. Our foreheads fell together, a meeting of minds, of madness, magic and memories of our past. It was like we were in a ceremony again, sisters of the Seventh Tribe, seekers of the way. We clung to each like vines, afraid of drifting apart, of being swept away, while we waited on the world to spin out of balance and fling us off. Our need for touch was deeply intertwined with what we did not receive in our childhood, but we had each other. In this tender moment, we were kids again, two small saplings with shallow roots planted in disturbed soil, in our kingdom behind the pine curtain. Like those Loblolly pines Maw Sue always talked about, we were just trying to survive, adapt and thrive despite our surroundings.

Meg let go of my hands and leaned up. "Cass…," she said, tender and breakable. "I need to tell you something."

I flinched. "Okay." And braced myself.

"The night you went to the river…" she paused and fought back tears. She began to shake and stutter, barely able to speak.

"Meg. What is it? If you're worried about me, I'm fine. I'm getting help. It's okay," I said worried about her. It was unusual for Meg to express any form of emotion. "Just tell me." My heart suspended in my chest.

"Okay, okay. It's not you, it's me. I can do this. I can. Shhhhit. I get so crybaby when I'm drunk!" Her hands pressed hard on the carpet and the anticipation was killing me.

"I knew about Mark," she said, "I knew what he did to you before you told me."

"What?" I said, confused. "How? What do you mean *you knew?* I never told anyone. Wait, wait a minute, did Mark spread it around school? How did you hear about it?" My heart beat fast as if I was in high school drama again.

"No. No, Cass. Just listen. Calm down. It's not that way. I heard you sneak out. You were never good at it. I thought you were going to meet the guys at the river as usual, and I had a crush on Terry, so I wanted to go but I didn't think you'd let me, so I waited a while."

"Terry?" I say shocked, "You had a crush on Snuff?"

"Yes. I know, crazy, huh? He was so nice, nothing like the other guys. I waited then I headed through the woods down the trail. It was scary as hell. I jumped a thousand times when I heard noises. And I got lost and off the trail a bit, because at night it looks different and I had a tiny flashlight, so that scared the bejesus out of me, so I turned around and went back to the beginning, and thank God, I found it or y'all would still be looking for me. I lost track of time. I was almost there, or close when I heard you screaming. It scared me to death. It was pitch dark except for the flashlight and the critter sounds in the woods seemed to scream with your scream, which made it worse. I just took off running as fast as I could. I got to the edge of the woods where I saw the fire, but I couldn't see anyone. I kept walking toward the noises and then I heard you scream louder. I knew it was coming from the water. I saw Mark's car, put everything together and…"

Meg started crying suddenly as she remembered. I cried with her, because I know what she saw. I closed my eyes and tried to hold it together, but knowing that my sister witnessed such a horrible event, made it ten times worse. It's as if we both were reliving a nightmare.

"You were screaming NO over and over." Meg's lips were quivering hard now, so much her voice was shaky. "I—I couldn't move. I couldn't speak. I wanted to help. Do something, but I couldn't move. My God, Cass, it was like I was out of my body or something. Maybe in shock. I don't know."

Hearing Meg took me back. I felt woozy and disoriented till I thought I might black out. Float to the void where all is numb. No feelings, tears, just nothingness.

"Then I'm just running. Cass, I'm running like the wind back to the house. I didn't stop till I got there, then I called Snuff."

"Youuuu WHAT?" I shouted in shock.

"I called Snuff. I had to. He was your best friend Cass. He was half-asleep and I was so out of breath and babbling, he thought it was a prank at first. But when I said your name, he woke up quick. Snuff and Pepper hauled ass.

"What? Pepper knows too?" I started to panic if I was reliving my high school gossip mill days. "Jesus ever-loving…" I sighed.

“He was the only one with a car Cass. Just listen.”

I rolled my eyes dreading the rest of the story as Meg continued.

“I hung up the phone and ran back down the trail as fast as I could to the dirt road where Snuff said they’d meet me. I had been running for a while when I heard a car and saw headlights coming from the river. I knew it was Mark. I don’t know what come over me, Cass, but this dark thing in me, this anger for what he did to you took over. I was scared he would get away with it. Then I saw a thick tree branch, still green, half the size of a two-by-four. I grabbed it. The next thing I know, I’m standing in the middle of the road holding a branch, possessed of something unnamed. And I was not moving. The grill of his car slid to a stop a few feet from me. The dust cloud made me choke but I didn’t move. I had an angry cry in me, Cass. One of those strange cries from another world. Broken, maddening, animalistic cries for revenge. I screamed for him to get out but he just laughed. I stormed over to his front windshield and told him on the count of three I was going to start swinging at glass. He got out when he thought his precious car was in danger. I was shaking all over. He could see it too.

“He looked me up and down and said, Well, well, what do we have here? So you’re the youngest Collard girl, aren’t you? Was it Mug, Mig or Mag? I stared a black hole of silence right through him as he walked closer. The more he talked with his big fat mouth, the angrier I got. Then he said, did you come to join your sister tonight? That’s some double trouble. A big ‘ole bowl of collard greens, whoo-wee. His eyes were hungry and dead. That’s when I swallowed the dark. The only sound I could hear in my head was your screams, and all I could see was his smug face, and flashbacks of him forcing his body on you. I snapped like a twig. I remember walking toward him like some battle-drawn soldier and I don’t think he expected it at all, like it was a game or something, which is why he didn't move. I had a stable target. I think he even laughed at me, which made me madder. Before I swung at his fat head I made a clarification. Loudly I said, you are a piece of shit. And by the way…my name is Meg, motherfucker.

"The next thing I remember is screeching tires. Then Snuff and Pepper pulling me off Mark while he was writhing in the dirt crying like a baby, all bloodied up."

"Damn Meg…your mean ass ways paid off." I laughed darkly just to keep from crying.

"Yeah, I was a mad porcupine with clawing nails and punching fists and swinging limbs. I was so fueled with adrenaline and anger, Snuff said I went at Mark a second time. So this is why I was in your bed that morning. I wanted to tell you after you got out of the shower, and I tried to, but you were long gone. I could tell."

"The scratch on your face, was it from the scuffle?" Hot tears streamed down my cheeks while my voice cracked.

"Yep, but did you see him?" Meg laughed.

I nodded, remembering that day in the hallway. I felt as if I was there again, facing the shadow that shifted my life. My insides were in knots.

"Snuff warned Mark if he even so much as glanced your way, Cass, he'd come after him and finish the job."

"I can't believe this," I said jarred with emotions. "All these years and I never knew. Why…why didn't you tell me? Why didn't Snuff say something? This is unbelievable."

"Cass, he did. He called and called. Plus, I tried to tell you even days later, but you refused to talk to anyone. You were in your own world of pain. After that, you know, we just grew up and it just never came up. I figured you tried to put it behind you."

"Oh, I put it behind me all right," I said, sighing. When I gathered my wits and came to terms with what Meg had actually done, I grabbed her hands. "Meg. You were so brave. I'm in awe you stood up to him. I guess your mean streak paid off." I smiled and cried at the same time.

"I should have done more, Cass. I should have stopped him before…you know…but I just…"

"Stop it, Meg. There was nothing you could have done to prevent it. *Nothing.* What you did was the bravest thing I've ever heard. I ran into Mark at school and his face looked like a bruised banana. You put a hurt on him. The son-of-a-bitch got a pine curtain ass-kicking he'll never forget. A collard green ass-kicking! I bet every time he sees a tree limb he trembles." We both cracked up laughing and embraced each other in a long hug of weeping and tears.

I grabbed the bottle and poured us two shots.

"I want to make a toast."

We raised our glasses. "You ready?" I said, looking at Meg gleefully.

"Yeahhh."

"And by the way, my name is Meg, motherfucker!" I said, laughing. Meg laughed too as we clinked our glasses together and chugged the bitter and sweet memories of our childhood. After the laughing stopped there was the familiar momentary lapse of silence between us, as if we both had to settle into what we had just revisited. Re-lived. The madness of our past mixed with the mayhem of our memories. I subconsciously braced myself. According to Maw Sue and all her tales, magic always follows mayhem. I had no idea it was fixing to reveal itself in ways unimaginable.

I got up and zig-zagged my drunken self to the bathroom. For a few minutes, I looked into the mirror. Three shadows appeared. Replicas, versions of me in eras long ago, the little girl, the teenager and the woman. They were fading in and out, touching but not quite merging as one.

I stumbled to the living room, "I've had way too many drinks. I'm seeing shit!" I said plopping down on the floor and laying my head against the couch cushions as the ceiling tiles spun in my vision.

"Cass…" Meg said in a chilling tone that was unsettling, "I think you'd better have another drink. I have to tell you about Mom."

I sprung upward too fast in rebellion. A familiar call to arms this family knows all too well.

"Hell noooo," I said falling back dizzy. "Only one mother lecture a year. And I've had a lifetime worth…just saying."

"I have to Cass. You need to know. Do you want a drink first?"

"Goddddddd…I don't have enough pills for this" I said mustering a sigh from the deepest parts of me. "I'm going to need years of therapy to recover from this night, this one night alone. But go ahead Meg. It's evident you're going to do this, regardless of what I want or say, so just spill it. At least I'm drunk. Maybe I won't remember tomorrow. Hey, maybe my amnesia will kick in again. Lord knows that would be great in this case. "

"Ohh…gosh, I don't even know how to start Cass, let me see…I mean, it's complicated…"

"For the love of baby Jesus, Meg, my whole life is complicated. We just clarified that the last two hours. So whatever you have to say, it couldn't be worse than that."

"Well…I think…. maybe it might, but I just…"

I rolled my eyes and looked at Meg snapping my fingers. "Get on with it sister! Geeeshhhh!"

"She was molested" Meg said barely audible. Her words were so soft I had to still myself as to what I had actually heard. There was a long silence as we stared at each other, a familiar unbelievable form of nostalgia without words, spinning cells and molecules inside us trying to find a way to speak the words we knew we needed to say, but couldn't. Mayhem colliding with madness as with everything else in our lives. I was inside myself, deeply wrapped within the House of Seven and my broken mind, stunned and shocked and trying to find stability in the already complicated mess of my life, my sister's life and now my mother's life. It was all too much.

"Wait, wait, wait just a second, Meg. Explain yourself. I'm in serious shock right now, absolutely crazy town, I mean spill it before I loose it..."

"I know. I was morbid about it too." Meg's eyes darted left to right as if she was trying to locate a semblance of sanity. "From what Mother told me..."

"She TOLD you?" I blurted cutting her off, "As in words from her lips, told you?"

This didn't sound at all like the mother I knew. Tell Meg? I was a tad angry, because she never told me squat. In my mind, I had flashbacks of me in childhood begging for her attention, begging her to talk to me.

"Do you want to hear the story or not? I'm trying here, Cass."

I blew out a long gust of exasperation held up from the seventies, from the room inside the House of Seven, the lipstick kisses room. "Sorry, my fault, go ahead." I poured another shot. I wasn't drunk enough for where this story was heading.

"I'll start at the beginning. Mother said she was eight when her mother, Merdeen, left for the first time. It's possible there were other times, but she couldn't remember. Her mom just left. No goodbye, no hug, no why or what-for, no nothing. She said the last thing she remembers was her mother folding clothes in the bedroom while she was occupied with paper dolls in the hallway. She heard the front door shut, so she ran to see. She heard the car crank and opened the door to see her mother driving away. Later she heard her father say she went to Galveston, the city of big dreams to start a new life. Mom was confused by this. Her dad,

Ernest, went after her and left Gabby with a distant uncle. I hate even saying the next part. It makes me sick to think about it."

Meg stopped and took a shot. I could tell she was having trouble telling the rest of the story. I could feel the oncoming weight, an impending doom on my heart, much like I'd felt as a child, waiting on the world to fling me off, cast me away to darkness. I felt faint and woozy as if this huge, unimaginable loss was coming toward me like an unstoppable comet seeking to blow up my world.

"Then it happened," Meg said with a weary glance, both of us unable to make eye contact, "The unimaginable happened to mom."

My heart sank. I slumped on the couch barely able to breathe or swallow the thick saliva building up in my mouth. My lips curled inward until they were numb.

"Ernest returned later without Merdeen. Life went on as usual but mom was, you know, broke. Changed. I mean, how does one process perversion like that so young?"

"They don't..." I said bluntly having experience in more ways than I wanted to admit.

"Then, get this...Merdeen returned as if nothing happened."

"Hmpt...familiar traits." I said remembering how nothing ever got resolved or talked about in our family.

"Oh, and one month later, she's pregnant. Nine months later, out pops mom's sister, Symphony."

"We have an aunt?" I yelled even more shocked."Seriously? Are you kidding me? I'll be damned. Mother has a sister? And her name is Symphony? What the hell? Did Merdeen get laid at the opera or something?"

Meg laughed, "It sure sounds like it, don't it. Mom said after her sister was born, everything went downhill from there. Merdeen went into something like a deep depression, sleeping all the time, rarely getting out of bed, and when she did, she was out of it. Mom said there was no food in the house, and her father had to regularly try to keep up with it and still work and he could never get through to her, she'd just look right through him as if he wasn't there. Mom had a fear Merdeen was going to leave again, and she was right. She left them all. Mom, the baby, everyone."

My mind clicked and roared and screamed into the empty places that now described why my mother is the way she is. What if I'd known back then? Would things be different? Would our relationship have been better? Would it have made a difference?

"Then it was repeat and replay, Merdeen leaving, Ernest going after her, mom and sister left at uncles, Ernest returning without her, and the whole shit show repeated itself over and over again. Mom said Ernest even had Merdeen locked up in the mental hospital for a month or so. She didn't go voluntarily either. Mom said these men showed up at the house one day and they forced her into a truck kicking and screaming. It was traumatic for Mom. She only learned later it was a state institution for the mentally ill."

By this time, my head was spinning. My mind seemed to go dark with thoughts of places like Castle Pines, and the things Maw Sue went through at those places, and I felt a tinge of compassion for this grandmother we never knew. I wondered if it was possible to have the curse on both sides of the family tree? If so, I didn't stand a chance. I could hear the moans and creaks of Castle Pines growing closer and closer. I grabbed my shot glass and poured another drink. I was rattled to the deep core of my being, so much I could feel the heavy weight of the House of Seven within me, the sounds of the word bones, the little girls running rampant. I did not know if I'd recover from this night.

"I'm still not finished Cass."

"Bloody hell." I said laying deep into the couch cushions hoping I'd sink and disappear into the fibers.

"If I had to hear this story…you are going to hear it" Meg said jumping on the end of the couch closer to me. "Mom said she was about ten years old and finally got the courage to tell her mother what her uncle was doing while she was gone. But, Merdeen didn't believe her. She slapped her and told her to stop talking fifth. Then dragged her to the kitchen and forced her to drink a glass of castor oil mixed with soap for lying. Who does that? I mean, after hearing all this, I can't even look at Mom the same. It's all I see when I look into her eyes."

Meg poured another shot. "After that, I think she gave up a little. Mom got older, Ernest and Merdeen fought more, and Ernest began to drink more, which intensified things. Mom said that she learned the warning signs. Arguments meant one of two things; her mother's departure, or going to the uncle's. Sometimes her mother stayed gone for days, for weeks, even months. No one knew where she was. Ernest would go on drinking binges. Home wasn't normal for them. There were no celebrations, no holidays, no birthdays, and no gifts at Christmas, no talking, no hugging, no caretaking, it was basically Mom tending and raising her own sister and trying to protect herself and Symphony from the uncle. She was thirteen when she put her foot down and refused to leave the house. She never saw her uncle again. Mom took care of Symphony while her mother continued her run-away sprees. Then mom met dad and the rest is history."

A messy history I thought to myself. I choked down a lump in my throat. It was hard to hear this about my own mother. The pain in my gut felt as if it was rising through my throat and strangling my ability to breathe. For the life of me, I did not want to cry for my mother. I had long ago erected a wall of stone against such things. No crying for Gabby. *Never. Not as a child. Not as a woman. Not now. Not then. Not ever.* To cry for her was to admit my weakness in needing her.

"I'm sorry. I thought you'd want to know, Cass. I figured it would explain Mom's moods and why she acts the way she does."

She shrugged. "Or it did for me. I mean look at all she went through. And think about it, we have an aunt. When I asked about Symphony, mom said that some things are just better left alone. She did say she's in Georgia, happily married with a family, and they talk once a year or so, but I got the feeling there was more, but mom wouldn't go into detail. I think it was hard enough for her to even say what she did. If anything, now I understand Mom's need to provide for us, like when we got every single gift imaginable under the sun. *Remember?* Mom has always been a caretaker. It's why she cooks. Cleans. Cares. She told me she never had a birthday party, not one. No cake, presents, nothing. Plus, what I find amazing is no matter what she went through growing up, *for us,* she did something different."

"Did she?" I said angrily and passive aggressive.

"Well, she tried too. Think about it. She made sure me and you were taken care of. We had everything we needed."

"Everything…except her." I snapped. My past would not let me agree with Meg. I sat traumatized. Angry, sad, disabled, confused. A hot fire steamed in my gut. Tears ran like rivers down my face. I felt like hard stone. My cheeks felt flushed as if someone had slapped me repeatedly. I was in complete shock. My mind tried to process all this information at one time. First, my sister Meg knew about the rape, and turns out, Snuff and Pepper did too. My sister has mental issues just like me and has butchered her flesh as bad as I have butchered my soul. Then my mother, who I have sought with every molecule in my flesh to KNOW all my life, and who I thought hated me to the core and basically disowned me as non-existent in her world—IS NOT the mother I thought she was. And we have an Aunt. Nothing is what it seemed. And now I realized most frighteningly of all, that our stories connected us in disturbing ways.

I shot up from the couch. "Do you know how much goddamned therapy I've had? I mean seriously like…a whole lot, like almost a year already. Once a week. Sit, talk, dump it out, figure it out, confront it! This is maddening." My voice was slurred and disjointed. "I just can't, I just don't get it." I laughed a hysterical cackle that turned into a waterfall of weeping tears and sorrow.

"Shit! I thought it was me." I said to no one, staring placidly into the nothingness of the walls. Then I spun around wild and enraged and filled with something I couldn't describe nor discard.

"Oh my God. All that time I thought it was me." I mumbled in revelation and despair pacing the living room like a lioness in a cage. "All ME. It was *always* me. I'm the reason. Me. Me. Me. I'm bad. No one can love me. I thought it was me.... that's what I thought the whole time. I thought it was me."

"What are you talking about, Cass?" Meg said confused and concerned, following me with her eyes as I bounced from one end of the room to the other.

"ME! I thought she hated me. I thought my own mother hated my guts. And it was all my fault. I was the reason she couldn't love me. I was unlovable. It was me. I tried to understand, make it right, fix it, correct it, rewrite it. GOD! I could never put it together why she couldn't love me. I did everything I knew to make her love me. I blamed myself. I was the monster she couldn't love."

I looked up at the pine board ceiling and let out a blood curdling wail. Part woman, part child, part something unnamed.

"I THOUGHT IT WAS ME!" And then I collapsed to the floor.

"Cass. Oh, my God, no. You thought it was you?" She said rushing to my side. "I had no idea. It wasn't. No, oh no. It wasn't you. You took too much of this on yourself and it wasn't yours. It wasn't you at all. It was him, the uncle and the craziness, the whole family actually, except for the sister. I think parts of mom were just gone, lost from what happened. But she did try, Cass. I think she really did. And she loved us, she did."

Meg held me and rocked me as she spoke.

"I'm sorry I didn't tell you sooner, I only found out two years ago. There were times, I meant to tell you, but either you and Sam would have a blowup or me and Bill would have one, so it was never good timing. Then you and Sam divorced, and the…"

"Fire." I spat cutting her off.

"No…I mean…"

"Me losing my mind." My voice was cold. Blunt. Abandoned.

"Not really, I mean, I just didn't know what was going on with you, it was a bad time, and I didn't want to add to it."

"Umm-huh…" I said feeling my mind slip away. All I could think about was calling Doc and telling her everything, but that was an overreaction. The next thing in my mind madness toolbox was to take everything out with forced activity. My mind and body was buzzing with anxiety and information so deep all I wanted was to react, even in danger, do something to get all of this out of me. It was the exact opposite of what Doc taught me. Reacting always got me into trouble. Tonight was no different. The intense desire to find a body, the body of a man, to release my pain through wild and casual sex slid into the folds of my brain like an intense orgasm I hadn't had yet. My emotions were nerve endings, alive and on fire, stimulating my entire system to overload. A need to release, vent, to let go of what bound me. I felt crazed, on the edge of something destructive. At least being with Meg gave me a sense of protection I needed during this moment of impending doom.

"Why mom told me Cass, after all this time, I have no idea. It just came out of nowhere," Meg said breaking the awkward silence of secrets. "You know how Mom is. How stuff suddenly spews out of her from the past. It never made sense to us. We didn't know, of course. Normally, I just overlook it, but that day

—oh my god. I couldn't stop her. It was like listening to a little girl talk. I can't process it. What do you do when you hear something so horrible?"

Meg's voice faded—although I could still clearly understand her, I couldn't mentally absorb it. The heat of my internal organs overwhelmed me. The House of Seven convulsed and contorted. All the hate, anger, misunderstanding, sadness, confusion and rejection, sympathy and compassion I felt for my mother, past and present, clashed inside me. Her story, then my story all blended together. Would it have made a difference if I'd known—would it have changed things? The mere thought rocked me. The world I had been holding up with my little girl hands dropped and splintered into a million pieces, and I lay in the wreckage. Unable to withstand the onslaught of words circling in my head, the broken knob clicked and spun. I collapsed on the floor and bawled like a child. Meg rushed to my side.

"It wasn't me," I said in whimpers. "It wasn't me." Inside the House of Seven a little girl screamed to the heavens, past the clouds, the black angels, the stars, the Mother Moonshine I'd tried so hard to reach. Together we cried. My tears were unlike any I'd ever cried before. *For myself. For my mother. For the little girls we lost. For the women each of us had become through survival, through necessity—because of our past.*

We were not the reason for the chaos and the undoing in our family. In therapy I'd learned about projection. *What it meant. How it affected me.* I see it from another perspective now. It was my mother who projected her feelings onto me.

Her feelings. Not mine. *Her past…her pain.* Not mine.

It wasn't me after all.

In the moments following, when my mind settled into a quiet discontent, I began to ponder. I remembered Doc's words. Because I was a keeper of things, mostly words, intentions, life events and the like, I deeply internalize them. Keep them close to me. I cling, I grab, I desperately believe I can fix them. And so, I make them my own. They become part of me. This is what I did with my mother. From beginning to end. Every single piece of it. It was my mother's. Her feelings, her pain coming out. None of it was mine to fix, to keep, to hoard. *It wasn't me.*

As a child, for the longest time, all I could fixate on was why my mother hated me. Why she didn't talk to me when I begged her to? Why she couldn't love me—see me—hold me—kiss me. I watched other mother-daughter relationships with affection and love and yet, I couldn't get a word. The whole time I thought it was me. But it wasn't. My mother's issues were her issues. What's worse, my issues affected the whole of everything else, and meshed with all the other issues of the family. After the great sadness at the river, unbeknownst to me, I followed my mother's example.

It didn't happen, I told myself. Everything is okay.

I pretended. I pushed it down. I denied.

But it *did* happen. Everything *wasn't* okay. The horrible, awful terrible happened to me. Just like the horrible, awful terrible happened to my mother. It was neither of our faults—nonetheless, we were greatly affected by our response to the horrible, terrible. Now I understand why Doc puts so much emphasis on confronting, dealing, grieving and healing. To do otherwise will harm yourself and possibly others. Growing up I experienced my mother as a powerful and negative force in my life. I went to great lengths to garner her approval and put great effort into pleasing her, hoping to get love in return. I did the same with marriage and relationships. The horrible rape only intensified my own personal thoughts of unworthiness, and sealed my fate of re-enacting the event in hopes of righting it. My mother was unable to love me the way I desired and needed, because she herself had not received a form of love. Affectionate, hugging, embracing. Her idea of touch had been tainted, warped and damaged so she knew no other way, except caretaking, providing, giving gifts, tending, cooking and so forth. I never knew this to be a form of love until now.

I can only assume when my mother struggled with her past, she had nowhere to put the feelings of pain, she had no outlet of blue lines or therapy to help her. Instead, her negative feelings of self-worth spilled out on me, on Dad, on Meg. But mostly, on herself. In turn, and because I didn't know any better, I internalized the words and blamed myself. I was unlovable, unwanted, a bad little girl. I was the monster she couldn't love. But it was projection all along. If you never deal with and confront your past, Doc says it will come out somewhere, in some form. Doc calls it denial till death. Back then, people just didn't talk about their problems, and they certainly didn't go to therapy to talk to a stranger about them. Taboo subjects were to be denied, overlooked, and stuffed down. The issues with her own mother had to contribute.

Denial till death. My mother tried in her own way, perhaps, to rewrite her past and make it right. *Stay. Be the mom. Be the caretaker. Never leave. Never confront. Never confess.* But in doing this, shutting down her emotions, she also shut away her affection, her closeness to others.

The unearthing of family secrets shifted me. Altered me in ways I can't describe. It also changed my whole outlook on many things. I saw my mother. Really saw the essence of her. I understood her distance. Her withdrawal, her unavailability. Like both sides of the moon, I could now see the dark side and the Mother Moonshine. I saw the scared little girl. I saw the woman. I saw the mother. Underneath the parental role, my mother had a fear of abandonment, anxiety, worthlessness, and deeply misguided sexual issues she projected onto me. They were in no way *of me*—not at all. But as a child I had no way of knowing it. Her unavailability to love me the way I sought to be loved was not her fault. She loved the only way she knew how. *Survival mode.*

As a young girl, my overt desire to be a woman, along with my early exposure to pornography magazines, all set off a threat in my mother, an internal alarm to protect and defend. Who knows, she may have seen Symphony in me, or had flashbacks of the times she stayed with the uncle. I may never know, but under the circumstances, who's to say what one will do when it comes to our children? I cannot blame her anymore. She didn't have therapy, pink pills or blue lines. My mother had no one. She kept her secrets until she told my sister. Meg might be the only soul to ever hear the secret out of my mother's lips. I pray it will start a healing in her. As it is starting to do with me. It will take time for me to integrate this into my life and absorb the impact it had, and will have in the future. Words have power to destroy and to heal. I know this all too well. I have a whole damn cemetery full of word bones. Now, I'm just trying to process how a bottle of tequila and slumber party with my sister completely kicked my ass, transformed my life and I'll be damned, helped me deeply understand my mother…Mother Moonshine, for the first time. *Ever.* Oddly, what kept us apart is now what links us together, and more disturbingly connects us in ways we could have never imagined.

At bedtime, I took a deep breath as to let the night rest as one lone tear rolled down my face sideways and crashed onto the sheets. I spilled off into the twilight of sleep but not before I noticed that Meg had to be a tangled vine and hook her leg ever so slightly on top of mine like she did when we were kids.

The next morning, I didn't remember where I was. I sat up and my head was as heavy as a tree stump. I turned to swing my legs off the bed and my eyes focused on a glass of water and a bottle of aspirin.

"Oh, thank God." I said in a whisper. The echoes in my head pounded and my mouth was dry as cotton. Meg appeared in the doorway with two cups.

"Coffee, Ms. Sunshine?"

"I'll take the pitcher."

Meg laughed. "Don't worry. I'm right where you are. I've been up an hour, already took my aspirin. And girl, we damn near drank a whole bottle, can you believe it?"

"Yep…by the drums in my head I believe it. Mmmm…this is so good."

"It's a good kind of hurt though, right?"

"I suppose," I said gulping down the coffee and sitting up against the bed.

"Don't forget. We got the funeral today" Meg said frowning.

My heart sank. I forgot about the funeral.

"God. I don't think I have any tears left."

"Me too, Cass. Last night was rough for me. I mean it. I've been carrying around those secrets for so long I swear to God I think they started to eat me alive from the inside out. I feel a hundred percent better now, well, minus the hangover."

"I'm glad Mother told you, Meg. I'm glad we had this time together. We never do this enough, do we?"

"No…we don't. I think when Bill goes out of town, we'll have to have one again. What do you say?"

"Sure…. just give me time to recover from this one. I feel like I've been hit with a dysfunctional backwoods meteorite."

Meg started laughing loudly.

"Too noisy," I said. "Can I have more coffee?"

"It's in the kitchen. I'm heading to the shower. Don't leave, okay? Wait till I get out."

"Yeah, yeah…whatever." I nodded and made my way to the kitchen, my head heavy and wobbling.

It took me three cups of strong coffee and two more headache pills to feel a tad bit normal again. I still felt a little drunk and in shock from all the confessions.

I lingered at the kitchen bar nursing my hangover with coffee until an hour or so passed and Meg strutted out like a peacock all shiny with clothes and makeup.

"Not fair," I blurted, "I look like crap and you're all sparkly and shit."

"Well, believe me, I don't feel sparkly. More like the shit. The clothes deceive. You want more coffee? I'll make another pot?"

"No, no. I'm good. I feel like a drunk jumping bean I've had so much. I need to get home and mentally prepare myself, take a shower and get all sparkly like you." I smirked.

"Wait, Cass, before you go, I need to give you something. Don't move. Wait right here."

Meg disappeared into her bedroom. If she comes out and tells me one more secret, I thought, I swear to God I will render her a throat punch. I can't take another family secret. Meg came back smiling like a possum with her arms behind her.

"I can't deal with any more secrets, Meg…what is it?"

"Aww pooh! Cass, just close your eyes. You'll spoil it."

"Geesh. What if I fall off this barstool?" I whined.

"Then I'll get on the floor with you. Now close your eyes, smarty pants." I made a face and closed my eyes. Underneath my lids, I felt out of control, spinning in orbit, black time, spirits and flashes of shadows and secrets.

"Okay. Open your eyes." Meg said in a chippy voice.

I opened my eyes. I blinked. I blinked again. Surely what I was seeing was not real. Was I delusional? Did I black out suddenly? I was brought fully alert when Meg started clapping her hands like she did when we were kids opening Christmas presents.

"It's your mirror bin," she yelled. "Aren't you excited?"

I fell deep into my mind trying to recover memories of it, what happened to it. I just assumed it disappeared when I did. But there it was like a king on a throne, a long-lost idol waiting on me to bow to its majesty. The pewter mirrored lid on top flashed a prism of light I hadn't seen in ages. My heart squirmed. I looked up at Meg in disbelief.

"How? Where? When?" I blurted.

"Mom."

"Myyy mother?" I said baffled and pointed to Meg. "Like your mom…and my mother?"

"Yes. Isn't it exciting? Dad found it in the well shed along with some books and stuff Maw Sue left behind that apparently Mama C kept and then after she passed, Papa C boxed it up. And you won't believe what's in the other box. All kinds of old strange books and handwritten scrolls, diaries and other stuff. You know more about Seventh Tribe stuff than I do. It's yours now. I'll load it up before you leave. Mom meant to give it to you yesterday, but the cobbler incident had everyone undone. Oh…and I have my mirror bin too. It still had the green scarf in it. Remember?"

She reached underneath the bar and took out her mirror bin, the one that belonged to Aunt Raven. The room seemed to fill with magic, particles of time and place that made me dizzy and yet, hopeful. The mirror bins sat on the bar side by side, blood to blood, sister to sister, generation to generation. I stared at both objects in disbelief as if they had magically appeared, through some method of time travel, spilling out spirits of yesterday. My mind instantly flashed images, seven sisters, drops of blood, the sizzling amber glow of number seven, petal people and voices I didn't recognize. There was an odd hum in the air as if the whole room vibrated at a low level, like the buzz of a beehive from a distance. I felt like a little girl again. The one who believed in magic. I reached over to touch the pewter mirror on the outer lid of my bin and my heart did flip-flops. The energy of it was alive and filled my ears with strange whispers and noises. A glimmer altered my vision.

Seeing—hearing—knowing.

I knew deep in my soul and my spirit that my life was about to change. Touching the mirror bin was like touching the heart of a child and hearing it beat for the first time—but not *any* child.

The child.

The little girl.

The one I left behind the pine curtain.

CLUSTERS AND CASS

The mind is not a vessel to
be filled but a fire to be kindled
- Plutarch

My skin breaks out in a cold sweat as I turn into the cemetery. Noises filter in and out, car doors and low murmurs. A mass of people encroaches the funeral tent. I stare at Papa C's coffin while the preacher does his thing. *Yada-yada, blessings, Heaven, spirits, amen.* The bugle plays "Taps" since he was a WWII hero. I'm lost in an elegy of sorrows. The musical notes grow strong hands and clutch each person by the throat until they choke and break down. The last note holds on, refusing to say goodbye. *I understand.* I hate goodbyes. It bounces off head-stones, pewter vases and angelic statues with chubby faces. It splits rocks, cracks the earth, shakes the heavens and makes angels weep. I stare into the vast portal of scattered souls laid to rest through the ages. My vision blurs. I feel removed from everyone around me. I'm held inside a thin strip of space where two worlds intersect, each yearning for the other.

I wonder if this is how the Seventh Tribe felt when they conducted their ceremonies, feeling the space of time existing in this world and the next colliding, intermingling with in-between places. Did they feel like giving in? Did they touch the void? *The gap, the place of entanglement.* Were they taken by it, in ecstasy or madness? Maw Sue's voice enters in my tender aching ears.

"It's not your season, Cass. You keep moving forward. Be a seeker. Blessed. Anointed. Beloved. I am proud of you and Meg." The words stir up a plethora of childhood memories. A veil is lifted. My gift is accelerated. Never before have I crossed this line of enchanted dazzling interpretation. *I see things. I hear things.*

Across the cemetery there is a sea of people, a faint glow of souls dimly lit at each tomb. Each one is holding a flower, just like the petal people, the Everlasting Immortelles. Every facial expression holds a story, their eyes wet with memory, with joy and sorrow. My mind hears their voices and a thousand words rush in, poured out like sweet sap straight to my gifted ears. Their otherworldly faces are unlike anything I have ever seen, a candle glow lit from another world, an eternal flame consuming them, keeping them, as they wait expectantly for others to follow. And then I see her and him. My breath feels sucked from my body. May Dell and Papa C stand together behind the tombstone. They both are smiling with eyes glowing from another world. *I look.* I look with tears of joy and tears of pain. But mostly, I look with love.

The gravesite funeral is brief. Family and friends had left leaving only me and Meg and our parents. I can't help but stare at my mother differently. I wonder if she knows, that I know, and does my face show it? She catches my eyes while they are getting in the car to leave and holds my stare for just a mere moment, and then turns away. Meg waves to them and sits down beside me. In her hand is a white carnation.

"Petal people?" I say.

"Yes," Meg says, smiling. "I'm freaking exhausted though. I'm going home for a nap. How about you?"

"I'm heading out soon," I say, hugging her. "Thank you for last night, Meg. It's helped me. More than you'll ever know."

"Seventh Tribe, Sis. Bonded by blood." We high-five and hug. "Love you much."

"I love you too," I say, pondering the flux of information from the past twenty-four hours. After she drives away, the cemetery is silent, subdued. I go over to Papa C's casket and pluck a yellow rose. I place my hand on the flower arrangement over the casket and close my eyes to say a prayer. Before I can utter a word, pain jolts me undone. I jerk back to see blood trickle down my finger, spilling into my palm. It is thick and slow-crawling and unleashes a terrible, awful emergence inside the house, inside me. Flashes of the moss tree damsels with spirited eyes cross my mind, the door of the house blazes a fiery number seven, and a thousand screaming sirens are going off inside the walls, stirring up insidious commotions, a topsy-turvy, chaotic, spinning orbit of existence making me insane. Lights flick on and off, doors open and shut violently, windows pop open and close, glass breaks and boards splinter. Roses and flower petals explode like confetti, blood pools up from the floor joists while light beams turn into swords and battle the dark shadows. An assortment of hands prick, prod, reach and grab at me. As the lights flicker, I catch a glimpse of the shadows haunting me my whole life. *She* is standing amongst them. She is stronger and able to stand within them without letting them destroy her. She is an accumulation of every little girl I've encountered since my memories came back. In a blitz of images, it's me at five, at six, seven, at eight, at ten, twelve, fifteen and sixteen. A freaky carousel of little girls going round and round all looking at me. My vision goes black, then pushes me back to the cemetery in a blur. I grab the casket in front of me to keep from falling. It feels clammy. When my vision clears, I realize my hand is touching her hand. SHE is perched on top of my grandfather's casket like the DQ of the Dairy Queen. Immediately she has control of me, inside and out.

"It's just you and me, Cass," she says laughing and pointing to herself, then me. "You—me—us. Yeah, I know. It's kind of hard to understand and put into words since we are the same, huh? I'm a bigger part of you than you want to admit, since you've denied me half the time. I'm the main cluster, you can bet your life on it. Even your Doc lady would agree."

Something inside me uncurls and stretches its claws, awakened for the first time. "Oh…don't even try it. I can read your thoughts," the little girl says. "Make me seven—make me seven." Her tone is mocking and childish. She is holding a creepy, dried white rose, wicked almost, mangled and torn. Her battle worn eyes stay glued to me as if she is simply reading a book about my life, page by page, detailing every sin, every secret transgression, every single thought and deed. She is the exact replica of my dreams and nightmares, still dressed in hideous patchwork shorts and an orange t-shirt, freckled face and a cascade of limp dishwater hair. She is barefoot and her toes are spotted with peeling red nail polish.

"No. You're not imagining this," the little girl says. "This is real. Cass real. Cassidy Cleopatra Collard real. Cluster real. Seventh Tribe real. Seeker real." She spins the rose in her hands. I notice her finger is cut exactly where my finger is cut, identical blood drops from the thorn dripping one after another, and she has the same seven scar. I'm not sure if I'm hallucinating or daydreaming or if I'm going insane.

"Oh. You're seeing me all right, Cass. You do," she says, pointing her fingers to her eyes, then mine. "So…*now* that you've acknowledged my existence…and let me just say, gosh almighty and Lord Tarnation, you are a stubborn shit. I thought I was going to be stuck inside the House of Seven forever. It's about time you listened to me and let me out…finally."

She wipes the damp sweat from her face and pulls her hair off her neck. She leans forward and draws my eyes to hers.

"I encourage you to go forward and that means you don't have a choice, unless you *want* to remain stuck and circle the freaking mountain of stuck for the rest of your life. I tell you this much, I'M NOT going back in. I'm done with secrets."

She laughs in an extra sort of way that stirs up memories. "It's time to do what seekers do, Cass. You know the drill. Maw Sue taught you all you need to know and that therapist, Doc, she knows too. Do what she taught you. Work it out, Cass. Black angels, blue lines, you know the drill. Look into the void. Remember the magic is in you. It's always been in you."

The girl reaches out and touches my cheek in the way I want to touch hers. Her lips never move but my gifted ears hear her speak. There is a long-drawn-out silence in between what I hear and what I want to believe. Her hands lift toward the sky.

"Use the gift, Cass. Reach, reach, reach."

My right-hand lifts in response to a magical force. "*Make me seven—make me seven.*" Whispers fill the gap between my ears. A hard resistance fights me internally and externally. Shadows emerge but I don't engage them. I face the little girl. Our hands lift and clasp together. My ears fill with the sounds of a thousand voices, hers, mine, Maw Sue's, Papa and Mama C's, Big Pops', Jesus, the apostles, the prophets, the petal people, the seven sisters, the whole Seventh Tribe and so many voices from the graves. Words in unison, across time and death, across family lines and ages, centuries, generations, all speaking to form a cosmic intervention, inside me and outside me. *Beyond me.*

A bolt of electricity shoots through me. I fall slowly forward and emerge inside a thick fog, falling without control; I lose my balance and mobility. I go right through the little girl, her figure a transparent apparition, like seeing my own reflection in glass, *of me, of her, of us*, all tangled up. Step by step, second by second, the world I know, the world I seek, the shadows hunting me, the child I hate, and the child I love. We touch, we merge together, her visions, my visions, my fears, her courage, her fears, my weakness, our vows, our faults, our good, our bad, sweet sap, bitter sap, Southern sap, bleeding and healing, wild roses, drips of blood, voices from petal people speaking, talking, shouting, and telling twisted tales. Then a shuddering silence covers me.

My mind at rest. My madness stilled. It is a peaceful calm. I'm not sure how long I stayed in this state of relaxation, like floating. Perhaps I am dead and this is how it feels at peace, at quiet, at rest. When I come to myself, I am every bit alive and on my knees in front of the casket. The little girl is gone. I am alone. *Everything is different. Everything is the same.*

I had crossed a line in the sand, stepped over a barrier and entered a realm of magical oneness, and then fell back to earth, never to return to where I was. Or how I was. I hear a voice out of the earth, below and above, beyond and inward, internal and external, a whisper in the dust, a stirring voice so quiet, it is loud, and so overwhelming it calms nature to a deep sleep, a subtle trance. A connection of unity, transformation, and transcending pricks my soul with terrible, splendid wonders. Particles, little decibels of righteous fury enter the foundation of the cursed house within me, making a disturbance, throwing on light, spilling out truth and sending the shadows into chaos and turmoil. The wisp of spirit speaks like ferocious winds wrapping around trees and whipping the branches. *We are one. The girl and I are one. The adult. The child. As it should be.*

I accept the woman I was, the woman I am and the woman I should be. The woman I will be. I look and accept the little girl in darkness and light, in the good and the bad, I accept her. Her victories and her defeats. I love her unconditionally. I accept what I know and what I don't understand. I look to let go. I finally accept her, accept me—in fullness, all the clusters of Cass, black angels, broken knobs, and blue lines.

ALL IS SEVEN

For a man to conquer himself is the first and noblest of all victories* - *Plato

Weeks after Papa C's funeral and my partial acceptance of the little girl inside me, a valid part of my whole self, I began to have an influx of memory flashbacks, more vivid than ever before. The same scathing flashes, images, dripping blood, then the gentle rain followed by a memory.

It was a typical day in 1970-something. It must have been August because it was hot with scorching sun and dishrag humidity. Meg and I were riding in the front seat of Maw Sue's Ford Ranchero, which was a new concept in the automobile industry, a car with one full front seat but a bed like a truck, the best of both worlds. We had the windows down, on our way back from the Pick-N-Pack. Maw Sue skidded to a stop and Meg and I were catapulted to the dashboard and ended up in the floorboard. Maw

Sue opened the door and ran out. Meg and I untangled ourselves, jumped up and followed.

Lying in the middle of the road was a barn owl. Its wings were disjointed and its eyes aglow and it was still breathing.

"Did we hit it?" I screamed.

"No, child, we didn't but someone did and it's suffering," Maw Sue said concerned.

"It's hurting, Maw Sue, what do we do, what do we do?"

"Girls, quit your bantering." She said walking back to her car. She lifted the seat and pulled out a machete and began walking toward the owl. My eyes sprang from their sockets. Meg let out an awkward squeal.

"But…but can't you save it? There has to be something we can do."

"I am saving it." Maw Sue said just as the blade sliced through the neck bone. Air swishing, shifting and spiraling through a funnel until it hit my eardrums painfully.

"Girls…sometimes death *is* merciful." Maw Sue said glancing up at us, "Especially for the sacred."

My heartbeat wouldn't slow down and I couldn't catch air in my lungs. A strange fog fell upon the earth, engulfed us, and vaporized as if it had never been. The sky regained its bluish tint and the rays of torrid heat returned to punish us. Maw Sue picked the owl up in two pieces and chunked it in the back of her Ford. Meg and I watched it roll around in the bed of the truck with tears in our eyes. At dusk Maw Sue asked us to come over and bring our mirror bins. We were puzzled and yet fascinated as to what she was going to do.

Meg squinted and snarled, "I'm not eating an owl, Cass. I'm not."

I laughed. "Me neither."

We arrived to find a campfire out in the backyard lit with candles in the shape of a seven. We knew it was some sort of ceremonial tradition, attributing to the Seventh Tribe, but we didn't know what we were in for. Maw Sue had cut the foot talons from the owl which was kind of creepy. The long spiky tongs lay near the flames on a piece of white cloth surrounded by pieces of bone, feathers and twine. Suddenly, my heart leapt backwards as my eyes focused on the fire. Squished between the logs the owl carcass was eaten up by the leaping flames, now only bones and particles of flesh, its skull peering out at me with empty eye holes glowing yellow and orange. The smoke smelled like rosemary. Maw Sue was known to spice up fires with herbs and tonics. This was common in most of the ceremonies we've had before, but none of them involved roasting a dead owl. For a split second, I wondered if Maw Sue was crazy and the townsfolk might be right in their assumptions. And then I hated myself for even doubting her. *This is just tradition*, I told myself, *just ritual, pure and simple.*

Meg had gradually nudged herself as close to my side as possible and her right hand draped against my thigh for stability. I gulped a hard spirit of unknowing. We watched Maw Sue with curiosity. She was throwing spices and herbs into the fire. It glowed a prism of colors. I watched the owl's eye sockets turn from red to green to yellow and then blue. Maw Sue was praying and chanting the strange language of seven we seldom understood.

She had a small sharp knife in her hand. "Girls, set your mirror bins at your feet." We did as she said and placed the heirlooms on the ground. I swear I could hear a thousand whispers inside the mirror bin, words I couldn't decipher, the same voices that echoed inside my head at times. It was strange. I glanced down at the ground to the pewter mirror on top of the bin and saw reflections, swirling shadows of ghost people, human forms dancing and slinking, and moving in all sorts of ways. Floating all around them were the petals of a hundred different flowers swept up by the wind and the flames from the fire that leapt beside it. In this moment, I knew we were not alone.

"Your ancestors performed this exact ceremony years and years ago," Maw Sue said, her voice dark and mysterious like a spell. She stared deeply into our eyes with her gaze of gray. Hanging on her wrist were two necklaces made from owl bones and feathers wrapped with twine, and clinging to each one was an owl talon.

"I have been waiting for this moment for years, girls, I just didn't know when it was coming. But today is the chosen day. You see, girls… Owls have inner light." Her words seemed to disperse glitter fragments when they left her lips. "This is why they travel in the dark with the unknown. When others are blind and helpless and lost, the owl has wisdom in its eyes because the eyes are the inner light of its soul. Never leave a wounded owl to its own death. It will suffer needlessly. Tradition requires a sacrifice. The sacrifice allows the owl to pass its inner light of vision onto others. Today is a special day. From this moment onward, each of you will have the capacity to find your way in this life, no matter how dark it gets, no matter if you are lost, or without hope, look for your inner light. It is your wisdom. It is your heritage. It will guide you to the one true light. The one true lamb of God. The blood you spill tonight will mix with the blood of your ancestors who also shared the inner light. My ancestors did it, I did it and now you shall do it. I will place a symbolic number, a seven on your palm, like mine," she said, holding out her palm to show us the scar shaped like a seven. "Seven is symbolic of the ancient tribe. The divine wholeness of your inner light."

There was a mystery in the atmosphere. The necklaces, the owl carcass, the fiery flames, Maw Sue's words about blood and her strange seven scar. I was scared but even so, something inside me begged for it, as if it was meant for me. Meg brushed against me and we looked at each other. I gave her the big sister look of assurance it would be okay.

"I'll go first," I said, holding out my arm.

"This will hurt a little, girls, but only for a minute and then I'll spread some Immortelles healing salve on it and the pain will stop right away, I promise. Okay?" Meg and I looked at each other and nodded. Every scratch, cut, insect bite or scrape we ever got had seen that salve and it was kinda magic, because it stopped the pain and itch of just about anything. Meg and I called it Maw Sue's magic goo.

"I am so excited, girls. You are about to be joined with the Seventh Tribe. A spirit world of seven that few people ever experience." Her voice was raspy and she had a dip of snuff in her cheek but her voice held a sense of expectation to it I yearned for. I held out my palm and she wiped a thin clear salve across it. It had a strong smell like alcohol. She bent down by the fire and placed the knife tip inside the owl's eye bone while the flames licked it. She pulled it out and waved her arm like a flapping bird with one wing. I tried not to pant but I couldn't control my breath because my heart was beating so fast. Meg was nudged up so close to me she was nearly attached to my side. I put on a brave face as Maw Sue said some strange words and placed the knife tip on my palm and cut it into the shape of a seven. It stung and hurt a bit but not for long. The blood rushed out. I felt faint, yet oddly connected to something beyond me. Maw Sue turned my hand sideways while the blood pooled and seven red drops fell into the open mirror bin at my feet. Each drop of blood soaking into ancient wood gave me a sense of something I didn't have before. I felt a gleam in my eyes, an inner light flicker. A lightness in my chest and a spring in my step. My face felt as if it was shining. My lips parted slightly and a calmness of breath exhaled. I felt a flutter in my belly and a jolt, then a floating sensation as if all my burdens had been removed. Mostly, I had a sense of belonging. I was a part of something bigger than me.

Maw Sue was chanting her strange language, prayers and incantations. The abundance of shadows inside the mirror bin were now in the world around us, circling the fire like shadow dancers, all holding mason jars full of assorted dried flowers. They spoke the same words Maw Sue was speaking, in unison, till it sounded like the whole world was speaking.

When the last drop of blood spilled, it stopped. The voices, the chanting, the sounds, the dancing shadows, all of it ceased. Maw Sue's face turned to stone momentarily, and then back to her usual self. I felt a sense of unsteadiness, wobbly on my bare feet. Maw Sue grabbed me and said, "Well done, my child, well done. Welcome to the Seventh Tribe."

The atmosphere seemed odd, as if I had drifted from the netherworld. I could hear crickets and the fire crackling and the wind howling across the pines, but the shadows and sounds were gone. I felt a tinge of sadness, of longing. I did feel different, changed, almost re-born.

"Girls, I need you to keep your wound hidden until it heals. Others don't understand our old ways. Can you do that?" We both nodded. We knew a long time ago to keep the secrets and the stories Maw Sue told to ourselves because other people think Maw Sue is crazy, but we knew the truth. She had just finished doctoring my wound with magic goo and a bandage and I felt no pain. Meg was practically a zombie attached to my shoulder now.

"Just a pinch. No worries, Meg. It's over quick. It's worth it. I swear." I said reaching out to hold her hand to give her some reassurance. I watched Maw Sue carve a seven into Meg's palm and drip the blood into the mirror bin, the amulet of our ancestors. My sister was wearing Aunt Raven's green scarf around her neck, and slung over her shoulder. To my surprise I got to see the dancing shadows again, as if the magical vision was in me to stay. It was

Aunt Raven's shadow who caught my attention, dancing around Meg admiring her old scarf. I recognized her from old pictures I found inside the old Seventh Tribe Scrolls and books in Maw Sue's closet. Meg noticed it too because her eyes were as wide as pies as she followed the shadow dancers around. With the last drop of blood, the vision stopped. "You did wonderful, Meg. Welcome to the Seventh Tribe family," Maw Sue said, bandaging Meg's hand.

"Girls, now we shall finalize the ceremony with the wisdom of the owl. First we shout. We scream like an owl into the night. This is how you do it. Listen to me and then join me, okay?"

We both looked at her intently with wonder and glee. She started hooting like an owl, then a barking hoot, a whistling hoot and a screeching hoot. It was wild and one with nature and we loved it. We joined in with Maw Sue hooting and hollering and being one with the owls. We sang until we all fell out laughing. Once we caught our breath and sat in stillness of the darkness with only the sound of crickets and night creatures, Maw Sue asked us if we were ready for the rest of the ceremony. And we jumped up excited for more.

"We'll seal the amulet when we're done." She says bending down. She picked up a wooden bowl of blood and our hearts beat fast. She dripped seven drops into each mirror bin, then dipped her forefinger in the owl's blood and stirred it around. She turned to face us. "This is the blood of the owl who has sacrificed his inner light so you may have it in your journey of life." She stood in front of me first, and placed a streak on my face, one for every word, inner light, divine wisdom, vision and love. Then she drew swirls and designs. I looked at Meg and she looked at me. We laughed. Then she stood before my sister and repeated the process. Before it was over, Maw Sue said we looked like traditional Seventh Tribe warriors and our ancestors would be very proud.

We didn't know it then, but everything we just experienced would usher in a storm. A battle was coming that very night. A battle that would tragically upend us all.

Maw Sue sat the bowl down and bent down on our level. She was smiling and her gray eyes glowed milky white like they were lit from the otherworld. She placed the twine necklace of bones and feathers around our necks and placed the owl talon in our carved seven hands. She bent her forehead to ours and embraced us in a circle of three. A heaviness surrounded us, as if every shadowy presence was encircling us. I saw them in my inner vision; an embodiment of protection, love, spirit, enlightenment, vision, guidance, leading, wisdom—all our inner lights glowing at once. While Maw Sue prayed over us, I shook with the intensity of a thunderstorm, and in my mind, I saw the barn owl soar above us, outstretched wings, and eyes glowing like fire. I sobbed with gushes of tears and snot till I heaved with deep breaths. It was one of the strangest, most emotional and spiritual moments I've ever had. Of course, leave it to my sister to interrupt emotion. Miss Unemotional Meg could not handle a lick of heartfelt pain, so she created a diversion by singing our favorite tribal song and dancing around the fire holding up her owl talon. Maw Sue and I were not ones to turn down a good song and dance, so we joined her. We sang *Minnie the Moocher* so much over the years, we finally made up our own tribal song and we sang it to the heavens.

"Heyyyyyy-oo-ohhhh *(Whoa-oaaa-aohhh)*
Whoa-a-a-a-ahhhh *(heyyyyy-oohhhh)*
Whik-kiii, whik-kii, whik-kii *(it's getting kinda sticky)*
Heyyyy, whoa-oaah (the Gods are very picky)
Jiggy, jiggy, jiggy (get on down-touch the ground)
Crown, crown, crown. (and we don't mess around)
We are the Seventh Tribe (break it down, down, down)
Whoo-whaa-whaa, whoo-whaa-whaa
Heyyyyyy-oo-ohhh *(Whoa-oaaa-aohhh)*"

We danced and sang and laughed and held up our owl talons until we wore Maw Sue out. Meg and I collapsed in the dirt beside the fire and Maw Sue sat on her tree stump tuckered out.

In the silence we all stared into the fire with an alert gaze and a solidarity we'd never felt before. Just when I caught my breath, I turned to talk to Meg. I caught it in the corner of my eye. Out of the dark a shadow emerged, pale skin, black hair and angry blue eyes. Gabby stood in the mist of smoke like a deranged ghost. Our mother did not look happy. At first, she just stared blankly, no words, only a disconnecting glare which parted tree branches, made insects scurry, and night birds cry out. Something told me that we were toast. Everything spun out of orbit. She ripped off our bandages and kicked the bowls of blood across the lawn splattering it like a crime scene.

"Have you lost your mind?" she yelled and made a dodge at Maw Sue.

"Now Gabby…" Maw Sue stood up to calm her, but it was too late to reason. The whole world spun out of control. Our mother flipped smooth out and went toe-to-toe with Maw Sue, screaming and cursing all sorts of obscenities. Meg and I pulled on Mother's arms and begged her to stop and try to understand, but no matter what we said, she pushed us away and would not listen. The rattling necklace bones gave a clatter. Seeing them must have undone her. She reached down and jerked them off our necks and threw them in the fire. My eyes burned white hot. I lost all the air from my lungs. Meg fell to the dirt bawling. I was trembling to the core. I gripped the sides of my head as if to cover my ears from the animalistic sounds coming from my throat. A wail that pierced the night like the shatter of black glass. It shook the pines and made every primal creature scream within the deep, dark woods.

I watched in agony as the visions and enlightenment burned away the gifts bestowed to us in the flames of the campfire.

Beneath the logs, the owl's empty, hollowed-out eye sockets glowed like a haunt burrowing a hole into my soul, and the talons seemed to claw their way out without escape.

In my dreams I did not stop screaming. The rest of the night was a traumatic blur. The next thing we knew, we were dragged home kicking, screaming and crying. Maw Sue was pouring water over the campfire as the vision of her grew smaller. We passed Mama C and Papa C standing on the porch with confused faces.

Once she dragged us in the house, she slammed the door.

"Sit down and don't move!" She said storming over to the phone. She called Dad at his work. Then hung up and dialed another number and turned away so we couldn't hear her. The next thing we knew, there was a policeman at our door, and a van in our driveway. It was black and had a gold castle drawn on the side of it with the letters CPH. I heard mumbling and the door shut. I felt it in my bones. By this time, Mother was pacing the house talking all sorts of nonsense. How we were never seeing Maw Sue again, it was a goddamned massacre, and the crazy bitch better not ever touch her children again or there would be hell to pay. Meg was pale as a paper plate sitting beside me.

"I'll be right back. If she asks tell her I went to pee." Meg nodded but I could tell she was scared to death. I didn't waste a minute of time. I ran out the door cutting a swath through the darkness until I reached the edge of Maw Sue's yard. I could see Mama C and Papa C standing a distance away, and two men in white uniforms putting Maw Sue in the van with the castle on the side. It hit me like a timbering tree. Castle Pines Hospital. CPH. They were taking her to the mental hospital. My heart sank.

I barely remember the rest of the night. Just bits and pieces. I remember running after the van, hitting the sides of it, screaming at the top of my lungs, and Papa C pulling me off and wrestling with me until they got me to their porch. When they finally took me back to the house, I was a mute. I would not let my mother touch me. She had already scrubbed the blood off Meg's face, clean as a new cup till she smelled of lemon dish soap. Meg was saggy and limp as the dishrag. Her eyes were more lost and torn than I've ever seen them. I wanted to motion to Meg but she seemed preoccupied, and there was no way I was talking to my mother. I walked straight past them and into my room and slammed the door. I don't remember how long I lay in bed with my skin heated and my tears soaked with owl's blood and staining my sheets, but I was still awake when my door opened. The shadow of my mother approached me with a bowl and a washrag. All I remember is opening my mouth and screaming at the top of my lungs till the ceiling shook and she left.

I wore the owl's blood for two days and stayed awake as long as I could, afraid she'd come and wash me down, but on the third day I awoke to find my face clean and smelling like lemons. I had exhausted myself from protest and must have fell asleep. She had won. I was furious. Not only did she ruin our ceremony and burn our necklaces, but now she'd wiped away our tribal insignia until every trace was gone. And to top it off, Maw Sue was locked up in Castle Pines and I seethed with anger and hatred.

A day after the tragic events, I was still traumatized. My hand throbbed and the bandage was spotted with red blood. I unwrapped the gauze to see the cut perfectly sliced into the shape of a number seven, still raw and fresh. I realized I still had something my mother could never take. Emotions overtook me and I ran out of the room dragging the gauze attached to my hand like a snakeskin. My mother was standing at the kitchen sink washing dishes. I held up my hand and screamed from the hallway as loud as I could.

"YOU CAN'T TAKE THIS FROM ME. YOU CAN'T BURN THIS IN THE FIRE! YOU CAN'T WIPE THIS OFF, CAN YOU?" and then I stormed back inside my room and slammed the door as hard as I could. To make my point, I opened it again, then slammed it a second time till the walls rattled. I cowered to my bed sobbing. I was empty, lost and numb without Maw Sue.

For the next few days, and weeks, I did not speak to my mother. She talked to me as if nothing had happened, typical Gabby denial. I returned silence, my mother's native language. I worked her own method against her; avoidance, blank looks, distant gazes. I pretended she did not exist. I laughed out loud brashly and unashamed when she sat Meg and me down and told us we were to never tell of what happened to anyone. The story she told was the cuts on our hands were from playing with Coke bottles when we shouldn't have. I can't remember how long I flagrantly rejected any semblance of my mother's presence, but over time, a child wears down, and in the journey of my youth, I surrendered to the upheaval of adulthood and all its lies and manifestations of dysfunction. Whatever control or approval-seeking hoodoo my mother had over me sank in. Over time, and through her methodology of persuasion, I came to believe the lies and erased the truth. If anyone asked me how the scar came about, I told the Coke bottle lie. The ceremony and the rituals were erased. A month or so later, Maw Sue returned. Gabby tried to keep us away from her, but it was futile. That was one rule she finally gave up on. She couldn't keep watch over us all the time. It was exhausting and besides, we were too good at sneaking out.

PRESENT DAY

SEPTEMBER 1, 1988
NEWS YOU CAN USE
BY EDNA ROLLINS

TEXAS NEWS EDITION

The reverberating effects of the strange fire that rocked Pine Log months ago, and continues to wreak havoc long after the flames were put out cannot be understated. Ms. Poland still has nightmares. The quilting club has started a prayer chain in hopes that she will reclaim her peaceful rest and return to normal. As for Mrs. Holsomback, she declares there is a hex over her entire street, because one week after the fire, her grass died, and her flowers wilted limp and fell over and she says her green thumb is now non-existent. She has been added to the prayer chain as well. Mr. Ferguson, who witnessed the entire event, says he has strange dreams of the woman at least once a week, still dancing on the lawn and occasionally hears loud taps at his window. He now keeps his shotgun near his bed and garlic hanging on the windows. Regardless, she still whispers to him in voices that entice and tempt him, but he says he rebukes her in Jesus's name. I figure the only light we can see from this terrible event is that Mr. Bailey's donation pot totaled a whopping one hundred and fifty dollars to replace his flowers. He loaded his truck at the Hilltop Farmers Market with quite a selection. He may win this year, so watch out.

As you can see, community, we have a lot to pray about. We are the gatekeepers, the overseers and the lights that beckons and guards this town lest the devil come in and take it. Go sign the petition against spirits and go see Lola for your haircut and five dollars off. Until next time, tune into KTBR local radio news station 109.9. I'm Edna Rollins and that's news you can use.

BURN IT DOWN

It is finished.
~Jesus of Nazareth

It's killing me not to pick up the phone and dial Doc's number and tell her everything I've remembered, but I've come too far too regress now. I'm trying to apply the boundaries she has taught me. It is hard though. All I've been doing for the past twenty-four hours is trace the seven scars on my hand and stare at it, remembering the ceremony. My emotions are all over the place. I feel anger for what my mother did, and the lies she told. I feel this magnetic pull toward Maw Sue for instilling a sense of purpose and magic and the belief in something bigger than myself. I can also see, *in hindsight*, why my mother was pissed off. She saw her daughters cut with a knife in some blood ritual. In her eyes, it was sinister. Even if she were told every single fact, she wouldn't have understood. She was married into the family. She didn't have the gift. The Seventh tribe comes from dad's side of the family. So even if she did know, it wouldn't have mattered.

Having retrieved these memories made me sad and emotional, but also relieved that I finally knew the truth. I am also tired from reliving the traumas. Exhausted enough to lay down, I fell asleep rubbing the scar. I woke up inside my dream. It was surreal, so much I thought it might be happening in real time. Flames lit up everywhere, the couch, the rugs, the table, the curtains, my whole house was on fire, but when I reached out to touch it or put it out, I felt nothing. My hand went right through the flames. Everything was burning, everything except me. The door to my bedroom opens and I run towards it. Instantly I fall. Down a hole I go. Swallowed. Forever falling into the darkness like my flashbacks. In that moment, the memory returns. The descent and downfall of Cassidy Cleo Collard Reed.

Marrying Sam Reed was a mistake. We fought constantly until the fights grew tiresome and then we simply ignored each other. I could only go so long without trying to make up, but Sam would have none of it. He had moved on to some new shiny object and pushed me out of his life yet still manipulated me like a puppet. His cheating was only intensified by his lack of acknowledgment. It's like I wasn't there at all. The phone call to my mother in desperation was my last plea for help, for an answer, for someone to just say they loved me and everything was going to be okay, no matter if I stayed or left—all would be fine. At the time, I didn't know about my mother's history and past abuse. I only know that I needed someone that cared.

I was looking for answers, for affirmation, *something*. I reached out, the one and only time I reached out to my mother—and she shot me down. Make the bed—live the lie. And unconsciously, I did exactly what she said, somehow believing that I deserved to live this way. I made the bed and lived a lie until it almost killed me. Sam became my quest for approval, for love, for acceptance. It didn't matter he was still cheating; I thought I could change it. Love him more. Love him better. Love harder.

Not getting what I needed from my mother, only rejection, pushed me to the brink. Those little ghost girls with skeletons and word bones appearing to me were just the beginning of my descent into madness. Day after day they returned.

"Shall we bury them?" they'd say. Each era, each version of me pleading for answers.

"Shall we bury them?" The voices growing louder and louder until I shut my eyes and tried to make them go away. It got so bad I'd bury myself under pillows, or hide in closets, but the voices grew louder. Finally in desperation and insanity I answered them.

"Bury them!" I screamed violently. And they left one by one, disappearing into the walls like vapor, just like the day on the phone with my mother, when they first appeared. Of course, my mind was already damaged, broken, and I was slightly unhinged due to my marriage. I didn't know it was about to get worse.

One day out of nowhere, the broken knob clicked and I heard a distant roar. The sound was my life unraveling. It started with a deep depression that affected my whole mind, my body, my spirit. Dead zones, mind lapses, a thousand aches and pains, black holes of time missing, sleep disorders, nightmares, panic attacks; and this was just the short list of mind meltdowns. As I fell apart, in addition, the fixer in me, the chaos controller tried to mend the marriage, keep everything together. Hold the world up—for whatever dysfunctional reason I didn't know yet.

Sam cheated blatantly in front of me, as if he dared me to say anything. It was the ultimate betrayal. He continually mocked me and all my attempts at reconciliation. I was drifting to the end of myself, physically, mentally and spiritually. There were days I couldn't get out of bed. The earth felt as if it was swallowing me, holding me in its deep dark mouth beneath the ground where no one could reach me. This would last for days, or weeks, then reverse itself as if the earth vomited me out of its stomach. Instead of bed-locked depression, my body would fill with uncontrolled energy, an atom bouncing off the walls, wanting to split into a thousand fragments. I could no more control myself than I could stop the earth from rotating.

The breaking point came when I sat at a red light. Low and behold, pulling up next to me was Sam and next to him was his side piece, Cynthia Stubblefield. They weren't even hiding their relationship. They were flaunting it in front of me and God knows who else. I was made to look like a fool in my own town. Sam turned my way, emotionless in expression but his eyes told me everything I needed to know. He turned away and began to laugh and cut up with her. It was all I could do to maintain my emotions so they wouldn't see me cry. I didn't exist to them. Like everyone else in my life.

Cass didn't exist. I sat there weaving in and out of my mind. The light turned green and I couldn't move. Horns blew, cars sped by me and yet I still couldn't move. My mind spun, the broken knob clicked and in a waft of images and sounds, I replayed the last few months over in my head, all of the fights Sam and I had, the verbal abuse, objectification, mocking me, then the phone call to my mother, her rejection, make the bed, live the lies, the kitchen identity, the pots and pans, the drinking, the little girls asking, "Shall we bury them?"

Right then and there, at the intersection of Trinity and Grafton, I came undone. I went straight home in a manic neurotic trance as if someone else had control of my body. Walking inside the house was like stepping inside the house of Sam. *Him, him, him. It was never about me.* Triggers went off, little bombs exploding one by one of all the bad things Sam ever said to me. Provoking me, arguments, disagreements, cut-downs, manipulations, crazymaking, and pushing me away. Impulsively, I yanked his stupid trophy stuffed duck from the wall and plucked all the feathers off one-by-one with satisfaction. I took down the mummified bobcat he was so proud of killing and talked about constantly as if he was some great warrior. I hated animal trophies anyway. I never understood it. I had no problem with hunting for food or making items of use from the skins, bones, etc…

My dad hunted all his life, but the difference was, he ate everything he killed and had no need to glorify his skills by hanging a dead animal on the wall. The more I looked at the bobcat, the more he cried out to me. It was like he needed to be set free, to go back to the kingdom of which he came. I felt obliged to help. I stuffed my wedding ring inside the open mouth of the bobcat that was petrified into a frozen scream…*my scream,* a yell to be freed from the captivity of a dead relationship. I sat the taxidermy animal in the middle of the room and began making a pile. A plan was forming in my mind, unstoppable, and out of my control. The broken knob was in motion. I gathered a few scattered bones, a strip of leather and feathers from Sam's miserable collection and made a necklace. A symbol of freedom and resurrection and a little revenge. I placed it around my neck. The clattering of the bones as I walked sounded like applause to my ears, the spirits of ancestors edging me onward in my mission of emancipation.

I crammed garbage bags full of Sam's animal trophies, clothing, hunting jackets, T-shirts, shoes, boots, accessories, pictures, knickknacks, belts, magazines, basically everything I could stuff into a bag, until there was nothing left but duck feathers and furniture. I knew I could not stuff all the bags into my '89 Buick, so I phoned a coworker and asked to borrow her pickup. We exchanged vehicles, and on the way back, I stopped at the hair shop and bought a long blonde number 14 wig with curls. I went back to the house, loaded up the truck and changed into black pants and a black shirt. I put the wig on and stared into the mirror reflection. My eyes were blank and lost, lonely and sad. The mirror revealed an assortment of faded people, ancestors and Maw Sue, and a whole slew of little girls of every age. They shimmered in and out of the silver reflections like my past self, intermingling with my future self. It was weird and oddly comforting.

And then it appeared in the mirror, fading in and out as if someone was drawing on my face. Stripe after stripe across my cheeks. In my head I heard whispers telling me what to do. *A warrior going into battle needs insignia, a mark to distinguish and intimidate the enemies.* The next thing I knew, the seven scar on my palm was sliced open and there was splatters all over the sink, the bone necklace and bloody designs painted across my face. I was now a spirit warrior.

I could hear drumbeats in the distant calling me. Sounds, whispers and songs, tribal lyrics and music. I was ready to be free. Ready to battle. My pupils erupted into tiny flickering flames. I saw them in the mirror image of myself. They burned hot tears and steam as I walked to the refrigerator and took out the bowl of uncooked collard greens. I grabbed a box of matches and walked to the truck. I loaded bags of Sam's stuff till the bed of the truck was a heap. I was halfway crying and halfway laughing. The crying was grief for what I never had, for expectations, and dreams, but the laughing wasn't my normal laugh. It was one of those long, maddening, psychotic, lost-your-way kind of halfway howls, halfway cries, halfway laughs—that somehow never find their way back. I barely recognized it as my own. It felt like many pieces of me all wrapped together to snap. And I was broken, beyond broken, hidden inside fragments of the House of Seven deep within me.

The next day I was oblivious to what happened. My memory was blank. My mind was catatonic. The broken knob had finally broken all of me. I remember drifting in and out consciousness, fog and feathers, faces and fire. *Knock-knock.* I am drifting, floating. *Knock-knock-knock.* It sounds like thunder in the distance. Then a rush of people standing above me, circling, leaning in and back. Shadow people I didn't recognize. I thought I heard Sam's voice but wasn't sure. Drifting in and out, I scanned the room but it was a mist in my sleepy eyes. I felt a tickle on my arm. I turned my head sideways until my cheeks were flush on the cold hardwood floor. A broken mirror lay slant against a wall and my reflection stared back at me. There I was. Sprawled out in a pile of feathers, couch cushion stuffing and animal bones in Sam's office. People leaned in and out, faces enlarging and shrinking, lips moving with garbled words. It was dreamlike. Until it was black. Then I woke up and I could hear them, and feel them around me, touching me, asking me question after question.

Are you okay Mrs. Reed? Can you hear me? Are you hurt? Did you cut yourself? How did you cut yourself? Can you tell me? Did you start the fire? Mrs. Reed? Mrs. Reed?

Hearing them call me by my married name, lit something within me. I went at them like a cat. The next thing I know I'm being restrained by the shadows, who turned out to be police and paramedics. My mind drifted. My lips yelled. But I had no idea what I said—my universe was muddled. They put me on a gurney and rolled me out. When my eyes hit daylight, the bright sun blinded me but I did catch a hazy glimpse of a small crowd gathering. Sam was there and he wasn't alone. Trembling, I felt myself withdraw deeper inside the House of Seven until it was dark and safe.

I cannot be sure of how much time passed. I woke up in the hospital and for the first five-seconds, I thought for sure I was in Castle Pines. I started screaming and tossing bedsheets and pulling out wires and tubes. A policeman and nurse ran inside trying to calm me down. After a few minutes of intense questioning on my part, I understood how I came to be here. I wasn't in Castle Pines, but Grafton Hospital. *There was a fire. I had a deep cut on my hand. Police stood guard at my door.* I was alarmed but that wasn't the worst of it. I looked down at the bracelet on my wrist with my name and the words that sent a rack of chills through my bones.

5th Floor Psychiatric Ward

Confused. Puzzled. Scared. I had no memory of coming here. And what fire? And why was my hand bandaged? And the guard? Was I in trouble? What happened? I began to panic, begging the nurse for answers. The next thing I know, the nurse inserts a needle in my IV tube and my panic subsides immediately. I'm calm, subdued but still lucid enough to understand what's going on. My mind is tossing and turning still. Some time passes before a tall, lanky gray-haired woman wearing a navy pant suit walks in with a manilla file. She flips out her badge, opens the file and fills me in.

Arson, criminal mischief and trespassing? *That can't be me,* I said. Until I looked at my palm all wrapped up and bloody. *Why can't I remember? What is wrong with me?* But all I could ponder was Castle Pines and Maw Sue. My worst fears were coming true.

Startled by a quick explosive whoosh, I sprang up from the couch. I was in a cold sweat. I blinked a few times to make sure I was awake. The last thing I saw in my dreams was a woman dancing around a fire. Her face zoomed in closer and closer. It was me. I am the woman. I eyeballed my surroundings and felt the fabric of the couch and my own skin to make sure where I was. Assure myself this was my house and not some hospital or God forbid, Castle Pines.

"Holy shit." I said to myself, realizing what my memory had conjured. "I remember. I remember everything. I did it. I set the fire. I did it all. Oh my God, it was me." There was a sense of relief and also panic. What would happen to me now? I went to the kitchen sink and poured a glass of water and gulped it down. I ran to the phone and quickly dialed Doc's number but realized it was three in the morning. I hesitated but decided to leave a message anyway. This was different than all the times before. Pearl's bland voice came on, then a beep.

"Pearl. I know it's late. I know. But this is important. SERIOUSLY, PEARL. I need you to tell Doc to call me. Or not. Hell, you can call me. Just PLEASE move my appointment up a day or two. And guess what? *I know what I did.* I got my memory back. I know, I know, I get it. I've called before with bullshit, but this, this is the truth. Okay, Pearl? Good. Okay, thanks, you're the best, really, okay, bye." I hung up before I could tell her who it was. I laughed out loud because she would know exactly who it was. My voice was her damn nightmare. I tossed and turned the rest of the night, barely able to sleep. It was clear to me now that I had set the fire. It was all me. Guilty as charged. I was the crazy-town arsonist. This didn't bother me half as much as the fact Edna Rollins was right, probably for the first time in her life.

The next morning I walked into Doc's office full of adrenalin. Pearl was able to move up my appointment since I was so urgent. She stared at me with a mixture of curiosity and trepidation. I paced the floor like a caged animal. I was so full of information I was about to bust. I heard the door open from the small hallway, and Doc appeared. I rushed her like a football quarterback. I coiled myself around her like a python. I hugged her so tight I thought she was going to drop my file.

"Cass are you all right? It's okay, calm down. Let's go in my office and talk." She patted my back as I unhinged myself from her. My eyes were already leaking as I started talking the second Doc closed the door. She quickly sat down and started writing with her hoodoo pen. I was so ready to talk, I spilled out everything. I paced the floor with open lips revealing all the secrets of my past, the memories of the ceremony, the owl, the meaning of it, my mirror bin, all the rituals of the Seventh Tribe, the stories I was told, my belief in them, our locust crowns, my inability to accept the reality of my parents' relationship woes, the seven scar on my palm, my mother showing up at the fire ceremony and freaking out about the cut, the lies she made up afterwards that I learned to believe were true, along with the horror of what happened, the trauma it caused me, the terror of the unknown. Maw Sue and the white van, her going to Castle Pines, my hatred for my mother because of it, which eventually led to me slipping in my mind, my actions, the anger I felt. I pushed the memories down. *Repressed. Erased.* Then over time, the depression and lonely teen years, compulsiveness of marrying Sam, the cheating, the fights, the replications of my childhood repeated itself in my life all over again. I couldn't see it then, even though deep down, a part of me knew something was off. Probably the combined pain of having to relive it twice, reenactments, first with my parents, and then in my own life.

There I was attempting to fix my life, fix my childhood hurts, fix my broken mind, mend the messes, heal my parents. But as Doc always said, we can't fix other people, only ourselves. Eventually, everything came to a halt. My mind, my body, my spirit could no longer accept it. I know without a doubt it started long ago in my childhood, but it increased slowly over time and intensified with trauma. It finally exploded into a full-fledged mental breakdown when I made the phone call to my mother. It was then I really knew my sham marriage was over, if it ever existed at all. When it didn't work out like I dreamed it would, nor did I get motherly approval, that is when the little girls came in. I'm thinking to rescue me. Lead me back to my roots. It was necessary pain. My overwhelming need for acceptance from my mother went deep. Her rejection ran deeper. It triggered the broken knob to finally go off the entire door hinge. *Click. Clatter. Broke. The whole house was in turmoil.* Utter mental breakdown. Instead of leaving like a sane and confident person would do—I stayed. I endured the abuse and betrayal because I was determined to love them enough to make them love me. *Fix it Cass! Make it right!* So I stayed just like my mother stayed. Make the beds—live the lies.

Doc continued to write in my thick file while I continued to pour out the descent of madness which provoked me to become a pyro. Make the bed. Live the lies. Stalk the cheating husband. Make it work. Be the Southern wife you should be. Everything is so clear to me now, as if I see what was hidden from my mind, the pine curtain pulled back to view reality—not what I thought it was.

The little girls, versions of me appearing with their bones, word skeletons, redemptive words they desired to hear, to fix, to mend, to repair, were all created in childhood out of pain, survival and denial. The Hush cemetery was created to bury the word bones, because they were dead, unused words, unfulfilled dreams and desires. Since I was incapable of withstanding anymore disappointment, I instructed the girls to bury the word bones. My mind state of denying reality. Denying what I'd never receive.

Things came to a head the day I saw Sam and Cynthia Stubblefield at the intersection living a life that should have been mine. My mind snapped. When the light turned from green to yellow to red—all I could see was flames. Everyone knows what happens after that. Just read *The Pine Log Gazette*. Edna fills everyone in on all the details.

Once I had finished spilling my guts to Doc, I felt emptied of all emotions. I took a long-winded gasp and leaned back on the couch. I was exhausted from lack of sleep but it felt good to finally know the truth. It didn't seem to matter to me that I was guilty and in a heap of trouble for the fire. For me, knowing the story behind it, the *whole story,* was more important.

"Well Cass," Doc said with a glint in her eyes, "It seems you've been listening to me all this time and you've obviously did the hard work and now it's paying off. You have your memory back. Well done."

"Yeah, I did listen. I did Doc…I can't believe it but everything the eyewitnesses said must be true. I think it was exaggerated to a level where Edna exceeded her creative writing liberties a little too far. I suppose from a bystander point of view, it was a bit odd." I chuckled.

"But…I wasn't devil worshipping and I'm not part of some cult, although some people wouldn't understand my great-grand-mother's rituals. I mean I get it. I do. And I *did* set the fire with Sam's stuff, and the animal trophies make sense now. The owl connection, along with the bone and feather necklace. I was recreating my childhood ceremony, in my own way, to cleanse myself of Sam, using his trophy animals in place of the owl sacrifice. I mean they were already dead and all, but I was making a point. It fit the narrative, so to speak.

"It's so weird now that I remember bits and pieces of that night, coming and going. It's like I dreamed it, but I know it actually happened. I think it was part of my mind separating it from me, maybe to protect me, I'm not sure. I did sing and dance. The neighbors were right. At first I had a tape in the truck playing our old song, *Minnie the Moocher*, but as the night progressed, I began singing our tribal song that Meg and I made up as kids.

"And yes, I hooted and howled and sang out just like we did with Maw Sue as kids. I was trying to put my life back together. The only way I knew how. I wanted to feel the way I felt the night before the hell, that was my mother, showed up to ruin it. *I wanted to feel alive, important, anointed, loved.* Just like Maw Sue made us feel that night with our crowns and mirror bins, and stories. I don't think I've felt alive in a long time. Maw Sue was the only one who had the magic to make me feel like I was made for something bigger. I admit, there was eccentric rituals, blood stuff and ceremonies, old family stories and traditions, but it was pure magic, the kind you never want to vanish, even after you grow old. It connected me to my kin, to people I feel I know, a bloodline deeply intertwined, although I've never met them. It matters to me. It did then. It does now.

"I do remember feeling oddly disconnected the night of the fire, as if guided by things outside my control. Maybe to find ME, the girl I used to be, or *was,* back then. Not sure but I knew I had to have a ceremony. So yes, I set Sam's belongings on fire in Cynthia Stubblefield's yard. This is my confession, I guess. I was ridding myself of my marriage and cleansing myself, of myself, so I could be the person Maw Sue said I could be. Who I've always wanted to be. Was it wrong? Could I have done it differently, sure, I see that now, but my mind is different now too. I think differently because of you. Therapy has opened doors that would have never been opened otherwise. Am I ashamed of what I did? *Not really.* Honestly, it doesn't compare to the brutality that Sam put me through. Was it all his fault? No. Would I do it again? Knowing what I know now, absolutely not. But I'm not the same person I was, when I first entered your office.

"BUT I will say this…if it was the only way back to my true self, then yes, I'd do it all over again. Those ghost girls, the ones who appeared to me in the mirror that night, along with Maw Sue were guiding me. I believe that. Call it crazy or superstitious mumbo-jumbo, it doesn't matter. In my mind, in that moment, it was real. I saw them. I listened to them. I did exactly as they said. We had us a ceremony. They were there. Because you see, they had to be. Each of them represented me at different ages throughout my childhood and teenage years. *They knew me.* They were all part of the process back to wholeness. They were the puzzle pieces to put me back as one. Weeks ago, I wouldn't have shared this with you out of fear. But now I'm laying it all out. I'm telling you this, because I trust that you will help me continue to put myself back together. I hope there is some minuscule part of you that believes in magic and supernatural experiences that change a person. Could you send me to Castle Pines as mentally unstable? *Yes.* You could very well do that, but knowing my whole story, I hope and pray that you won't. I mean, was I hallucinating? I don't know, Doc, I really can't say, because it's a little fuzzy, but at the time, in *that* moment, I needed them to be real. That little girl inside me needed them all to be real.

"Doc, you are the one who told me of the existence of the inner child. I just happen to have an inner child that split into several pieces, that is all. Will she heal? I hope so. I hope I heal with her. I pray I can put her back together. All of it is who I am now. It's who I've always been. I just didn't know it until now. It's like the masterpiece hanging in your lobby that I love so much. The painter has black angels. He wouldn't be his true self without them. I am the same. I have a broken knob. And you have helped me find my outlet, my art, my blue line."

I paused and took a deep breath. I had been rambling so much I lost track of time and place, but there was *still* one pertinent question on my mind.

"So, am I going to jail? Since I've confessed to arson?"

Doc sat her pen down and leaned forward on her elbows. She had a quirky edge to her smile that sent mixed signals. I wasn't sure if it was good or bad.

"First of all. Bravo. I'm so happy your memory came back, along with the others. It does seem to fall in line with everything else we've spoken about. It actually makes a lot of sense. But we'll talk about that at the next session. Now to answer your question." She pursed her lips and stretched back against her chair. I was about to die of curiosity. I could see myself in an orange jumpsuit along the side of the highway picking up trash while Sam and his girlfriend drove by laughing. Or Doc just as well, might send me to Castle Pines.

"Cass. Listen, I am fixing to tell you something important. Brace yourself."

Fear shot through me. My eyes rolled back in my head and I slumped on the sofa in preparation for the worst. My eyes closed and I held my breath. *Don't panic, don't freak out, stay calm.*

"You are not going to jail. Nor are you going to Castle Pines. I wasn't going to tell you until the last month of therapy because I didn't want it to affect your growth, but I think today is as good a day as ever. The charges were dropped."

"WHAT?" I said gasping and lurching forward on the couch. "All of them? Just dropped? How does that work, what happened?"

"Yes. All of them. There is one catch and it's teeny, but get this. Interestingly enough, Cynthia Stubblefield, the girlfriend, found out the hard way about Sam and his cheating ways, just like you did. I'm unaware of the details, but apparently it wasn't good, and she sent him packing. She sent word from her attorney last month that she was dropping all charges. Sam could still file charges since it was his stuff you burned, but it's highly likely he won't. He's moved on to some other poor soul."

"Are you freaking kidding me?" I started laughing. And then I couldn't stop. "That is some karma shit right there." I laugh-snorted, which made Doc and I both laugh even harder.

"Wait," I said remembering, "What's the catch?"

"Well, apparently the neighbors were upset about their flowers being burned, so Cynthia had one stipulation for you to uphold. You have to donate at least one hundred dollars to the local Flower Pot Committee every month for one year to restore and fund the community gardens."

"DONE!" I said smiling.

"Good. I will let them know. Now, Cass, are you ready to hear my evaluation of you? This is the last process of therapy, when I let you out into the world to live with what I've taught you and what you've learned about yourself. No late-night phone calls in panic. And Lord, Pearl will be happy with that part of it,"

"I'm all ears," I said, knowing it could be good or bad but no matter, I was ready to hear it.

"So, in my field of work I see a lot of people. Different problems, different patterns of growth, things of this matter, but in all cases, despite their psychological issues, there are other reasons. Everyone has faults but as humans, it bothers us to be flawed, imperfect, or different. We may not admit it, but it's true. We mold ourselves from others and have this ideal in our heads we have to be perfect. But we are not. The fact is we can sink so morbidly into sin and despair, it renders us incapacitated at times. We live our lives practicing perfectionism, always attempting to live up to some expectation in our heads, and not only ourselves, but we expect it from other people. They should be like us, we think. It is very easy to get lost in this world and it comes from losing our core identity, losing our true selves. Plus, you add burdens and addictions and trauma to the mix, and then you add other people's problems, sins and mental incapacities. It can and it will affect us. Everyone else's lies, truths, lifestyles, belief systems, gifts, curses, betrayals…the list goes on and on. Our surroundings can form our journey. Our perceptions of who we are and what we can become. When we're little, and I'm referring to the child in us, we're still trying to find our place, and most often we put the people we love up high on a pedestal. I call it the throne cycle. We place people on a throne to look up to for a model of perfection, for how to do it right, how to make life better, more convenient, less painful, but they are human, like us, and when they fail, or fall from their throne, which they will, it's devastating to us because we set expectations. We expect more from them, so we can be more. If they succeed then we have a chance, but it they fail—then we fail. In the throne cycle we set people up so they can never, ever fail. Not in our eyes, anyway. The truth is, we all fail one way or another, big and small. Even Maw Sue taught you the concept in her own way. With every story she told, she put *into* you something she lacked inside herself. Thus, enabling you to do better than her. We all do this. Maybe it was something she had failed at—but instead she wanted to make it right for you. She instilled those stories of magic and hope into you, so you could choose better."

Row after row of goose pimples shot up my arms. The air around me grew cloudy and mysterious, otherworldly. I smelled lemons and a fire, felt a charge in the air around me, and could hear a crackle of flames. In my mind, I could see the colorful shadows from the mirror bin dancing on the walls in and out from the bookshelves and emerging from Doc's paintings. It was the petal people. The shadows had always been the petal people. People who have gone before me, passed on to the otherworld. People I recognize and others only from old pictures. My mind was a foggy enchantment as I listened to Doc speak.

"Cass, in psychotherapy, the expression 'feet of clay' doesn't refer to character defects or weakness, but actually the understanding we can and will screw up our lives. Sometimes it's our own decisions, sometimes others. It's a failure clause in our DNA. It's the original sin the Bible speaks of. We all have it. It's going to happen. More so, when other people fail us, we are disappointed. Or sad, or rejected. We may have greatly admired or looked up to this person for protection or safety. Children need substance, a nurturing form of identity, a bonding needed to grow. We turn our parental figures into gods and demand things from them, without ever knowing their own journeys. We demand the broken cup with the crack in it hold the water for our thirst, when it just can't. It's not possible. A cup with a hole will leak. And it leaks on anyone close. We expect perfection from a broken mold. It's a survival method we adopt as children, clinging to the ones who mean the most.

"Our fathers and mothers are mere mortals—a man, a woman with just as many faults and shortcomings as ourselves and others. All of us are capable of making grave mistakes. We have the ability to hurt others, terribly and painfully, sometimes to the point of death. The *denial till death* metaphor applies here. Putting people on a throne only to be knocked off is painful and misinterpreted. In order to cope with the failure and the loss of what we thought was reality—it can clearly be misplaced. Misdirected. Mistook. Altered perceptions. We see what we want to see. We do it as protection for ourselves. In addition, we might blame ourselves. We turn to drugs, alcohol or choose to self-medicate—pick your poison. Every single one of us has clay feet." Doc leaned over and sat my thick protruding file on the desk next to the bell. I was lost in the moment soaking up her words, line by line, item by item.

"In your case, Cass, it was misdirection. Especially your mother. It is highly possible it happened with her mother as well. A passed-on trait of nothing but pure survival. Sometimes trauma is generational. The energies of all your ancestors traumas are passed on, and on and on. Straight down the line. Who knows how far it goes back, until someone decides to break the cycle. You did what you had to do. So did your mother. You both held secrets inside, and the unknowing of them tied you together in destructive ways. The expectations you had of her growing up were unrealistic to her because she could not give what she didn't experience or know how to give. Her traumas erected your own. But now you know why and it makes sense to you. When before it didn't because you had no idea of the history behind the traumas, the people and events behind them. You used to blame, but now you have compassion. You blamed yourself as well, and now you know it wasn't you at all. It was her past, her upbringing, her fear of abandonment, her being the sole provider and caretaker of her younger sister, along with other issues. It was her traumas reenacting themselves onto you. Her throne cycle.

"It's generational, yes, but it doesn't have to end in this pattern. It takes work, lots of work but it can be done. I'm actually thankful your mother was brave enough to tell your sister, or this mystery would continue to be hidden and we'd never have known. When your mother spoke it out loud, it became real to her. This trauma was denied for years but once she spoke it—it ushered in the first fruits of healing. In fact, just because she hasn't sought therapy of healing, doesn't mean she hasn't broke some of the curses. She did. She broke the denial by death cycle. She spoke the horrible out loud. Sometimes sharing it with one person is all it takes. Healing might begin. Now, whether or not you speak to your mother about it is up to you. But you do need to know people who are traumatized this deeply and for this long, *cannot* mend instantly by a few talks. It also may damage the relationship more. I know you don't have much of a relationship with your mother, but now, at least you know why she is the way she is. Healing and confronting our past take time, lots of patience, therapy and work. You take care of yourself and leave others to do the same. Remember you are only a fixer of you, not others. It will always be in you, and it will come out, but you have to realize it and stop it before you repeat patterns of old. Again, your mother may not be capable of what you have done in this last year. Remember, perceptions and expectations. It's a different generation, with so many nuances. Her life is her own to heal or to keep or to destroy. Your life is to heal you, set boundaries, healthy goals. But that journey can begin by forgiving your mother, and most of all, forgiving yourself."

Doc's words were heavy and heartfelt. I sank inside the House of Seven with the little girl, the inner child. We simmered over the words, the meaning, and the message.

"And something else..." Doc said smiling. "When we realize the humanity of our own substance, throned and dethroned, whatever it may be, we realize we all have feet of clay —*we don't have to be perfect*—we can be ourselves. I can be me. You can be you. *Cass with clay feet. Cass with clusters.* It's that realness that makes us human. It's what makes us unique and gifted. We're authentic. We're real. And when we're real—we allow others to be real too."

I was spellbound. Dots connected inside me. I lost myself for a second as if I didn't know where I was. A place of darkness and light. They stood in front of me at a distance. I saw an assortment of shadowy petal people. I recognized them as my ancestors. Standing in the middle with a crooked smile and holding a mason jar full of roses was Maw Sue. Mama C and Papa C were there too. Starbuck Adams, Maw Sue's lifetime love, was there as well. Standing in front of them, twin boys, and twin girls, and the seven sisters, lined up one through seven, and beside them their parents, Brue and Simon and others I didn't recognize, only through old family photos. Above them, flying in silence was a large barn owl with encrusted clay feet and glowing eyes of inner light. When I came back to myself, Doc began to speak again.

"You've grown so much, Cass. I am proud of who you are, who you've become, who you've always been, the child, the adult, the woman. If Maw Sue were here, I think she'd say you were as close to seven as you've ever been. Queen of the Pine Curtain. Think about it. You have a belief in yourself, your true self. You can move forward now. As you do, you'll continue to grow, to heal, to live a life of your own choosing. Now...let's talk about that, shall we. You only have a month and two weeks to go, and I know you'll do just fine out in the world. You only have to check in with me every three months for medications. And of course, if anything arises, feel free to call me or leave a message with Pearl."

I snickered under my breath. Pearl will love that. But Doc was right. For the first time, I believed in me. All of me. I could channel the darkness to the blue line. The black angels would have a place to rest. A center. A belonging. Blue lines and black angels were part of me, who I was yesterday, who I am today, and who I will become tomorrow. The words on the blue line give meaning to my world, they shape my reality, my internal makeup, the shell of me, inward and outward, my perceptions of my past, my present and my future. Even the petal people have their place. Long ago, their whispers drove me mad, but now they find a place on the blue line, in stories and books, and journals and inside my mason jar. Writing is my purpose borne out of pain and suffering. A necessary pain of growth and enlightenment. It is my gift and my curse. The word skeletons I buried in the hushed cemetery as a child were resurrected and brought to life on the blue line of my journal. They are at rest now. I know my gift has the power to lift me like an owl with clay feet or plunder me in darkness with my black angels, but either way, I transform and channel it into creativity.

I think of Maw Sue's life and how much she struggled with the madness, the gifts, and the curses. It's a shame she didn't have a Doc in her life to help her through it. Regardless of her difficulties, Maw Sue managed to work a magic in Meg and me. She put in us what she could not do for herself. I got teary eyed when I realized the magnitude of what she had actually done. It's what she said all along. Four words. *Make lovely your losses.* Maw Sue made lovely her losses through stories and magic and belief in the unbelievable. If she had not the courage to do what she did, all those years, even in her own mind sufferings, I would have surely been a statistic. A denial through death statistic or worse.

It was emotional leaving Doc's office knowing there was a finality to it, a change, a different road ahead. I'd see her for an hour every three months, so it wasn't ending for good, but after sharing this journey with her this past year, it seemed strange to part ways. I checked out at the counter like I normally did. Pearl fidgeted with paperwork behind the desk and was taking longer than usual, so I glanced around the room to take it all in until I heard whispers.

"I have information I think you'll find interesting," Pearl said in a soft breath. I turned to face her almost in shock that she spoke.

"I'm sorry?" I said making sure I heard what I heard. Pearl pushed her glasses upwards, and rubbed her nose, all the while shuffling papers.

"I said I have information for you." She said a little louder than before but still in a whisper.

"Why are you whispering? Did my insurance reject the claim? What is it?"

"No, no, nothing like that."

"Well, what is it?" I said impatiently. "Wait. Hold on." It just dawned on me that Pearl was having an actual full blown conversation. *With me.*

"Pearl, I'm just thrilled that you're talking to me. I was a little mean to you at first. I'm sorry. I apologize for that. I was... different then. I'm better now. Ask Doc."

"Yeah, yeah...I don't care about that, Cass, I'm talking about something important."

"Oh," I said thrown off by Pearl's sudden backbone.

"Edna Rollins." Pearl said anxiously. "I have information about Edna Rollins."

I stared at her blankly. My mouth was open a bit in confusion.

"I'm sorry. I'm just shocked you're suddenly so talkative to me. I've been coming here almost a year and you barely said a peep. Now you say you have information about Edna Rollins, of ALL people. Why in the world would I—the woman she has made the main topic of her gossip column—want ANY information about Edna Rollins? I mean, even though she was partially right, it didn't give her permission to stir the pot. She's a blabbermouth busybody. Always has been. She talked about me, my great-grandmother, and damn near everybody in town since the sixties. That woman needs to get a life. I couldn't give a rat's ass about that cottonmouth or anything you have to say about her."

"Uhhh, yeah," Pearl said, shrugging. "I know I don't talk. Sorry, I'm kind of socially awkward." She tugged at her ears and moved her body as if she was a noodle loosing up in a pot of boiling water. "My boyfriend says I should really start getting out more, but ecckkkk…people, crowds, can't do it." She pushed her thick glasses upwards and snarled her nose.

"I know you don't like Edna, nobody does. But my boyfriend works for her, or rather he's kind of like family, her godson."

"Too bad for him." I said uncaring.

She bent her face into the counter and cupped her lips as if no one was supposed to hear her even though there was no-one else in the room. I was overtly curious even though I didn't want to be.

"Okay, listen." She said in a mysterious tone. "George has worked for Edna for years, and he edits her columns, and then copy prints them on the old news printer that was supposedly her father's, who was also a journalist. Anyway, George sees a lot. And hears a lot…" she exaggerated her voice low as if this was dire information. I was puzzled as to where this was heading. "Plus he reads her letters."

"Pearl for God's sake. Are you going to tell me a story about Edna? What has this got to do with me? Get on with it, I have a new life to live, in freedom, so I'm sort of ready to scram. You know what I mean?"

"Edna's a scam!" Pearl blurted out of character. It was so outside the lines for her, it took her a minute to gather her bland bearings back. It threw me off as well. We both looked at each other momentarily in shock until she continued the story.

"What I'm saying is everything she writes about, you know what other people do, is pretty much exactly what she has been doing for years. George found letters, lots of letters, and he has downtime a lot, so he reads them, and talk about gossip! They are steamy, and supposedly from one of the Moon Wanderers that Edna took up with back in the seventies. Plus, there's a particular journal he found that details the events that happened when Edna went to one of their camp gatherings in California on vacation, which no one knew about. George saw pictures back in the day of Edna drinking, dancing, flowers in her hair, half-naked, even smoking, plus she had relations with a tribe member named Hadnot which apparently has been going on for sixteen years or so. They talk on the phone regularly, and she travels to other towns to attend gatherings with him every year. George wants to flip the tables on her. He wants to re-write an article and expose her for who she really is. She'd never know what hit her until it was too late."

"So Edna's a wild child? A closet Hippie?" I said wanting to laugh uncontrollably. "She smokes the devil's lettuce too?"

The more Pearl talked, the more unbelievable it sounded. But if it was true…the gall of that woman to carry on like some high and mighty savior talking and spreading gossip and lies, and yet she carries on like some scandalous bohemian tramp undercover.

"You know what Pearl. It sounds like a great idea. Whatever it is. I'm all in. What do I have to do?" I said with pure satisfaction.

"Nothing, you don't have to do a thing. George wants to do it. He's been looking for a way out of that job for years, but he's tied by family. He wants to go to college and she keeps saying she'll let him go, but she hasn't. George's mother won't let him quit because of some old family squabble that Edna hogtied them into, so George feels like her servant mostly. He just wants out and saw this as an opportunity. She'll be so mad, she'll fire him and run him so far out of town, he'll finally get to do what he wants. I just thought you'd want to know who she really is. Since, you know, she wrote stuff about you and all. And it might not change what she's already wrote, but she'll get what's coming to her. When George finishes writing up an article on Edna, and prints it, instead of what she wants to print, by the time she finds out, it will be too late. It will be distributed all over town. George knows what he's doing. He's smart."

"Well look at you, Pearl," I said shaking my head. I was kind of proud. I had misjudged this little under-the-table firecracker. Pearl had some gumption to her after all. And George sounded like a prize. This was just too good to be true.

"How many people know about this? I just got off temporary probation, you know, so I can't have anything to do with this if it has blowback. Understand?" In the same thought I wondered if this was a good thing for me to be involved in, since revenge didn't seem like the right course for me to take now that I've actually healed and on a new journey. I was perplexed as to what to do, plus asking Doc was out of the question, so I left it all to Pearl to just give me information. I'd decide later if I wanted to pursue any recourse. But it did gnaw at me a bit. Lord have mercy, I think I'm becoming a responsible, non-compulsive adult.

"Of course, sure, yeah, yeah that's not a problem." Pearl spoke with her hands. "I told George I wanted you to know, because of the article she wrote about you, that's all. And we are the only three people that know. Pretty soon, the whole town will know who Edna really is." Pearl spoke in a tone that was way to Sherlock Holmes and it cracked me up.

"You are something else Pearl," I said meeting her hand in the air to hive-five. "When is this covert mission happening?"

"As soon as Edna decides she wants to write another article. She's been off and on with the writing, and George isn't sure what's up with that, but she'll eventually write something because she always does, and that's when NEWS YOU CAN USE is going down."

"My, my, my Pearl. You are one bad girl," I said laughing as I walked towards the front door.

"I got my ways," she said with a mischievous heckle.

"Well, I like it. Just don't strike a match." I said leaning on the door, "We all know how that ends." I winked and walked across the parking lot. This was a new beginning and I could feel the weight of it pressing me, the unknowns, the unfamiliar and the fears of change.

MASON JARS AND MIRROR BINS

The more we try to deny who we are,
the more we become what we fear.
~ Freud

It was three months before I saw Doc again. The court system was tied up in paperwork, so my dismissal was delayed, but it wasn't a big deal. I was laying low and staying out of trouble. Pearl told me at my last appointment that George was still working the magic on Edna and she'd call me once it goes down. It's hard to get one over on the gossip queen. Either way, I was healing slowly and dealing with my life, where I've been, where I'm at now.

There is one thing I haven't moved past yet. It's been sitting in the middle of my living-room floor since I brought it home from my sister's house. I hadn't the heart to open it yet. With the funeral a few months ago, the dismissal, me getting my life back, and just basically dealing with all the memories, I truly didn't think I could handle anymore. To be truthful, I am fearful of what I might find hidden.

When I got close to the heirloom, I could feel it. All the power and energy of the people of the past seemed to rise up from it. Those strange flashes hit me like before; ceremony, crackling fire, leaping flames, terrifying screams, the slice of the blade, seven distinct drips of blood, Maw Sue's red forefinger on my cheeks, the smell of the owl's blood, the shadows dancing and voices singing. *Can I open it? Am I prepared for what I'll find?* I wasn't sure. All I could hear was Doc's voice in my ears: "Confront it, Cass."

I poured a glass of wine and contemplated. I paced a bit and then sat on the living-room floor in front of it. I felt the stirrings of the past coming alive in the glimmer of the mirror reflections, as if it had held every snapshot of my life. I downed half the glass of Cabernet Sauvignon and prepared myself. Time to face the magic of a childhood I put away, lost, forsook, denied. The ancient talisman of the Seventh Tribe sat before me, anticipating my awakening with a gentle hum. In my childhood vision it was a God, larger than life, blood of my blood, seeker to seeker.

I popped open the lock. It made a loud swishing sound like air escaping. Dust particles spiraled in a cloud and I could smell old tarnished scents, oil of rosemary, honeysuckle and lemongrass. I took a deep breath and opened the lid. Sitting on top was a satchel of herbs I collected on walks with Maw Sue behind the pine curtain. I lifted it to my nose. Rosemary, sage and mint intoxicated my senses. Underneath was a handful of pine needles tied in a bundle with a blue string. After all these years it still smelled like home. The little girl, Southern sap, the Queen of the Pine Curtain. I laid it on the rug and tears welled in my eyes for what was next. They were laid out like corpses wrapped in burlap waiting to be resurrected. The petal people, wilted flowers, *Immortelles,* the Everlasting representation of my loved ones. Big

Pops, May Dell, Maw Sue, and me, the dead one. The wild, white rose, the spirit rose represented the little girl taken at the river, the night of the great sadness. I thanked God the little girl is no longer dead, no longer hidden in darkness, inside me, inside the House of Seven where I kept her imprisoned, robbed of voice, denied life and love. Tenderly, I removed the fragile dried rose and held it to my heart and wept. I felt the weight of grief the rose carried in its petals all these years, because I could not bear it myself.

The more I held it, the lighter it got. I opened my wet eyes and laid it aside, and winced. There on top was the rose for my mother. The mother I erased. The mother I replaced with this rose. When I couldn't revive our relationship, she didn't exist to me. I submitted her to the petal people. It was sad but necessary. *For the child. For emotional survival.* But now, the adult in me has to resurrect what I did. *But how?* Maw Sue wouldn't approve of me using the ritual for my own personal judgment. I'm figuring out that revenge isn't my thing. I sat the roses aside till I could process and figure out how to reverse the curse. Next was a tattered and stained letter. I didn't recognize it to be the Seventh Tribe poem till I opened it and could hear Maw Sue's voice reading it for the first time.

Immortelles. The Everlastings. This poem touched me deeply as a child and its waxing poetic spell stayed with me throughout my journey. Reading it after all these years made me smile and weep.

Next were my tiny journals and scrap pieces of paper with scribbles of words. Some disturbingly dark, some comical, others confusing and riddled with pain and big questions. Some I remember, some I don't. I laughed and finished off my wine.

It seems I was a writer all along. Words resonated in me, so much they had to have a place to rest. As a child I buried the word skeletons inside the Hush cemetery beside the House of Seven. It was a survival method. It was the only avenue where I could maintain some form of stability and function. Today, words have found their rightful place on the blue lines of my journal. I can see the child so clearly, the one I was then, the one I am today, even now. With the wonder of a child's eyes, I pulled out feathers, rocks, and other objects I collected behind the pine curtain of my childhood. And then my ears splintered with the sound of a creature.

"Oh my God. It's the crackle," I said out loud, spilling over with laughter. The lone cicada crackle was brittle and so fragile with age, I thought for sure it would crumble in my fingers. In my childlike ears, I'd hear the terrible, awful crunching sound of the brokenness I avoided in childhood when we accidentally crushed one. Memories of Meg and me flooded my thoughts, collecting boxes of crackles, dressing them up, and the infamous prank on Maw Sue. I laughed so hard my belly hurt. This memory provoked another memory. *My childhood vow.* I made a solemn vow to never grow up. It was laughable now, but as a child, it was frightening to see the life of grown-ups falling apart around me, and I wanted no part of it. I scrambled through the journals until I found it. Reading it again made me feel alive. I did grow up but not in the way the little girl expected. I'm an adult…but I kept the little girl's promise.

I am her. She is me. Inner child and messy adult. We are one.

It was then I noticed a pink fabric tucked in the corner and bound with ribbon. When I untied the ribbon, it was like heaven raining down in my lap. My heart swelled so big I thought my chest would explode. Scattered like hundreds of rose petals were *Kisses for Cass,* lipstick kisses from my mother's lips. Tear after tear flooded my hot cheeks as I picked them up one after another. My mother used to put on lipstick and take a torn piece of paper and kiss it, leaving her imprint, then tossing it away in the car, in the bathroom, or on top of the dresser. I'd have scavenger hunts to find each one. I'd look at her and see what shade of lipstick she was wearing and then off I'd go. They were kisses from my mother's lips to mine. I held on to them as a child, hoping, wishing, and praying I'd find enough lipstick kisses to uncover Mother Moonshine. The mother I knew existed, but rarely saw. All around me, lipstick kisses, imprints of my mother's withheld love, shades of passion pinks, ruby reds, crushing corals. The weight of the emotions in those tiny pieces of paper came crashing down. I broke into sobs. The adult in me cried. The child in me cried. And I'd like to think even Mother Moonshine cried.

Knowing what I know of my mother now, even in understanding, didn't make the pain any less. I still yearned for a mother I would probably never have, or experience as I did one precious night under the moon.

Perceptions. Thrones. Expectations. Cycles. Clay feet.

I heard all of Doc's words running through my mind. I saw my mother, parts of her, now, and I realized she gave what she had to give, in the only way she knew how. Did she get it all right? No. But who does? I certainly didn't. Maybe we learn the best and the worst from people so we can clearly see the best and the worst in ourselves…a mirror of reflections, of failure, and of redemption.

Doc said to look at the good, deal with the bad, and move on. Mother did teach me good as a child, even though I couldn't see it then. How to cook, to skimp and save money so that I could one day travel the world. Every summer we went on vacation, hitting the highway to visit other states. She loved to travel. We went one place every year in the summer. I forgot about all the good times we had on those trips. My eyes could only see the bad. Mother also taught me when you don't have fireworks you make your own. She taught me to cut loose. Dance on the lawn barefoot and bang pots and pans. And maybe, just maybe, I want to think she left those lipstick kisses just for me, because it's the only way she knew how to give them. I may never know everything there is to know about my mother, her deeper story, who she is, but I know enough to forgive. My mother and I are more alike than we are different.

And my father, he had clay feet too. Rebel clay feet. My best and worst from him as well. My drinking habits come from his bootlegging bark, a little too much alcohol in the sap of the tree limbs. He did inspire me to use my own head, to wonder, observe, dream, explore, question and seek adventure. *Go out knowing,* he'd say. Use my imagination. Don't leave this world a wasted life. If you're going to leave it, then leave it knowing something. Did he have faults? You bet. One of his dark vices became mine. I'd like to think this cycle will be broken with me.

No one knew about mental illness back then, the way they know of it now. I was as messed up as Maw Sue—it's just no one recognized the signs, because you know, those damn perceptions Doc talks about. Lord, dealing with my clay feet had to be double-trouble. And Meg? Well, I discovered a lot about my little shiny diamond sister. She was a sore loser in card games but she had a hell-fire streak in her that terrified me. In the end, she protected me at the risk of herself. She stood for me at the river. For someone so little, she was brave and fearless. Sharp as a diamond's point and shiny as a midnight star.

It was a surreal moment when the past emerged with the present, my mirror bin, the amulet of a Seventh Tribe, my tokens, a child and an adult wrapped in one, finally together to remember, forgive and move forward. I could only do one thing which seemed right. Surrounded by my version of love, paper kisses, I took each one to myself, one after another. I accepted a kiss from my mother's paper lips to mine. A lipstick kiss to my cheek, my forehead, my lips. I could almost feel her ghostly flesh near me, mother to child. Kisses for Cass. It broke my heart and healed it at the same time. In my vision two little girls danced and beat on pots and pans with silver spoons with their Mother Moonshine. With each coral crush kiss, with every lipstick smudge, I made peace with our grievances. Suddenly, like magic and warmth from the heat of the pine curtain at sunset, I felt the presence of the divine. Maw Sue was right. God, the great majestic one in the Michelangelo painting with his sacred fingers reaching to Adam's fingers, were now my fingers reaching—up, up, up, because in reality, God had never left me.

When I gathered my wits about me, and wiped the snot and tears, I collected each paper kiss and put them neatly back inside their pink sachet with ribbon and sat it with the rest of the stuff. I had reached the bottom of the mirror bin. It sat in awe and wonder as if it was just made. There it was, my childhood locust crown waiting for its queen. The queen of the pine curtain. The locust crown leaves were brown and cracked, the brambles twisted and aged, the honeysuckles dried and crippled, the sap brittle and dark, the flowers and stems curled and the thorns held it all together. The precious gift of nature made from Maw Sue's hands. I reached inside tenderly and lifted it out, gently and so focused I felt the air leave my lungs. Tear after tear flooded down my face as I remembered the words, the ceremony, the anointing from my great-grandmother. I could barely swallow without feeling lumps in my throat. I felt breath and redemption and tasted glory on my tongue. It was the crumbs Maw Sue talked of; crumbs of my past, of my present, of my future. I knew at that moment what I must do. I sat the crown down and ran to the phone.

"Meg, do you have your crown?" I said full of anxiousness.

"Whaaat?" she said thrown off.

"Your crown…the locust crown Maw Sue made us when we were little."

"Are you okay, Cass? You sound rattled."

"DO YOU HAVE YOUR CROWN?"

"Yes.... okay. Calm down. Yes, I have it. It's in the mirror bin. What is wrong with you? Why are you so loud?"

"Because! I just opened mine. Everything is still there."

"I have the green scarf in mine, and yes, I have my crown too, but it's almost falling apart. Why?"

"You ask too many questions. Can you bring the mirror bin and the crown with you and meet me on the old dirt road by our parents' house? Just park at the intersection and I'll meet you there."

"What in the Tomfoolery are you up to Cass?" Meg said with worry. "What are we doing exactly?"

"Trust me. I know what I'm doing, Meg, I promise."

"That's what I'm afraid of."

"Come on..." I said trying to be convincing.

"As long as it doesn't involve a fire." Meg said mischievously.

"No promises." I said in a smarty-pants big sister tone.

"Fine. I'll meet you there. I'll have to take Bill's piece of shit hunting truck because he's out of town in my car."

"I don't care if you ride a horse. Be there." I said hanging up.

A half-hour later, I bailed in the cab of Bill's old rattling Ford truck while Meg scratched and shifted gears. We spun off down the old road of our past towards what was once our childhood gathering place that turned into my worst nightmare. I wasn't sure how this was going to turn out—but I had to try.

I sat my mirror bin next to hers. There was a bottle of vodka and a long machete in the floorboard. I looked at Meg and picked it up.

"Are we going to get drunk and kill somebody?"

She laughed. "We might see a snake, you never know. It is the river bottom. And that's some good drink right there. Bill got it from a client. Expensive spirit. And he doesn't know we're drinking it." She laughed wickedly. "Plus, I need to drink since I have no idea what you are up to."

I smirked. "We'll both need drinks. Especially after I tell you what all has happened."

Meg looked at me, intently curious. "Whaaatttt?"

"It was me. I set the fire."

"No shit. You remembered?"

"I sure did. Along with a whole lot of other stuff. But the best part is, get this, Meg. The girlfriend ditched Sam and she dismissed the charges. I pay some money to a flower fund, that's it."

"Hell yes, sister! That's drink worthy Cass. Go ahead."

I grabbed the vodka, opened it and burned down a swallow and passed it to Meg. I glanced behind us. It was almost dark. A large cloud of red dirt stirred in the gloom of the taillights as we entered our pine curtain kingdom. It was the first time we'd been together under the pines since we were kids. Everything felt familiar. A shiny diamond and Southern sap. Road trip rebels. Together again behind the pine curtain.

Out of nowhere a thud hit the front bumper of the truck. Meg squealed and hit the brakes. We skidded till we were sideways in the road.

"What the hellfire was that?"

"I don't know," I said unsure and looking around. "Did you see anything?"

"No. Did you?"

"No, I was looking behind us but I heard it hit." We sat in stillness and silence as if neither of us knew what the next move was.

"Fine." I said huffing. "I guess I'll get out and look. If I get murdered it's your fault." I opened the door hesitant.

"My fault? You called me sister! So…it's on you." Meg

cautioned in slow whispers. "Plus I can't see anything?" She leaned across the seat apparently waiting on my next move. I gave her a glare straight out of our preteen years.

"Meg, why are you whispering?"

"I don't know, it's what they do in movies, you know, right before someone is whacked" she said smiling and giggling.

"Oh, you're hilarious, Meg. Get out of the truck. You're coming with me."

"Fine. We die together. I accept my fate." Meg replied like a queen on the way to the guillotine.

"When did you get so dramatic?" I said looking at her curiously.

"Hmph…" She shrugged as we made our way to the beam of the headlights. Our shadows were long and stalky beside us on the ground. I stopped in my tracks. My heart skipped. Meg stopped too. Her face went pale.

"Shit…" I said gasping and looking up at her. All at once, we were brought face-to-face with our childhood. A dead owl lay on the ground circled in blood and entrails, still alive and twitching. It was painful to watch but more painful to realize what it meant for Meg and me.

"Nothing is coincidental." I said looking at Meg sternly. "Maw Sue used to tell us that. We can't leave it here. It will suffer. Death is merciful. Remember that's what she said. Never leave a wounded owl behind. Remember, Meg? It's sacred."

"Yeah, yeah…sacred." Meg said more scared than emotional. I felt a fluttery feeling in my belly. I knew without a doubt what I had to do. I turned and walked back to the truck. I pulled the machete out of its leather sleeve and felt my chest hitch. My balance was poor and my eyes tunneled. I walked toward the light beams and the crumpled feathers, all the while hearing whispers in my head, *they fly silent*, over and over. Meg was bouncing on her heels with more energy that I could withstand. She was babbling all sorts of words, but I could not filter them in. All I heard was the inner realm, the whispering words of the owl's inner light.

I raised the blade and swung. It was quick. When it was done, the whispering in my head stopped. I could hear Meg's low moan again and her pacing in the dirt. By the look on her face, I knew she remembered. This night was guided by someone beyond me and I had to follow its lead. Come what may.

"Come on, Meg." I handed her the machete while I picked up the owl and tossed it in the bed of the truck. "Drink some vodka. It'll calm you." She stood frozen in memory, locked back in time to our splendid and tragic childhood.

You remember, don't you, Meg?"

"Of course I remember our savage childhood. Who wouldn't remember cutting an animal in half and wearing its blood? That was Easter, wasn't it?" I busted out laughing.

We climbed in the truck not sure of what our next move was, but I was pretty sure it was going to be a repeat of the familiar. Meg passed the vodka and I took several swigs while she cranked the truck and we barreled down the dirt road laughing like we were kids again. A few minutes later Meg stopped and killed the engine. The headlights shined a beam of light over the edge of the riverbank. There was a stillness inside the cab. In the silence we both braced ourselves. What used to be a wonderful, whimsical fun place for us as kids, and teenagers, had long ago turned into something ugly. After the night of the great sadness, neither of us returned. *Until now.* My stomach turned flip-flops. I reached for the vodka once more and stared out at the lapping water, quiet and silent, my eyes barely blinking. Inside my head, the broken knob clicked and all I could hear were my own screams reverberating back to me from another time, held captive by the wind, the pine trees, the disturbed soil, and the water that haunted me.

"Cass, what are we doing here?" Meg said stoic and reserved. I grabbed my mirror bin and opened the door.

"Give me a minute." I said walking straight to the edge of the riverbank, the exact place the great sadness took me. Meg followed but stayed a safe distance behind. The woods had changed over time. Brush had grown up thickly covering where our fire pit used to be, and new trees had sprouted and grown tall, adding a shrouded look to what used to be open and airy. The river seemed wider but the pool of water, our old swimming hole had not changed, it had only birthed a smaller pool below the crest, eaten up from erosion. A small and beautiful waterfall trickled down from each pool and slowly made its way down the river. The way I see it, Mother Nature had to recover from the violence committed here that awful night and drown out the sounds of my screams and the bad energy left. It was replaced with the sounds and beauty of a waterfall.

I sat down on the ground, my mirror bin beside me, it's pewter lid reflecting the galaxy of stars in the deep, dark sky. While I stared into the water, I threw handfuls of dirt in simmers of anger rising up in me. Then it subsided and grief overtook me. In a brutal siege of suffering, I lamented my loss of innocence. I wept until everything grew silent in my mind and all I could hear was the faint rushing trickle of the waterfall. I turned and motioned to Meg sitting on the hood of the truck.

"Let's get on with it." I said in a better frame of mind. My tears had dried. It was time to make things right.

"Get on with what? What are we doing?" Meg said as she walked up.

"This is where I lost myself. It may seem crazy, but I am STILL HERE. I may have physically walked away, but the spirit of me, that little girl is still here. I know you didn't believe much in Maw Sue's rituals, her strange ways, but once upon a time, I did. Back then, I had some connection to myself that I don't have now, and I need to find it again, reconnect, get it back. You don't have to say anything, you don't even have to participate, but I really do need you to be here for me. Can you do that, Meg?"

"I'm right here. I'll do whatever it takes to help you, Cass. You just lead the way."

"Thank you." I said reaching out and hugging her.

"Okay, okay, enough mush, let's do this." Meg said not wanting to show emotion.

"Okay, well, since therapy, I've had an abundance of childhood memories return. One of them was at Maw Sue's at night, with a fire ritual, and the owl ceremony, and the cutting of hands." I bared my arm in front of me and rubbed the seven scar. "Do you remember that night?"

"Is that the night we were playing with Coke bottles and cut ourselves?" She stuck her palm out.

"No, Meg. No. That is *not* the truth. That is what I'm talking about. Mother lied to us. We were so little, and she was so upset with Maw Sue for her rituals, and for cutting our hands that she had Maw Sue locked up in Castle Pines. We were told over and over again that these scars were made by me and you playing with Coke bottles, until eventually, we both believed the story. What she didn't know is that Maw Sue had the same seven scar. All the years later I questioned it, and the memories were vague and spliced until recently."

"What? You mean we didn't play with bottles?"

"No, Meg. Maw Sue made these cuts. You really don't remember?"

"Apparently not. Why did she do that?" Meg's voice was conflicted as she stared at her palm.

"Well, I didn't remember it all these years, until I basically lost my damn mind with Sam, and reenacted the ceremony with a cleansing fire at his girlfriend's house, and got arrested for it.

Then comes therapy and poof! Memories like a madhouse. I went through hell to find them, so now that I know the truth, I'm telling it like it is. I'll give you the short version. That day in nineteen seventy something, we were riding with Maw Sue, driving home from the store, and Maw Sue found a wounded owl in the middle of the road…"

Meg gasped with a hissing rasp. "Oh. My. God." She turned and pointed to the truck.

"We just hit an owl. I hit an owl. I killed an owl." Her voice grew shrill, loud and fast.

"Meg, calm down. I know. It's okay. It's part of it. Just slow down and let me finish and you'll understand."

"But…"

"No. Listen," I said grabbing her hand. "Maw Sue said owls are sacred and shouldn't suffer. To our ancestors in the Seventh Tribe there is a deeper meaning. Maw Sue took the owl home, and that night we had the ceremony, she made necklaces, she put the owl in the fire, she mixed the blood with our blood after she cut our palms into a seven. Everything was great, we danced, sang and celebrated. It was fun. But…a bit later, Mother showed up. She threw a hissy fit and went batshit crazy when she saw our hands and called Maw Sue a mad butcher. She threw our necklaces in the fire and dragged us back home and had Maw Sue committed to Castle Pines. It was a nightmare. I snuck out and saw it all. Now, hear me out. This is important. I believe everything has led us to this moment tonight. Bad or good and all the in-between, even the owl you hit earlier. Are you listening, Meg?"

"Yes, yes, I'm listening, but I'm going to need a drink real soon because this is a little too much for me to process."

"Yeah, me too. Okay, so…the mirror bins. They were made for the seven sisters, their individual ritual, consecration, cleansing and empowerment to seal it with each daughter's own persona of self. Which is what Maw Sue was doing that night, but we didn't finish it. We got interrupted. Maw Sue told us we'd seal it with three words at the end of the ceremony. But everything went wrong when Mother showed up. Our mirror bins were open. I have replayed this memory over and over again, trying to figure it out. *That* is what happened. It has to be. I tried constantly to think of three words that Maw Sue would say. I racked my brain senseless going over everything, time and time again, until now. *Until the owl.*

When you hit that owl tonight, it just came to me, all the memories, and Maw Sue's words. *They fly silent.* It has to be it. I vaguely remember Maw Sue closing my bin a few times, when I had it with me at her house a few summers when we stayed with her. It was if she relived something from her own childhood, her times with the mirror bin as a child, and she'd whisper, *they fly silent* and close it. Maw Sue told us the amulet or the mirror bin, as we know it, is in many ways a miniature encapsulation of each person, in spirit and embodiment, our true persona, the owl's wisdom and the omnipotent power of something beyond us, something bigger, Godly, majestic. So, for instance, my mirror bin belonged to sister number one, which is Maw Sue's mother, and our great-great grandmother Joseymae. So her energy, her spirit, and persona is in there, her blood soaked in the wood, so is the owl they sacrificed for wisdom. Then it was passed to Maw Sue, same thing. Then passed to us. The night of the ceremony, my spirit and energy, along with my blood and that of the owl, was joined to the wood as well. But, here's the kicker. Because of the chaos that night—it wasn't finished."

"How in the hell do you remember all this?" Meg said astounded and shaking her head.

I cracked up laughing. "Therapy and pain. Believe me, it wasn't easy."

Meg sprawled out on the dirt. "Now that you're saying this,

some things are coming together, but I don't have a memory like you do. Mine is fragmented. I wish I could remember."

"Here's my theory, Meg. Because of the terrible events, Mother showing up, Maw Sue carted off to Castle Pines, both of us traumatized, the made-up lies, all of it disrupted the ending of the ceremony. Our ritual wasn't sealed. The door was left open, so to speak. Because of that, I believe a great deal of chaos was allowed to enter in our lives, that ordinarily wouldn't have been allowed had we sealed it. Because of that, it wreaked havoc, upturned life as we know it. Left it off-kilter so to speak. It's a long shot but I've had a lot of time to think about this, and tonight when you hit that owl—in one millisecond, it spiraled together in my head. The pieces lined. We have to finish the ceremony tonight. We have everything we need, the mirror bins, an owl sacrifice, and one thing we didn't have back then."

"What's that?" Meg asked.

"Alcohol." I smiled. "Are you ready to make it right? Seal the amulet. Finish it."

"I barely remember that night, Cass. But hey, what the hell, if you say so, then I'm ready to help you. You've been through more than me. It's creepy with the owl though, but I'm all in, sister. Let's seal the amulet by God."

We high-fived each other and giggled like we were little kids again playing with crackles and the world was our oyster. We scrambled around trying to set up the area with as much as we could remember. We gathered some fresh flowers for our locust crowns, some brambles, honeysuckles, pine cones, pine needles and some vines, and drew a circle in the dirt with a fire pit in the middle. I opened my mirror bin and pulled out two roses, the petal people, the *Immortelles* Everlastings, the broken me, the dead flower me, the one I plucked off the wild rosebush the night of the great sadness. The other petal flower is the one I picked for my mother back then, the mother who never saw me, who I erased from my life because she made me feel non-existent. I sat the roses aside and took out the brittle locust crown and placed some fresh flowers beneath the thorns. I placed it on my head and felt a rush of air. Room to breathe, as if for the first time since my childhood. The damp air in the Texas heat beaded my skin with pellets of sweat. My heart felt heavy like stone.

"Now it's your turn, Meg."

"Most certainly. I am a diamond queen, after all," she said royally and winking. She opened her mirror bin and pulled out Aunt Raven's green scarf and threw it around her neck and shoulders. Then placed assorted flowers throughout her locust crown and placed it upon her head. She bobbled from side to side as if she was enjoying the childlike moment with new eyes. The moment was magical as if we had the whole forest to ourselves. The night sky anointed us with bright stars and a faint glow of the moon creeping through the pines. I thought of Mother Moonshine and knew part of her was here, whether she knew it or not.

"Wait!" Meg shouted and took off running to the truck. She came back with the machete, and both head and body of the owl carcass. She would have looked wild and wooly, almost primal, if it were not for the green scarf blowing behind her. It was then I knew Meg had begun to remember her past. I watched the shiny diamond show off like she always does. She took a stick, poked the fire and inserted the owl's head between two logs. The flames erupted. Smoke suffered upwards while the feathers smoked, singed and curled. The sounds took me back and I would have gotten lost in the glow of roasting eyes if it hadn't been for Meg distracting me with her newfound Seventh Tribe knowledge. I couldn't help but rib her a little like I used to do.

"This is great, Meg, that you're remembering and all, but you DO KNOW we ate an eyeball." She stopped abruptly and turned to look at me.

"We did not," she said with an unconvincing eye twitch. "I

would have remembered an eyeball. I would have proudly told every kid at school."

"No doubt about that." I said laughing. Then she went back to her primal roots of being a fashionable Daniel Boone with a green scarf. I watched her with amazement. Dad raising her like a boy was coming in handy because she knew her stuff. She stripped off a piece of bark from a nearby tree to make a bowl and plucked a few feathers from the carcass, respectfully as Maw Sue had taught us, in awe of the owl's magical presence. The owl flies silent, they are like ghosts—they could be near us and we'd never know it. It was so mysterious to me, even saying the words made a chill go up my spine.

Meg laid the carcass on a large log, hacked the feet off and drained the blood into the bowls of bark she had made. I watched as she replicated almost every ceremonial move Maw Sue made. At times, I saw her ghost intermingle within as if she was watching to make sure we did it correctly. It was hard for me not to tear up seeing her. There were other times I'd get caught up in the flames of the fire, the owl skull, its hollow eyes, and the memory of childhood ceremonies mixed with the current events, me setting fire to Sam's stuff, the animal trophies, my own ceremonial cleanse and the way life turned out, for me and Meg, and how everything is connected. It all led to the here and now.

I had yet to read any of the manuscripts, scrolls, journals and books from the Seventh Tribe, but it will happen in time. When they are ready, I will hear them call. They are tucked away in my closet safe and secure in waiting.

I watched Meg place the bowl on the ground near us. She went back to the fire and put the sharp knife edge in the flames. She returned and said, "This might hurt a bit and I don't have any of Maw Sue's salve to numb it, so are you sure you want to do this?"

"This is necessary pain, Meg. It's nothing compared to the pain I've already suffered."

I held out my palm and took a deep abiding breath. The seven-scar glowed under the moon and the crackling firelight. There was a sharp pinch and a sting when she pierced the scar open. This would be the third time it had been cut. Seven blood drops fall. The sound of the dripping almost drove me to madness, hearing them repeatedly in my mind for months, and now, in reality. It validated my childhood memories, my flash-backs. I glanced down and watched the mirror bin take in my full-ness, my energy, all of me, my blood absorbed into the veins of the wood while a shudder ran through my body, a unification of oneness I hadn't felt before.

"My turn," Meg said cheerfully. She seemed distant, almost removed from the circumstances of what we were doing but then again, Meg had always been reserved, never one to show emotion. I wrapped the bandage around my palm and took the knife. Her seven-scar pulsated as it awaited its fate. I glanced up at her to make sure she was on the same page.

"You're sure about this?"

"It's too late to second-guess now, sister. Let's do this. Rock and roll."

My smile turned serious and I made the cut. My ears heard all sorts of sounds, like portals opening, water gushing, windows slamming, strange and eerie sounds, and I could not fathom what they actually were. The blood dropped, *drip, drip, drip, drip, drip, drip, drip.* Seven drops into the mirror bin that used to belong to Aunt Raven. I glanced up and Meg was emotional, although she was fighting not to be.

"You did great," I said handing her a bandage.

She smiled with confidence. "Well, what can I say, I'm kind of a warrior. I ate an eyeball once."

We giggled so hard, blood gushed from our wounds. It was a good long laugh with wet eyes and sore bellies.

"Oh. Lord. I need a drink before we finish this shit," I said, looking for the vodka bottle.

"Me too. A double. Why not a triple?" Meg said.

"Sounds good to me."

We shed our shoes and grounded with the earth. The fire roared with the owl's remnants burning in the flames while we stared out across the river. It was pitch of dark in the distance with the large dreadful pines standing watch over us, and the river was slick like black glass while the trickle of the waterfall and the sounds of the night soothed our wrecked souls. We drank the expensive vodka and sat in the silence of nostalgia.

"You remember what's next? Or is this it? Do we close the mirror bins now or what?" Meg asked breaking the quiet.

"I do remember. We're not through, sister. There's more," I said smiling and taking another swig. I jumped up and did a little jig.

"We get to be warriors because we are in the Seventh Tribe. Now…let's do some face painting."

Meg smiled and grabbed the bark bowl of owl's blood. She dropped seven drops into my mirror bin, mixing with my own blood and those of generations ago. It was perfect. Then Meg and I faced each other. She dipped her finger into the bowl and placed stripes and designs on my face as she spoke the ancient words, our rites of passage.

"Inner light, divine wisdom, vision…" She paused and her lips trembled. A big tear puddled in her eye and she sniffled. "And Love. The greatest of these is Love."

When she finished, I shed a few tears.

"Awww…so perfect Meg. You added your own swag to it, you sparkly diamond you!" I punched her in the arm. I was a proud sister. She had come so far.

"Now it's my turn, where's the bowl?" We quickly switched roles. I held the owl's blood proudly like my ancestors must have done centuries ago. I dripped seven drops into Meg's mirror bin. The earth seemed to rumble and shake and turn loose of things shackled in darkness for ages. It was exhilarating. I dipped my forefinger in the blood and painted Meg's face as I recited the words I hadn't spoken since I was a little girl. It made me emotional and warmed my heart at the same time. I knew that we were surrounded with the company of angels, ancestors, and the petal people, all witnessing the ceremony that should have been, long, long ago.

"Divine wisdom, inner light, vision…" I paused and smiled. Meg's eyes were lit like two diamonds. "And Love. The greatest of these is Love." I marked the final stripe across her face and sat the bowl at my feet. We stood sister to sister, face to face, arm to arm, blood to blood, flesh to flesh, bound by ties from the past, unified by things we may never understand, yet through it all, love held us. Built us. Broke us. Brought us back. We put our foreheads together, and closed our eyes in a wordless prayer. In my head I imagined the whole tribe observing in wonder and approval while a flight of owls watched in silence. We were one. One with ourselves, one with our pasts. One as women, as adults, as sisters, as children once lost, now found. A kingdom reclaimed. Redeemed. Restored. The locust crowns on our heads interlocked with their tiny sword soldiers. We were safe. We felt powerful. We were queens. We were warriors. We were recipients of inner light, divine wisdom, vision and most of all, love.

"Wait." Meg blurted and rushed away. I jumped.

"You have *got* to stop doing that, Meg. I am still a jumper, you know the complex PTSD aftermath. Fight or flight stuff."

"Yeah, yeah, sorry. But look, we should have used the talons." she said whining and holding up the owl's feet.

"Ehhhh…I think it's fine without them. It doesn't have to be exactly like it was back then. The mirror bins were most important of all. I mean, Maw Sue had herbs back then too, and we don't, so I think we're good."

"Good," she said relieved.

"You're the pioneer woman, not me." I laughed.

"Well, I have my limits," she said, tossing her green scarf like a drama queen.

"Okay, queen sparkle diamond slash Daniel Boone, ha-ha. Whoever you are. Let's finish this." I said getting up and walking to my mirror bin. Meg followed behind me. I had no idea if three words would seal the amulet and seal the ceremony. I hoped and prayed it would, so Meg and I could feel whole, complete, seven, as the initial ceremony was supposed to do, way back when, before the chaos hit and we left the lid open, never sealing it. We had nothing to loose at this point. We had to try. We sat on the ground facing the fire, our mirror bins expectant in front of us.

"On the count of three we'll say it together and close the lid.

"Okay Cass." Meg said agreeing to agree. I wasn't sure she believed at this point.

"Three, two, one."

"They fly silent." We said simultaneously closing the mirror bins. Neither of us lifted our hands from the mirror bins. We were each hopeful, expectant of something to happen, something we had missed that night long ago, something denied us, taken from us. Our eyes rolled around and scanned our surroundings for clues, anything that might connect us to the otherworldly we so much wanted to catch a glimpse of. Something to comfort us, validate us, and certify that we were not half-baked crazy Southern sisters with a penchant for the dark side. The woods were eerie and there was a black curtain folding in on us as the dark night, grew darker. The fire dwindled down to an amber glow as we waited in wonder, taking in the sounds of the night. Then I heard a crack.

"Sorry," Meg said as she popped her neck. "Are we done?"

"Well, it's not like anything is happening."

"Maybe it's not supposed to, Cass. Maybe it is what it is. It happens like it happens."

"Profound words, Madam Meg. I'll remember that nugget of wisdom." I rolled my eyes in slight disappointment. In my childhood mind, I expected something magical to present itself, something mysterious and unexplainable. In retrospect, I also thought about what Doc said about clay feet—and high expectations. Maybe Meg was right. *It is what it is. It happens like it happens.* Never a way with words, that one.

I was just happy we completed the ceremony. We sealed the amulet. We did our part. It gave a finality to everything past and present. I was positive Maw Sue was proud of us. As for me…I had other business. It was time to take my Kingdom back.

I walked over and picked up the two roses I had laid on the ground. Meg had put some logs on the fire and the bright light from the flames lit up the riverbank. I got closer to the edge and bent down to sit and meditate. I could hear the ripple of the water but it did not drown out what was in my head. I heard my screams, felt the pain, the sounds, the splashing water, me fighting, the flashbacks, the great sadness as it entered like a possessed demon of the dead. I glared at the place where it happened. It was time. I steadied myself and leaned over, placing each rose in the water. In my vision it might as well have been myself as a child back then, and my distant mother who exiled me from her life. They were simply roses, but in the Seventh Tribe, they were more. They were the grief takers and had they not been there, to help me in my life through my troubles, I'm not sure I would be alive today. Across the water, they floated like mangled corpses, Viking burials without the flames, slowly drifting the bends of the river. I took a deep, abiding, redemptive breath—and let it all out. Maw Sue said salvation, the deeper meaning of the word, meant

Room to breathe. And letting go of the dark past meant I had room to breathe freely, unbound, safe and forgiven. I inhaled and exhaled deeply. I felt peace again.

Meg sat down beside me quietly as to not disturb my meditation. She put her bare feet in the water and swirled them around. The sounds stirred me. I closed my eyes and whispered the words my soul needed to hear.

"Birds of the air, lilies of the field, great stars of Heaven. I want to be me, whole and complete. Make me seven. Send me crumbs so I may consume and make my life a beautiful bloom." I felt the atmosphere fill with the presence of God, the space of time between the void, the gap between the fingers. In my head I could see the masterpiece painting of those godly hands reaching out and human hands stretching to touch. Unite. Merge.

"In honor of seven. Amen," Meg said as she grabbed my hand and squeezed it like she did when we were kids. The air around us was magical, yet tranquil. We were kids—we were women. A little closer to God than we'd been since childhood when our belief was innocent, untouched by life and trials. In sequence, with warrior-painted blood-streaked faces of inner light, we reached upwards with our branded seven palms like two kids plucking out stars from the deep black sky. We reached to touch the realm, the gap of the great void, the space between Adam's and God's fingers. Together we braced ourselves for the journey ahead. We were grit and courage, moon and stars, faith and hope.

We look. We love. We let go. We surrender our past, our present and our future to a higher power. Like the suffering servant, Jesus, the rusty nails in his hands, his pierced bloody feet, the betrayed sword slicing his side and the thorns of his humble crown piercing his head—for the first time, in all these years, I understood forgiveness. Of myself, and others. *Clay feet forgiveness.* Instead of clinging and being a keeper of things that were not mine to keep—*I let go.* I surrendered. When I tossed the two petal people roses in the water, a representation of the damaged teen, and the other rose, the distant mother I thought abandoned me, I was able to forgive. This was my release, and my redemption. The more I let go, the more I saw the bright light of God's presence as I did as a child. But most importantly, the wide, long gaps of space between my mother and me suddenly grew closer, as if we'd never been far apart at all. Sitting in the exact place of the great sadness, I had to forgive the boy who took my innocence that night long ago. I didn't forget…but I forgave to release myself from the bondage. By surrendering the rose to the river, I reclaimed my crown, my right to my body, myself, my soul. I took back the crown stolen from me as a child. I was no longer a victim.

I am a little girl—I am a woman. *I am enough.*

After our silent childlike ritual, we gazed out into the river. The moment had put an intensity in the air that was about to choke both of us, so I lightened the mood.

"Heyyyyyy-oo-ohhhha *(Whoa-oaaa-aohhh)*
Whoa-a-a-a-ahhhh *(heyyyyy-oohhhh)*
Heyyyyyy-oo-ohhh (Whoa-oaaa-aohhh)"

I sang and pushed my shoulders against Meg's. In a few seconds, I was on my feet circling the fire and enticing Meg to join me. She glanced at me as if I had lost my mind. I sang loudly, coaxing her with laughter and teasing her face with a pine straw limb. She got up and walked near the fire. Her face showed me that she was about done with my childhood games. But I kept singing, I kept dancing. All of a sudden, when I spun around, Meg jumped forward, her body crouched low to the ground and her arms spread-eagle, circling and bobbing. She cut in right on time in Meg fashion.

"Heyyyyyy-oo-ohhhh."

"Whoa-a-a-a-a-ooohhhh," I answered in fire and spirit.

"Whoa-a-a-a-a-ooohhhh." Meg sang louder as her voice echoed through the forest. Two sisters lost in a moment, a song, a place where our past and our present intermingled. As we sang and danced, the spirit world around us came alive and the dust swirled up with sand ghosts. The Seventh Tribe joined in; the seven sisters, Maw Sue, her mother, and all the ancestors. It was electricity surging and energy moving, the earth, the wind, the water, the fire, the moon, the dark. Then as if my mind willed it into being, she appeared. Though Meg would not see her, my mind's eye knew she deserved to be there. My Mother Moonshine formed from the beams of light shining down upon us. She looked right through me as if we held a mutual understanding, without words. I fell into the deep blue sea of her eyes. I looked. I gazed. I saw love in the only form she could provide it. I took in all of her touched by the moon. Feeling her fissures and her cracks and the great flaws of her embodiment, I felt her shine. She joined right in with her pots, pans and silver spoons. Mama cut loose as my daddy liked to say. Hooting, howling, yipping and yelling. Banging, clanging, shimming and shaking. In the middle of the pine woods, around a roaring fire, the past emerged with the present and it was glorious.

Our lyrics could be heard from the tops of the bottle brush loblolly pine trees to the depths of the disturbed soil. Meg and I danced till we collapsed in laughter, followed by solitude and the familiar silence. Somehow, now, it didn't seem as maddening as it used to be. We lay on the ground beside the crackling fire, looking up at the twinkling sky and its wonders. The night gave its sacrifice of sounds, its wildness, the creatures of the night, the coyotes howling, the cicada crackles humming, the crickets chirping, the frogs croaking and owls hooting. *We had our kingdom back.*

A half hour later, Meg was waiting in the truck while I went to pour water on the fire. When I turned to walk away, I heard a sound coming from the forest. I stopped and listened. It was coming from the edge of the thicket and then I heard voices. My eyes swirled and scanned the area in fear someone or something was out there. For a second, it took me back to the night of the great sadness. I sat the empty vodka bottle down by the fire and walked closer to where the sound was coming from. The voices got louder, the snapping and popping branches got closer, and I began to shake.

"Shall we bury them?" the voice said. My body convulsed tip-to-toe. *No, no, no,* I thought. *I can't do this. I'm healed. I've had therapy. I'm done with this.* The voice gave way to a shadow, and the shadow turned into a little girl. I recognized her as me when I was five. Her face still young and innocent. That was me before it happened. Seeing her broke my heart. And then suddenly another one appeared. *No, no, no, this can't be happening. What is wrong with me? I've settled this. It's all over now. Forgive and move on. I can't be having a breakdown again. Why is this happening?* But *it was* happening in plain sight. Every age of me as a child appeared.

"Shall we bury them?" they asked repeatedly.

I wanted to scream into the deep black pitch of the pine woods because I knew my mind could not take another breakdown, not after what I'd been through. Back when I called my mother, during my meltdown with Sam, they appeared to me the same, all of them burdened and carrying my past on their backs, the word bones, the skeletons, etched and branded with scribbles and things to fix my life and the lives of others. I needed them back then. But I deal with life and problems differently now. There are no longer any word skeletons to bury. No burdens to carry to the Hush cemetery. No unspoken words to keep hidden. No voices to silence. No little girls to protect anymore. And then it hit me. I know this...but they don't. I've released everything in my life, *except them*. In mere seconds, they were all standing before me. Every age, ever era, ever pain. All of them carrying the burden of word bones on their backs, asking in repetition, "Shall we bury them?" The boney skeletons were blazing with amber glows from another time and place, still waiting to be fulfilled, answered, validated, comforted, embraced. They had been buried and dug up countless times over the years waiting for their moment. Tears gushed down my face. The magnitude of what I had to do overpowered me.

I hitched, heaved, shook and wept, looking inward and through each age of myself. They were only doing what I created each of them to do, back then, when I needed them to survive. But like me, they yearn to be set free. They are not keepers. They were never meant to carry the burdens I gave them. They came back tonight because the ceremonies Meg and I performed beckoned them to me. It was their turn. They were waiting on me to give them permission to be free, unbound, unconfined. Released from the House of Seven and the Hush cemetery. To live. To finally live as they always should have.

I bit my lips while my body convulsed at the savage weeping of my soul. I thought I had cried heavily before, but no. This was a new undoing. A snot-slinging, body-shuddering, soul-rattling Southern howl that split the seams of the Earth. I hesitated and wept so hard, because deep inside, I knew what would happen once I let go for good. It's debilitating to the mind, body and spirit when you finally release all you've ever known, the comfortable parts of yourself, the things that hold you back, the things you've outgrown, the hidden things that stifle, or control you, the coverings, the masks of your childhood, the molds you've build with small hands to survive because it's all you've ever known. I was able to live because of these little girls. Every one of them had a purpose in my life growing up. Each one provided strength or support when I had none. If I had no voice—they spoke for me.

When I was silenced, they were my lips. All my questions about life, and love, and injustice, and anger, and family, and the universe. Every desire fulfilled and unfilled was written on the dry bones, a voice from a childhood journal, spoken and unspoken. Then they'd carry my burdens. Each one would hoist the skeletons on their shoulders and ask, "Shall we bury them?"

And I'd say, "Yes, bury them." One by one, they'd march to the Hush cemetery behind the House of Seven with the oak trees and upside-down moss children with their knot eerie eyes glowing and they'd dig a grave for the word bones. But in my heart of hearts, I knew there'd come a day of reckoning, a day of redemption, of resurrection, of confrontation and digging up bones.

I stood before each of them and took back the wholeness that was in them, to myself, it's rightful place. As I embraced each one, I touched their cheek and looked deeply into their eyes. It was a tender connection but also painful. I saw and felt their sacrifice and relived it in my mind. *Survive. Adapt. Thrive.*

And for the last time each one asked me, "Shall we bury them?" I could see the deep unresolved yearning in their eyes. I sobbed and sniffled barely able to keep myself together.

"No, child. Don't bury them. Not today. Not ever again." A glint of light sparkled in their eyes for the first time. They looked at me, at each other, then back at me, confused, yet hopeful and curious.

"No more burials," I said halfway crying and raising my arms. "No more silence. The words have a voice now, because of you." My own voice was breaking and my throat locked up with sadness. "You were the word keepers and it is time to let them live. Let them have their VOICE! Let them speak. Let them be written. Let them be stories and tales. Let them be love. Let them be loud. Let them scream if they want to. Let them sing. Let them be praise and let them be worship. Let me be light and let them be dark. Let them be the child. Let them be the adult. Let them free to be the voice they've always been. You *were* my keepers. You were my survival. For the word bones…and me. You kept me safe. I am thankful. You helped me survive. Your job is done. You are free. You are coming home to me, my heart, my spirit, your rightful place. Let the words, the bones, the skeletons, the roaring voices of every question, every letter, every word that Cassidy Cleo Collard ever had be set free. LET THEM FOREVER BE FREE! You can rest now. Come home."

The air was mystical and filled with a dark enchanting vibration that echoed in the forest. The tree tops swayed and the ground tingled and the river water splashed. Words flowed from inner places within me, long ago hidden and unspoken. I didn't want it to end, but I knew it had to. Because with every ending, starts a new beginning. Each girl I created out of happenstance to survive, to keep the voices and the written words alive. Now I must let them go. Each girl met my eyes one by one, a meeting of the mind, a smile, a knowing—the word bone skeletons on their backs disintegrated into dust. The little girls bounced around weightless and fairylike and then placed their hands on my heart. I felt their fullness enter me, return to me as if it never left and then they faded away, like fog in the night. When they were all gone, a familiar silence filled me. At first it was unsettling. I was alone now. I had nothing to fall back on, as I did when I was in survival mode as a child. I must now handle this a new way. I closed my eyes and wept but not for long. I was different now, no longer tossed about like a leaf in the wind. I'm a healing adult with a beautiful inner child. I have a voice now. My true authentic voice. I will be okay. *We will be okay.*

I turned and walked back to the truck. I stopped by the fire and picked up the empty bottle and scattered trash but something made me stop and look up. I glanced into the deep, dark, tranquil sky and suddenly out of nowhere the owl was there, as if somehow, it wasn't there at all, blending in with the wind, shadows, slinks and blackness, meshed and united with silence. I smiled so hard I thought my heart would explode. For the longest time, silence had been a burden to me, a terrible madness eating me from the inside out. *Until now.*

Broken knobs, black angels and blue lines. All three blended imperfectly to form me. Maw Sue was right all along. Words have power. And so does silence. And I now understand more than ever, what she meant by those four words that haunted me as a child. I think I finally did it Maw Sue. I made lovely my losses.

TWO BUCKETS, ONE CHOICE

And now these three remain:
faith, hope and love.
***But the* greatest of these is love.**
~ 1 Corinthians 13:13

A week later, the phone rang. It was Pearl out of her mind with rambling speech.

"Oh my God, Cass, you're not going to believe what happened."

"What? Is everything okay, is Doc all right?"

"Oh, no, no. That's not why I called. Doc is fine. It's Edna. George did it."

"He did?" I said, surprised. I never read the *Gazette* anymore but I might make an exception in this case.

"YES, HE DID!" Pearl said, excited and short of breath. "Well, it didn't go as he expected. Not exactly, but it worked. He got caught, actually. And it was bad at first. Edna gave him the notepad as she normally did, and George typed it out, and she proofed it and gave her go-ahead, but then he felt bad and started having second thoughts because Edna hadn't been in the same mood for months now, and he knew something was different or she was struggling with something, anyway, he knew it was off. He waited until the next day, then he decided to go ahead and go for it. He typed a new bulletin, exposing Edna of her faults, but not in a mean-spirited way, it was more of a, let's say, revealing nature of what Edna had been doing, because he did it in Edna's voice, as if she had actually written it in a confession to the town.

"It was ready to go to print by lunch. George sat the document on the table underneath a book, turned facedown. When he returned, Edna was sitting in his chair with tears running down her face, and holding the document he wrote. George felt bad, but told her that he was tired of working and wanted to go to college. He didn't care anymore about people's feelings, because he'd learned not to from Edna. This really set Edna on fire. They had a knock-down argument but both stood their ground. It was tense for a while, until Edna broke down. She asked for time alone and for George to wait till the end of the day to finish his shift and then he did not have to return, ever. So, George waited. One hour before closing, Edna returned with a new edited document in a style similar to what George had actually written, confession style, but it was the truth of Edna's past in her own words. She asked George to read it and tell her what he thought. He did. And it went to print. They parted ways, but not before Edna told him she'd pay for his college. George almost fell out. Anyway, you're not going to believe this article. Seriously, not going to believe it."

"Wow, that is some powerful stuff right there. I'm going to go pick up a *Gazette* right now. I can't wait to read what Edna has to say about her life, *for once*, and not someone else's."

"Wait," Pearl said, "When you pick up the *Gazette* and read it, I want you to drive by her house. You MUST."

"Okay, but why?"

"You'll see. I'm telling you. Drive by there."

"Okay, Pearl. I'm heading out now. I can't wait to read it. Did I just say that? My-my how things change."

Pearl laughed. "Yes. Who knew?"

I hung up and drove to the corner store. It was full of chatter and an abundance of people buying flowers. *Did I miss Mother's Day, a holiday or something?* Hmm, it must be a town event. I shrugged it off and grabbed a *Gazette* from its wooden display case. I opened the cooler for a coke and walked to the counter.

"Would you like a flower with that?" the gentleman clerk said nicely.

"No," I said pondering. "No flowers for me."

"You *sure* you don't want a flower?" The clerk seemed annoyed by my refusal.

"Uhm…I'm sure I don't want a flower, but thank you," I said pleasantly but firm.

"But everyone is buying flowers, *not* pencils, but flowers," he said, trying to convince me. *Why would he mention pencils and flowers in the same sentence? What in the world?*

"Uhh no sir, no pencils OR flowers for me, just a Coke and the *Gazette* please, but thank you again."

"Suit yourself." He shrugged and rang me up. I walked away puzzled. I sat in my car wondering what the hell has gotten into everybody. People were toting out flowers by the dozen. And what's the deal with pencils? I made a note to check my calendar when I got home. Obviously, I'd missed some weird event I'd never heard of. I drank down my cola and started reading the *Gazette*. Enthralled with Edna's content for the first time in my life, I was flabbergasted. All sorts of emotions pinged through me, from the past to the present but finally settling into a wide smile and a shake of my head.

"Might as well." I said laughing out loud and opening the car door. "This is going to be fun."

"Sir, pardon me."

"You're back." The store clerk lit up.

"Yes, I am. I've changed my mind. I'll take that flower now."

"Glad to hear it. Everyone loves flowers today, yeah?" he said pulling them from the vase.

"They sure do," I said smiling and halfway laughing. "Wait. I'll take a dozen, one of every color if you have it."

"I have plenty. Here you are." He sat the bouquet on the counter while I paid. I giggled like a school girl and walked towards the door but stopped halfway. "Sir, can you tell me something?"

"I'll try," he said.

"How many pencils have you sold today?"

"Zero. Not one pencil, imagine that."

"Figures," I said grinning, "Have a good day, sir."

I threw the flowers in the seat and backed out. As I pulled onto the highway, I noticed an old man in a lawn chair next to a vegetable stand off the roadway. Little sparks erupted in my mind. I knew what I had to do.

PRESENT DAY

MARCH 2, 1989
NEWS YOU CAN USE
BY EDNA ROLLINS

TEXAS NEWS EDITION

Dearest Pine Log community. I started helping my father with this bulletin when I was twenty-one, and full-time by twenty-three. In 1940 I married my sweetheart Jimmy Don and we had eighteen wonderful years together and one adorable son, James. When the Lord allowed them both to be taken from me in

1958 from a terrible fiery car crash, the Edna I used to be was burnt up in the flames and rose to the heavens with them, never to be the same. Their deaths changed me. I grew hard-spirited. I stopped writing. I stopped living. I wandered around in my pajamas talking to birds in my yard trance-like for a year. Inside, I paced room to room, looking at old photos, reliving old memories, smelling my son's clothing, my husband's aftershave. My grief overcame me until I was no longer a person, just a shell of something unnamed. I tried long and hard to regain my composure, get a new routine, start over—but the old one was so familiar I literally could not function without it. I wandered around without going anywhere. A homeless soul within a home. I had no idea that years later, the Wanderers would be the very thing that would save me and bring me back to a life worth living.

I knew I could not let my father's business go under because I was a loose cannon. Slowly, I started writing again. All I had is this column in the *Pine Log Gazette* and you followers who read it. I found my way back in writing and it truly did bring me out of the pit after my family passed, but I do admit now that I was still a bitter soul, and I took it too far sometimes. I stepped over boundaries without care or concern of other's feelings, I made terrible accusations without facts, and I hurt people with my words that I should have been using to help. Looking back now, I promise you that I did not do it intentionally. I have learned a lot about myself, the Edna who was, and the Edna I want to be. To be truthful, I was angry with the God that I said I worshipped. I was mad because He took my loved ones away and left me alone. *What am I to do with that?* I said over and over but got no answers from God, which made me even more sour. It had nothing to do with anyone in the community. It was me. I was hurt and I hurt other people. For that, I am truly sorry. This column was my lifeblood. I clung to it like a leech sucking the blood off of everyone for no other reason than to fend off my loneliness, insecurities and my anger for all the things you folks had, that I didn't. I offer my deepest regret. I've heard that you all know me to be uptight, self-righteous, judgmental, a nosy busybody and many other flaws that no one likes to admit. I would like to add one to the list, if I may. I have been living a lie. An outright, big, fat lie. Let me explain further.

In 1971 the Moon Wanderers showed up a few miles from Pine Log at one of their yearly campsite gatherings. I went on a mission from God, I thought, to do an article on what I deemed as heathens invading our lands and I had every intention of stirring the pot. I got to see them in their native free-spirited hedonistic way of life; and I was appalled. Yet, deep inside, something was awakening in me and I didn't even know it yet. What jolted me happened afterwards.

Billy Ray Thomas was my bodyguard and went along on the trip and unbeknownst to me, met a woman there and fell in love. Weeks later, he disappeared with her. Even though the whole town had no idea of his whereabouts, he was actually gallivanting with the Moon Wanderers, and here I was putting out all-point bulletins about his sudden departure thinking something terrible had happened. All the while he's in love. Later, when the truth was revealed, I was mortified that he could take up with a jezebel woman of that nature. I did not know that one year later my life would flip upside down with the same tangled love thoughts that would rule me for the next sixteen years.

In 1972, I was on vacation in California celebrating my 55th birthday alone. I was God-smacked when I heard the locals talking about a tribe of nomads at the nearby campgrounds. When I asked about them, imagine my surprise when they said they called them the Moon Wanderers. I couldn't help myself. I had to find out if Billy Ray and his woman might be there, maybe talk to him, find out about his life and such. I knew I needed to blend in with them, not the old Edna, but a new version. I went to a dress shop and bought a dress I would have not worn in a million years. I looked like I came straight out of Woodstock.

There was a long trail leading to the camp,

and along the way, wildflowers grew abundant, so I picked a few and tucked them into my hair. Within ten minutes of wandering around inside the bustling confines of the activity and people going here and there, I stopped to take it all in. A few feet away, a man stood still as stone and stared right through me. It rattled me at first but I continued to look around, discounting his piercing eyes. To the left and right I took everything in, but no matter where I looked, the man was there, still staring, until I had no choice but to meet his gaze. When I did, his mouth curved up in a smile. I tensed and did not smile back. I looked away pretending I did not see him, but clearly, I did. He was shirtless with a purple peace sign painted on his chest, a scruffy graying beard and soft blue eyes. He was holding a metal water bucket with a big silver dipping cup. Suddenly, I felt awkwardly giddy. An emotion I am not used to feeling, believe me. He passed by several people filling their cups with water, but he always looked back up, and when he did, our eyes continued to meet until he was standing in front of me.

"Water?" he said rattling me undone with his deep voice. I felt something inside me shift.

"I don't have a cup," I said shyly and looking away. Before I turned back, he had a fresh cup from his pack and was offering it to me.

"Ohh…okay." I said reluctantly.

He began to pour the water from the dipper into my cup and inside my body, the dry dusty dunes of my thirsty soul began to crave companionship, although I fought it vehemently.

"Thank you," I said as I drank a swallow. All the while he never took his eyes off me, which made me exceedingly nervous.

"You are Adsila. Beautiful Adsila," he said.

Immediately, I thought with relief, Oh, that's it. He thinks I'm someone else. Either that, or he's intoxicated.

"No, no. I'm Edna. Edna Rollins from Texas."

"You are Adsila. Adsila from Texas," he said, putting the dipper in the bucket. Then he reached up to touch my hair.

I reacted by walking backwards. "Okay, buddy, enough with the handsy-pansy stuff." By this time, I was sure he was drunk. But this dude did not let up. He continued the word game, calling me Adsila from Texas and I argued right back with him, for some odd reason, until he surrendered in angst.

"Edna" he said, "Edna from Texas. If you are going to be a part of this tribe, you must have a tribe name, and Adsila is the name for blossom, like the ones you have in your hair. I am Hadnot from Virginia. But here in the tribe, I am Dakelh which means water traveler." He raised up the bucket of water. "Get it now?"

"Ohh..." I said, exasperated and irked. "*Why* didn't you say that to begin with?"

"You wouldn't let me."

And he was right. This water traveler pegged me from the get-go and it rattled me undone. For some strange reason, whatever I drank from that bucket had me head over heels for this nomad and from that point onward, I was a part of the tribe. The rest of the week, I stayed with Hadnot and the Moon Wanderers doing all the things they did. I felt alive for the first time in years since my husband and son died. I am here to tell you that I am in love with a water traveler, a Moon Wanderer.

Every year since our meeting, I have gathered with them across the country in every state across the continental US. We are complete opposites. We butt heads, we argue, but we make it work. He knows the real Edna from Texas, the pained, heartbroken, ugly parts of her. Yet he loved her to wholeness again. I never thought I would love again, but here I am.

However, there comes a time when you have to make a hard choice. Each year, after the gatherings, I returned to Pine Log to live a lie. I am a stubborn old goat and Hadnot knew it. Even though I had found a well of water to fill me up and make me whole, loved, complete... I wasn't ready to let go of my past life. After all, my father built this business up from scratch. I was raised here, married here, had my son here. It felt like home, even though they all were long gone. I'm not sure what I was holding on to. Maybe it was the fact that you folks are all I had left. By entering your lives, through my little column of words, I felt a part of something, I had a family again, in a small way. I know I didn't do it right most times, and I'm sorry for that. I want you to know that you are family to me. Thank you for filling the spaces of emptiness in me for so long after I lost Jimmy and James. Throughout the years, I went back and forth as to what I should do; leave with Hadnot and see the world, or stay in Pine Log with everything I am familiar with. Hadnot and I stay in touch with letters and phones calls; however, this year was different than all the rest.

You see, I am hesitant. I am scared of change. I have a million doubts. I'm an introvert. Hadnot is a social butterfly. He takes risks. I hold back. He loves wildly. I love in bits and pieces. He sees the world as this grand vision to be explored, and I see it with fear and trembling. He is patient, kind and long-suffering. I am compulsive, often mean-spirited, and suffer nothing if I don't have to. He walks on the grass barefoot and climbs trees with abandon. I walk on the sidewalk with shoes and scream at the tree climbers as childish and immature. We are obviously different in every way imaginable, and that is why I am afraid. In fact, I've been afraid of this moment for years. I knew it was coming, I just didn't know when.

Hadnot laid out ultimatums. He is serious. I know he is. Either I leave with him and start a new life or walk away forever. He will not play half-and-half. I am wrecked with emotions. The mere thought of NOT having him in my life overrules all the unknowns and fears. I have lost way too much in my life already, and I will not lose the one thing that has made me exceedingly happy. For weeks I have pondered. Hadnot is patient, but he is no fool. My heart feels like a dry, dusty dune without my water traveler, and the prospect of not seeing him again overwhelms me.

Fine folks of Pine Log, I need your help. I am sixty-one years young and there is no sense in wasting precious time. Tell me what you think. I rarely ask anyone for their opinions because I have so many myself. I know you are all laughing at that one. It is true. However, this time, I am seriously open to hearing what you think, since you have been my family all these years.

Edna or Adsila?

- Should Edna from Texas stay in Pine Log and continue writing and serving the community?
- Or should Adsila the flower blossom join Dakelh the water traveler and see the world?

Who do you choose? If you choose Edna from Texas, drop a pencil in the bucket. If you choose Adsila, drop a flower in the bucket. It's all going down at the corner of 421 Hollis Avenue.

Front porch.

Two buckets.

One choice.

What's it going to be, Pine Log community? Help me decide.

I look forward to seeing your decision. Thank you for being such a wonderful part of my life. Either way is a win-win. This *may* or *may not* be the last time you see my column or hear me on KTBR Radio News Station 109.9, but for old times' sake, I'm going to sign off either for the last time, or like always, I'm Edna Rollins, and THAT'S NEWS YOU CAN USE.

QUEEN OF THE PINE CURTAIN

Make lovely your Losses
~Maw Sue

After leaving the garden stand, and reading the gazette for the second time in disbelief, I quickly went home and rummaged through my kitchen cabinets. Once I found everything I needed, I hopped back in my car with a heightened sense of purpose, hope and mischief. The entire drive I listened to the radio and sang loudly to God, country, and pastured cows, my own rendition of Fleetwood Mac's song, *Say You Love Me.* As my body moved to the beat, my mind's eye released a series of flashbacks from the past that streamed joyful tears in my eyes.

...Meg, mother and I under the big drop moon dancing, shimmying and shaking, beating the hell out of pots and pans while the sky filled with hundreds of burst firework flames.

...Maw Sue, Meg and I dancing around the ceremonial Seventh Tribe fire, faces painted, blood bound, throwing caution to the flames, talons in our hands uplifted to the stars and singing till our lungs were hot.

...We were Goddesses. Unhindered. Spellbound. All the while, in stealth fashion, flying high above with outstretched wings and eyes like yellow sparks of fire, the sacred ones joined in. They had always been there, flying in silence.

I rounded the corner of Beechnut Avenue and drove three blocks till I found Hollis Street. Edna's house wasn't hard to find. You only had to look for the traffic jam. Apparently, everyone else in Pine Log had now read the *Gazette* and they were helping Edna with her decision. I found a parking spot on the side street a few houses down.

I walked the sidewalk in amazement. The whole front porch of 421 Hollis looked like an outdoor flower stand. Sprouting and growing from the doors and windows were all sorts of blooms and flowers, flowing down the steps and into the driveway, and sprawled out on the lawn. I never even saw a bucket, much less two. And there was not a pencil to be found, anywhere.

I sat and watched throngs of people drive by and drop flowers off one after another. I couldn't help but laugh and think about how much I used to despise Edna Rollins since my early youth for all the things she said about my great-grandmother, and other people who ended up at Castle Pines, for the fire story, for myself. But now...I felt nothing but empathy knowing her story. All she lost, of her family and herself. Just like me, Maw Sue, my mother, and even my sister; all reacting according to our own pain, our losses, our deepest rejections, all in an attempt to just survive. Maw Sue's words come to mind. *Adapt, survive, thrive.* A seed, a sapling, everyone trying in their own way to grow in disturbed soil.

Each of us reacted differently, but nonetheless, through it all, a portion of love was found in the mix, waiting on us to claim it, take it back. Honor the process. Forgive ourselves, and others. Heal the pain. Love ourselves through the loss.

In a way, Edna didn't think she deserved to be loved in her true form, but Hadnot showed her differently and that made all the difference in the world. It's inconceivable to imagine someone could love us in our raw, ugly, unmasked authentic form, but when it happens, it transforms us. It allows us not only to accept and receive that love from others, but to also love ourselves. Maybe for the first time and that in itself may be the hardest part.

At the end of the driveway, I lay claim to my spot. I sat the silver bowl containing a bouquet of colorful flowers wrapped with fresh collard greens tied with a white bow. In the middle of the bow was a single unlit match. Leaving my signature and saying what I wanted to say, without *actually* saying it, left me gleeful. My smile turned to laughs as I skipped down the side-walk. Adsila got her answer.

But most of all, like me and Maw Sue…

Edna made lovely her losses.

A SPECIAL NOTE FROM THE AUTHOR

For those of you that had meltdowns, felt panic or triggered by a prior trauma you experienced, I am truly sorry. Just know that I prayed for you in advance. I *have* been there. I understand trauma well. Facing it is incredible hard. I sincerely hope that you will rise up from the hardships you have faced, like Cassidy—like myself and others I've known along the journey to finding wholeness and healing. This story takes on a lot of challenges; hard subjects, mental illness, rape, dysfunctional relationships, emotional abuse, family dynamics, and more. I hope above all, it opens the door to more serious discussions. All in all, I pray the story changes you, impacts you, rattles you the core, makes you cry and laugh, and think a little differently than you did before. I hope you experience the supernatural reality that is beyond us, bigger than any of us imagine. I pray you rediscover the child within you and the magic she still holds. She is key to recovery and finding your true authentic self, so that you can begin your journey home. Together, as one embodiment, adult and child, hand in hand.

You **can** heal. You **can** recover.

You can rise above anything that has tried to beat you down or destroy you. And please remember that we often do not know the whole story behind other people's actions. There may be a deeper vault of things you do not know. More so, they themselves may not know. Other people's battles are not yours to fight. It's hard not to take it personally, and I cannot say which route is the best to take in every situation. I know that most of all, your journey is about you, so if you concentrate on your recovery, you can deal with just about anything else that comes along. However, you **cannot** do it alone. Seek the help of a professional. Then and only then, can you begin to see the road to recovery and use the tools you've learned to grow, heal, survive and thrive. It is then you will know yourself, your voice of authenticity. It begins with you, and your inner child. The true voice. Listen to her. You CAN make lovely your losses. May all the good come to you as you begin your journey.

Thank you again for reading.

~ Barb Lanell

If you are struggling, please seek help. The National Suicide Prevention Lifeline is a United States-based suicide prevention network of over 160 crisis centers that provides 24/7 service via a toll-free hotline with the number 1-800-273-8255. It is available to anyone in suicidal crisis or emotional distress. If you are a victim of sexual assault, get help now. Don't wait. Call 800.656.HOPE (4673) to be connected with a trained staff member from a sexual assault service provider in your area.

A NOTE ON OWLS AND OTHER BIRDS:

Although this story is fiction, it talks about dead or injured owls used in sacrificial ceremonies that are tribal in nature. It's a made-up story, fiction, a product of my imagination but I feel in this sensitive climate we live in, that I need to address this officially in case others are not aware of the wildlife laws.

In the US and Canada, the 1918 Migratory Bird Treaty Act made it illegal to trap, kill, possess, sell or harass migratory birds, and the protection includes their eggs, nest and feathers and other parts. There are exceptions to the law and special permits may be given, game birds taken in season and for researchers, Native Americans also are allowed to possess certain eagle and hawk feathers. For more information on specifics, see the 1918 Migratory Bird Treaty Act.

ACKNOWLEDGMENTS

In memory of my great-great grandmother. Although you are long gone from this world, your presence in my childhood made an impact on my life that has never left. Your storytelling abilities greatly inspired this novel, along with our long walks in the pine woods, two locust leaf crowns and one majestic story that has been the cornerstone of my life since the age of five. Thank you for introducing me to Jesus.

DIY IMMORTELLES EVERLASTING

THE PETAL PEOPLE

The Immortelles Everlasting flowers are a traditional ritual of mine, as well as the characters in the book. They make beautiful dried flower arrangements for your home, or you can use them to remember a specific loved one who's passed on, or commemorate a special event, a ceremony, or maybe you need to let someone go. The symbolism is all yours, a personal and heartfelt choice, so just make it your own.

Step 1: Select your flower petals. This can be plucked from a bush, bought at a store, from a funeral, special event, etc…

Step 2: Whether you have a bunch of flowers or one flower, tie a ribbon or twine around the ends of the stem.

Step 3: Place the flowers upside down to hang in a dark closet or area where it is dry (no humidity) and no light for up to two weeks.

Step 4: After two weeks, check the flower for dryness. Be very careful in touching it, dried flowers are fragile.

Once dried, place the petal people in your favorite vase, on your bookshelf, or hang them upside down in bunches, along with other dried herbs. The beauty and symbolism of dried flowers for me, is much like the poem by Sessa Ainsley in the story. They are the grief takers, the memory makers, and they symbolize eternal life where we will one day join those who have gone before us. Whatever they symbolize for you, I hope you find the petal people beautiful and everlasting.

Have you made your own Immortelles Everlasting Petals? Snap a pic and share them with me on social media. I'd love to see them and hear your story.

FOLLOW THE SAGA

Follow the continuing Saga of the Seventh Tribe and its beginnings, along with all your favorite characters, Cass, Maw Sue, Aunt Raven, and the Moon Wanderers.

Coming Soon!

ABOUT THE AUTHOR

Barb Lanell is an American author. She lives in the South and is currently writing the continuing saga of the Seventh Tribe. THEY FLY SILENT is her first work of fiction. When she's not writing, she's happily an introvert at the farmhouse studying herbalism and tending to her large apiary of honeybees.

Follow her on social media or BarbLanell.com

Made in the USA
Middletown, DE
24 August 2024

59175979R00241